JL   ⁰,⁵⁰

"FASCINATING . . .
THIS BOOK IS FUN . . . .

Grift sense refers to the instinct for spotting a scam and
Tony has plenty of opportunity to use his skills in this
entertaining read."
—*The Tampa Tribune-Times*

"*Grift Sense* is one of the best debuts I've read in years.
It has a great plot, wonderful characters, and a slick,
subtle wit."
—*The Toronto Globe and Mail*

"The hard-nosed dialogue and the fast-paced, serpentine
plot deliver a page-turner of a mystery. Just when read-
ers start to relax, thinking it's clear sailing to the end,
Swain throws yet another curve."
—*Canadian Press*

"A knowing, lively plot surrounded by a kidnapping, a
return from the dead, a promise of May-December ro-
mance, as many curves as a Vegas showgirl, and a
shower of what even the hard-bitten gambling profes-
sionals in [the] cast describe as epiphanies."
—*Kirkus Reviews* (starred review)

"Billed as one of the best card-handlers in the world,
Swain packs this first novel with enough tidbits on the
art to back up the claim. Combine that insider's knowledge with clean writing and a reasonable con, and the
result is a fun read a la Elmore Leonard."
—*Publishers Weekly*

"Well-crafted, dryly humorous, and highly enjoyable."
—*Library Journal*

P9-CKC-904

By James Swain
Published by Ballantine Books:

GRIFT SENSE
FUNNY MONEY
SUCKER BET

James Swain
Grift Sense

BALLANTINE BOOKS • NEW YORK

Grift Sense is a work of fiction. Names, places, and incidents either are a product of the author's imagination or are used fictitiously.

A Ballantine Book
Published by The Ballantine Publishing Group
Copyright © 2001 by James Swain

This book contains an excerpt from *Sucker Bet* by James Swain published by Ballantine Books. Copyright © 2003 by James Swain

www.ballantinebooks.com

ISBN 0-345-46383-8

This edition published by arrangement with Simon & Schuster, Inc.

Manufactured in the United States of America

First Ballantine Books Edition: April 2003

OPM 10 9 8 7 6 5 4 3 2 1

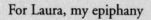

For Laura, my epiphany

Special thanks to Chris Calhoun at Sterling Lord, my agent Jennifer Hengen, also of Sterling Lord, Emily Heckman, and Shawn Redmond.

And God said to Moses,

"Moses, come forth."

And Moses came fifth,

And it cost God

Two hundred and fifty bucks.

—old gambler's joke

Fifteen Minutes of Fame

It was February, cold, and Al "Little Hands" Scarpi was pumping iron outside his double-wide on the outskirts of Las Vegas. Raising the bar over his head, he watched a ponytailed kid on a Harley roar up in a swirl of dust. Parting his leather jacket, the kid removed an airline ticket and spun it like a Frisbee, nailing Little Hands squarely in the chest.

"How much you bench?" the kid wanted to know.

"Five hundred, sometimes more," Little Hands said, wiping his sweaty face with a stained towel. "You lift?"

The kid laughed and revved his hog, as if that was all the muscle he needed.

"You on 'roids or something?" the kid asked.

"Steroids are for pussies," Little Hands said.

The kid left and Little Hands went inside his trailer. The ticket was for a noon Nevada Air puddle-jumper to Reno, the return for later that night. Printed on the sleeve was the confirmation number of a Hertz rental, a four-wheel-drive Jeep Cherokee. Printed beneath that were cryptic instructions. Cal-Neva Lodge—ask for Benny.

Inside the sleeve was money, five grand in thousand-dollar bills. Little Hands clutched it while thinking about the flight his employer had booked him on. It would be filled with businessmen. Then he imagined himself standing on line at the Hertz counter. More businessmen. Shredding the plane ticket, he went outside and tossed the pieces into the wind.

The drive to Reno took eight hours, another hour to navigate the treacherous mountain roads to Lake Tahoe. A light snow had dusted the highway, and he did thirty most of the way. It was a different world up here, the air thin and difficult to breathe, and a pounding headache soon filled his skull.

The Cal-Neva Lodge straddled the state line, which was how it got its name. It was dark when Little Hands parked at a casino called Lucky Lil's, then jogged down the road to his destination, his broad muscular back lit up by oncoming headlights.

He entered the Cal-Neva to the happy sounds of a slot machine paying a jackpot. At the front desk, he learned Benny was on break. Going outside, he found his contact having a smoke by the tennis courts. To his surprise, Benny was a she.

"My mother wanted a boy," Benny explained, blowing a smoke ring that hung eerily in the frigid air. "Ain't you cold?"

Little Hands shook his head no.

"Guess all that muscle keeps you real toasty, huh?"

Benny winked, coming on to him, and Little Hands got up close and breathed in her face. She swallowed hard. "Hey, I was just kidding, okay? Don't act so crazy. If you don't know it, this job is going to make you famous."

"Quit blowing me," he said.

"The guy in Bungalow ten—the guy you're going to whack. You know who he is?"

When Little Hands said no, Benny smartly said, "It's Sonny Fontana, that's who, big boy."

Little Hands didn't believe her. Sonny Fontana was

the poster boy of professional hustlers and forever banned from stepping foot in Nevada. He'd ripped off every major casino and never done time. The notion that he'd be hiding out in this crummy dump was too much for Little Hands to swallow. Sonny Fontana, his ass.

Sensing his doubts, Benny said, "Don't you get it? The bungalows are technically in California. Nobody can touch Fontana as long as he doesn't cross the state line." Producing a newspaper from her pocket, she said, "See for yourself."

Little Hands held the paper up to the moonlight. It was a photograph of Sonny Fontana taken outside a federal courthouse in Carson City several years ago. Jet-black hair, bushy eyebrows, big Roman nose. A real street guinea.

"You positive this guy's in Bungalow ten?"

"Sure am." Benny stamped out her butt. "Enjoy your fifteen minutes of fame."

"Right," he grunted.

Beneath a smiling half-moon, Little Hands crossed the grounds. Bungalow ten was surrounded by fir trees. He stuck his face in a side window. A guy in his birthday suit stood inside a tiny kitchenette. Loud music was playing on the radio and an open pizza box sat on the kitchen table. In profile, the guy looked like Fontana, but so did a lot of guys. He took a bottle of vodka from the freezer and left the room.

Circling the bungalow, Little Hands found a rear window with light streaming out and resumed watching. Inside, a woman with a shaved crotch sat upright on a four-poster bed while the naked guy refilled her tumbler. Licking her lips, the woman said, "Okay Sonny, let's see if you've got any more bullets in that thing."

Little Hands gripped the windowsill. So it really was him. He'd always dreamed of whacking a big shot and

making a name for himself. He watched Fontana mount
the woman from behind. They went at it like a couple
of porno stars. Just as he was about to climax, Fontana
grabbed a cream-colored Stetson off a poster and stuck
it on his head. Slapping the woman's buttocks, he said,
"Let's cross the finish line together, honey!"

Little Hands backed away from the window. Standing
in the lonely gathering of trees, he fought back the urge
to cry. At the tender age of six, he'd caught his mother
screwing a fireman wearing a red helmet. His mother
had picked the fireman up in a bar where he'd come
after battling a four-alarm blaze. Seeing her son's
stricken face, his mother had burst into tears; the fireman just kept screwing. With his little hands, Little
Hands had beaten on the fireman, to no avail.

Little Hands went around to the front of the bungalow. He'd thought about the fireman every day since.
And his red hat. Like his mother wasn't worth hanging
around for. The anger had been building inside of him
for a long time.

He knocked on the front door. From within, he heard
feet shuffling. A light on the porch came on. He could
feel someone watching him through the peephole.

"Hotel security," he said.

The door opened and Fontana stuck his head out. He
still wore the Stetson, only now it was perched rakishly
to one side. Reeking of vodka, he said, "Yeah, what's
the problem?"

Little Hands stared at him, just to be sure. It was the
same guy from the newspaper article; there was no
doubt in his mind. He'd killed many men in his life, but
this one was going to be special. Grabbing Fontana by
the throat, Little Hands closed the door on his head.

"This is for Mom," he said.

Six Months Later

1

Everybody cheated, at least everybody Tony Valentine had ever known. They cheated on their income taxes, on their spouses, on the phone and cable company, and if they had balls, in a Friday-night poker game or on the golf course. Everybody did it at least once; it was human nature, and a forgivable sin. But those who developed a taste for it, they were the problem.

And there were a lot of them. The number of professional con artists and hustlers working in the United States was at epidemic levels, and legalized gambling was to blame. With thirty-eight states having legalized wagering in one form or another, cheating was as rampant as it was during the early days of the Wild West. There was no lottery that could not be scammed, no slot or video poker machine that couldn't be rigged, no casino dealer who couldn't be compromised. The cheaters made sure of that; they were human scum, lower than any common thief or hoodlum, and Valentine had never regretted putting a single one behind bars until one fateful August day that made him think twice about the work that he did.

The day had started routinely enough. Up at eight, he'd eaten a bowl of Special K while reading the box scores; taken the usual shit, shower, shave; then hit the front porch of his Palm Harbor home with his second cup of joe. Sitting in a rocker beneath the cool breeze of an overhead fan, he supposed he looked like every other retired fart in his neighborhood, the only difference being that he was far from retired.

"You're late," he groused to the FedEx driver at nine-thirty. Taking the clipboard from the driver's outstretched hand, he hastily scribbled his name.

"Got stuck behind a funeral procession," the freckle-faced driver explained, exchanging the clipboard for a padded envelope. "It's that time of year. Got to run. Stay healthy, Mr. Valentine."

Valentine froze in the doorway as the orange, white, and purple van sped away. What was the driver insinuating—that old people died in bunches like leaves falling off a tree? Florida, he'd discovered on retirement, had two things in great abundance: nice weather and lots of mighty stupid people.

The envelope was from the Acropolis Resort & Casino in Las Vegas, and he tore it open, remembering his chat the day before with a moronic pit boss named Wily. A player had taken the Acropolis for fifty grand and Wily had begged Valentine to look at the surveillance tape to see if the guy was cheating. He'd sounded desperate, so Valentine had said yes.

The envelope held a video cassette, a check, and a note. Most pit bosses had never graduated high school, and Wily's scrawl was barely legible. From what Valentine could decipher, Wily thought the dealer was involved. Pit bosses always thought that, and he tossed the note into the trash.

Popping the video into the VCR, Valentine settled into his La-Z-Boy. Black-and-white images materialized on his thirty-six-inch Sony. A fuzzy young lady was dealing blackjack to an equally fuzzy man. The Acropolis was one of the oldest joints in Las Vegas and needed to get some updated surveillance equipment or risk losing its license. He fiddled with the tint control and the picture gradually took shape.

Watching surveillance videos was a unique experience. The cameras filtered twice as much light as the human eye, and as a result hairpieces looked like rugs, cheap suits took on zebra stripes, and women wearing red dresses became naked. It was like entering the Twilight Zone.

Soon Valentine found himself yawning. Normally, the tapes he viewed were action-packed and filled with plenty of people. That was how most casino scams worked, with someone causing a distraction while three or four members of a "mob" did the dirty work. This tape was different. One guy, playing alone at a blackjack table, was winning hand after hand. Valentine studied his play, then the sweet-looking blonde doing the dealing. Everything looked legit, except how the guy seemed to know exactly when to take a hit and when to stand.

Twenty minutes later, Valentine still had no idea what was going on. If he hadn't known better, he would have thought someone was putting him on. *No one on the planet is that good.* Stopping the VCR, he retrieved Wily's note from the trash. The pit boss had written *Dealer flashing?* and underlined it. Valentine knew when a dealer was flashing her hole card to a player, and the blonde on the video wasn't doing it. Wily was dead wrong.

But that didn't mean something crooked wasn't going down. The guy on the video was winning way too much. Grabbing a pad and pencil from his desk, Valentine knelt on the floor so he was a foot from his TV, then hit Start on the VCR.

"Okay, mister," he said as the tape started to roll, "let's see what you've got."

The guy had plenty—so much so that Valentine soon nicknamed him Slick.

For sixty minutes, he kept a record of Slick's play, noting every time he won, lost, or played to a draw with the house. Slick's strategy was erratic, at times plain dumb, yet he won way more than average. The sixty-four-thousand-dollar question was, how much over average? A few percentage points could be attributed to luck; anything over that meant darker forces were at work.

When Slick had played one hundred hands, Valentine added up the X's beneath his three columns: fifty-eight hands won, thirty lost, twelve tied. Nearly a two-thirds winning percentage. That was unreal.

He went to his desk and booted up his PC. It was time to do the math. A program called Blackjack Master filled the blue screen. Blackjack Master simulated the game of blackjack with any strategy a person chose to play. Once the strategy was entered, the program would play it for one million hands, then spit out the odds. Several updated versions had come out over the years, but Valentine had stayed loyal to the original. So what if it was slow? It got the job done, and that was all he wanted from a computer.

Slick liked to hit on seventeens when the dealer was showing a ten, and Valentine decided to run it as a separate strategy, just to see where it got him.

Blackjack Master Simulation

A. Set number of hands (1,000,000)
B. Clear statistics
C. Fix player total (17)
D. Fix player's first card (10)
E. Fix dealer up card (10)
F. Begin/continue simulation
G. Display statistics by hand type
H. Display statistics by adjusted count
I. Display card deal statistics

J.   Print statistics
K.   Write statistics to disk
L.   Simulation log file
M. Return to first menu

Done, he hit Enter, then listened to his hard drive whir. A minute later, Blackjack Master made its opinion known.

Hands:	1,000,000
Shuffles:	148,400
Wins:	213,600
Losses:	753,330
Net chips:	-43,770.0
Expected return:	-0.7672

It was a bad strategy, producing worse odds than if Slick had stayed pat, and not drawn a card. His eyes shifted to the numbers on his pad. According to his less-than-scientific calculations, Slick had won seventy percent of his hands in this situation.

Unreal.

The other strategies played out the same. Blackjack Master gave them the thumbs-down, yet Slick managed an impossibly high winning percentage. You had to be smoking something to believe that a player could maintain these percentages over the course of several hours' play. Which meant Wily was right about one thing. Slick was definitely cheating. The question was, how?

Valentine ate lunch the same time every day, standing over the kitchen sink wolfing down a sandwich while gazing at his postage stamp of a backyard. Sometimes he listened to the radio, big bands on 106.3, but not often.

Tony, he could hear his wife say, *sit down. It's bad for your digestion to stand while you eat.*

Old habits die hard, he'd say. *You walk a beat, certain things stay with you.*

You haven't walked a beat since being promoted to detective, she'd reply, the lines coming out like a *Honeymooners* skit. *That was twenty-five years ago.*

Twenty-five years? he'd exclaim, shaking his head in wonder. *God, it feels like yesterday.*

He sipped a Diet Coke while thinking about his conversation with Wily. The pit boss had called Slick a nut; now he knew why. Slick hadn't just cheated the Acropolis, he'd rubbed everyone's face in it. No hustler with half an ounce of common sense ever did that. It just wasn't healthy.

But there was another dynamic that was equally disturbing. Even if Wily didn't know what Slick was doing, he still should have barred him once his winnings started to mount. Nevada casinos were private clubs that reserved the right to prohibit anyone from playing. It wasn't commonly done, but this would have been a smart time to exercise the option.

Only Wily hadn't. He'd let the casino's losses get out of hand, which meant either he was a total jackass or he thought Slick was on a lucky streak that would eventually run its course, and the Acropolis would win its money back.

Suddenly the soda didn't taste so good. Something was wrong with this picture. Then it hit him like an anvil: Professional hustlers were like nuns when it came to exposing themselves. Slick had broken a cardinal rule of his own profession.

Why?

Mabel Struck materialized on his back stoop, looking tropically resplendent in her orange polyester slacks and high-wattage parrot shirt. Seeing the Tupperware container between her liver-spotted hands, Valentine realized that, bless her heart, she'd brought him dinner.

"Anybody home?" she said, nose pressed to the glass. "Hey, Tony, I can see the TV on. You sleeping on the job again? Wake up, sonny boy."

He unlocked the back door. "Come on in, Mabel."

"Don't tell me you were standing there the whole time," she said, entering his kitchen.

"Afraid I was."

"I can't see a thing without my glasses anymore," she said, jabbing him in the gut with the container. "You know, this old-age thing really sucks."

"It beats the alternative. I was just having lunch. Want a ham-and-Swiss?"

"No thanks. You sound stressed." Fishing her glasses from her pocket, Mabel fitted them on her nose and gave him the once-over. "You *look* stressed. You feeling okay, young man?"

"Great," he said without enthusiasm. After Lois had passed away, Mabel had started leaving hot meals on his doorstep, country-fried steak and mashed potatoes or fried chicken and cornbread. It was food for the soul, and he'd eaten every bite, even when he'd had no appetite. He took the container and put it on the top shelf of his refrigerator. It was heavy. He said, "Lasagna? You shouldn't have."

"It's no bother, really. What's eating you?"

"I'm having a problem figuring something out."

"Can I help?"

"Sure. Have a seat while I finish lunch."

Mabel took her usual spot at the kitchen table. A sixty-four-year-old retired AT&T operator from Cincinnati, she'd raised two children by herself and had come to Florida when they'd tried to move back in. She despised retirement and had embarked on a new career that brought her a surprising amount of notoriety.

"Know anything about blackjack?" he inquired.

"Not really. But I used to play bridge."

"Competitively?"

"Yes, tournament level."

"Ever catch an opponent signaling cards to a partner?"

"Well, now that you mention it, yes. Back in 1968 in a tournament in Boise, I saw Ethel Bell signal her husband that she had five trump cards. I called the referee immediately."

"That's enough qualification for me," Valentine said. "I'd like you to look at a videotape a casino sent me."

"Sure," Mabel said, "but before we do that, I want you to critique my newest ad. I think it's ready."

From her purse Mabel removed a piece of manila stationery and slid it across the table. Her anonymous classifieds had been running in the *St. Petersburg Times* for over a year and had turned her into a minor celebrity. Newspaper editorials now quoted her witticisms and local politicos used her jokes in their long-winded speeches. She had become a voice, a responsibility she did not take lightly.

"Be honest," she told him.

Depressed, overweight, domineering older woman, slight drinking problem, hyper, on food stamps and oxygen. Would like to meet a cute young professional man with big abs and a foreign sports car, low mileage. Please send current résumé, blood test results, and nude photo for a platonic relationship.

"Haw, haw, haw," Valentine brayed, holding his sides. To think that his sweet-faced neighbor possessed this kind of wit was beyond him.

"You like it," she said.

"You've outdone yourself."

She produced another sheet. "This one, too. Be truthful."

"Two? You're going to run two ads in one day? I don't think the locals are ready for this, Mabel."

"Stop acting retarded. Just read it."

"Yes, ma'am."

Tired of phone sex, sweet boys? Call Grandma Mabel and I will tell you about my arthritis, my bills, how people are better drivers up north, how hard it is to live on a fixed income, my ex-husband, grandkids, last operation for gallstones, and lots more. No crackpots, please.

"You're killing me," he said, swiping at his eyes. "This is a classic."

"You really think so?"

"You're taking practical jokes to a new level."

"I want to leave something behind," she said, dead-pan.

"You sure you want to use your real name?"

"I could use some groupies. But enough about me. Tell me all about your problem. Maybe Grandma Mabel can help."

"Maybe you can," he said.

Mabel was one of the best judges of character Valentine had ever known, her instincts honed from years of talking to strangers on the phone. He escorted her into the living room and helped her get settled, then started the VCR and knelt beside her.

"Something unusual's going on here," he explained. "The guy on this tape is cheating, and the people who've hired me think the dealer may be helping him. Tell me what you think."

Mabel pulled her chair up within a few feet of the TV and stared at the screen for several minutes, then cleared her throat. "Well, she's definitely interested in him."

"Define *interested*."

"You sound just like a cop when you talk like that."

"Excuse me. Please—define *interested*."

"As in she likes him. Would like to know him better."

Valentine was surprised. If anything, the dealer seemed to be holding back. It was too bad the tapes didn't come with sound; if he could just hear them talking, he might get a better feeling for what had gone down.

"She seems pretty reserved, if you ask me," he remarked.

"Oh, Tony. Sometimes you act like you just crawled out of a cave. Any woman with an ounce of class acts reserved when she's around men. Women show their interest in the opposite sex in *little* ways. Take this young lady. She's interested; you can see it when she makes eye contact. And when she smiles. You can definitely see it in her smile."

Valentine had noticed that, too. As a rule, blackjack dealers did not smile or interact with patrons. But Slick was the only player at her table, which made not having a conversation pretty much out of the question.

"There you are," Mabel said, pointing at the screen.

"What?" he said, staring.

"He just did it again," Mabel said.

"Did what?"

"Did you see the corners of her mouth turn up?" Mabel said. "She was going to laugh. The guy keeps making her laugh. I counted three times. He's definitely got her number. I know it's none of my business, but why would a casino worry about someone winning a few hands of blackjack? Don't they make millions a day?"

He paused the tape. "They do. And a guy like this can put them out of business."

"Out of business? Oh, come on!"

And that was the shame of what Valentine did for a

living; no one understood the seriousness of his work. So he explained.

"Let's say our friend bets a hundred dollars and wins twenty hands in a row. If he parlays every bet and the house doesn't stop him, by the end of the twentieth hand, he'll own the casino."

Mabel paused. "Is the man we're watching capable of that?"

"Definitely."

She consulted her Mickey Mouse watch, then stood up. "Time to run. I've got to fax my ads to the newspaper's classified department by two."

"You going to run both?"

"Read tomorrow's paper and find out," she replied.

He walked Mabel down the front path to the narrow sidewalk that connected the row of New England–style clapboard houses. It was a straight hundred-yard shot to her place. She patted his arm and said, "Heat the lasagna in the oven at three-fifty for thirty minutes. Don't use the microwave; it makes the cheese runny."

"The guy's a real lady-killer, huh?" Valentine said, never one to leave loose ends dangling.

"A regular Don Juan."

"You think she's helping him?"

"Could be," Mabel said. "Later, Tony."

It was an angle to which he hadn't given much thought, and he went back inside. The VCR was still on, and he slipped into his La-Z-Boy and resumed watching. Slick was on a roll, and as he won hand after hand, Valentine focused on the blonde doing the dealing. After a while, he began to see what Mabel had seen. There was a chemistry between them. She didn't seem upset that he was winning so much, and that wasn't a good thing.

2

Three thousand miles away, Nola Briggs was practicing her riffle-shuffling, her brain on autopilot. Curls of hours-old cigarette smoke did lazy contortions over her blackjack table, the bluish haze lulling her to sleep.

It was eleven a.m. and the casino was as dead as a church social. A big computer convention was in town, but none of the action had spilled over to their tables. Too bad—she needed the dough. Like most dealers, Nola earned fifty bucks a shift and made up the rest in tips. When it was dead, she barely earned enough to pay her rent and eat at McDonald's once a week. Maybe the casino could survive on little old ladies playing the twenty-five-cent slots, but she sure as hell couldn't.

A native of Queens, New York, Nola had pulled up stakes and driven to Las Vegas ten years earlier, chasing a dream. She'd win a super jackpot or meet a successful guy and end up living on a beautiful spread raising horses or some breed of large dogs. As dreams went, it was a tall order, and the fact that none of it had materialized didn't faze her. Life was a gamble, and she'd played the hand she'd been dealt accordingly.

"Hit me," a man's voice said.

Nola blinked. The world's cutest guy had materialized at her table. Their eyes met, and she saw the corners of his mouth curl up mischievously.

"Remember me?" he asked.

Of course Nola remembered him. He'd sat in the same spot the night before and the night before that. A computer software salesman from upstate New York. She'd been mesmerized by his looks until he'd started drawing on stiffs and beating her when she was holding eighteen and higher. He'd taken her for twenty grand the first night, thirty the second.

"Hit you where?" she inquired.

His smile grew into something more, and Nola's heart began to melt. He was terrific looking without being handsome: soft mouth, gentle eyes, the New York accent having none of the usual rudeness. He drew a wad of hundreds from his pocket.

"Come on, Nola—don't you want to win your money back?"

"Sure, Fred," she said.

"It's Frank," he said, ruining the smile with a little frown. "Frank Fontaine."

Nola knew damn well what his name was. Frank Allen Fontaine, age forty-four, divorced, no kids, star salesman for a computer outfit out of Poughkeepsie, no criminal record. Once he'd started winning, security had called the Mirage, where he was staying, and gotten his credit card number. Within minutes, the results of a complete financial and personal check were spitting out of a fax machine.

"He's a choirboy," Wily had told Nola during her break, the printout clutched in his hand. "Mr. Clean."

"What did you expect?" she replied, firing up a cigarette. "Ted Bundy?"

"I don't like his play," the pit boss declared.

The employee lounge overlooked the casino floor, and they stared through a tinted two-way mirror at Fontaine sitting at Nola's table, awaiting her return.

"What don't you like about it?" Nola said.

"It doesn't feel right. He's hustling us."

"How?"

"The fuck I know. But he is."

"People get lucky."

"Not this lucky."

"So bar him."

"And let him walk out of here with our dough? You don't get it, sweetie. I want to break this paesano."

"Well, you probably will," Nola said when her cigarette was gone. "He's no player."

"He's sure soft on you."

"Well, he is kinda cute. And polite. And he tips great."

"You sucking his dick?"

Nola stuck her tongue out. "Go sit on a spike, fatso."

But Wily hadn't given up. Pit bosses were required to make quotas. It had been a rough week and Fontaine's score was going to put Wily's take on the negative side, and that was unacceptable. So Wily had come up with one of his famous stupid ideas. Because Fontaine was attending the computer show, Wily figured he must have some kind of computer device on him. And because it was illegal in Nevada to bring a computer or calculator onto a casino floor, Wily believed he could relieve Fontaine of his winnings without any fear of legal repercussions.

So Wily had frisked him right at the table the second night. Fontaine took it like a real gentleman. Not once did he raise his voice or threaten to sue the casino.

"Perhaps you could tell me what this is about," Fontaine had said when his pockets produced nothing.

His face beet red, Wily had stammered a lame apology. "I'm *really* sorry, but you're a dead ringer for a guy who robbed us a while back."

Fontaine's face betrayed a hint of skepticism.

"On my mother's grave," Wily swore, putting his hand over his heart. "You could be brothers."

"I'm surprised I made it through the front door," Fontaine had replied, giving Nola a wink.

And now he was back, dressed in a navy silk sports jacket with mother-of-pearl buttons and a choirboy smile lighting up his face. Nola pushed him his chips. "Good luck."

Shuffling the cards a final time, she offered them to be cut, then dealt. She worked a two-deck game, hand held. A lot of casinos on the strip had gone back to hand-held games. The players seemed to like it.

"Insurance," she said, her face card an ace.

"That's a sucker's bet, isn't it?" he inquired.

Nola looked at his bet. Five blacks: five hundred bucks. He was starting off heavy. It was against the rules to coach, but Nola saw no harm in passing along a little knowledge.

"Not really," she explained. "Insurance protects your bet if I have blackjack."

Fontaine looked at his hand, exposing his cards to her. He had a fifteen, a stiff. "Naw," he said.

Nola bit her lip. When it came to strategy, her dream boy was a dope. She peeked at her hole card. A nine. She had twenty. Fontaine was a goner.

"Guess you don't have blackjack," he said, smiling.

Nola pursed her lips. The odds against his drawing a six and beating her twenty were astronomically high. *Let's see you wiggle out of this one,* she thought.

"Hit me," he said.

Nola dealt him a deuce.

"Again," he informed her.

Nola stared at him. He had a seventeen, a pat hand. Drawing another card was the wrong play unless he somehow knew what her hole card was.

"You sure about that?" she asked him.

"Positive."

Nola dealt him a four, giving him twenty-one. She turned over her hole card.

"Look at that," he said, his face begging forgiveness while laughing at the same time. *"I win."*

Nola took a deep breath. Was Frank Allen Fontaine going to turn into her own personal *Groundhog Day*?

Wily sauntered over to her table, a toothpick twirling in his teeth. Earlier, a couple of Asian high rollers had dropped seventy grand shooting craps, meaning he was going to make his weekly quota despite Nola's previous losses. In a show of good sportsmanship, he slapped Fontaine on the back.

"Mr. Fontaine, welcome back. How about a drink?"

"That sounds great," Fontaine said. "Give me a 7-Up."

"Can I interest you in something stronger?"

"Thanks, but no thanks."

Wily summoned a toga-clad cocktail waitress. Her name was Bonnie, and she took his order with a syrupy smile on her face. She was new and still enthusiastic about working in a casino.

"I was wondering," Fontaine said to the pit boss. "Do you have any of those terrific cigars left?"

"The Paul Garmirians? I think I can rustle one up."

"I'd really appreciate it," Fontaine told him.

When Wily returned ten minutes later, he didn't have Fontaine's cigar. Instead, he was accompanied by Sammy Mann, the ancient, pasty-faced zombie who headed up casino surveillance. Sammy spent twelve hours a day parked in front of a wall of video monitors that watched every square inch of the casino. If someone started winning too much, it was Sammy's job to zoom in with the eye in the sky and start taking pictures. Sammy had been shot in the leg years ago, and as he limped alongside Wily, the two men appeared joined at the hip.

They halted behind Nola's table. Since Wily left, she'd lost twelve hands in a row and over fifteen thousand dollars. In an angry whisper, Wily said, *"Take a break!"*

Visibly shaking, Nola clapped her hands and stepped back from her spot. Sensing trouble, Fontaine put his arms around the fortress of black chips in his possession and pulled them close. Tossing Nola a hundred-dollar toke, he said, "Thanks, honey."

Sammy plucked the chip out of the air. Sammy's eyes were as smooth as glass, and he breathed heavily through his crooked nose.

"I know you," Sammy declared.

Fontaine's eyebrows shot up inquisitively. "Stony-brook, class of '76?"

Sammy shook his head violently.

"Poughkeepsie High, class of '72?"

"Don't think so," Sammy snapped.

"You want me to guess," Fontaine said innocently.

"I know you from the road," Sammy said. "You're a hustler."

An ugly look clouded Fontaine's handsome features. Nola felt the whisper of intuition crawl up her spine. There was something familiar about him, yet she couldn't place what.

"You calling me a faggot?" Fontaine spouted angrily.

"No," Sammy replied. "I'm calling you a cheat."

In another lifetime, Sammy had earned his livelihood ripping off casinos. At sixty, he'd retired to Palm Springs, become a full-time drunk, and squandered his money. After cleaning himself up, he'd come to Las Vegas and auctioned his ability to spot other hustlers to the highest bidder. He'd gotten religion and was not ashamed to rat on players he'd known from the road.

Fontaine pointed an accusing finger at Wily. "First,

this bozo has me frisked; now you're calling me a crook. The problem with this place is you're just a bunch of sore losers."

Fontaine began stuffing stacks of black chips into his pockets, but Sammy grabbed his arm.

"You and I worked together . . . your laugh hasn't changed."

"My laugh?" Fontaine shook free of his grasp. "Touch me again and I'll knock you into next week."

Sammy backed up. Wily barked into a walkie-talkie and two beefy security guards came charging across the floor. Jumping to his feet, Fontaine grabbed the back of his chair.

"This is going to make a great lawsuit," he announced.

Nola swallowed hard. Now Fontaine's voice was starting to sound familiar. It was spooky; she knew him, yet she didn't know him. Perhaps their paths had crossed back in Queens. *That's it,* she thought, *when we were kids.*

"You're real cute," Sammy said, eyeing him cooly. "Sooner or later, I'm going to remember where I know you from. If you're smart, you'll get out of my casino while you still can."

"I won this money fair and square," Fontaine shouted indignantly, still holding the chair. "Pay up, or I'll call the police and have you arrested."

"You'll do *what*?"

"You heard me. For stealing."

"Get *him*, boys!" Sammy bellowed.

The security guards' names were Hoss and Tiny. In their formative years, they had played football at Michigan State, both all-American. Fontaine was a lot smaller than the quarterbacks they'd run over during their heyday, and they brusquely wrestled him to the floor and emptied his pockets.

"Count those chips," Sammy ordered.

A mob had formed around the blackjack pit and Nola combed the familiar faces of her coworkers. It happened every time: one little fracas and everyone but the crippled change girl came running. She watched Fontaine being pulled to his feet, his pockets hanging inside out. He flashed her a funny grin, and Nola flipped him the bird.

Then Hoss and Tiny dragged Fontaine across the casino and out the sliding front door, tossing him harshly onto the pavement like the sack of human garbage that he was.

Wily let her go home early.

Nola changed into jeans and a faded polo shirt in the employee lounge, then exited through the casino, waving to a couple of dealers she knew on her way out. Passing the sea of slots, she stopped at an alcove near the front entrance that housed the most famous slot machine in Las Vegas. Its name was One-Armed Billy and its progressive jackpot currently stood at a cool twenty-six million. Billy stood nine feet tall and took only five-dollar tokens, and Nola had seen countless little old ladies hang monkeylike on Billy's arm to set the reels in motion.

"There you are," Nola said.

Joe Smith sat on a high stool beside Billy, looking bored out of his mind. Proportionately, Joe was the right person to be guarding Billy, as he was easily the largest casino employee in the world, standing seven feet tall and weighing three hundred pounds. Nola planted a kiss on his ebony cheek.

"Heard you had trouble earlier," Joe said.

"Man, did I ever," Nola replied. "I thought the guy was going to break a chair over Sammy Mann's head."

Joe said, "Sounds like it got pretty wild."

"You should have come running. Everybody else did."

"I'm sure Surveillance got it on video."

"Maybe they'll let you check it out for the night."

"You mean like Blockbuster?" he asked.

"Yeah, like Blockbuster."

Joe found this amusing and his whole body shook with laughter. He'd played hoops at University of Nevada, Las Vegas for three seasons before his inability to read and write was noticed by an English professor not in tune with the university's athletic program. The Acropolis had hired him the day he'd been kicked out of school, and he'd been married to One-Armed Billy ever since.

"So what was this guy doing that got him bounced?" Joe asked.

Nola shook her head. "I've never seen anything like it. He must've won eighty percent of his hands."

"Wow," Joe said.

"But Sammy said he was cheating, and *he* should know."

"You're right about that," Joe said. "Sammy can smell a hustle a mile away. How's biz?"

"Crummy. Got any ideas?"

Joe scratched his chin. "Well, maybe Nick should put new greeters in the fountains."

"Try telling Nick that," Nola said.

The greeters were the brainchild of the Acropolis's flamboyant owner, Nick Nicocropolis. Originally, Nick had wanted to put ancient statues from Athens in the fountains that lined the Acropolis's entrance. The Greek government, which had to approve the deal, had howled. Undaunted, Nick had commissioned a famous sculptor to carve toga-clad statues of his ex-wives—two beauty queens, two showgirls, a stripper, and a retired hooker who'd run for mayor and gotten six votes—and had put them out front instead. At night, colored water sprayed them in orgasmic bursts, raising the ire of women's groups across the nation.

Nick had loved the bad publicity. Soon the greeters became the casino's motif and popped up on doorways, matchbook covers, cocktail napkins, even gaming chips.

That had been eight years earlier. Las Vegas catered to families these days, and Nick's big-titted harem was a big no-no. The Acropolis needed a new gimmick, in a hurry.

"Well, I'd better run," Nola said. "You take care."

"Drive safe," Joe said.

Home sweet home was a development on the north end of town called the Meadows. Never buy a new house in Las Vegas, someone once told her. Nola hadn't listened, and now she regretted it, her place worth less than what she'd originally paid for it.

She pulled up her driveway and hit the automatic door opener. Over the years, boyfriends had left punching bags and barbells and other testosterone-producing equipment in her garage, leaving barely enough room for her car. She squeezed in and rested her head on the steering wheel as the door fell and her garage grew dark. *Please God,* she prayed, *no more days like this.*

Her first stop was the refrigerator. Her choices for lunch were endless: cold pizza, cold spaghetti, cold Chinese, half a turkey sub, and Schlitz beer. The sub had the most potential, and she took it out of the fridge along with the mustard.

The answering machine was blinking. Either Sherry Solomon, her best buddy and fellow dealer, had heard the news and wanted to know the gory details, or her boyfriend had called to talk dirty. She hit the replay button and the melodious sound of Frank Fontaine's voice sent a shiver down her spine.

"Hey, Nola," he said. "I forgot to say good-bye. Hope you don't get into any trouble. See you."

See you? Picking up the phone, Nola punched in *69, a service that allowed her to track the source of the last call. An automated voice spit out a number and Nola dialed it.

"Brother's Lounge," a gruff voice answered.

Nola knew the place. It was a stone's throw from the Acropolis and was a real dump. "Lemme speak to Frank," she said.

"Lots of guys named Frank here, lady."

"Frank Fontaine."

"Describe him," the bartender said.

Nola did. The bartender seemed to know exactly who she was talking about.

"Hey, Frank, you still here?" he bellowed across the bar. Coming back on the line, he said, "Sorry, lady— he's gone. I can take a message if you like."

"No, thanks."

Nola ate her sub and watched *Road Runner* cartoons with the sound muted. She couldn't stop thinking about the call. It was so crazy, yet typical. A real guy thing. Women apologized when they won big at her table; men liked to rub her face in it. She made a mental note to call the phone company and get her number changed.

Soon the sub was nothing but a pleasant memory and she was sprawled facedown on the couch, counting sheep.

Nola awoke to the sound of a battering ram taking down her front door. She rubbed her eyes, thinking this was TV mayhem, but it was a real SWAT team that burst into her living room. Before she could sit up, a half dozen automatic weapons were pointed in her face.

"On your stomach," one of the SWAT team shouted. He was big and had the letters *LVPD* stenciled in blazing white letters across his Kevlar vest. Nola hit the floor.

"You've got the wrong house," she protested. "The crack lady lives three doors down."

"Shut up," the officer replied angrily.

Nola kissed the carpet as her wrists were hog-tied behind her back with a set of plastic cuffs. While her rights were being read, her house was torn apart. More police poured through her open front door while the precious air-conditioning escaped into the stifling afternoon.

Soon she was sitting on the couch, dripping perspiration. She watched an officer come into the living room and drop a bag of pot, some prescription medicine, the message pad that sat beside the phone, and a stack of unopened mail onto her coffee table. She finally found her voice when her diaphragm hit the growing pile of her belongings.

"I want a fucking lawyer!"

When she didn't shut up and her protests became too loud, she was hoisted to her feet and led outside past a crowd of gawking neighbors, including the mail carrier. Then she was shoved into the back of a cruiser, where she began to sob uncontrollably.

A dark sedan pulled up her driveway. Through her tears, she saw Wily and Sammy Mann get out and walk across the lawn, still joined at the hip. They stopped to stare at her, before entering her house. Their faces, normally warm and friendly, were openly hostile.

Only then did Nola have an inkling as to what kind of trouble she was in.

3

In his dream, Valentine is a young man and his body still knows how to sprint. It is winter and he is running down the Boardwalk in Atlantic City, his lungs gripped by the wet bronchial cold of the sea. He passes Mel's Famous Foot-Long Dogs and the shuttered cotton candy stand. It is a moonlit night, and down by the shoreline, he sees a gang of men taking turns kicking a fellow police officer, who is lying in the sand. The officer is his brother-in-law, Salvatore, and he jumps the railing and draws his gun, firing in the air. The gang scatters.

"Oh, Jesus, Sal," Valentine says.

His brother-in-law is spitting up blood. Valentine kneels in the sand and cradles Sal's head in his arms. Soon the flow of blood stops and Sal's breathing grows tortured. Valentine gently shakes him, but his brother-in-law does not respond. Something warm seeps from Sal's body, and Valentine realizes it is Sal's soul he has encountered.

Voices fill the air. The gang has reappeared on the Boardwalk. Their leader, the notorious Sonny Fontana, jumps the railing and approaches him. He is holding a gun and makes Valentine drop his weapon. Then he makes Tony get to his feet.

Valentine has been hunting Fontana since the day the casinos opened in Atlantic City. Fontana has committed dozens of crimes, and now he can add murder to his résumé.

Fontana smiles at him, like Sal's passing is no big deal. He puts his hand on Valentine's shoulder.

"You and I need to come to an understanding," he says.

Valentine cannot help himself. He knocks the gun out of Fontana's hand, then puts his hands around Fontana's throat. The gang members jump the railing, drawing their weapons.

Valentine squeezes hard, Fontana's eyes bugging out of his ugly face. It is suicide, but Valentine cannot stop himself.

It is a dream in which he has no control.

"What's up?" Valentine said, rubbing sleep from his eyes as he unlatched the screen door. Embarrassed, the freckle-faced FedEx driver stepped onto the porch and stuck a padded envelope into Valentine's hands.

"Sorry, Mr. Valentine, but I found this floating around my van," the driver explained sheepishly. "I rang the bell a few times. When you didn't answer, I got worried."

"Why?" Valentine asked crankily.

"You're the biggest customer on my route. I don't want to lose you, Mr. Valentine."

Lose me? The driver's knocking had ruined his nap, and Valentine was too groggy to come up with a clever comeback *and* fire it off, so he said, "Glad to hear it."

The driver handed him a clipboard and said, "If you'll just sign on the bottom line, I'll let you get back to bed."

"Won't sign anything I can't see," Valentine replied, fitting his bifocals on. "And I wasn't in bed. I was in the living room, working. Am I really the biggest customer on your route?"

"Just about."

Signing the form, Valentine asked, "Got a name?"

"Ralph Gomez," the driver replied.

Valentine stared at the driver's milky white arms and checkerboard face. "You don't look like a Gomez. I would have pegged you as a Murphy or an O'Sullivan, not a Gomez."

"What's a Gomez supposed to look like?"

"I don't know. Spanish, maybe Mexican. You've definitely kissed the blarney stone."

Gomez realized he was being complimented, and a thin smile creased his face. "My mom. Dad was Cuban—came over in the fifties. So what are you? Italian?"

Was he Italian? What kind of question was that? Even in his earliest baby pictures, Valentine looked Italian.

"No," Valentine snapped, "I'm Mongolian."

"Beg your pardon?"

"Chinese, like the fortune cookie."

Gomez's smile disappeared and his freckled face twisted in puzzlement, then outright confusion. The joke had flown right over his head and off the screened porch and was now spinning somewhere high above the stratosphere.

"Your mom or dad?" he inquired.

The envelope contained a surveillance tape from a casino in Reno, plus another frantic note from a pit boss. Every day across America, casinos were getting ripped off, the losses totaling millions of dollars. So much work, so little time.

Going to the kitchen, Valentine fixed his third cup of coffee of the day. Normally, two was his limit, but he'd slept so hard that he didn't think he'd fully wake up if he didn't get some caffeine into his system. Filling his cup from the tap, he poured the contents into the back of the Mr. Coffee maker, then placed his cup directly on the hot pad.

Thirty-five years married and you still act like a bachelor, Lois would say, watching the ritual each morning as she fried his egg and blackened the bottoms of his English muffins.

It's effective, he'd reply.

And frugal, she'd say.

That, too.

I bet it saves us, what, fifty cents a month on coffee beans, she'd say. *Maybe more.*

It's all I want, he'd say. *Why fix more?*

You make being wasteful sound like a crime, she'd say, spooning sugar into his cup, a smile on her face.

Maybe it is, he'd reply.

He sat at the kitchen table and sipped the scalding brew. Coffee just didn't taste right if it didn't take the skin off the roof of his mouth. The phone had rung earlier and he stared at the blinking answering machine. One of the great things about being retired was not having to call people back if you didn't want to. And right now, he didn't want to.

He glanced at his watch. Nearly dinnertime. Yet what he felt like eating was a big breakfast. The diner on Alternate 19 served a good one, twenty-four hours a day, but he didn't like sitting at the counter alone, looking old and pitiful.

Mabel materialized on his back stoop. He unlocked the door and she strolled in wearing canary yellow slacks and a flowered shirt right out of an old Sears catalogue. Because of the heat, she changed clothes several times a day, each outfit more garish than the last.

"I'm going grocery shopping and thought you might need a few things." Opening the refrigerator, she peered at the vacant shelves. "How about some Italian bread to go with your lasagna? Publix has a wonderful bakery."

Trying to put mom-and-pop delis out of business, the local supermarket now sold fresh bread and rolls. They almost tasted like the real thing, so he said, "Sounds great. Want a hot drink?"

"Tea, if you have it."

He put the kettle on, then extracted a ten from his wallet and slipped it into Mabel's shirt pocket.

"What's that for?" she asked.

"Gas money. How was your afternoon?"

"I watched the ball game. The Devil Rays won. It was so *exciting*."

Among the locals, it was a source of constant amazement that Tampa Bay's new baseball team was capable of winning a single game. Every time they did, it made the front page of both newspapers, with new heroes being christened every day. Valentine found the whole thing very perplexing. He'd grown up bowing to the Yankees, who were expected *not* to lose.

"I also worked on a new ad," she said. "Want to see it?"

"I'd be flattered," he said.

She produced a square of paper with borders and fancy type, the proud product of a home PC.

Old? Tired? Forgotten?

Has retirement got you singing the blues? Want to get even with your kids? And all those pesky credit card companies? Enroll today in Grandma Mabel's school of financial insolvency. You too can live like a millionaire. Remember: Dying broke is the best revenge!

"It's different," he said, sliding the ad back.

"You don't like it."

"It doesn't tickle my funny bone. It's . . ."

"Come on—I can take it."

"I don't know. A little extreme."

"Jokes are supposed to be extreme." Her mind was made up, and she tucked the ad away. "It's going to cost more to run, but Social Security is sending me two hundred extra a month, so it won't be a stretch."

"Then go for it," Valentine told her.

"So what did you do this afternoon?"

"Believe it or not," he said, "I watched the tape I showed you earlier today."

"Still got you stumped?"

The kettle was singing. Valentine fixed Mabel's tea, spooning in a half-teaspoon of honey, and served his neighbor.

"Right now, I've got two theories," he replied, sitting down again. "The first says the guy's reading the dealer's body language each time she peeks at her hole card. In those situations, his winning percentage is unbelievably high."

"Really?" Mabel sounded amused. She sipped her tea. "What does she do—stick her tongue out each time she has blackjack?"

"It's a little more subtle than that."

"Try me."

"Well, there are two types of dealers: those who want you to win and those who don't. If a player can peg which type of dealer he's got, he has an advantage."

"You're losing me. Why do certain dealers want you to win and others not? Why should the dealer care?"

"Tips," he explained. "The ones who want you to win expect a tip when the night is over. The ones who don't are usually so jaded that no amount of money will make them happy. They *want* the players to lose because it makes them feel good."

"And the dealers give their feelings away by their body language?"

Valentine sipped his coffee and nodded. "They're called tells. Poker players use them all the time. I've never seen them used at blackjack, but there's always a first time."

"He'd have to be very good, wouldn't he?"

"Damn good."

"What's your second theory?"

"The girl is signaling him."

"How?"

"I have no earthly idea."

"How can that be a theory if you don't know how it's being done?"

"Because it's logical," he explained. "Experience says lean toward the simplest theory. Maybe she's doing it with her eyes or her lips or the way she flares her nostrils. I'd have to see her in person to know for sure."

"So the girl's guilty?"

"It's a distinct possibility."

Mabel put her cup down, her eyes fixed on the blinking answering machine. Valentine fidgeted uncomfortably.

"Not to change the subject," she said, "but have you spoken to Gerry lately?"

"He called over the weekend," he mumbled.

"Did you have a conversation, or did he have to leave a message on that horrible machine?"

If Mabel had a flaw, it was her unwillingness to let sleeping dogs lie. Six months before, he'd lent his son fifty thousand dollars to buy a bar in Brooklyn, New York. His son had been in and out of trouble over the years, and Valentine had always begrudgingly bailed him out. The bar, Gerry had promised him, would be a new beginning. So when Valentine had gone to visit a few weeks ago, he'd been shocked to find Gerry sitting at a desk in the back room, running a bookmaking operation. "You're early," his son had quipped, a phone pressed to his ear. Removing his belt, Valentine had whipped his son's butt good—and had not talked to him since.

"What's so horrible about my machine?" he asked.

"You need to change the message."

"I like the message. It's me."

"Are you going to answer the question or not?"

"You know," he said, "when you talk like that, you sound just like my dearly departed wife."

"I'm sorry. Would you *please* answer the question?"

"I was out in the backyard."

"Did you call him back?"

"I haven't gotten around to it."

"Tony, I'm ashamed of you."

"That makes two of us."

"And what is that supposed to mean?"

"I'm ashamed I dislike my son as much as I do."

"Then why won't you call him?"

"He's not worth it," he said, ending the conversation.

Valentine escorted Mabel down the front path to her car, an old Honda Accord with a vanity plate that said spoofs. She got in, and as he closed the door for her, she said, "At least listen to your machine."

"All right, all right," he said.

"And call your son."

"No," he said as she drove away.

Going inside the house, Valentine hit the Play button on his answering machine.

"Hey, Tony—Wily here at the Acropolis. Love the message. I've got a big problem, buddy, and I need your help."

Valentine winced. He hated it when total strangers

called him buddy. *Pal* was acceptable; *Hey, friend,* okay; *Yo, chief,* borderline; but never *buddy.*

"Believe it or not," the pit boss went on, "the guy on the tape showed up again. He started beating us, so we tossed him. Our head of surveillance watched the tape and decided our dealer was signaling him. We had her arrested this afternoon. We showed the tapes to Gaming Control, and they're not convinced. They think we should drop charges." The pit boss coughed nervously. "It's a real fucking mess. I'd like you to fly out here and have a look. I know this is spur of the moment, but my ass is on the line."

"I'll bet it is," Valentine said to the machine.

"Money's no object. I'm begging you, Tony. I'm having an airline ticket couriered to you. Call me."

Valentine erased the message. Vegas in August? Who was this joker kidding? Besides, what could he do? The Gaming Control Bureau was the single most powerful entity in Las Vegas and was responsible for prosecuting any cheating taking place inside a licensed casino. They were the knights on the white horses who were entrusted to keep things honest. Without their support, Wily didn't have a pot to piss in.

He stuck Mabel's lasagna in the microwave while thinking about the young woman on the tape. She was a sweet-looking kid and not the type he'd normally suspect of cheating. Now that she'd been arrested, her career dealing blackjack was over. It would be a crying shame if she was innocent.

The kitchen phone rang. Dinnertime was the witching hour for solicitors, and he let his machine pick up.

"This is Tony Valentine. I don't answer my phone because too many jerks call. Leave a message or a fax. Or you can go away. It's up to you."

"Hey, Pop, it's Gerry," his son's voice sang out.

"Guess I missed you again. Glad you're leading an active social life down there."

"Get on with it," Valentine said to the machine.

". . . anyway, it looks like I'm coming down to your neck of the woods. I scored some tickets to the Devil Rays and Yankees game tomorrow, and I figured we might catch a game. Whaddaya say? It would be fun, like old times. I'm flying down in the a.m. on Delta. Call me at the bar, okay?"

Valentine took the lasagna out of the microwave and stuck a fork in it. A baseball game sounded great, only not with Gerry. His son had been making his life miserable for years, and he wanted him to suffer and do a little penance. He did not think that was so much to ask.

His doorbell rang. His place was turning into Grand Central Station. Valentine went to the door; through the window, he saw a *Tampa Express* van parked in his driveway.

He opened the door, and the strangest-looking courier he'd ever seen waltzed in. Shaved head, with a dozen silver pins connected by silver chains adorning the side of his face. The name tag above his pocket said Atom. Had his folks actually christened him that?

Atom handed him a thin envelope, then produced a pen from behind a pierced ear. "Sign on the label."

Valentine scribbled his name, and Atom tore off the receipt.

"Atom, mind if I ask you a question?"

"Not at all."

"How much did it cost to have those pins put in your face?"

Atom smiled, thinking he was being paid a compliment. "I got it done in Ybor City at Pin & Pierce. Three hundred for all twelve. The chains were extra."

"Atom, if a man came up to you in the street,

knocked you down, and pierced your cheek with a hat pin, they'd put him away for ten years."

Atom looked puzzled. Then his face reddened; Valentine almost could've sworn that the pins also changed color. "This is different," he spouted defensively.

"I'm glad one of us thinks so," Valentine said.

Atom refused a tip. Valentine shut the door and tore open the envelope. Inside was a ticket to Las Vegas on Delta, the departure the next morning. He checked the seat assignment. Wily had sprung for first class.

The phone rang and he let the machine pick up.

"Hey, Pop, it's Gerry. I just spoke to Mabel Struck on her cell phone. She says you're home and that you're probably standing in the kitchen sticking your tongue out at the phone. Look, Pop, enough is enough. I'm coming down to Florida whether you like it or not. We need to hash this out. Like men."

Like men? What were they going to do, Greco-Roman wrestling on the floor? Gerry didn't know how to act like a real man; that was the fundamental problem. "Get serious," he shouted at the phone.

"I mean it, Pop. I'm coming down."

The line went dead. His son sounded hurt. Good. Their rift was finally getting to him. His mother had coddled him, and now that she was gone, he was finally faced with having to grow up, whatever that meant these days.

Valentine checked the ticket again. The return had been left open. Neat—he could fly home once Gerry was safely back in New York. All of a sudden Las Vegas in the middle of August sounded like a nice weekend getaway.

He went to the bedroom and pulled a suitcase from the closet and started tossing clothes into it.

4

Nick Nicocropolis's father had been a sponge diver in Tarpon Springs, Florida, as had his father before him. It was dangerous work, perhaps the most dangerous profession in the world, and both men had died a few months apart while plying their trade, his father from the bends, his grandfather from a hammerhead's bite. Neither had carried insurance, leaving Nick to support his mother, three sisters, and an elderly grandmother at the tender age of sixteen.

Quitting high school had been much easier than finding gainful employment. He was small, five-six and one-forty, and because most Greeks were inherently superstitious, no one on the sponge docks would employ him as a diver, which happened to be the only decent-paying work around. So he'd taken to hustling pool in tourist bars and cheating at cards and loan-sharking and running a sleazy escort service and stealing rental cars at Tampa International Airport just to make ends meet. It was nickel-and-dime crap, and he'd humped it until his mother and grandmother were pushing up daisies and his sisters were in school or hitched. Then he'd packed his bags and headed west. The year was 1965.

Thirty-four years later, Nick Nicocropolis could look back and be proud. His childhood had been hardscrabble, but so what? Losing Gramps and his old man in the same year had been rough, but their losses had also taught him lessons that he might otherwise never have learned. It had hardened him, and in that hardness Nick found a strength he had not known he possessed. A callous had formed over the aching hole in his heart, and from that he had grown strong.

"Fontaine disappeared," Nick said, repeating Sammy Mann's words. "In broad daylight, he walked into the parking lot and vanished. How does that work? Trapdoor?"

"I think they use mirrors," Sammy said.

"Who?" Nick said.

"Siegfried and Roy. You know, the elephant."

"*Sigmund Freud?* Why the hell are you bringing them up?"

"I thought that's what you meant."

In anger, Nick slapped the expansive granite desk in his penthouse office. Biting off the end of a cigar, he spit it into the trash. "Every day, I look out my window at those two Krauts stealing the crowds from my casino. You think I give a rat's ass how they make the elephant vanish? What I'm asking you, numb nuts, is how Fontaine managed to shake the tail you had on him."

Sammy shrugged his shoulders, wishing he knew. Fontaine had sauntered around the casino into the covered parking lot, ducked behind a concrete pillar, and vanished into thin air. The tail never saw him again.

"We think he changed clothes and ducked into another car," Sammy explained. "That's all we can figure. He left his rental with the keys in the ignition."

"Yeah, yeah, yeah," Nick said sarcastically, "changed his britches and ran. What am I paying you for, anyway? I spend thirty years working my balls off trying to do someone a favor and you let a guy who's ripping me off take a walk. Jesus Christ."

Sammy hung his head in shame. His employer was the last of a dying breed, a hard headed little jerk who'd refused to sell out to the big hotel chains and was now paying the price for his hubris. The Acropolis could not afford to be ripped off on a regular basis without Nick's getting a distress call from the bank.

"Sorry, boss," he said.

"What about the girl?" Nick said.

"We had her arrested this afternoon."

"She post bail?"

"Not yet."

"You sure she was in on it?"

"Sure, I'm sure," Sammy said. "I've got the whole thing on video."

"I saw it," Nick reminded him, sticking the unlit cigar between his teeth, "and I didn't see her doing a frigging thing."

"She was signaling him," Sammy said defensively.

"You're sure?"

"Of course I'm sure."

"Then why didn't you bust Fontaine when you had the chance?"

"Because I wanted to watch the video a few times. I didn't want to accuse either of them before I was sure."

"But now you're sure."

"Now I'm sure."

"One-hundred-percent-positive sure?"

Sammy grunted. There were times when he'd prefer starving on Social Security than listening to Nick's line of crap.

Nick sensed Sammy's displeasure. His unlit cigar took on the appearance of a living thing as it wiggled in his mouth. "What about Gaming Control?" he asked.

"They're not on our side on this one," Sammy said.

"You're shitting me."

"Look," Sammy said, "I can *prove* Nola was cheating. Every time she checked her hole card, she signaled its identity to Fontaine."

"How?"

"When she was pat, she leaned on the table with her nondeck hand. When she was stiff, she pulled back."

"Will it hold up in court?"

"Wily hired a consultant to back me up. Some retired dick from New Jersey."

"From Jersey? You're shitting me."

"He's supposed to be the best."

Nick chewed away, not liking it. Without Gaming Control on their side, he'd probably lose in court. But that didn't mean he wasn't going to press charges. If word got out he was going soft on hustlers, his joint would be labeled a candy store, and he'd have more cheats at his tables than an outhouse has flies.

"How long she been working for us?" Nick asked.

"Almost ten years," Sammy replied.

"Any trouble before?"

"No, sir. She's been faithful."

"Yeah, yeah, yeah," Nick yammered like an old Beatles song. "Quit blowing me. Dealers don't turn rotten overnight. She's probably screwed us before."

Sammy's eyes had gotten sore looking through Nola Briggs's evaluation reports. A sheet was filled out by the pit bosses each week that served as the dealers' report card, with marks for attitude, appearance, customer comments, and most important, the dealers' win and loss percentages. Nothing in Nola's records suggested that she'd been anything but a model employee until now.

"I don't think so," Sammy replied.

"You contradicting me?" Nick asked sharply.

"You pay me to tell you the truth," Sammy said. "I'm just earning my money, that's all."

"Glad to hear it." Standing, Nick turned his back on Sammy and looked out the picture window behind his desk. Two weeks ago, he'd had to fire the grounds crew; now the lawns were the color of cinnamon. Once upon a time he'd owned the swankiest club in town, the house of the highest high rollers; then he'd blinked and found himself running a dump that catered to losers and tour groups.

"Why you think she did it?" Nick wondered. "Money?"

"We checked her bank records. She was making ends meet."

"You think it was greed?"

"No," Sammy said. "Spite."

"Toward who? That pinhead Wily?"

"No. Toward you."

Nick stared at Sammy's ghostly reflection in the window. His head of surveillance looked ready for a rest home.

"Come again?"

"Toward you," Sammy repeated. "You fucked her."

Nick did a snappy one-eighty and tossed the unlit cigar, which hit Sammy square in the chest. "Watch your fucking language."

"Yes, sir."

"In what way did I fuck her?"

"You *fucked* her," Sammy said, "as in sticking your male part into her female part."

"I don't need a fucking anatomy lesson," Nick roared. "Who the hell told you I fucked her?"

"Wily," Sammy said.

"Did he say when this alleged fucking took place?"

"Wily said she showed up on your doorstep about ten years ago. Drove out to Vegas from the East Coast and her car broke down in our parking lot. You happened on her and invited her up to your suite. Next thing you know, *wazoom*."

"Wazoom?"

"As in you fucked her."

Nick put his hand on his forehead, struggling to find a memory. "Let me guess. This was before I stopped drinking."

"Wily said it happened right before."

"Another ghost in the closet, huh?"

"Afraid so, boss."

Nick shook his head sadly. He had quit the sauce a decade ago and was still paying for it. A drinker of legendary proportions, he'd effectively erased whole portions of his memory, including most of his first two marriages and several torrid affairs, forcing him to rely on Wily and several other longtime employees to remember the wrongs he could not. "You said this girl's worked for me for ten years. How come her face isn't familiar?"

"She works the graveyard shift. She was subbing for another girl when this happened."

"She's worked the graveyard shift for ten years?"

"By choice, according to Wily."

"This is some strange chickie. You sure I screwed her?"

"Wily said it wasn't a big deal," Sammy explained. "It lasted a week. Then something happened and you split up. But Wily said it ended friendly; you gave her a job dealing blackjack and she's been a model employee ever since."

"Until now," Nick said.

"Yeah, until now."

"Let me see the little lady's file."

Nola's file was as thick as Nick's thumb, filled with vacation forms and work evaluation sheets. A recent photo was stapled to the inside page, and he stared at a tasty-looking blonde with high cheekbones and capped teeth. Nothing about her looked familiar, and he found himself wondering if it had been anything more than a one-night stand. An orange GoGo tour bus pulled up in front of his casino and he watched a mob of white-haired geezers pile out and form a conga line, itching to get inside and take a shot at One-Armed Billy. Then it would be off to the Liberace Museum and a box lunch at the Hoover Dam. Across the street at the Mirage, a dozen stretch limos filled the entrance, the high rollers lining up to squander their dough.

"Here's what I want you to do," Nick said. "You track this Fontaine character down and beat him to within two inches of his life. Redo his face, break his legs, whatever you want. Just make sure you hurt him."

"That shouldn't be too hard," Sammy said.

"Good. And make sure everyone in town hears about it."

"Yes, sir."

Nick watched Sammy grow small as he crossed the office.

"Hey," he called after him.

Sammy stopped on a dime. "Yeah?"

"You sure I banged her?"

"Lola in Housekeeping confirmed it," Sammy replied.

Nick winced as his head of surveillance left.

Catching hustlers was the toughest job in Las Vegas, as Sammy liked to tell anyone who cared to listen. They acted just like normal people, came in all shapes and sizes, and could talk their way out of just about any tight situation.

Take the little old lady playing blackjack down below. Using a portable camera with a zoom lens, Sammy had been spying on her from the catwalk for twenty minutes, waiting for her to make her move. She was a sweet old gal, with blue hair and bifocals, somebody's grandmother for sure. She had a nice way about her, too, with a consoling word for her fellow players when they busted, a smile and little burst of applause when they won. Unfortunately, she was a hustler, and it had taken Sammy a while to spot her.

The guy posing as her son was also a hustler, an athletic type in his early thirties with a hundred-dollar haircut and a Ralph Lauren wardrobe. Hanging on Mom's chair, he complemented the old gal perfectly.

His mother had been increasing her bets and now had three hundred dollars on the table. Through his camera Sammy saw the son's shoulders tense, and he zoomed in on his mother's hand. Unlike most casinos, the Acropolis let the players touch their cards. It was old school, but Nick wouldn't have it any other way.

Mom peeked at her hand. A king and a six—a stiff. Tucking the cards under her bet, she expertly copped the six in her left palm, her left thumb remaining motionless during the move's execution. *A lot of practice had gone into that,* Sammy thought.

Taking her left hand off the table, Mom dumped the six into the open purse in her lap. Her son, who'd been gripping the back of his mother's chair, removed his hand and scooped up the lone king. "But Mom," he said loudly, "you've got blackjack!"

In one continuing action, he added the ace of spades palmed in his hand and turned over both cards. It was pure poetry, and Sammy caught it all in three quick pictures.

"Oh my," Mom squealed with delight. "Would you look at that. Is there a special name for this?"

The dealer, a green kid who'd started the previous week, flashed her a dopey grin, oblivious to what had gone down.

"They call it a snapper," he replied.

"A snapper! How cute!"

The dealer paid her two and a half to one. Pocketing her winnings, she flipped him a fifty-cent toke.

"Get them," Sammy barked into a walkie-talkie.

Hoss and Tiny had been hiding in the emergency exit and came barreling through the door like a pair of hungry bears. Reaching the pit, they pinned the son to the table while knocking Mom out of her chair and onto the floor.

"For Christ's sake, take it easy," Sammy shouted.

The son started yelling like a stuck pig and covered his head with his arms, a telltale sign that he'd been busted before. Mom was lying on the floor, screaming, and Sammy adjusted his earphone, wondering if the reception was off. Mom no longer sounded like a lady, and as Tiny pulled her up, Sammy saw why: Her wig had fallen off along with her bifocals, revealing the shaved head of a local hustler named Doovie Jones. Snatching his wig off the floor, Doovie stuck it back on his head.

"How dare you strike a woman," he shouted indignantly.

More security appeared. Sammy ran up and down the catwalk, checking the other tables. More than one casino had been ripped off by a pair of hustlers creating a diversion while a third hustler switched a shoe or cleaned out a rack of chips.

The tables looked secure. Out of the corner of his eye, he spied Joe Smith poking his big black head out of his alcove.

"Joe," he yelled into his radio, "what the hell you doing?"

"Nothing," Joe replied, his voice riddled with static.

"Get back to your goddamned chair," Sammy ordered.

"Yes, suh."

Wily came on the radio.

"I've got everything under control," the pit boss said reassuringly. "Nothing to worry about."

Sammy could hear him gloating. Nailing two teams of cheaters in the same day had given Wily a swelled head.

Sammy knew better: For every pair they caught, ten more were lurking beneath the surface, sniffing the water for blood.

"Don't kid yourself," Sammy told him.

"There are hustlers all over this town," Sammy said ten minutes later when Wily entered his tiny office in the surveillance control room. "You gotta stay on your toes."

"Yeah, yeah, yeah," the pit boss said sarcastically.

"Keep that up, and Nick will can you."

Sammy slid the report on Doovie across his desk for Wily to read. The report would be given to the Gaming Control Bureau along with a copy of the videotape to be used as evidence in court. Without the tape, the case would be thrown out, as there was no jury in Nevada that would convict a player solely on the basis of sworn testimony. The casinos were not liked, and the locals paid them back whenever they could.

"Looks good to me," Wily said, scribbling his name on the last page next to Sammy's. A button on the phone on Sammy's desk lit up. Punching the button, Sammy took the call over the squawk box.

"Mann here."

"Sammy, so nice to hear you still have a job. This is Victor over at the Mirage."

"Hello, Victor over at the Mirage," Sammy said, gritting his teeth. "What brings you out of your cave?"

"I heard you got whacked for fifty big ones by one of our guests. I called to give my condolences."

There was not an ounce of sincerity in Victor's voice. Victor's boss had once tried to buy the Acropolis and turn it into a parking lot. The establishments had been at war ever since.

Sammy said, "You should screen your guests a little more thoroughly. This guy was a pro."

"He was screened," Victor replied. "Clean as a whistle. You shouldn't have let him keep coming back. Three times? What the hell were you thinking?"

"We were trying to catch the son of a bitch . . ."

"I heard you let him walk."

"Up yours, Victor."

The line went dead. Sammy had just been anointed chump of the month; he could see Victor on the other end, laughing himself sick.

"We need to find Fontaine," he said. "I'm open to suggestions."

Wily parked his rear end on Sammy's desk, which nearly tipped it. Righting a paperweight, he said, "I've got an idea. Once Nola posts bail, we pay her a visit and have a little chat."

"You mean slap her around?"

"If it comes to that."

"Are you serious?"

"Nothing rough—just enough to scare her."

"That's illegal," Sammy said.

"So?"

Sammy noticed that Wily had become preoccupied with something stuck to his necktie. It looked like a small chunk of steak smothered in yellow béarnaise sauce. The Acropolis served the best $4.99 buffet in town, and Wily never missed it. With a deft touch, the pit boss plucked the offending morsel off the garment.

"Don't," Sammy said forcefully.

Wily hesitated, the piece of meat inches from his open mouth. With a shrug, he let it fall into the wastebasket.

"Any other ideas?" Sammy asked.

"You still think Fontaine's someone you know?" Wily said.

"I sure do."

"Well, this consultant I hired keeps a database of every known hustler around. Maybe he can finger him."

Sometimes Wily surprised Sammy with a smart idea.

This was one of those special times. "Who is this guy, anyway?"

"Tony Valentine."

Sammy had to smile. Before he'd gotten religion, he had run with a cooler mob; he had been switching decks on unsuspecting blackjack dealers in Atlantic City when Valentine had busted him one Christmas eve at the old Resorts International. As cops went, Valentine had been a real gentleman about the whole thing, no rough stuff or threats. A pro.

"Let's hope so," he said. "I've got a bad feeling in my gut about Fontaine."

"How so?" Wily asked.

"Think about it," the head of surveillance said, shifting uncomfortably in his chair. "Fontaine whacked us three nights in a row. A smart hustler wouldn't have been so blatant."

The dull look on Wily's face indicated he wasn't connecting the dots. Sammy finished his thought. "He was trying to get caught."

"But that's stupid," Wily said, clearly perplexed. "He had to know we'd nab him or Nola."

"Him, no; Nola, yes."

"You think he used her as bait?"

Sammy scratched his chin reflectively. On the surface, it didn't add up, but who knew what Fontaine was really up to? "He was trying to create a diversion and it didn't work. He bolted, and Nola got left holding the bag."

"What a lousy prick."

Sammy nodded, hearing Frank Fontaine's taunting laugh ringing in his ears. Of the fifty-odd casinos in town, Fontaine had chosen theirs, and Sammy wasn't going to sleep soundly until he knew why.

"He's a shark," Sammy said, "and we'd better find him before he bites us again."

5

Vegas's McCarran International Airport had grown up since Valentine's last visit. Movable sidewalks, celebrity voice-overs on the PA system, upscale boutiques and jewelry stores, splashy promo films for the casinos on digital screens at the baggage claim. It was a regular amusement park, complete with video poker and banks of gleaming one-armed bandits.

"They say the casinos cheat their customers," a fifty-ish woman wearing an I LOVE LEONARDO DiCAPRIO T-shirt and support hose remarked as they waited for their bags. "You think that's true?"

"Absolutely not," Valentine replied, noting the plastic bucket filled with silver dollars clutched to her bosom. No luggage, and she was already betting the rent. "The state of Nevada wouldn't permit it. The casinos are the single biggest source of revenue the state has. They make sure everything's on the square."

"On the what?"

"On the square. As in legit."

"Oh. You some big-time gambler or something?"

"I don't play," he admitted. "It's a poor man's tax."

A flashing red light on the baggage carousel went off. The woman's eyes brimmed with hatred and Valentine got the feeling he'd ruined her vacation before it had started. Their bags came off the carousel together, dead last.

Valentine lugged his suitcase outside and stepped into an oven. High noon, and the desert was burning up. Standing on line at the taxi stand, he heard a man call his name. Without his glasses, Valentine wasn't very good at recognizing people anymore, and he watched a tall, well-tanned individual approach, his cigar-store-Indian face gradually coming into focus. The off-the-rack suit had *law enforcement* written all over it.

"Bill Higgins. Fancy meeting you here."

The two men warmly shook hands. It had been years, but Higgins hadn't changed. As head of Nevada's Gaming Control Bureau, he had forged a brave new world by joining forces with the New Jersey Division of Gaming Enforcement in the prosecution of a team of suspected hustlers. The alliance had worked, and the two bodies had been talking ever since.

"How's life treating you?" Higgins asked.

"Can't complain," Valentine said. "Nobody listens."

"Let me give you a ride."

"You don't know where I'm going," Valentine said as Higgins dragged his suitcase over to the curb. Then added, "Or do you?"

"The Acropolis, right?"

"Yeah," Valentine said, unable to hide his annoyance. "Who told you?"

A white Volvo was parked in the fire zone, a bored-looking guy with a buzz cut at the wheel. Higgins tossed the suitcase into the trunk. Valentine slid into the back-seat and Higgins got in beside him. The car edged into bumper-to-bumper traffic.

"To the Acropolis," Higgins told the driver.

"The back way?" the driver asked.

"That's probably a good idea." To Valentine, he said, "Traffic's gotten so bad you have to drive five miles out of your way just to get anywhere."

"Who told you I was coming to town?" Valentine said.

"One of my sources," Higgins replied. "It's funny, because I was going to give you a call."

"You were?"

"Yeah. I need your help."

The Volvo took the entrance ramp and edged into traffic on the Maryland Parkway. Bill wasn't the type to ask for help unless he was drowning; so much for the fun weekend away from home. Yet at the same time, it felt good to hear someone say he was needed.

"*Help*'s my middle name," Valentine said.

"Retirement treating you well?" Higgins asked as the Strip's gaudy casinos came into view.

"Depends on your definition of *well*," Valentine replied. "Lois died nine months ago, my son and I don't talk, and I seem to be clocking more hours than when I was a cop. Otherwise, it's not so bad."

"I'm sorry about your wife," Higgins said after a pause. "At least you haven't lost your sense of humor."

"I'm told it's the last thing to go."

The driver circled the Strip. It had grown into a real city, the old stalwarts like Caesars Palace and the Trop dwarfed by silly-looking pyramids and medieval castles, each new property standing belly to butt with an established hotel, the new kids pushing out the old. Sin City was morphing into Disney World.

"How'd you get into the consulting racket?" Higgins asked.

"After Lois died, I had nothing to do. One day the phone rings. Head of security for Trump Casinos in Atlantic City asks if I'd be interested in viewing some surveillance tapes. I explain to said gentleman that I'm retired and no longer among the living. Said gentleman offers me a hundred bucks an hour, minimum thirty hours a month, and my business was born."

Higgins whistled through his teeth. "They're paying you three grand a month to watch surveillance videos?"

"They sure are."

"You working for other casinos?"

Valentine nodded. His uncanny ability to sniff out hustlers had saved Atlantic City's casinos millions over the years, and his opinion was eagerly sought. Along with Social Security and his pension, he now made the kind of living he'd always dreamed about. If only Lois were here to show him how to spend it.

"How's things by you?" Valentine asked.

"Crazy," Higgins replied. "I always envied you guys in Atlantic City. Protecting twelve casinos is nothing compared to the sixty-two I've got out here."

"Running a skeleton crew sure doesn't help," Valentine said.

The driver let out a laugh. Higgins didn't see the humor; a scowl twisted his face. When it came to gambling, Las Vegas bested Atlantic City in every department but one—gaming control. Higgins's bureau employed a measly three hundred agents to do everything from collect taxes to prosecute cheats, while Atlantic City employed twelve hundred strong. Compared to the Garden State bureau, Higgins's operation was Third World at best.

"What's gotten into you?" Higgins wanted to know.

"I want to know who told you I was coming to town."

"A snitch on my payroll told me," he said icily.

"Someone I know?"

"I don't think so."

The Acropolis's legendary fountains came into view. Nick Nicocropolis's voluptuous harem of ex-wives looked as unappetizing as Valentine last remembered. Making one mistake in your lifetime was acceptable, but six was a crime.

"I want to warn you," Higgins said. "Nick Nicocropolis is running a shaky operation. He's not filing CTRs with the IRS on high rollers, which can only mean he's skimming money to stay afloat. If we decide to nail him, I'll give you a heads-up so you can get out of town."

"I really appreciate that, Bill."

"No problem. Now, let me ask you a question. I'm sure you've seen the tapes of this guy who beat them. Any idea what he's doing?"

"Either he's reading the dealer's body language," Valentine said, "or she's signaling him."

"You don't think he might be doing something else?"

"Like what?"

"I don't know. Maybe he's come up with a new way of beating the house. Like card counting."

It had not occurred to Valentine that Slick might be doing something new. No wonder Bill was biting his nails. A third of the people who gambled in Las Vegas did so at the blackjack tables. If Slick had developed a method to beat the house, the game of blackjack would have to be drastically changed, or worse, discontinued altogether.

"I don't think so," Valentine said. "If this guy had a new system, he wouldn't have come back three times. My instincts tell me the girl's involved."

"You think they're a team?" Higgins asked.

"It crossed my mind."

His friend breathed a sigh of relief and looked straight ahead. He was part Navajo and rarely made eye contact while speaking. "Well, that certainly puts a whole new light on the situation."

"Why? You weren't thinking of dropping charges, were you?"

"I was until now."

"Did you grill her?"

"A detective over at Metro is interrogating her right now," Higgins said. "That's where I'm heading after I drop you off. You can join me if you want."

"Sounds great," Valentine said.

They had reached the Acropolis's front entrance. Years ago, it had been something special, but now it was a borderline dump. Higgins leaned forward and spoke to the driver. He retraced their route and soon they were back on the Maryland Parkway.

"You miss the work, don't you?" Higgins asked.

"Every goddamn day," Valentine replied.

For someone who'd never been arrested, spending twenty-four hours in a holding cell in the bowels of Metro LVPD headquarters was a nightmare with no point of reference. It did not compare to a rotten day at work or getting fired or a head-splitting hangover. It was more like all of those experiences rolled together and then doused with gasoline and lit on fire. And because Nola Briggs didn't know better, she'd allowed a slinky black transvestite named Jewel to befriend her.

"This your first time, ain't it, honey?" Jewel had asked, her homespun Southern drawl dripping sincerity.

They sat on a bench in a steel cage with eleven other desperate-looking women. Nola nodded her head.

"Well," Jewel went on, "these bitches might look mean, but we're all the same deep down inside. You understand what I'm saying?"

"I guess," Nola mumbled.

"You keep your chin up," Jewel said, patting Nola's knee. "To survive in here, you got to be strong."

Nola nodded, fingering the tiny St. Christopher's medallion the police had missed during her strip-down. It had been her mother's and her mother's before her.

"Who's the little guy?" Jewel asked.

"My bodyguard," Nola said, pulling the pendant from her shirt so Jewel could have a look. "He goes wherever I go."

"He sure is pretty," the transvestite said, nearly drooling.

Hooking her manicured forefinger around the pendant, Jewel popped the chain, tossed St. Christopher into her mouth, and swallowed him. The cell erupted in jeers and catcalls.

"Give it back," Nola cried, bouncing her tiny fists against Jewel's chest. "Goddamn it, give it back!"

"Next time I shit," Jewel said, hopping off the bench.

A short time later, a bald detective led Nola upstairs to a windowless interrogation room and handcuffed her to a steel chair bolted to the floor. She laid her head on the pocked table and cried herself to sleep.

When the detective returned, Nola's boyfriend Raul was with him, his arms and legs manacled together. Raul's cocoa-brown eyes briefly met hers, then stared gloomily at the floor. A second chair was brought in. The detective handcuffed Raul to it, then departed without a word, slamming the door loudly.

Nola leaned on the table, trying to get as close to Raul as possible. He was the prettiest man she'd ever known, with high, sensual cheekbones and skin the color of toffee, as good outside of bed as he was in it, with a smile for any occasion and a laugh as uplifting as a hit song on the radio. So what if he wasn't educated and made his living washing dishes for five-fifty an hour? Let her friends make all the fun of Raul they wanted: He was the real thing, an honest-to-goodness man who treated her with respect and kindness and constant affection, and she was going to hold onto him as long as she could.

"Oh my God," she whispered. "What happened?"

She saw his feminine eyes well up with tears.

"I'm screwed," he said.

"Why? What on earth did they say?"

"They're going to deport me," he moaned.

Nola nearly bit her tongue.

"I went to your place after work," he explained. "The cops were there. They sat me down, started asking questions. One of them wanted to see my papers. I showed him, and he saw my green card had expired."

"You let it expire?" Nola said, starting to cry. "No! No! No!"

"He said you cheated the casino," Raul went on, "and if you didn't come clean, they were going to screw me."

"It's a lie," Nola spit angrily, her tears bouncing off the table like drops of rain. "I didn't cheat anybody. How can they say such a thing? I've worked there for ten goddamn years."

"I know," Raul said, his voice a whisper. "I told them: My baby, she's never cheated anybody; her heart's as pure as gold. But they don't want to listen. They say they know you're guilty. They say you're guilty as sin."

"I didn't do *anything*," Nola screamed defiantly, the tears bursting from her eyes and splashing her lover. "I swear on my mother's grave I wasn't in on it. The guy somehow knew the cards I was holding." She began to bawl, her chin touching her chest. "I couldn't do anything. Why didn't Wily take me off the table if he thought I was cheating?"

"I don't know, baby; I don't know," Raul said, his voice as soothing as a morning dove's coo.

"He's trying to pin it on me so he can save his ass," she sobbed, lifting her head and looking at him, her eyes red and distorted. "He's so fucking stupid."

"What you going to do?" Raul said.

"I'm sticking to my story," Nola replied, her fear turning to rage. "I didn't do anything. I don't hang around with hustlers; my record is clean. I've won Dealer of the Month ten times. They have no evidence, no proof. They let the guy who was doing the cheating go and arrested me. Well, that won't stand up in court."

"I already told them all those things," Raul said.

"And what did they say?"

"They said if you don't help them, they're going to screw me." Raul paused, hoping she'd change her story. Back in Tijuana, he had a mother and two baby sisters who stood by a mailbox each week, awaiting his check. "You sure you don't know this guy?"

"I swear to God, Raul—I've never seen him before."

Her boyfriend found the strength to laugh.

"Well," he said, "then I guess it's adios, baby."

"You know why a Mexican is like a cue ball?" the Metro LVPD lieutenant handling the investigation asked, his open mouth fogging the interrogation room's two-way mirror. A few feet away, Higgins and Valentine sat on folding metal chairs. Higgins made a face. "Watch it," the GCB chief said.

"Because the harder you hit them, the more English you get out of them."

The chubby lieutenant's name was Pete Longo, and he was a scumbag. Instead of interrogating Nola properly, he'd chosen to haul in her boyfriend and use him to blackmail her. It was the dirtiest trick in the book and the type of thing that had given the Metro Las Vegas Police Department its sordid reputation.

"That's not funny," Higgins said testily. "Maybe I should sign you up for the cultural diversity class my department's conducting."

"Fuck cultural diversity," Longo said. He lit up a cigarette and blew smoke in their direction. He didn't appreciate Higgins's bringing another detective to the interrogation, even though Valentine was retired, and he was intent on showing his displeasure.

"Your humor is offensive," Higgins said.

Longo inhaled pleasurably on his cigarette. "I'm thinking of dropping charges."

"Like hell you are," Higgins snapped.

"You told me this morning she was innocent," Longo said.

"That was this morning," Higgins replied.

"Let me get this straight," the lieutenant said. "This morning you said the GCB wasn't interested in prosecuting Nola Briggs. Now you're telling me to hold her. I don't get it."

"I changed my mind," Higgins said. "You got a problem with that?"

Longo chuckled. "You're like that song. Should I stay or should I go? Make up your mind."

"I just did."

"But I don't want to press charges," Longo said stubbornly. "Your case sucks."

Higgins stood up and stuck his face within inches of the chubby lieutenant's. "Stop jerking me around, Pete. I'm telling you to treat this like any other case of cheating. I'll go directly to the judge if I have to."

Longo's face turned into one big sneer. In a measured tone, he said, "It's your call, Bill, but let me tell you something. I'm sick and tired of having the likes of Nick Nicocropolis telling us who we should and shouldn't arrest. It's bad enough my people spend their time dealing with crimes the casinos are causing, and not on the street fighting the drug dealers and street gangs that have migrated from L.A. during the past decade. The fact that this case is bullshit doesn't seem to bother you. Well, it bothers me. But, like I said, it's your call, my friend."

What a nice speech, Valentine thought. Longo had probably been waiting a long time to get on his soapbox and use it. The problem was, he had no right giving lectures. Judging by the size of his enormous gut, the lieutenant wasn't spending any more time chasing drug dealers than he had to.

"I'm glad we agree on something," Higgins said.

"Your case *sucks.*" Longo jabbed his thumb at the

sobbing lovebirds next door. "It doesn't add up. She rips off the Acropolis, but does she run? No, she goes home, fixes a sub, and watches the Cartoon Network. Am I the only one seeing an incongruity here?"

The blood had risen behind Higgins's tan, giving his face a dark, menacing quality. This was about to turn into a first-class pissing contest, and Valentine found himself wishing he'd checked into his hotel and turned on a ball game or, better yet, taken a nap. Smothering a yawn, he stared at Nola Briggs, who was still crying her heart out. She was really pretty, the kind of girl that got the little mouse on the treadmill going. He glanced at the clock hanging over them; her boyfriend had come into the room more than ten minutes earlier.

Fishing two shiny pennies from his pocket, Valentine tossed them to the floor. Longo looked at him like he wanted to bite his head off. "What?" the detective snarled.

"I want to say something."

"So say it."

"I just had an epiphany," Valentine announced.

"A what?" Longo said.

"A vision; a moment of truth."

"And you just had one," the lieutenant snarled.

"That's correct."

"Well, please share your epiphany with us."

"Nola is guilty as sin," he said.

Longo threw his arms in the air. "How can you know that, sitting there?"

Valentine got up and went to the mirror, eyeing Nola through the tinted glass. She was still bawling like a kid who'd lost her lunch money. He pointed at her.

"This isn't how innocent people act," he explained. "Look at the predicament she's in. Anyone else would be screaming for a lawyer. Not her. She just sits there, knowing we're watching, proclaiming her innocence.

Who cares what we think? Telling the police she's innocent won't change her situation one bit. She's trying to convert us. Innocent people never do that."

Truth was the great elixir. The anger disappeared from Higgins's and Longo's faces.

"For argument's sake, let's say you're right," Longo said, the rancor gone from his voice. "You think the tapes are enough to convict her?"

"Probably not," Valentine said.

"Then I have to drop charges."

"Not right away. If I were you, I'd ask a judge to post a reasonable bail. Let her walk and put a tail on her. Fontaine will eventually show his face."

"You seem pretty certain about this," Longo said.

"I'd bet my reputation on it," Valentine replied.

Longo scratched the top of his balding crown. Officers of the law could be led to water but never made to drink. The lieutenant glanced at Higgins and said, "You agree?"

"If Tony says she's guilty, she's guilty," Higgins said. "I think it's a darn good idea."

Longo snorted contemptuously. "Two minutes ago, you were telling me to hold her. I hope you know what you're doing."

Higgins slapped Longo on the arm. The blow did not make a friendly sound. "I do. I want her watched twenty-four hours a day. Anything suspicious, call me. Think you can handle that between drug busts?"

Longo's face reddened; he knew Higgins was going to make him regret his little speech for a long time.

"Sure thing," the chubby lieutenant said.

6

The Acropolis was just as Valentine remembered it—
an old-fashioned gambling joint with a silly motif
that had endeared itself to enough old-timers to keep it
afloat. It had nothing to recommend it over the new
kids on the block except lots of character, and that
didn't count for much these days.

It was after three when he checked in and found two
messages awaiting him at the front desk. He read the
first while riding the elevator to the fourth floor, his
nose twitching at the fifty-year-old bellman's repugnant
cologne. It was from Wily, and his chicken scratch had
not improved. From what he could make out, the pit
boss wanted him to touch base once he'd gotten settled,
and he had left his pager number.

The elevator doors parted and he followed the bellman down a twisting hallway with as many turns as a
carnival fun house. His room was adjacent to the service elevators, and as the bellman unlocked the door,
Valentine peered over his shoulder into a depressingly
dark space with as much charm as a cave.

Valentine parted the blinds as the bellman described
the amenities. He had a wonderful view of a gray concrete wall.

"Where's the toilet?" he inquired.

"You're in it," the bellman replied.

"What are you, a comedian?"

"Right," the bellman said. "I carry bags for exercise."

He was funny in a pathetic way, so Valentine tossed him a five-dollar bill. The bellman stuffed it into his vest without a hint of gratitude. After chaining the door, Valentine peeled off his clothes and took a shower.

There was a special ugly to Las Vegas, and his bathroom was a monument to it. Neon blue walls clashed with a urine-colored sink and john, the moldy shower curtain a map of ancient Greece. After a few minutes, the hot water ran out and he found himself dancing under the bone-chilling spray. Getting out, he heard the phone.

He took his time getting dressed. Being retired had its privileges; not hurrying was certainly one of them. When he went into the bedroom, the message light on the phone on the bedside table was blinking like a beacon on a stormy night. He sat down on the rock-hard bed and dialed voice mail. An automated voice greeted him and soon he was listening to his message.

"Hi, Tony. It's Mabel. Glad to see you made it in one piece! I know how you hate flying. Listen—Gerry came by earlier, and he was hopping mad when I told him you'd flown the coop. I guess he had a big weekend planned with his father. . . . Anyway, to make a long story short, I'm going to the ball game with your son this afternoon. He was going to scalp the tickets, and I said hey, I'm great company. So we're going. I hope you don't mind."

"Jesus H. Christ," Valentine muttered. Gerry and Mabel on a date. The thought made him shudder.

"I like your son, I really do," she went on, as if anticipating his reaction. "I know he's put you through a lot of grief, but I just can't be mean to him. I hope you understand."

"Not really," he said.

"Anyway, the real reason I called is, I'm going to scrap the 'die broke' ad. You were right—it doesn't work. I mean, it's clever, but so are most five-year-olds. The good news is, I've come up with something really funny. By the time you get this message, I'll have faxed it to the hotel, so if you don't mind, I'd like you to take a look at it and give me a call. I'll be waiting by the phone. Ta ta."

Valentine hung up remembering the time he'd tried to take Gerry to see the Yankees in the play-offs only to have his son say no and go off with his dope-smoking friends. It had been some of the bitterest rejection he'd ever tasted. What goes around comes around, he supposed.

He felt the room tremble as the service elevator docked next door. Two Mexican chambermaids got out, chattering loudly as they pushed a squeaky laundry cart down the hall. He could hear every syllable. The phone rang again.

"Mr. Valentine, this is Roxanne at the front desk," a friendly female voice said. "I have a fax for you."

"I'll be right down," he said. "And Roxanne, I need to be put into a new room."

"New room?" She sounded offended. "What's wrong with the room you're in?"

He lowered his voice. "I found a body under the bed."

"*A body?*"

"Yeah. I think it's Jimmy Hoffa."

"Well," she said, her fingers tapping a computer keyboard, "let me see what I can do."

On the long walk back to the elevator Valentine took stock of the carpet's muted orange and red checkerboard design. He'd read several studies conducted by casinos to quantify the effects of really bad carpet. The goal was to find out which patterns were so upsetting to the human eye that it actually coaxed a customer into looking up from the floor and into the eyes of a dealer or gleaming slot machine. The idea was to trigger impulse play. No one had ever determined if it really worked.

On the way down, he remembered the second message in his pocket, and he unfolded the fax that had been given to him when he'd checked in.

Valentine,
You old fuck.
Take some advice from a friend and stay retired.
No job is worth dying over, is it, pal?

"What the hell," he said aloud.

The elevator doors parted, but Valentine did not get out. Over the years, he'd been threatened by several hustlers, and a couple had actually tried to do him harm. The doors closed and the elevator rose on its own accord.

Soon he was back on the fourth floor. He punched the Lobby button and again descended, then read the fax again. Whoever had sent it knew him well enough to know he was retired. Had Bill's snitch told everyone in town he was visiting? Or had someone he'd once busted in Atlantic City spotted him at the airport and overheard his curbside conversation with Bill? Whatever the answer, he was going to have to stay on his toes or risk going home in cargo instead of first class.

To reach the front desk, Valentine had to pass through the casino, and he stopped briefly to get the lay of the land. The casino floor was designed like a hub of a wheel, with the gaming tables and slots in the center of the wheel, and all other destinations flowing from that center. A person couldn't get anywhere inside the

Acropolis without passing through the wheel, and, it was hoped, dropping a few dollars. Twenty-five years earlier, every casino in Las Vegas had been designed this way. He suspected that today, the number was less than a handful.

Roxanne awaited him at the front desk. She was a vivacious gum-chewing redhead with muted brown eyes, his favorite kind of girl. She pegged him right away and said, "I thought Jimmy Hoffa was buried in Giants Stadium."

"That's Walt Disney," he said.

"I thought Walt Disney was being kept in a refrigerator down in Orlando."

"That's Adolf Hitler."

She slid the fax across the marble counter.

"You're a real piece of work, you know that?"

Valentine grinned. "Where're you from?"

"I was raised in New Jersey. I came out here five years ago."

"I'm a Jersey kid, too. You mind the heat here?"

"It's okay so long as you don't wear any clothes."

Valentine's eyes grew wide and she grinned. He sensed that she was enjoying this as much as he was. How many years separated them? At least thirty. It was nice to see he could still ignite a spark, however brief.

"You in for a convention?" she asked.

"I'm doing some work for the casino."

"You don't say."

"Listen, I need to ask you a favor. If my son calls, could you tell him I checked out?"

Roxanne raised an eyebrow. Her pleasant tone vanished. "You don't talk to your own son?"

"No," he said, "and neither should you."

"And why's that? He murder someone?"

"It's nothing like that."

"If he didn't murder someone, why can't you get over it?"

It was Jersey logic if he'd ever heard it. There would be no winning with this young lady, so he retreated from the front desk. Frowning, she went to wait on another customer, casting him an evil eye as he hurried away.

He slipped into the lobby bar for some privacy. It was called Nick's Place and was cozy dark. The bartender stood behind his empty bar polishing a highball glass. He looked about Valentine's age, rail thin and silver-haired, and did not get annoyed when Valentine ordered a glass of water with a twist of lemon.

"Sparkling or Evian?" he inquired politely.

"Tap, if you have it."

The bartender treated it like any other drink, setting the glass on a coaster and sliding it toward him. It was the first classy thing Valentine had seen anyone in the Acropolis do, so he tipped the man two bucks.

He unfolded Mabel's fax on the bar. Why had Roxanne assumed that he should be civil to Gerry? What gave her that right? Sipping his drink, he perused Mabel's latest assault on the funny bone.

Tired of the same old grind?
Enroll today in Grandma Mabel's school for begging. Become a pro. Special classes for TV evangelists and career politicians. Learn the pitch and never work again.

Mabel Struck
President Emeritus
813/PAN-HAND

Valentine grit his teeth. What was Mabel doing? This wasn't funny at all. The ad had *Gerry* written all over it. In the smoky mirror behind the bar, he saw a meaty-faced palooka sauntering toward him. He was too soft-looking to be a mobster. As he slid onto the adjacent stool, Valentine said, "You must be Wily."

"That's me," the pit boss said, rapping his knuckles on the bar. "Roxanne said I might find you in here."

"She's some girl."

Wily ordered a bourbon and water. Under his breath, he said, "She's got a thing for older guys, if you hadn't noticed."

"Now that you mention it," Valentine said, "I was wondering what she was doing in my room."

Wily guffawed like it was the funniest joke he'd ever heard.

"I'll use that one," the pit boss said.

His drink came. Valentine told him about being picked up by Bill Higgins at the airport and seeing Nola interrogated. Then he explained his theory of why he believed Nola was involved in the scam. Behind Wily's muddy cow eyes, he saw a flicker of something resembling intelligence.

"Sammy Mann said the same thing," Wily said. "He thinks she's guilty as hell. To tell you the truth, I didn't spot it right away, and I know this girl very well."

"Sammy Mann's living out here?" Valentine said, the threatening fax still in his thoughts.

"Sammy Mann is head of the casino's surveillance. He's my boss."

Valentine nearly spit water through his nose.

"He got religion," Wily explained. "He's one of us."

"Did he tell you I busted him once?"

"Sure did. Said he beat the rap."

"My ass, he beat the rap. He'd still be in prison if he hadn't paid off the judge."

That really got Wily laughing. "Sammy bribed a judge? Oh boy, that's really good."

Their talk drifted back to work. Wily pounded the

bourbons in an attempt to keep up with Valentine's
need to quench an insatiable thirst he'd had since stepping off the plane. Soon the pit boss's face resembled a
big red blister.

"Sammy thinks this weasel Fontaine set Nola up,"
Wily said, his tongue thickened by the booze. "Sammy
thinks it was all a smoke screen. He thinks Fontaine had
something else in mind."

"Like what?"

"A big score."

"Fifty grand is a big score."

"Not anymore," Wily said, eyeing something floating
in his drink. He fished it out with a spoon. "Of all the
joints in town, he picked ours. There has to be a reason."

"And you want me to find out what that is."

"And him, if you can."

"That's a tall order."

"If it's any help, we think he's still in town."

"Bill Higgins tell you that?"

"Uh-huh."

According to a billboard Valentine had seen at the
airport, the population of the Las Vegas metropolitan
region was hovering at just over one million. As big
cities went, that wasn't very big at all. With Nola out of
jail and the police watching her, Fontaine was sure to
show up sooner or later, and Longo's men would nab
him. It was a no-brainer.

"Double my fee if he gets caught?"

Wily was too polluted to think it through. Normally,
Valentine didn't take advantage of drunks, but this one
had comped him the worst fucking room in the house.
Raised a Catholic, he believed in making amends, the
sooner the better.

"Sounds good to me," the pit boss declared.

7

It was Nola's best friend Sherry Solomon who bailed her out of jail later that afternoon. Sherry was a Southern California blonde with a great face and killer legs. She had migrated to Vegas the same week as Nola, her '79 Volkswagen van stuffed with her things. They'd gone to dealing school together and for a while shared a crummy one bedroom, until they'd both gotten on their feet. Sherry was a survivor and Nola had called her first, knowing that even though Sherry didn't have five grand to post bond, she probably knew someone who did.

"My ex-boyfriend's brother is a bail bondsman," Sherry explained as she handed the parking attendant three bucks. "Saul Katz. He runs those ugly billboards you see around town. You know: 'Don't bawl—call Saul!' I told him you were square and wouldn't run and leave him holding the bag."

"Thanks, Sherry," Nola said, wiping tears from her eyes.

"Hey—you going to be okay?"

Rummaging around in the glove compartment, Nola extracted a Kleenex and honked her nose savagely. "I spent the last six hours in a room handcuffed to a chair. You know what that feels like? Every guy who looks at you, it's like he owns you. I feel like a piece of meat."

Ten minutes later, Sherry pulled the car into the Jumbo

Burger and ordered their usual fare, extra-large crispy fries and diet orange sodas. Back on the highway, her mouth stuffed, Sherry said, "Raul's screwed, isn't he?"

Nola punched a straw through the plastic lid in her soda, the sound like a small gun going off. "Sure looks that way."

"I asked Saul to post his bond . . ."

Nola laughed bitterly. "And he said, 'For some stinking wetback? Get real, honey.'"

"It wasn't like that. Don't get so down on everybody."

Nola took a long swallow of her drink, then shot her friend a hard, unforgiving look. "In case you hadn't figured it out, *I'm fucked,* my dear. At least Raul gets to go home. Vegas is home for me. Nick is never going to hire me back, and if they somehow find me guilty, I could do time in the state pen."

"You going to hire an attorney?"

"With whose money?" Nola asked. "My house isn't worth squat. Whatever equity I have is in profit-sharing from work, and I can't touch it." Nola put her chin on her chest and fought back another wave of tears. "I don't know what the hell I'm going to do."

Sherry took the exit for the Meadows and drove past the vacant guardhouse. The identical two-bedroom houses were lined up in neat rows, the sharply pitched roof lines making tepees against the burnt-orange desert. Some days it looked pretty as a picture, others ugly as sin, and she supposed it all depended on your frame of mind. She hit the brakes when she saw a school bus unloading some kids in front of them.

"There's an ugly rumor going around the casino."

Nola perked up, a worried look on her face.

"Wily told one of the dealers that Sammy Mann has a videotape of you and Fontaine having a conversation in the casino parking lot."

"In the parking lot?"

Sherry nodded. She drove down Nola's block, the driveways filled with identical Japanese imports. "Nick has cameras everywhere, even outside."

Nola was sitting up very straight, her face taut and expressionless. "And when did this supposed conversation between me and Fontaine take place?"

"Three days ago. After we got off our shift."

Nola stuck out her tongue and let out a Bronx cheer.

"What's that supposed to mean?" Sherry said, clearly perplexed.

"It means 'So what?'" Nola said, crossing her arms defiantly. "For the love of Christ, I talk to a hundred people every day when I'm working."

"But Sammy Mann's got it on video."

"*So what?*" Nola said, starting to fume. "The *Enquirer* runs pictures of famous people standing next to criminals. It doesn't mean they know them."

"Wily's saying you did it out of spite, that you hate Nick for what he did to you ten years ago."

"Yeah, yeah, yeah," Nola said, perfectly imitating Nick's annoying yammer.

"Do you?"

"Hate Nick? No more than anyone else who works for him."

"Wily says you were sweet on Fontaine."

"Fontaine was a nice guy. Aren't those the ones we're supposed to like?"

"Did you meet him in a bar or something?"

"For the love of Christ, Sherry. I don't know the guy," Nola practically shouted. "I'd never seen him, and that's the God's honest truth."

Sherry pulled the car up Nola's driveway and put it in park, letting the engine idle. "Sammy and Wily are putting the heat on everyone in the casino. They're asking lots of questions."

"Tell them anything?" Nola asked sarcastically.

"I told them you're the squarest dealer in the joint."

"Thanks for the thumbs-up."

Sherry put her hand on her friend's knee and gave it a squeeze. Once, on a stormy Friday night when no decent man in Las Vegas would have them, they'd shared a bed, an experience that had spiritually bonded them, if only briefly.

"You'd level with me if you knew this guy," Sherry said softly. "Wouldn't you?"

"You sound jealous," Nola teased her.

"Come on. I'm trying to help you."

"Of course I'd level with you," Nola insisted. "You know I can't keep a secret. So the next time Wily bugs you, tell him the truth. I don't know Fontaine."

Nola's lips brushed her best friend's cheek, then she opened her door. "Thanks for the save, Sherry. I really appreciate it."

"What are best friends for?" Sherry said.

Sherry watched Nola disappear into her depressingly plain little house. Her friend was doomed and wasn't doing much to help herself. It made her sick to see Nola throwing her life away, and she put the car into reverse and backed it down the drive.

Sherry did care, almost as much about Nola as herself, and she waited until she was a few blocks away before sticking her hand beneath the seat and switching off the tape recorder.

The police had ripped Nola's place apart, then put everything back where it didn't belong. Going to her bedroom, Nola knelt on the floor, pulled a thin cardboard box from beneath the bed, and removed its flimsy lid. A cry escaped her lips.

Her diary was gone, along with stacks of letters and bank statements and other useless paper she dutifully stored for the IRS each year. Whatever the police hadn't known about her personal life before, they certainly knew now.

The clothes Raul kept in her closet were also gone, and she guessed the cops had packed a suitcase for him, having decided to deport him once they'd realized she wouldn't play ball. What Nazis they were! Without evidence, they'd resorted to breaking the same laws they were sworn to protect. But Raul would get even. Thousands of illegal Mexican immigrants were slipping into Texas every week, and it wouldn't be long before he'd be back on her doorstep, panting like a lovesick pup.

The bathroom had been turned upside down. Towels on the floor, her prescription medicine in the sink. She put the bottles back into the cabinet and tossed out those medications that had expired. Done, she ran her finger across the labels, sensing something was amiss.

"For Christ's sake," she swore.

Her prescription Zoloft, the little blue happy pills that kept her afloat, were gone. Nola's eyes welled with tears. What were the police trying to do, make her go crazy?

In the kitchen, a blinking answering machine awaited her. Six messages. She listened to the first five seconds of each before hitting Erase.

"This is Chantel with MCI—"

"Hi, my name is Robyn with Olin Mott Studios—"

"This is a courtesy call—"

"Fred's Carpet Cleaning here. We're having a special in your—"

"This is AT&T—"

The last message was a guy breathing. After ten seconds, the line went dead. Barely able to control herself, Nola punched *69 on her phone.

"Brother's Lounge," a man's gruff voice answered.

"Tell Frank Fontaine to leave me alone," she screamed into the receiver. "Do you understand? Tell him to stop calling me!"

"Frank's not here," the man said, his tone indicating he was used to such calls. "Wanna leave a message?"

"Yes. Tell that pond slime to climb back under his rock and leave me alone. And he can go fuck himself while he's at it."

". . . 'fuck himself while he's at it' . . ." the man repeated, as if writing it down.

"And you can go fuck yourself, too," Nola exploded.

". . . 'go fuck yourself, too' . . ." the man echoed.

Nola slammed the receiver into the cradle, then ripped the phone out of its jack. Comics. Las Vegas was filled with comics.

Off the kitchen was a closet she'd converted into a study by laying down a square of cheap carpet and sticking an Office Depot secretary in the corner. It was her private space, and Nola slipped inside the tiny room and shut the door, the sudden darkness calming her down like it always did.

She booted up her Compaq Presario, the darkness pierced by seven and a half inches of blue iridescence. Entering Windows, she hit the File button. The program had a function that let her view the last eight files that had been opened. Scrolling through them, she realized that the police had already been here. There wasn't much to see, mostly letters she'd never gotten around to finishing and her finances on a Lotus spreadsheet, but their invasion of her in cyberspace seemed the ultimate insult. She erased everything.

Exiting Windows, she logged onto the Internet through AOL and typed in her password.

"You've got mail!" an automated voice cheerfully announced.

Nola looked in her mailbox. One message had arrived dated this morning. The return e-mail address was unfamiliar. She took a deep breath. Who was looking for her now?

> Nola,
> Heard you got busted. Sorry (really).
> You've never been through this before. Here are some things you need to know.
> The police have bugged your phone. They have probably moved into an empty house nearby and are watching you right now.
> It doesn't matter that you are innocent. In their eyes, you are guilty, and since they're the law, you *are* guilty, unless you choose to do something about it.
> You need to act fast. I dropped a key in your mailbox. It opens a safe deposit box at the First American Savings & Loan near your house. Use the money to hire a good lawyer. I forged your name, so you have access.
> Love,
> Frank

She fell back in her chair. *Love, Frank?* Who did this shark think he was? And how had he gotten her e-mail address? It was a setup, plain and simple. Deleting the message, she shut down her computer.

She sat in the air-conditioned darkness and stared at the screen's muted afterglow. It faded slowly, a great metaphor for her own predicament. Fontaine was right about one thing. She was screwed. She'd been *suspected* of cheating, and in this town, that was enough to lose your sheriff's card. Without that little piece of laminated plastic, she couldn't work in a casino. And as sad as it sounded, dealing blackjack was the only real skill she had.

This is another fine mess you've gotten yourself into.

Yes, it was. Her inner voice was great at stating the obvious. Another sad chapter in the sorry life of Nola the Victim, an epic novel of stupidity and needless suffering. See Nola lied to, spit on, and treated like a human doormat, only to come back for more like a washed-up fighter who's grown fond of eating punches.

She needed some air. Going out the back door, she stepped barefoot on the patio and started dancing, the bricks hot enough to fry an egg. Hopping onto the grass, she crossed onto her neighbor's property. The owners, a husband-and-wife dance team called the Davenports, had retired to Palm Springs and left the house with Century 21. It had been vacant for months, and Nola put her face to a shuttered back window and tried to peer in, wondering if the police really were inside.

She felt the wall hum; something electric was running inside. Curiosity killed more than just cats, and she crept around back and retrieved the spare key from a rock in the garden.

Clutching the key, Nola contemplated unlocking her neighbors' back door and marching inside, just to see if the police really were there. Did she have the guts?

No, she decided, she didn't. Instead, she went to the Davenports' two-car garage, unlocked the door, and slipped in.

Parked inside was an unfamiliar Chrysler sedan. Nola pressed her face to the driver's window. A two-way radio was mounted to the dash. Cops. She shuddered. Score another round for Fontaine.

Inside the house, she heard a man talking on the phone, his voice gravelly and mean. Nola tiptoed across the concrete floor, remembering all the times she'd watched her neighbors practice their intricate routines, and stuck her ear against the flimsy particleboard.

"The fuck I know what she's doing. It's been silent since she made the call. Can you believe it? Home ten minutes and she calls a bar where Fontaine hangs out. Of course I got it on tape. The guy's got a twelve-inch schlong is what I think. She neeeeds him."

Nola brought her hand to her mouth. How in God's name was she going to convince the police she didn't know Fontaine now? The fact that Fontaine had called her first would be irrelevant in their eyes. She was doomed.

Okay, Frank, she thought, *you win.*

She slipped out the garage door and locked it. Retracing her steps, she went into her own house and marched down the hall. Opening the front door, she made a beeline for the mailbox at the curb.

Despite the heat, it was a beautiful day without a cloud to mar the bright blue sky. She worshiped the sun and fresh air and had stayed in Vegas probably longer than she should have because she got to enjoy these things every day. She would not do well in prison, if it came to that.

Her mailbox was jammed with junk mail. One envelope stood out. Her address was hand written, and there was no return address. She tore it open and a steel key fell into her palm—and with it, a note.

Nola,
This is how I signed your name.

She examined Fontaine's forgery. It didn't look anything like her signature, but that wasn't the point. It was written in simple script and would be easy to duplicate. As crooks went, he was awfully smart.

But why was Fontaine throwing her a life preserver? What did he gain by helping her prove her innocence? He was a hustler: There had to be something in it for him.

The sun was making her feel like one of the French fries she'd eaten for lunch. Back inside, she grabbed her keys and entered the garage from the kitchen, hopping into her Grand Am. She kept the garage air-conditioned, so the car was ice cold. For the longest while, she sat behind the wheel, thinking.

The conclusion she came to was a simple one. Like it or not, she needed a lawyer, a real good lawyer, one that could buy her time until she could straighten the police out. If the safe deposit box was filled with cash, then she was going to take it. What other choice did she have?

She fired up the engine and hit the automatic garage door opener. Sunlight flooded the interior. A sense of urgency overcame her, and she threw the car into reverse and skidded down the drive, barely able to see.

She braked at the curb to check for the neighborhood kids and saw the cops' Chrysler backing down the Davenports' driveway.

She did thirty through her development, the Chrysler fixed in her mirror. Braking at a stop sign, she watched the car pull up. Inside sat two dudes in their midthirties, one black, the other Hispanic, both wearing *Terminator* shades and hip street clothes. She wasn't fooled for a second.

She slowed down, forcing the Chrysler to hang back. The guard booth in front of her development sat vacant, just as it had since the day it was built. A quarter mile away was the entrance ramp for the Maryland Parkway. She spun the radio to her favorite station, classic rock for whining boomers, and with the Stones' "Satisfaction" pumping adrenaline through every vein in her body, punched the accelerator to the floor. The Grand Am let out a beastly roar and she blew past the empty guardhouse.

Her tires were smoking as she flew onto the six-lane superhighway and was immediately challenged by a sleek Porsche Boxster whose driver was determined not to give up the lane. Freedom was a glorious thing, and Nola was not about to relinquish hers anytime soon.

Blowing past the Boxster, she was soon doing one hundred and twenty. The cops in their Chrysler were nowhere to be seen.

8

The fifty-year-old bellman was waiting when Valentine returned to his room. Without a word, he retrieved Valentine's suitcase and escorted him upstairs to his new digs, a twelfth-floor suite with travertine floors, red leather furniture, and a Jacuzzi sporting eighteen-karat gold fixtures. It was high-roller heaven, the kind of room money couldn't buy, and Valentine called the front desk and left a thank-you message for Roxanne.

Exhausted, he went to bed early and slept as soundly as he had in a long time. The next morning, a Mexican busboy appeared at his door at eight A.M. with scrambled eggs, toast, fresh OJ, a pot of coffee, and the local paper. He had finished reading the box scores when there was a tapping at his door. He opened it to find a grinning Sammy Mann.

"Remember me?" the head of security asked.

Old age had robbed Sammy of his debonair good looks, his face gaunt and unhealthy. Gone, too, were the tailored clothes and silk neckties, replaced by beltless polyester slacks and a tacky madras shirt.

"If it isn't Sammy 'The Whammy' Mann, last of the red-hot deck switchers," Valentine greeted him. "Come on in."

Sammy limped in and took a seat at the head of the dining-room table, a chrome-and-glass monster big enough to seat twelve. As he got settled, Valentine poured two cups of coffee and pulled up a chair. Sammy tipped his cup, his dark eyes twinkling. They seemed to be saying, *Isn't life filled with little ironies?* Sammy was one of the classier cheats Valentine had ever arrested, and for a while they reminisced about the old days and the various hustlers they'd both known.

Their mutual acquaintances were many. Like most hustlers, Sammy had switched partners as often as he changed shirts, and the array of talent he'd plied his trade with was a venerable Who's Who of Sleaze. Jake "the Snake" Roberts, Whitey Martindale, Larry the Lightbulb, Sonny Fontana, Big J.P., and on and on.

"I probably ran with every great hustler of the last twenty-five years," Sammy boasted, working on his third cup.

"Who was the best?"

"Sonny Fontana, hands down."

"They ever catch the guy who murdered him?"

"Not yet."

"Looking back, you have any regrets?"

"I just wish I'd gotten to Atlantic City sooner."

It was a common lament. In the late seventies, Atlantic City had put a new rule into play at its blackjack tables. It was called Surrender and allowed players to look at their cards, and if they had a bad hand, surrender half their bet. Someone had forgotten to do the math, as Surrender actually put the odds in *favor* of the players, especially those who knew how to card-count. Overnight, the word went out that the little city on the Jersey shore was a candy store, and hustlers from around the globe had come running. Surrender was eventually banned, but by then the damage was done. The casinos had lost millions.

"A lot of boys retired after visiting Atlantic City," Valentine said.

"Until you came along," Sammy said ruefully.

"Someone had to stop them."

Soon the conversation drifted to the topic of Sammy's bribing a judge. He was not ashamed to talk about it. "I was scared as hell of going to prison. You hear stories. Every prison has a crime boss. If the boss finds out you're a hustler, he puts you to work. Believe me, I wasn't about to start cheating other criminals."

"That could prove hazardous to your health."

"No kidding."

"How much did it end up costing you?" Valentine asked.

"Thirty grand and a condo I owned down in the Caymans. I was facing five years minimum, so I didn't mind paying."

Valentine topped off Sammy's cup with the last of the coffee. He'd heard the same complaint from hustlers over the years: Prison was tougher on cheats than other criminals. "So tell me about this Fontaine character. Wily says you know him."

Sammy corrected him. "I think I know him. His play reminds me of someone from a long time ago. His attitude strikes a nerve."

"How so?"

"He's arrogant. Like he's daring us to catch him."

"Think about what you just said," Valentine said, passing the cream. "You paid a judge a small fortune to avoid prison, and this joker Fontaine dares you to nab him. Doesn't make sense."

"I know," Sammy said. "Wily told me you keep profiles of every hustler you've ever arrested. Maybe Fontaine matches one."

"I already tried that," Valentine admitted. "Physically, he doesn't resemble anyone I've got in my computer. That means he probably had plastic surgery. If I'm going to make a match, I need to learn more about him. His habits, the way he dresses, what he drinks, that sort of stuff."

"I'll give you a list of everyone he came into contact with at the casino. Wily had a lot of interaction with him."

"Good."

Across the street, the volcano at the Mirage blew its stack, sending a giant doughnut of black smoke into the humid summer air. They watched it float lazily over their heads and burn a hole in the simmering sky.

"You've seen a lot of hustlers over the years," Valentine said. "How would you rate Fontaine's play?"

"One of the best."

"But no one knows who he is."

"Yeah," Sammy said. "Creepy, isn't it?"

The pager clipped to Sammy's belt went off. He checked it, then pulled out a small cell phone and made a call.

"That was Wily," he said, hanging up. "He's down in Nick's office. Looks like we have a breakthrough."

Valentine had never been fond of snitches. Although most law enforcement agencies depended heavily on them for information, they were still parasites, barely human types who spent their lives clawing on the glass, forever on the outside looking in.

The lady sitting in Nick Nicocropolis's lavish office was a perfect example. Her name was Sherry Solomon, and on the surface, she was a real dish—cute face, nice figure, an easy, engaging smile. A pretty nifty package until you looked hard and saw the bags under the eyes and realized she was pushing forty and the charms she'd lived on all her life were starting to fade. She was afraid for her future, so she'd taken to selling out her friends. Before Nick's secretary escorted her in, Nick Nicocropolis asked Wily if he'd ever slept with her.

"Never," the pit boss had replied sharply.

Nick looked relieved. He explained to Valentine that his memory was shot, and that he could no longer rely on it to keep a record of his sexual conquests. The legendary lover Don Juan, Nick's boyhood idol, had died being unable to name a single lover. Nick didn't want that to happen to him, which was why he'd kept Wily around for so long. Hearing this news, the pit boss tugged uncomfortably at his collar.

Valentine nodded and said nothing. Over the years, he had met his share of oddball casino owners, and Nick fit right into that group. A little guy with a Napoleon complex who'd probably jumped on every female who'd ever shown the inclination. Nothing new there.

Sherry played her tape for the four men. Wily sat beside her, nodding his head enthusiastically. Nick sat at his desk, rolling dice on the blotter. He smirked when the tape went silent.

"So?" the casino owner said.

Wily jumped in. "Nola hates you. You can hear it in her voice."

"A lot of people hate me," Nick reminded him.

"It shows motive," Wily said.

"She was laughing at me," Nick said, throwing a seven. "What's this 'yeah, yeah, yeah' crap? Is this some inside joke?"

His employees' faces turned to stone. Standing behind the desk, Sammy cleared his throat. "It's what you say when you get excited, Nick. 'Yeah, yeah, yeah.'"

Nick looked flummoxed. Valentine could tell that he had absolutely no idea what his head of surveillance was talking about. Never tell the emperor that he has no clothes.

Nick looked to Wily for help.

"'Yeah, yeah, yeah,'" Wily chorused like a parrot.

"Why are you saying that?" Nick said, getting furious.

Wily grinned oafishly. "'Yeah, yeah, yeah'. It's what you say when you get riled up."

"I don't say 'yeah, yeah, yeah,'" Nick said heatedly. "I never say 'yeah, yeah, yeah.' That's horseshit. I say 'yeah,' like everyone else. So don't go around saying that anymore, okay?"

"Sure, Nick," they all said.

"Now where were we? Oh yeah, the tape. I think you're going to have to do better, honey."

Wily nudged Sherry Solomon with his elbow. "Sherry, tell Nick what you told me this morning about Nola."

Sherry folded her hands in her lap and looked straight ahead, her pose reminiscent of that of a naive schoolgirl.

"Well," she began, "Nola and I roomed together for a while. This was right after you and she split up. I heard her say things that were scary. Nola has it in for you."

Nick's face turned serious. "She does?"

"She wants to ruin you."

Nick gave her a stony look. "Just what did I do to Nola Briggs besides give her a job and try to take care of her that made her want to hurt me?"

"You pierced her soul."

"*I did?*"

Sherry nodded solemnly. "She wanted to go to a shrink and get it off her chest, but she didn't have any dough, so she spilled her guts to me. Anyway, she talked a lot about paying you back one day. In spades."

"She's got revenge on her mind?"

"Yes. She said there was a flaw in the casino's security system, and if she could figure out a way to exploit it, she was going to take you for a bundle."

"Nola actually said that?"

Sherry Solomon nodded her bleached blond head.

Nick turned and looked at Sammy. "What flaw?"

"I don't know what she's talking about," Sammy replied.

Nick looked back at Sherry. "What flaw?"

"She never told me," Sherry explained. "But I do know this: She said you took her up on the catwalk one night, and while you were screwing her, she looked down and saw it. She was going to tell you, but the next day you dumped her."

"You don't think she was just talking tough?" Sammy said, clearly disturbed by this piece of news.

"That's not like Nola," Sherry said.

"But this happened ten years ago," Nick said. "I mean, time heals all wounds, doesn't it? Why now?"

"Something happened to Nola six months ago that triggered it," she explained. "She broke up with a guy and got real depressed. Started missing work, sleeping in all day. I stopped by one afternoon and found a pamphlet from the Hemlock Society in her house. She was thinking of killing herself."

"This is some messed-up chickie," Nick said, his gaze now fixed squarely on Wily. "How come you didn't pick up on any of this?"

"She seemed okay to me," the pit boss said sheepishly.

Nick fixed his gaze on Sherry. "So what happened?"

"She took a Mexican vacation," Sherry replied, "and came back a new person. I asked her what happened, and she told me she'd finally found a way to pay you back."

"Did she say how?" he asked.

"No, sir, she didn't. But then this Fontaine character showed up, and I started to wonder. I mean, he's her type, and it's her table he keeps going to."

"And what type is that?"

"Dark, ethnic, lots of fun."

"That's Nola's type?"

"Yeah. Gets her juices flowing."

"Yeah, yeah, yeah," Nick said, swiveling his chair around so he was facing the window, his brown and deteriorating empire laid out before him like a faded Hollywood movie set. "So what you're telling me is, she's a threat to me and everyone who works for me."

Sherry began to answer, then halted, her lips trembling. Opening the purse in her lap, she removed a cigarette. By the time it had reached her lips, Wily had a flame waiting for her. She took a deep drag and the tension melted from her face.

"What I'm telling you," she said evenly, "is simply this. Nola hates you. It's the kind of hatred men don't understand. You pierced her soul. She told me she could never look in the mirror after what you said and see herself the same way. So now she's paying you back."

Nick spun around, not appreciating his employee's lecturing tone. The dice hit the wall and came to rest on the carpeted floor at Valentine's feet. Snake eyes.

"For what?" he said angrily. "What did I do? Tell her she had bad breath? Call my bookie after I had my orgasm? You're killing me, honey. What did I do to deserve some chickie holding a grudge against me for ten whole years?"

"You told Nola her tits were too small," Sherry said. "When she wouldn't get implants, you dumped her."

Nick scowled, his darkly tanned face shriveling like a prune. He looked at Wily for help; when none was forthcoming, he stared at Sammy, then at Valentine, who'd been busy scribbling notes on a pad. Finally, in desperation, he looked to Sherry Solomon.

"So?" he said.

"I heard you were the best lawyer in Las Vegas." Nola's knees banged Felix Underman's polished mahogany desk as she pulled up a chair. "That's what everyone says—'Mr. Underman is the best.' Not that I ever needed an attorney before. But now that I have been arrested, well, you were the first person I thought of."

The legendary defense attorney said nothing, his eyes fixed on the attractive woman who'd buffaloed her way past the lobby guard and barged into his office unannounced. Normally, Underman avoided working on Saturdays in observance of the Sabbath, but he'd been in court all week and needed to catch up. He had a mind to show her the door, but her appearance intrigued him. This young lady *looked* innocent, and that was something he rarely encountered. He nodded for her to continue.

"Anyway, Mr. Underman—"

"Please, call me Felix," he said.

"Sure, Mr. Underman."

Underman frowned. There it was again. For thirty years, he'd practiced criminal law in Las Vegas and everyone in town had called him Felix. Then during a tricky triple-murder trial, he'd grown a goatee and the local newspaper started calling him Mister. The fact that Underman hated it didn't matter. It was who he had become, and he could do nothing to change it.

He watched Nola Briggs take a brown paper bag off the floor and drop it on his desk. She slid the bag toward him, and Underman obliged by opening it and peeking inside.

His breath grew short. Underman was a rich man, with a garage filled with fancy sports cars and a yacht in San Diego and a beach house in Acapulco, yet money still intrigued him. His father had toiled at two jobs all his life, running a synagogue and teaching elementary school, and had died with less money than was in Nola Briggs's paper bag.

"I'll give you ten grand if you'll just consider my case," Nola said. "I need help, Mr. Underman."

Underman closed the paper bag and slid it to a neutral corner of his desk. Over the years, he'd gotten good at visually counting bills, as most of his clients paid him in cash. Nola's bag contained close to fifty thousand dollars.

"I would be happy to discuss your situation," he replied. "If I think I can help, we can then discuss my fee."

"Oh, thank you, Mr. Underman, thank you," she gushed. "I've always heard you were a gentleman."

"My upbringing," he confessed. "My father beat it into us with a stick. Now, why don't you start at the beginning."

For the next twenty minutes, Underman let Nola talk. He had heard of her arrest through one of the snitches he employed on the Strip, as he made it his business to know who in Las Vegas was getting arrested, a tactic that allowed him to decide if he wanted a case well before it ever walked through his door. And Underman certainly wanted Nola's case. The crime she was being prosecuted for, called flashing or signaling, was difficult to prove, and the fact that the Acropolis had allowed her alleged accomplice to walk was the kind of hole he could drive a Mack truck through. Underman liked beating the casinos in court, as it was the only place he had an advantage over them.

An excellent witness, he decided when she was finished. Good teeth, soft voice, an engaging smile. Dealer of the month ten times. Perhaps, if he got the charges thrown out, he could convince her to file a libel suit against Nick Nicocropolis and take that little Greek Neanderthal to the cleaners.

"I need to ask you a few questions," Underman said.

"Shoot."

"Any previous disciplinary problems with the casino?"

"None," Nola said proudly.

"Not one?"

"No sir."

"How about the law?"

"Never. I've never even gotten a parking ticket."

"Let me guess," he said. "You don't drive."

Nola's face lit up, and Underman imagined the effect she was going to have on a jury. No record, a squeaky-clean past, and that wonderful smile. She was almost too perfect.

"Any problems with current or past employees?"

"Problems, no. Relationships, yes."

"You had a relationship with someone at the hotel?"

"I dated Nick Nicocropolis ten years ago."

Underman sat up very straight in his chair. He'd been divorced three times and knew that there was no greater wrath than a woman scorned. He gave his prospective client a hard look.

"And?" he asked.

"And nothing," she said, lighting a cigarette. "It lasted ten glorious days and then Nick dumped me. Later he offered me a job dealing twenty-one. I took it, thanked him, and went on with my life."

"So you don't have an axe to grind with Nick?"

"I wasn't happy then," she admitted. "But it wasn't the first time I'd been dumped. I've been around the car-nival a few times, Mr. Underman."

"Haven't we all, Miss Briggs?"

"Please, call me Nola."

"Of course. Nola, I'd like to take your case, but only under one condition."

"Which is?"

"I want you to take a polygraph test. If you pass it, I'll petition the judge who arraigned you. I'll argue that the Acropolis has made a grievous error. In their zeal to nab Frank Fontaine, their security people assumed you were his accomplice, something that often occurs in cases like this. I feel confident the judge will dismiss the case."

"I'll do it," Nola said.

Underman smiled. In his experience, only people with nothing to hide were willing to let themselves be strapped to a polygraph and grilled. This was going to be too easy. Consulting his desk calendar, he said, "Let's see. I have a deposition on Monday, an all-day meeting Tuesday. How about Wednesday morning?"

"I want to do it right now," Nola replied.

"Miss Briggs—"

"It's Nola, Mr. Underman."

Underman made a conciliatory gesture with his hands. "I have other clients, Nola, some of whom are sitting in jail, awaiting my services. I can't let them down."

Nola pulled her chair up, her knees again banging the desk. With trembling lips, she said, "Forgive me for sounding presumptuous, but your other clients are nothing but scumbags and two-time losers who've probably spent the better part of their lives behind bars. They're bad people who need a man of integrity like you to defend them. Well, I'm different. I'm not a bad person. I'm an innocent victim who's being wronged by a system that allows a powerful person like Nick Nicocropolis to trample whoever he pleases. Nick's already hurt me once, Mr. Underman. Please, don't let him do it again."

She was fighting back tears, and Underman found himself at a loss for words. He pushed a box of Kleenex her way and glanced at the bag of money. His poor father was probably rolling in his grave. When he looked back at Nola, she had regained her composure and was staring directly at him.

"Half now, the other if you get me off," she said.

His breath grew short. She was offering him a fortune for a day's work. He counted to five so as not to appear greedy.

Then he said, "Very well, Miss Briggs. I'll take your case."

9

Pumping the Acropolis's staff about Frank Fontaine proved a far bigger challenge than Valentine expected. Fontaine had visited the casino three successive days and had come into contact with dozens of employees, yet except for Wily and the giant African-American named Joe Smith, no one seemed to remember him. *Frank who?* the employees collectively asked. *Never heard of the guy.*

Not that Valentine could blame them. Nevada was one of the few states that vigilantly prosecuted its citizens for even *knowing* about a casino's being ripped off, the crime a felony and punishable by five years in a federal penitentiary. No wonder the staff had quickly wiped Fontaine from their collective memories.

By noon, he was finished. He slipped into Nick's Place and was disappointed to learn they didn't serve lunch. Sliding onto a stool, he laid his notes on the bar and reviewed them while munching on Goldfish and pretzels. His favorite bartender served him a glass of tap water with a lemon twist without being asked.

It was Joe Smith who'd given him the most new information about Fontaine. Each time Fontaine had visited the casino, he'd played One-Armed Billy and chatted with Joe about his hoop days at UNLV. During these conversations, Joe had noticed that Fontaine wore elevator shoes and guessed he was two or three inches shorter than he appeared. He also had a hair weave, something that was not apparent from the surveillance tapes. And he was a smoker. Joe had seen him toss a cigarette into the gutter before he'd entered and knew a nicotine habit when he saw one.

"Company," the bartender mumbled under his breath.

In the back bar mirror, Valentine saw Roxanne making a beeline toward him, her pretty features distorted by an ugly expression. Turning on his stool, he flipped his notes upside down on the bar.

"Fancy meeting you here," he said. "Thanks for upgrading me to a suite."

"You're welcome," she said through clenched teeth. "I hope you didn't find any unexpected girls in the room."

Valentine blanched, remembering his comment to Wily.

"He's used the line all over the casino," she said, seething.

"I'll kill him."

"Get in line."

She started to leave, and Valentine grabbed her arm. She resisted, but not as much as he'd expected. Was she really hurt, or just disappointed? Probably a little of both. Jumping to his feet, he said, "Roxanne, please. I'm terribly sorry. It was a stupid thing for me to say. I didn't mean to hurt your feelings."

She let him take her to a table and buy her a drink. Her shift had just ended, and she ordered a Bombay and tonic. The bartender served them and gave Valentine a sly wink.

"Heard from my son recently?" Valentine asked.

"He called three times this morning. I told him you didn't want to talk with him, but he kept calling back."

"That's my boy," Valentine said.

"You shouldn't hate him so much," she said, jumping

in where they'd left off the last time. "I mean, what's the harm of taking a few bets? Most bartenders I know do it. It's part of the business."

Valentine didn't know what to say. Leave it to Gerry to talk out of school. He could run from his son, but he couldn't hide.

"Roxanne," he said after a pause. "I don't want to discuss this. My son and I have been at odds for as long as I can remember. When my wife was alive, she played referee and kept things civil; now that she's gone, we can't be in the same room without going at each other's throats."

"Are you still mad he's a bookie?"

"Of course I'm mad. He's breaking the law. He's been breaking the law most of his life. And I gave him the dough to open the bar. He—" Valentine bit his tongue. "I just want to give him time to think about it."

"So you won't talk to him."

"That's right. I won't talk to him. But I do need to talk to you."

Roxanne brightened. "You do?"

"The hotel has hired me to conduct a little investigation."

"You a dick?"

"Ex-cop. I run a consulting business."

The news seemed to relax her. Taking a swallow of her drink she said, "No kidding. Wily said your company was called Grift Sense. What does that mean?"

"It's an old gambling expression," he explained. "A grifter was a cross-roader, a hustler. Having grift sense was the highest compliment a hustler could pay another hustler. It meant that you not only knew how to do the moves, you also knew when to do them. Sometimes that's the most important thing."

"And you have that."

"I can feel when a hustle's going down, even if I don't know exactly what it is."

"Grift sense."

"Right. Anyway, I need to talk to you about Frank Fontaine."

"Okay."

As Valentine fiddled with his pen, she said, "I knew there was a reason I liked you."

He raised an expectant eyebrow.

"My old man was a cop," she explained.

There was a lot more to Roxanne than met the eye. She was working on her MBA at UNLV's night school while holding down two part-time jobs, her days split between managing the front desk and balancing the hotel books. She was a savvy young woman with a boatload of ambition, and Valentine found himself liking her more than he probably should.

Early on, Roxanne had recognized the threat Fontaine posed to the Acropolis. A player who never lost could quickly put the casino out of business. She had been working the front desk the morning of Fontaine's third visit and remembered the encounter in vivid detail.

"Frank Fontaine may be the greatest blackjack player who's ever lived," she said, working on her second drink, "but when it comes to having class, he was a mutt trying to act like a poodle. My father always said, 'You want to see if a guy has class, look at his shoes. No polish, no class.' Fontaine didn't polish his shoes."

Valentine scribbled furiously. "What kind of shoes?"

"They looked like Ferragamos."

"Anything else?"

"His vision isn't very good."

"How could you tell?"

"He popped a contact lens and came up to the desk begging for some drops so he could put it back in. When he brought his hand to his face to put the lens in, he nearly poked his eye out."

He added *far-sighted* to his list of notes. He already had enough information to run another check on his database. Ten to one, it was someone they all knew.

"Did you get a good look at his eye?"

"Yeah. It was the same color as the contact."

Good girl. "Anything else?"

"No, I think that's it."

He put his pen away. The bartender brought another round without being asked. The guy was beginning to grow on him. Valentine drank the water in one long swallow. There was something about the desert heat that made his thirst unquenchable.

"You sure know how to pack them away," Roxanne said, wiping her lips with a frilly cocktail napkin.

"It's water," he said.

She took the glass out of his hand.

"Well, excuse me," she said, licking her finger. "It is water. You don't look like the type."

"And what type is that?"

"People who drink water are either alcoholics or Mormons."

Every interview came with a price. This one was getting a little costly, so he said, "There's a third category you're forgetting. It's called children of alcoholics. My father was a rummy. I saw what it did to my mother."

"So you don't drink."

"That's right," he said. "End of story."

"Hey. Sorry if I stepped out of bounds."

"Don't mention it."

He walked her out to her car. The employees parked in a giant macadam lot behind the casino, their cars baking in the desert inferno. Roxanne wrapped her hand in a handkerchief before daring to touch the handle of her gleaming white Grand Prix.

"Well," she said, "I guess this is good-bye. I'm sorry

for butting into your personal life. But your son just seems like a nice kid."

"Sometimes he is a nice kid."

"Then why all the hostility?"

He shrugged his shoulders. "I spent my life putting people like him behind bars."

"Oh. Well, I'm sure you'll settle things one day. I can't have kids, so I tend to mother people. I know it's a pain, but that's just me. See you."

Her lips pecked his cheek and then she slid behind the wheel of her car. Valentine stepped back as she fired up the engine. Being childless was no fun, especially when you wanted them. Had he known her a little better, he would have told Roxanne about the two-year struggle he and Lois had gone through to conceive his beloved Gerry.

The midday sun jumped out from behind the clouds, so he shielded his eyes with his hand to get a good look at Roxanne's license plate as she drove away. She seemed to be a wonderful woman, but who really knew these days? Taking out his pen, he jotted the license plate number down on the palm of his hand, then went back inside before he passed out from the heat.

His suite had been cleaned, and Valentine lay down on the circular bed and shut his eyes. Jet lag had suddenly caught up with him—he was dog-tired. He swam around in the sheets for a while, struggling to get comfortable.

It didn't work, his brain overloaded with all the things he'd learned that morning. The enigma of Frank Fontaine was slowly unraveling, one piece at a time. Opening his eyes, he stared at his reflection in the mirrored ceiling. He was a large man, a shade over six-one, yet he looked puny in comparison to the bed. Lifting his head, he noticed how inordinately large *everything* was in his suite. Big bed, big bathroom, big murals on the walls, big brass knobs on the doors, a big concrete balcony off the living room. It reminded him of old Miami Beach and its expansive Jackie Gleason architecture. A real time warp.

Rising, he went to the living room and got his notebook computer from its bag and booted it up. The dining-room table had been decorated with fresh-cut flowers and a bowl of fruit. He parked himself at its head and went to work.

During his twenty years working the casinos in Atlantic City, he had kept a profile of every hustler he'd ever come into contact with, jotting down their patterns, habits, vices, and idiosyncracies. A hustler might change his appearance, he reasoned, but he could never change who he was.

By the time he'd retired, he had amassed profiles of over five thousand hustlers, enough to fill up the hard drive on his ancient PC. The same information easily fit onto a Compaq notebook PC, which now accompanied him on every out-of-town job. The profiles, which he collectively referred to as the Creep File, were actually part of a program created by Gerry's first wife, a lovely computer expert named Lucille. Lucille had modeled Creep File after software called ACT, which was a basic database management program.

Booting up Creep File, Valentine hit Search and a blank profile filled the screen. Reading from his notes, he typed in what he'd learned about Frank Fontaine.

Name: Fontaine, Frank
Sex: Male
Height: 5'7"–5'10"
Weight: 150–160
Age: 40–45
Heritage: Italian
Hair color: black, weave

Facial hair: none
Identifying marks/tattoos: none observed
Disguises: none observed
Right- or left-handed: right
Smoke: expensive cigars, cigarettes
Drink: club soda
Nervous habits: none observed
Dress: designer, expensive
Attitude: cool, relaxed
Game(s) played: blackjack
Is dealer involved in scam? yes
Are other players involved? none observed
Player's betting habits: erratic
Range of player's bets: $100.00–$1,000.00
Does player conform to basic rules of game
being played? no
How is player cheating (list all possible
methods)? NA
Other known information: far-sighted; likes
basketball

Done, Valentine hit the Enter button. Creep File would
now take Fontaine's profile and compare it against every
hustler in the database. Those who matched Fontaine's
description in four or more categories would be pulled up
in a separate file.

Within seconds, the program was done. Valentine
scrolled through the matches and counted forty-eight
profiles. Fontaine was finally going to get his mask
ripped off. It was about time, for Valentine had come to
the realization that if he didn't make this guy, he would
never get to the bottom of what was going on here.

For the next hour, he read each profile while sipping
on a Diet Coke. Thirty-six of the hustlers were serving
time or deceased. Of the remaining twelve, he omitted
nine because of age and one who'd had a sex change.

That left two hustlers: Johnny Lonn and Frank "Bones" Garcia. Valentine knew each man well.

He jumped back and forth between their profiles, which included mug shots from recent arrests. Johnny and Bones were both Italian, were both world-class card counters, and they bore strong physical resemblances to Fontaine. Each man had also run with a gang and knew the ins and outs of orchestrating a major rip-off.

But with each man, there was a problem. In 1993, Johnny had lost his right thumb in a freak car accident; Bones had recently contracted a rare skin condition that had rendered him completely hairless. Neither man could be Fontaine. His hand slapped the dining-room table in frustration.

Pushing his chair back, Valentine went to the suite's picture window and stared down. Like an ugly woman without any makeup, the Strip was all warts and moles in the harsh daylight, and he watched a line of traffic slither snakelike past the hotel. Fontaine's cocky play was his calling card, and Valentine felt certain that he belonged to that elite club responsible not only for ruining casinos but also for fixing major sporting events, even bankrupting a small country or two. Fontaine was somebody special and had gone to a lot of trouble to keep his identity secret.

Calling room service, Valentine ordered a hamburger and a bucket of ice, then sat back down at the dining-room table. The computer had gone to sleep, and he impatiently tapped the Shift key with his finger. Finally, the screen lit up and he scrolled to page one of Creep File.

His eyes fell on the profile of Devon Ames, a Philadelphia-based dice scooter of some renown. Valentine began to read, determined to miss nothing. Like a bloodhound, he was going to sniff Fontaine out, even if meant reading all five thousand profiles in his computer, one at a time.

10

"What do you mean, you're dropping charges?" Sammy Mann bellowed, his face a few inches from Pete Longo's.

"You heard me," the chubby lieutenant replied, parking his butt on his trashed desk and firing up a Marlboro. It was Saturday afternoon, and he wanted to watch some college football; the last thing he needed to hear was this shriveled-up old hustler telling him how to run his investigation. "I'm dropping charges. If you were smart, you'd hire Nola Briggs back ASAP."

"Are you crazy?" Sammy howled. "She ripped us off!"

"That's debatable. Look, Sammy, her defense attorney, the one and only Felix Underman, had Nola take a polygraph test a few hours ago. The man who administered the test is an ex-detective and a pal of mine. He was kind enough to messenger over a transcript of her questioning. Care to hear it?"

"I sure as hell would," Sammy said, making the springs sag on the lumpy couch in Longo's rat-hole office. Wily, who sat on the other end, rose a few inches.

"He asked her fifty questions," Longo said, flipping through the typed transcript. "I'll just share the juicy stuff with you gentlemen. Here's one. 'Miss Briggs, before he walked into your casino and sat down at your table, had you ever met a gambler named Frank Fontaine before?' Answer: 'No, it was the first time I ever saw him.'"

Longo looked up into their faces. "The polygraph says she's telling the truth. Here's some more. Question: 'Do you know what it means to flash?' Answer: 'Yes. It means that the dealer is illegally flashing her hole card to a player.' Question: 'Were you flashing your hole card to Frank Fontaine when he was sitting at your table?' Answer: 'No, I did not flash my hole card to Frank Fontaine.' Question: 'Have you ever flashed a hole card to a player?' Answer: 'I'm sure I have, but never intentionally.' Question: 'Was Frank Fontaine sitting in such a manner that he would have been able to glimpse your hole card?' Answer: 'No, he was upright. You have to drop your head on the table to glimpse a dealer's hole card. He wasn't doing that.' Question: 'Did you signal Frank Fontaine in any fashion?' Answer: 'No, I did not.' Question: 'Did Frank Fontaine solicit you in any way before this incident took place?' Answer: 'No, he did not.'"

Longo put the transcript down and gazed tiredly at his two guests. "Her answers are all reading true. I'm sorry to spoil your party, but I've got to let her walk."

"Maybe she took speed and got her heart racing before she took the test," Wily suggested, a worried look distorting his blunt features. "Maybe everything she's saying is actually a lie."

Longo shook his head wearily. "The examiner took her pulse before and after the test was administered. Seventy beats a minute before, eighty-two after. That's within the normal range that the heart rate jumps when someone's strapped to a polygraph."

"You're saying she's telling the truth," Sammy said, his face deadpan. "You're saying we're screwed."

"I don't know if you're screwed or not," Longo said,

glancing impatiently at his watch. "I do know that the guy who administered this test worked for Metro LVPD for eleven years and is the same guy we use when we want a second opinion. He's the best."

"Nick's going to kill us," Sammy said. He glanced sideways at Wily, who was nervously scratching a stain on his necktie. "He'll fire us for making him look bad. We're fucked."

"Don't let her go, Pete," Wily begged, standing up to plead their case before the chubby lieutenant. "If she walks, we get the blame. We'll never be able to work in Las Vegas again. I got a wife and two kids; Sammy's ready for retirement. You can't make us walk the plank."

Longo held his palm up like he was directing traffic. "Guys, stop—you're killing me. Evidence is evidence, and you don't have any. I gotta drop the charges."

"You can't," Wily insisted.

"Hey," Longo said, "you should be thanking me. And so should Nick."

"Thanking you for what?"

"If I drop charges and get you guys to say you're sorry, Nola says she won't sue for false arrest and slander. That lets you boys off the hook."

"She's threatening to sue us?"

"She sure is. Seems she's got a pretty good case. After all, we arrested her on the basis of evidence you gave us, and that makes Nick liable."

"You're shitting me," Wily said.

"No, I'm not. If she can prove that Nick had it out for her and you two were following Nick's orders . . ." Longo shook his head sadly. "I hate to think of the consequences."

It was Sammy's turn to stand up. Every time he got together with Longo, the lieutenant made him feel two feet tall. He was always shaking them down for fight tickets and comps and an occasional suite so he could hire a college-age hooker to give him a blow job or entertain his girlfriend of the month. Whoever said gangsters no longer ran in Las Vegas had never been worked over by this lowlife two-bit mutt. It was the experience of a lifetime.

Digging into his pocket, Sammy begrudgingly extracted a Ticket Master envelope. It contained a seat for Tuesday night's Evander Holyfield heavyweight title fight at Caesars, third row center. Scalpers were getting five grand and more for seats this good. He handed it to Longo.

Longo removed the ticket and examined it. "Only one?" he asked innocently.

Wily shot Sammy a helpless glance.

"For the love of Christ," Sammy swore under his breath. From his other pocket, he removed a second ticket and handed it over.

"You know, I've always been a big fight fan," Longo said, slipping the two tickets into his sharkskin wallet.

"Me, too," Wily said. "So's Sammy. Aren't you, Sammy?"

Sammy didn't say anything. They were his tickets. Now he'd have to watch the fight at home on Pay-Per-View or go to a bar with a bunch of other clowns who couldn't afford a real seat.

"What are friends for," he said through clenched teeth. "So, are you going to help us or not?"

"I can buy you a few days," Longo said.

Sammy jerked his head around to stare at Longo. "*A few days?*"

"I should let her walk right now."

"*A few days?*"

"Here's what I'll do," Longo said. "I'm going to ask the judge who arraigned Nola to stall Underman until next week. Tomorrow's Sunday and Monday's a state holiday. That gives you three days to come back to me with hard evidence. Bring me something credible, and I'll gladly lock horns with Underman on Tuesday morning."

Sammy ran his hand through his thinning hair, not believing what he was hearing. He'd known hoods with better manners than this sorry excuse for a law enforcement officer. Biting his tongue, he said, "We really appreciate it, Pete."

"You da man," Wily said apishly.

"It's been a pleasure doing business with you," Longo said, shaking their hands at the door. "See you boys at the fight."

"I wish I was going to the fight," Wily said, pouting as Sammy paid three bucks to get his car out of the lot. "How about you?"

"I'll probably go to a bar or watch it on Pay-Per-View," Sammy admitted. "I love the fights."

"Pay-Per-View sucks," Wily said.

"Well, you can see it on cable. They usually show it a week later."

"Cable sucks, too. I won't watch cable."

It was rare for Wily to have an opinion about anything. He was vanilla and proud of it. When they were on the Maryland Parkway, Sammy said, "You got something against the cable company?"

"How many times you seen the fights on cable?" Wily asked.

"I don't know. Say a thousand."

"A thousand even?"

"No, a thousand and one. Get to the fucking point."

"You've seen a thousand and one fights, and how many ring girls have you ever seen? Bet you can't count them on the fingers of one hand. The best-looking broads at a fight are the ring girls, and they never show them on cable."

"And that's why cable sucks."

"Sucks the big one," Wily said.

Reaching beneath his seat, Sammy removed a flask of whiskey and removed the top with his teeth. He took a long pull, licking his lips when he was done.

"Why are you drinking again?" Wily asked.

"Because we're screwed."

"You think Nick will can us?"

"He should."

For a while they rode in silence, each man considering what that meant. For Sammy, it meant retiring to someplace cheap like Arizona or Florida where he'd spend his days hustling loose change at cards so he could afford to buy premium cigars. Wily's future was not as bleak; for him, there was always a decent-paying job at an Indian reservation casino or on a cruise ship. He'd survive, but he'd do so knowing his best days were behind him.

"Nola was in on it," Wily said. "You agreed with me."

"Stupid me," Sammy said.

"What is that supposed to mean?"

"It means I didn't think it through. If I'd known this broad was holding a grudge against Nick, I never would have had her arrested. I would have watched her, figured out what she was up to. The scam with Fontaine was a smoke screen; something else was going down, a big con, and we didn't see it."

They were back at the Acropolis. Sammy lapsed into silence as he passed the busty statuary that illustrated Nick's checkered marital history. He thought about Nola driving past the fountains each day, her hatred ignited by the sculpted mountains of silicone. No wonder she had it in for the boss.

Sammy pulled his car up to the front doors and threw it into park. The casino was dead, the uniformed valet nowhere to be seen. Letting the engine idle, he said, "What the hell is Valentine doing anyway?"

"I talked to him a few hours ago," Wily said. "He's holed up in his suite on his computer."

"Did he make Fontaine?"

"Not yet."

"Who put him in the suite, anyway?"

"I sure as hell didn't."

Sammy drummed his fingers on the steering wheel. "What's he charging us, anyway?"

"Thousand bucks a day, plus expenses."

"Jesus Christ," Sammy muttered, getting out as the valet came running. "What a thief."

Sammy found Nick alone on the catwalk, hunched over the railing, his attention consumed by the torrid action on a craps table below. Shadows danced on his face, tiny angels of light coming off a big-chested woman dripping with cubic zirconias. She was trying to make eight the hard way and kissed the dice like she was planning to make love to them if they pulled through.

"Sometimes I wake up in the middle of the night," Nick said after she crapped out, "and I lie in the dark and think about all the crummy things I've done in my life. At least the ones I can remember. They gnaw at you, especially the ones that ended up being worse than you had in mind."

"Like Nola," Sammy said quietly.

"I swear to God I don't remember her," Nick said, breathing heavily. "Now, with her clothes off, it might be a different story."

Sammy was in no mood to laugh. If Nick was trying to make a confession, it certainly wasn't coming across that way.

"Anyway," Nick went on, "Nola is a good example.

Sherry said we dated for ten days. My guess is we fucked like bunnies for nine, then finally got down to talking. Maybe I did ask her to get her tits blown up; stupider things have come out of my mouth. But the truth is, I was being honest with her. I like my women a certain way. There isn't a crime against that, is there?"

"Not that I know of," Sammy said.

"So look where my honesty got me," Nick said, glancing briefly at Sammy before returning his attention to the tables. "I've got a real enemy in this broad."

"You think Sherry's leveling with us?"

"She's not clever enough to make something like that up," Nick said. "Nola definitely has it in for me."

Sensing Nick's reflective mood, Sammy gently broke the bad news to him. "The police want to drop charges. Seems she passed a polygraph with flying colors."

"Beautiful," Nick said.

Nick began to take a walk. Sammy followed, their footsteps echoing in the cavernous space. They stopped at the blackjack pit and both men put their elbows on the railing. The tables were half full, the action light.

"I do know one thing," Sammy said after a minute.

"Only one?" Nick said.

"It's a figure of speech."

"I know what it is," Nick snapped. "So what's this one thing you know?"

"I know there isn't a flaw in our security system," Sammy replied. "Nobody can waltz in here and start robbing us without the alarms going off. No one's going to ruin you, boss."

Down below, a dealer had busted and was paying off the table. Several players had doubled down on their bets and the two men silently added up the house's losses: over twelve hundred on the turn of a single card.

Nick said, "It won't take much. Fifty grand here, a

hundred grand there. It all adds up. You hear what I'm saying?"

Sammy swallowed hard: It was the first time Nick had come out and admitted his financial shape was nothing to write home about. If the Acropolis had to shut down because of losses at the tables, he and Wily would never find work anywhere ever again.

"I won't let you down," Sammy promised him.

Nick thumped him fondly on the back.

"Glad to hear it," he said.

11

It was past nine o'clock when Valentine scrolled up the last profile in Creep File. He stared at the computer screen, his eyes aching. Outside, the neon city had come alive, and he was itching to go downstairs and take a walk, his brain fried by his notebook's little blue screen.

Staring him in the face was Chan Zing, a notorious card marker from Taiwan. Using the finely sharpened nail on his left pinky, Zing would edge-nick all the high cards in a blackjack game, allowing him to know if the dealer's hole card was high or low. Zing was a crafty guy capable of many things, but turning himself into a sweet-talking Italian was not one of them.

Valentine exited the program and shut down the notebook. This was turning into a nightmare. Frank Fontaine was hiding in his computer and he couldn't find the guy. Was old age robbing him of his powers of deduction, or was Fontaine a hell of a lot more clever than he'd originally thought?

Neither thought made him feel particularly comfortable. Rising, he stretched his legs while staring at the madcap carnival down below. Hordes of skimpily dressed tourists jammed the narrow sidewalks, giving him second thoughts about his walk. He needed some fresh air, and the Strip was probably the last place he was going to find it.

Moving into the living room, he hit the couch like a dead man and punched the remote. A black monolith rose from the floor, its doors parting as if by magic. A split-second later, CNN filled the thirty-six inch screen. It was just the balm he needed.

It was a slow news day. He watched the sports ticker on the bottom of the screen. The Devil Rays had clobbered the Bronx Bombers, with Boggs picking up five ribbies. Oh, to have been in the stands, watching Gerry eat crow each time a Devil Rays player crossed home plate. His son was not a good loser and would have taken the Yankees' loss to an expansion team particularly hard.

The phone rang for a while, then went silent. Moments later, the message light started blinking. He dialed into the hotel's voice mail and retrieved the call.

"Wily here. Just wanted to see if you hit pay dirt. I'm working the floor. You know, I was thinking about Fontaine—" A commotion erupted on the casino floor. "Gotta run," Wily said excitedly.

Valentine replayed the message. The commotion sounded like a big payout at roulette. Every game attracted different players who made different sounds when the action got hot. He'd always assumed it was something tribal that dated back to the beginning of time. His own tribe, he'd assumed, were the guys who'd sat around the campfire drinking coffee and talking. He listened to the crowd erupt a second time. Definitely roulette.

He called down to the floor and paged Wily.

"You make him?" Wily asked breathlessly when he came on.

"Still digging," Valentine replied. "So what were you thinking about Fontaine?"

"I don't know. Maybe it's nothing."

"Try me."

"I was thinking about his play."

"And?"

"It was like . . . well, like he was toying with us."

"How so?" Valentine said.

"I mean, it wasn't even competitive," Wily said. "He had us beat the moment he walked in. You know what I'm saying? And he wasn't sneaky about it. At one point, he actually laughed at us."

Valentine gripped the receiver, feelings its cold plastic freeze into his palm. Only one hustler he had ever known had laughed while ripping the house off. Only one.

"You're kidding me," Valentine said.

"Not at all," Wily said. "It was how Sammy made him."

"Sammy made his laugh?"

"Yeah. Said the moment he heard it he knew it was someone from his past." In the background, a craps table was going wild. "Gotta run. Call me if you come up with anything."

Valentine killed the power on the phone. Out of the mouths of babes and idiot pit bosses come the most amazing things. It didn't make sense, yet at the same time, it made all the sense in the world. World-class hustlers didn't just appear out of nowhere. They plied their trade for years before attempting to rip off a casino. Frank Fontaine had been around a long time.

Taking out his wallet, Valentine dug out the threatening note he'd received the day before and reread it. Hustlers had threatened him over the years, but only one had actually tried to kill him. And for good reason: because *Valentine* had wanted to kill *him*. And that adversary had possessed a laugh as wicked as the Devil himself.

Of course Sammy Mann thought he knew Frank Fontaine. Everyone in the gambling world knew him.

Only there was one problem.

He was dead.

Valentine thought about it some more, then dialed the front desk. Roxanne picked up.

"Don't you ever go home?" he asked.

"I wish," she replied. "Three of my coworkers got the flu. I'm working double shifts until they come back."

"Poor you."

"Yeah," she said. "Poor me."

"Has my son called recently?" he inquired.

"Only about ten times," she said.

"Did he leave a number?"

Roxanne hesitated, clearly startled. "No. Why?"

"I don't know. I was thinking about what you said."

"You were?" Another pause. Then, "I mean, that's great."

Valentine laughed silently. He was getting an inordinate amount of pleasure out of baiting this young lady. As to where he planned to take this, he had no idea, but the ride was certainly fun. He said, "Well, I'm sure I can track him down. Take care."

"You, too," she said.

His next call was to Mabel. It was three hours later on the East Coast, which made it dinnertime. Because his neighbor was a passionate cook, he assumed Gerry had weaseled an invitation and now sat at Mabel's dining-room table with a napkin shoved down his collar, utensils in hand, drooling as he eagerly awaited Mabel's next culinary masterpiece.

"How was the game?" he said by way of greeting.

A five-minute soliloquy followed. To hear Mabel describe it, it was the greatest Saturday afternoon of her entire adult life. And Gerry, his degenerate son, was the reason why.

"Is he there?" he asked.

"Your son? Why yes, he's sitting right here."

Stuffing his face at that very moment, Valentine guessed. "Put him on. Oh, Mabel—I got your fax. It was funny, but not your best. A little off, if you ask me."

"Gerry and I came to the same conclusion," she informed him. "He talked me into scrapping it. I'm composing a new ad right now. It's *very* funny."

Valentine felt his face grow hot. Being Mabel's sounding board was his job, not his son's.

"Here he is," Mabel announced.

"Hey, Pop!"

"Hey, yourself," Valentine said.

Gerry's voice was garbled, his mouth stuffed with food. He began to make awful choking sounds into the phone, and then Valentine heard the steady whacking sounds of Mabel pounding Gerry on the back. Soon his son was sipping water, breathing heavily.

"How many times am I gonna have to tell you not to talk with your mouth full?" Valentine bellowed into the receiver. "For the love of Christ, Gerry. Chew your food, then swallow, then talk. It's what separates us from the monkeys, you know?"

"Aw, Pop," his son said, sounding pitiful.

"Your uncle Louie—"

"Choked to death on a piece of veal on Christmas day," Gerry recited by heart, "and you and Gramps couldn't bring him 'round. I know the whole story. It runs in the family, and I'm the latest in the line. Stop making a federal case out of it."

Valentine took a deep breath. A few weeks off, and they'd both come out of their corners swinging like a couple of kids in an amateur boxing match, all anger and no form.

"Hey," he said. "I'm sorry."

His son didn't know what to say. Valentine tried another tack. "So how was the game?"

Gerry was not used to getting second chances from his old man, so he picked his words carefully. "Great. I mean, the Yanks got clobbered, but we had a good time anyway. I rented a little TV from a guy at the concession booth so we could see what was going on in the outfield. It was a blast."

"Sorry I wasn't there," Valentine said.

"Me, too."

A brief silence followed. Valentine wasn't really sorry, but he felt better for saying it. He cleared his throat.

"Listen, I need you to help me with a case I'm working on. I want you to go to my house—Mabel's got a key—and turn my computer on. Boot up Windows and pull up a program called DCF. Think you're up to it?"

Valentine bit his tongue the moment the words came out of his mouth. It was the first decent conversation they'd had in a long time, and now he'd gone and spoiled it. Gerry was trying—he'd give him that—whereas *he* was doing his best to burn another bridge.

"I mean, would you mind?"

"Not at all, Pop," his son said quietly.

Valentine had already booted up Frank Fontaine's profile on his Compaq notebook when Gerry called back ten minutes later.

"You need to fire your cleaning lady," his son informed him.

"Don't have one," he replied.

"That's what I mean. There are piles of crap everywhere. You're living like a hermit."

"It's *work*," Valentine replied. "I'm running a business. Don't touch any of it."

Normally, his son would have said something, and

Friday Night at the Fights would have resumed. But not tonight; Gerry was different, more subdued. Maybe Mabel had said something, or perhaps flying down to Florida and finding his old man gone was a much-needed reality check.

"I've got the C prompt on the screen," Gerry said.

"Good. Type in *shell* and hit Enter. Five or six icons will come on the screen. Double-click on *DCF.*"

"Done," his son said. "You need to get a new mouse."

"Don't use the one I've got."

"You don't use your mouse?"

"I can't see that damn little arrow."

"Suit yourself," Gerry said. "What's *DCF* stand for anyway?"

"Dead Creep File. Your ex-wife convinced me that instead of deleting a file every time a hustler died, I should transfer it to another program, in case I needed to reference it one day."

"That sounds like Lucille. She never threw anything away."

What about you? Valentine wanted to ask. He reined in his desire to insult his only child and said, "Here's the deal. You're going to create a profile with some information I'm going to give you, and then you'll run a match against the other profiles in the DCF file. I want you to print whatever DCF spits out and fax it to my hotel. It shouldn't take more than ten minutes."

"Hey, I'm happy to help. Can I ask you a question?"

"Shoot."

"Why are you interested in looking at profiles of a bunch of dead hustlers?"

"It's a long story," Valentine said. "I'll fill you in when I get back home."

His son paused, and Valentine realized what he'd just

said. To fill Gerry in, he was going to have to either call or go see him. His son had won this round.

"Sounds great," Gerry said.

The casino was jumping when Valentine ventured downstairs fifteen minutes later. It was a no-nonsense kind of crowd, guys in torn jeans and stained denim shirts, women in tank tops and Day-Glo shorts, their jewelry bought off the TV. Out of hunger, they'd made their way to this city in the desert with money they could not afford to lose—either begged, borrowed, or stolen—to chase the dreams that radiated from every billboard and storefront in the country. They were the worst class of gamblers, their knowledge so minimal that it made their chances of winning infinitesimal, and because other casinos would not allow them through the door in their blue-collar clothes, they ended up at the Acropolis, the poor man's gateway to heaven.

Roxanne awaited him at the front desk. She'd tied her flowing hair in a bun—*pretty* no longer described her. She was now in another league of beauty, and his heart did a little pitter-pat.

"Did you and your son kiss and make up?" she asked.

"Sort of. Thanks for the pep talk."

She slid Gerry's two-page fax across the marble counter. "You know, deep down, you're a pretty decent guy."

"I'm just old-fashioned," he confessed.

"I like old-fashioned," she said.

Her coal-dark irises looked ready to ignite, and Valentine felt his heart speed up. There was no doubt in his mind what was on *her* mind. It would be one hell of an experience, only he just wasn't ready. He'd abstained from sex since Lois's death, knowing the next woman he bedded would forever cut the tie to his late wife. It would have to be someone special, not a woman he'd known less than twenty-four hours, so he backed away from the desk.

"I bet you've seen *Jurassic Park* ten times," he said.

Roxanne frowned, not getting his drift.

"You like dinosaurs," he explained.

Back in the elevator, he unfolded Gerry's fax and read the scribbled message on the cover page.

Hey, Pop,
Only one file came up. Doesn't look like a
match, but what do I know?
Gerry

Valentine flipped the page. The single profile DCF had pulled up contained a mug shot, the face instantly familiar. Closing his eyes, he mentally compared the face to that of Frank Fontaine.

Facially, the two men were as different as night and day, one handsome and debonair, the other smarmy and uncouth, and it was easy to see why no one was making the connection. The fingerprint that bonded them was Fontaine's play, which was smooth and deliberate and absolutely flawless, the play of a man who could memorize every card dealt in a six-deck game of blackjack or go to a ball game and determine batting averages in his head, the play of a man who knew not only the odds on every game of chance ever invented but also every possible way to turn those odds in his favor, through either deceit, outright trickery, or sheer mathematical genius.

It was the play of a cold-blooded, ruthless individual born with the most terrible of gifts, a perfect brain.

If anyone was capable of rising from the grave, Valentine thought, *it would be him—the one, the only Sonny Fontana.*

12

Valentine decided to call the Gaming Control Bureau and break the news to Bill Higgins first. Sonny Fontana had been the bane of Bill's existence since the late eighties, when he'd burst onto the Las Vegas scene like a meteor shower. Bill had acted swiftly and gotten Sonny banned from every casino in the state, but Sonny had not gone away. Instead, he'd gone underground and begun training other hustlers who in turn paid him a percentage of their winnings. Along with cheating at blackjack, Sonny's students had learned the latest methods of dice scooting, rigging slot machines, and altering the outcome at roulette. He'd created a small army of clones, and the casinos had been on the defensive ever since.

Higgins's cell phone was on voice mail. Valentine didn't like leaving bad news on tape, so he said, "Bill, it's Tony. Call me once you get this. It's urgent."

The next person he called was Sammy Mann. He tried Sammy's home first, and when no one answered, he took a chance and called the casino's surveillance control room. To his surprise, Sammy was at his desk, and Valentine asked if he could come down.

"This must be important," Sammy said.

Valentine told him it was.

"We're on the third floor," Sammy told him.

Valentine took the stairs. He made it a point to take a vigorous walk a few times a day and get his heart pumping. It seemed to make him more alert. On the third-floor landing, he found two chambermaids having a smoke. They directed him to the surveillance control room, which was tucked away behind Housekeeping.

The door was unmarked and made of steel. He knocked and took a step back, knowing it was against the law to enter without proper clearance. Moments later, the door swung in and Sammy ushered him into a high-ceilinged, windowless room.

"I'm usually off Saturday nights," Sammy explained, locking the door behind him. "I was crashed in front of the TV when Wily called. A little old lady from Pasadena got hot at the craps table and Wily thinks she's past-posting. So I came in."

"Is she?"

"Hell no," Sammy said. "Wily's dreaming."

Valentine's eyes adjusted to the room's muted light. Every casino in the world had a surveillance control room, and he supposed they all looked something like this one. At one end stood an eight-foot-tall semicircle of video monitors. Each monitor was connected to an eye-in-the-sky downstairs in the casino. The monitors were watched by five security experts, all men, who sat at a master console, their desks covered in maps, telephones, two-way radios, keypad controllers, and dead coffee cups. The people in these jobs usually had law enforcement backgrounds and took great pleasure in busting cheats. Tonight's crew appeared hypnotized by the monitors' ghostly black-and-white images, their faces expressionless.

Sammy's office sat in a partitioned corner. They went in and Sammy shut the door. The call button on his phone lit up. He answered on the squawk box. "Mann here."

Wily's voice filled the room. "So what do you think? Is the old broad past-posting or what?"

"You're seeing things. She's clean."

"Clean, my ass," Wily spit back. "She's taken us for ten grand."

"Would you like a second opinion? I've got Valentine standing right here."

"Sure," Wily said. "Let him look."

"Screen six," Sammy said.

Valentine went and had a look. Screen six offered an aerial of a craps table. It was easy to spot the offending party: Her stack of chips dwarfed everyone else's. Someone at the console hit a toggle switch and the camera zoomed in on her. She was eighty if she was a day, and her hands were shaking with arthritis. Valentine could not imagine her palming a chip and secretly adding it to her bet after the dice had been thrown. What was Wily thinking?

"Clean as a whistle," Valentine announced on his return.

"No fucking way," Wily said over the box.

"Look, Tony's got something to tell us," Sammy said. "Why don't you come up?"

"I'll come up later."

"This won't wait. And leave the old broad alone. She isn't cheating."

"I'm tossing her anyway."

"You're an asshole."

"I won't deny that."

"Bad night?" Valentine asked when Wily sauntered in ten minutes later, a butt in one hand, a glass of Johnny Walker in the other, his necktie ringing his collar like a noose.

"Rotten," the pit boss admitted. Sipping his drink, he eyed Sammy, whose hand nursed an aching gut. "You okay?"

"To tell you the truth, I've felt better."

"Stomach acting up again?"

"My stomach, my head, my back," Sammy complained. "If it's not one thing, it's the other."

"Maybe it's cancer," Wily said, bursting into laughter.

Sammy looked ready to hit him. "Is that supposed to be a joke? You're sick in the head, you know that?"

"Hey, my kid told me that joke," Wily said defensively.

"Your kid told you that and you didn't hit her?"

"Hit my kid? Are you nuts? I could go to jail."

"You've punched enough morons in the casino."

"That's different," Wily said.

"Which kid?"

"The youngest, Michelle."

"She's twelve, right?"

"Eleven."

"You poor bastard."

Valentine stood mutely in the corner. During the wait, Sammy had told him about Wily's miserable home life. His kids were the casualties of his wife's first marriage and as mean as junkyard dogs. By working double shifts, Wily saw them only two weekends a month, which made the situation tolerable.

"Tony has some bad news," Sammy announced.

Wily looked Valentine in the eye. "You made Fontaine?"

"He sure did," Sammy said.

Wily continued to stare at him. "And?"

"It's Sonny Fontana," Valentine told him.

Wily slammed his drink on the desk. Miraculously, not a single drop escaped. "*What?* That's horseshit. Sonny Fontana is dead. Everyone and his brother knows that. We're paying you a thousand clams a day and you turn up a dead guy? Get serious."

Sammy tossed Wily the DCF profile and said, "Forget what you know. Tony made the match."

Valentine watched the blood drain from Wily's head as his eyes absorbed what was on the page. Looking up, he said, "Didn't some guy in Lake Tahoe crush Fontana's head in a door so hard his brains came out of his ears? That's the story I heard, and the guy who told me swore to God it was true."

"I heard the same story," Sammy said.

Valentine had heard the story, too, his source none other than Bill Higgins. Which was why Sonny's file had been retired.

"Then this can't be him," Wily said.

"I don't want to have an argument about this," Sammy said, growing annoyed. "I knew when I heard Fontaine laugh that he was someone I'd run with. This confirms it. We got robbed by the best cheat who's ever lived. Now we gotta make sure it doesn't happen again."

"Jesus." Wily took another swallow of his drink, set it on the desk, and then pushed it in Sammy's direction. The head of surveillance raised the whiskey to his lips.

"*Salute,*" he said, downing it.

"Didn't you once run with Fontana?" Wily asked.

"A long time ago," Sammy said, wiping his mouth on his sleeve. "Sonny's got no loyalty to me now, if that's what you're thinking."

Wily looked to Valentine for help. "Why us?"

That was a good question. Why would Fontana waste a good face-lift to hit a dump like the Acropolis? Fontana would know the casino would sweat a big loss and lean on him.

"I don't know," Valentine admitted.

"You ever arrest him?" Wily wanted to know.

"No," Valentine said.

"Tony's got a grudge against Fontana," Sammy informed him.

"You do?" Wily said.

Valentine nodded that it was so.

"Well," the pit boss said, "maybe now you can settle it."

"So who's going to tell Nick?" Wily asked a few moments later.

"You are," Sammy said.

"Me? I think Tony should. He made him."

Sammy shot Valentine a weary look. "You up to that?"

Normally, Valentine would have declined; being the bearer of bad news was not in his job description. Only, Sammy looked terrible and Wily was a little drunk. "Okay," he said.

"I'll toss you for who gets to chauffeur," Sammy said. He fished a worn Kennedy half-dollar from his pocket and flipped it into the air. The coin rotated lazily above their heads. Catching it, he slapped it against the back of his hand. "Call it."

"Heads," Wily said.

Sammy lifted his hand. "Tails. You lose."

"How come I never win with you?" Wily asked.

Valentine nearly laughed. Like seventy percent of the population, Wily probably always called heads. Which was why hustlers carried around double-sided coins.

"Who knows?" Sammy said.

"Looks like Nick's entertaining," Wily said, pulling his Buick up the driveway of his boss's palatial estate. It was nearly eleven and the manicured property was lit up like a used car lot.

"How can you tell?"

"The driveway's empty. Nick's got a staff of four. He

gives them the night off whenever he brings a lady home."

"Classy guy."

Wily parked by the front door. Valentine got out, counting eight polished pillars supporting the marble portico. History either praised or ridiculed men who built shrines to themselves, and Nick had set himself up for a lot of abuse—not that Valentine thought the little Greek cared.

Wily rang the bell. A gong sounded dully behind the door. When no one answered, he punched the intercom button.

"Yeah?" Nick barked over the black box.

"It's Wily and Valentine," Wily said.

"I know who it is. I'm watching you with a camera, you moron. Why aren't you home sleeping?"

Wily brushed a spider's web away before placing his mouth next to the intercom. He did not know who Nick was with or whether that person should hear what he was about to say. It was the smartest thing Valentine had seen the pit boss do.

"We need to talk," Wily said, dropping his voice.

"Isn't that what we're doing right now?"

"Face-to-face."

"*Mano a mano?* Why, you want to punch me out?"

Nick's giddy laugh filled the box. A woman's giggle accompanied it. Valentine got the picture. Sex was Nick's narcotic. When he was getting it, there was no happier male on the planet.

"We've got some bad news," Wily explained.

"How bad?" Nick asked, sounding worried.

"I think we should tell you in person."

"This must be serious."

"Yeah, Nick, it is."

Valentine heard what sounded like the splashing of

water and then the front door buzzed open. "Wipe your feet," Nick told them.

They did, then entered the ten-thousand-square-foot palace that Nick had somehow salvaged through six messy divorces and countless out-of-court palimony settlements. While questioning the hotel staff, Valentine had heard all about Nick's home, but nothing could have prepared him for the sheer horror of it. Built by the same crazy Greek fairy who'd designed the Acropolis, the house had dozens of false windows that looked onto painted scenes of the Greek countryside, the flora and fauna enhanced by anatomically inflated nymphs and nymphets engaged in every conceivable act of fellatio and intercourse.

"For the love of Christ," Valentine muttered under his breath.

"It's something, isn't it," Wily marveled. Heading into the living room he said, "How about a drink?"

"Water would be fine."

The bar was marble and shaped like a cock. Wily filled a glass from the tap, then plucked a pair of O'Doul's from the fridge and opened them. An unfinished cocktail sat on the bar, the glass smeared with burnt-orange lipstick. "Someone new," he quipped.

Drinks in hand, the pit boss marched down a hallway to the master suite. He paused at the door before knocking.

"Come on in," they heard Nick say. "We're all friends here."

The suite was massive, with more square footage than Valentine's entire house. It also had more stuff in it. Wily stood in the room's center, looking for his boss.

"Over here, stupid."

Wily started grinning. Valentine followed his gaze. Through an open door, he saw Nick in the Jacuzzi with

a young miss perched on his lap, still in the act of screwing her.

"Attaboy," Wily said under his breath.

Nick waved to them. The woman's shoulders tensed
and she spun her head around like Linda Blair in *The
Exorcist* and gave them a wicked stare. It was none
other than Sherry Solomon.

"Make yourself comfortable," Nick called to them.

The suite had a living room at one end. Wily took the
L-shaped leather couch; Valentine, the cushy chair designed like a hand. Under his breath, Wily said, "I wish
Nick would stop screwing the help. Someday it's gonna
ruin him."

"You should talk to him," Valentine suggested.

"Right," the pit boss said.

While they waited, Wily talked about Nick's sex life
like it was a matter of public record. To hear him tell it,
the thing that had gotten Nick into trouble his whole
life was the same thing that made him great. It was the
way he treated women. He loved every single one he
could get his grubby little hands on. If they were legal
and willing, he'd show them the best time they'd ever
had, lavishing gifts and attention and limos and the best
seats at the best shows and fresh-cut roses every day,
and just about everything else their little hearts could
desire or ever hope for.

And it was this wonderful display of affection that got
Nick into so much trouble. He was *too* nice to the
women he slept with. After a few weeks of being treated
like a princess, the poor ladies were not ready for him
to take off the magic slippers and tell them the ball was
over. It was a big letdown, and their reactions usually
ranged between hysteria and suicide.

Sometimes, Nick would cave in and marry one of
them, and he'd end up forfeiting another chunk of his
fortune to extricate himself. Wily had seen it coming

every time, the last wife leaving him on the exact day Wily said she would.

Nick came out of the bathroom in a red satin robe, his curly hair dripping wet. He snatched an O'Doul's out of Wily's hand. Sitting in a leopard-skin recliner, he took a guzzle.

"So how bad did we get hit?" he asked.

"Hit?" Wily said. "Who said anything about getting hit?"

"It's a pattern," Nick said. "Whenever the casino gets hit, you show up on my doorstep."

"I didn't know I was so predictable," Wily said uncomfortably.

"Well, you are," Nick said, the bottle never leaving his lips.

"Tony made Fontaine," the pit boss said.

Nick leaned forward, his robe parting and exposing his swollen genitals. "You interrupted the best lay I've had in six months to tell me that?"

Wily bit his tongue. "That's right."

"What's so goddamned funny?"

"I can see your balls."

Reddening, Nick covered himself. Wily put his serious face back on. Valentine sipped his water, trying not to laugh.

"Tell him," Wily said.

"It was Sonny Fontana," Valentine said.

"Stop blowing me," Nick said, killing the fake beer. "Fontana's dead. He got his head stuck in a door in Lake Tahoe."

"That's the story we all heard," Valentine said. "Trust me, Nick. It's definitely him."

"You're sure?"

"I am."

"One hundred percent positive sure?"

"That, too."

Nick did not want to believe it. Eyeing Wily, he said, "Are you and Sammy in agreement on this?"

"Yeah. That's why we came over."

Nick stood up and began pacing the room. Valentine heard Sherry Solomon brush past, then the bedroom door open and close. If Nick heard her leave, he gave no sign of it.

"Sonny Fontana," Nick said, punching his fist into an imaginary target. "My life is turning into a disaster movie. Why the hell would Sonny Fontana rob me?" Spinning on his heels, he pointed an accusing finger at his pit boss. "Any ideas?"

"I still think Nola's involved." Wily hesitated, then added, "Tony does, too," knowing Nick was more interested in Valentine's opinion than his own.

"That true?" Nick asked him.

Valentine nodded. "Get the police to haul Nola in and make her take another polygraph."

"You think we'll learn something?" Nick asked.

Valentine nodded. One of Fontana's trademarks was that he always worked with inside talent. "Nola said she'd never met Fontaine. Maybe not, but I'll bet my paycheck she knows Fontana."

"Jesus H. Christ," Nick said, his anger spilling over. The empty brown bottle left his hand and flipped lazily through the air, shattering against the head of the porcelain replica of the Venus de Milo standing inconspicuously in the corner of the suite.

"How come I can't remember this broad?"

Nick looked at Wily, as if expecting him to know the answer. The pit boss shrugged his shoulders.

"She sure remembers you" was all he could think to say.

13

Sunday morning found Nola circling the covered parking garage at McCarran International Airport. The lot was full, and she parked a half-mile away in Long Term, then hiked to the terminal, her shoes nearly sticking to the baking macadam.

A pregnant-looking jet roared overhead, arcing gracefully so as to give the passengers a last look before ascending into the cottony clouds. Growing up on Long Island's south shore near Queens, Nola had spent many afternoons at Kennedy Airport, smoking joints and lying in a hidden spot off the runway, watching the jets take off. How could her youth, which she'd hated, now seem so warm and fuzzy?

The terminal's freezing cold air snapped her awake. Someone who liked to walk had designed McCarran's terminals, and soon she was wishing she'd brought more sensible shoes. She'd dressed up nice, and her pumps were killing her feet.

By the time she reached security, she'd removed her shoes and was walking barefoot. She passed through a metal detector and an alarm sounded. A sleep-walking guard ran an electronic baton up and down her legs. Her keys.

The new terminal, D, required a tram ride and two long walks to reach its last gate, and she stopped along the way, bought a pretzel, and tossed four quarters in a Quartermania slot machine. Her horoscope had called this her lucky day, and she pulled the arm, thinking it was certainly about time.

Five minutes later and twenty dollars richer, Nola reached gate 84. The booth was deserted; the next flight not until noon. Slipping her pumps back on, she removed a pair of binoculars from her purse and gazed out the window. A quarter mile away, a bus with barred windows was parked on the tarmac, the words U.S. Immigration stenciled on its side. Standing in the bus's shade, twelve chained Mexicans awaited deportation. She studied each man's face. Raul was not among them.

Her breath grew short. Raul was a Houdini when it came to getting out of tight jams; maybe he'd talked his way out of this one and at this very moment was sitting on her living-room couch in his Jockeys, anxiously awaiting her return.

Then she saw him, and her happy ending shattered into a thousand pieces. The police had shaved his head and put him in drab prison garb. Her eyes burned with tears. It didn't take much to get her blubbering, and when she did, she usually got livid. This time, her anger was directed at the government. *We're a nation founded by immigrants,* she thought. *What gives us the right to deport someone for trying to feed his family?*

A cargo plane appeared on the tarmac and taxied toward the bus. Nola glanced at her watch: 7:15, just like the message on her e-mail said. Thank you, Frank Fontaine, whoever you are.

Nola saw Raul say something to the Immigration officer in charge. The officer laughed, his broad chest heaving up and down. A cigarette was produced, put in Raul's mouth, and lit. Nola wiped at her eyes. What a charmer.

Movable stairs were rolled up against the cargo plane,

and the prisoners went up them. At the top of the stairs, Raul stopped and let the cigarette fall from his lips. He crushed it out with his shoe, then went inside.

"Good-bye, sweet boy," Nola whispered.

The cargo plane took off toward the south, the sun's blinding rays balanced on each wing like a dagger. She watched the plane until it was no bigger than a pinprick, the man who had restored her faith in love swallowed up in deep blue sky.

"I love you so much," she whispered, her lipstick smudging the warm glass. "We'll be back together soon. I promise, baby. You just take care of yourself. And don't forget me. Please don't do that."

She was blubbering again. Stuffing the binoculars into her purse, she searched for a tissue.

"Here," a man's voice said.

Nola jumped a few inches off the ground, then did a full one-eighty. She had an audience.

It was Lieutenant Longo and four uniformed officers, plus Sammy Mann and Wily and an older Italian guy with salt-and-pepper hair and an interesting face. A gawking crowd had assembled behind them. Nola took the Kleenex from Longo's outstretched hand and blew her nose, her eyes never leaving the lieutenant's face.

"Planning to take a little trip?" Longo inquired.

"You see any luggage?" Nola asked. She opened her purse for everyone to see. "Or a ticket?"

"I'm taking you in," Longo informed her. "Let's go."

"Taking me in? For what?"

"The charge is fleeing prosecution," he said, unsnapping a pair of nickel-plated cuffs from his belt. "Put out your hands."

Nola stepped back, her shoulders pressing the glass. "I can't come to the goddamned airport and see my boyfriend be deported? What kind of inhumane assholes are you?"

"Give me your hands," the lieutenant demanded.

"I wasn't going anywhere," she protested, playing to the growing crowd. "You're throwing my boyfriend out of the country and now you're persecuting me. Leave me alone."

Longo wagged a finger inches from her face. "Now, you listen to me. You can walk out of here like a little lady or you can be dragged out like a raving bitch."

"You mean I have a choice?"

"You sure do."

"I'll take raving bitch," Nola said.

From her purse, Nola produced a can of pepper spray. She doused Longo, then dug her knee into his groin and bent the detective in half. Someone screamed, and the crowd showed its colors by heading for the exit.

Thirty seconds and three downed officers later, Nola found herself kissing the carpet, the older Italian guy having used a clever judo move to wrestle the pepper spray from her grasp, then kicked her legs out from under her and taken her down. Her pal Wily, whom she'd nailed right between the eyes, was being restrained by one of Longo's men as he attempted to kick her in the head.

Nola stuck her tongue out at him.

Felix Underman was jumping up and down, his movements as animated as a puppet on a string. His voice was loud, his protests extreme. He flew about the courtroom in a rage and shook his fists. The judge listened to his diatribe with a pained expression on his face. His name was Harold Burke, and normally he did not put up with nonsense in his courtroom. Only this was Felix Underman, his friend, so he did not tell the bailiff to toss him.

Judge Burke was pushing seventy and had known Underman most of his adult life. In their youth, they'd played handball together and gone to basketball games. They also shared a passion for the sweet science, often sitting together at prizefights. They respected each other, or so Burke thought.

"Your honor, never in my forty-five years as an attorney have I had a client's rights violated as Nola Briggs's rights were violated this morning at McCarran Airport," Underman proclaimed, waving his arms indignantly.

"She was violating the conditions of her bail," Longo interjected, standing motionless before the bench, his bloodshot eyes still smarting from being sprayed.

"My client was seeing her boyfriend deported," Underman insisted. "She had no luggage, no ticket, not even a credit card. All she had was sixty dollars and a lipstick on her person. Yet the police acted like gestapos when they arrested her."

Burke's face grew taut. Gestapos? This was not like Felix at all. To Longo he said, "There was an altercation?"

"The suspect pepper-sprayed me and my men," Longo explained. "We had to restrain her in self-defense."

"They broke her wrist and blackened her eye," Underman bellowed for all he was worth. "It was eight against one."

Burke thumbed through the arrest report. To Longo he said, "Does the suspect have a violent history?"

"No, your honor," Longo said.

"How many times has she been arrested?"

"This was the second time, your honor."

Underman howled like a terrier. "Your honor, my client's first arrest was two days ago. She has no proven criminal record of any kind."

Burke removed his glasses and rubbed the bridge of

his nose. Underman was getting on his nerves, the way good attorneys usually did.

"Is this so?" he asked the lieutenant.

"Yes, your honor."

Burke fitted his glasses back on. Ninety-nine percent of the people who stood before him had lengthy arrest records. The fact that Nola Briggs had been a model citizen up until a few days ago was certainly worth considering. He paused to stare at the motley crew of hookers and crack dealers that filled his courtroom. Many of the faces were familiar, as were their attorneys. Someone in back was talking trash, and he banged his gavel forcefully, killing the noise.

"Detective Longo," Burke said, "unless you can show me good reason not to, I'm going to let the suspect walk."

"I can, your honor."

Longo approached the bench. Sensing disaster, Underman edged up beside him, his eyes glued to the lieutenant's face. Lowering his voice, Longo said, "Nola Briggs has been identified as an accomplice of a known hustler."

Burke scratched his chin. "And who might that be?"

"Sonny Fontana."

Burke looked at Underman. His friend appeared to be at a complete loss for words. Burke savored the moment, along with a sip of coffee, then proceeded.

"Wasn't Sonny Fontana banned from ever stepping foot in Las Vegas?" he asked.

"That's correct, your honor," Longo replied. "He got a face-lift and now goes by the name *Frank Fontaine.*"

"And how did you come by this information?"

"He was identified by a consultant hired by the casino."

"This consultant is reliable?" the judge asked.

Longo turned and motioned to the gallery. Rising

from his aisle seat, Valentine approached the bench. His heroics at the airport had not come without a price. On reaching the courthouse, he'd discovered his wallet missing from his back pocket. It had put him in the darkest of moods. The plastic, he could replace; the money, he didn't care about; but the honeymoon snapshot of him and Lois at the Steel Pier, it broke his heart to realize that another piece of her was gone.

"Your honor," Longo said, "allow me to introduce retired detective Tony Valentine from Atlantic City. Detective Valentine is an acknowledged expert in the field of casino cheating. He made the match."

Burke motioned Valentine closer. "You're certain Frank Fontaine is actually Sonny Fontana?"

"Yes, your honor. I'd stake my reputation on it."

Burke rubbed his chin reflectively. "I see. That does put a different spin on things. Felix, what's your take on this?"

If Underman had known how to tap-dance, he would have started doing so. His take on the situation was that Sonny Fontana was dead. He knew this for a fact. A client of his, a three-hundred-pound sociopath named Al "Little Hands" Scarpi, had crushed Fontana's head in a door at the Cal-Neva Lodge in Tahoe, and half the casino owners in Vegas had thrown him a party. *Everyone* in Vegas had heard about it, only no one had talked publicly for fear of becoming an accessory to murder.

"I find this allegation hard to believe," Underman mumbled.

Burke waited for him to continue.

"That's it?" Burke said after a lengthy pause.

Underman hesitated. He was in dangerous territory. He'd heard of Valentine and knew he wouldn't have made such a claim without some kind of proof. Stranger things had happened in a court of law than a dead man rising from the grave. He recalled Nola Briggs pushing the bag of money across his desk and realized how easily he had been seduced.

"My client passed a polygraph test," Underman said, playing his last card. "I used a recognized expert in the field."

"We'd like to give Ms. Briggs a test of our own," Longo said, facing the bench. "Mr. Underman can be present, if he'd like."

"Sounds fair to me," the judge said. "Felix, does that sound fair to you?"

Burke was making this as painless as possible. Underman appreciated the gesture. "Yes, your honor."

"Good. Give the defendant another polygraph test, and I'll review the results. Are we in agreement?"

The lieutenant and the defense attorney nodded simultaneously. Burke brought his gavel down with resounding force and all heads snapped in the courtroom.

"Next!" the bailiff sang out.

Valentine stood on the courthouse steps, awaiting his ride. Wily had promised to have a car waiting at curbside. After ten minutes, he realized a car wasn't coming. It didn't really surprise him. He'd been offered several jobs in Vegas over the years, mostly working surveillance and training security. The money was right on, but he'd always passed. It was the people that had ultimately turned him off. It was a rough-and-tumble town, with everyone out for him- or herself. Telling lies was a way of life here.

A familiar white Volvo pulled up to the curb. The driver's window rolled down and he saw Bill Higgins gripping the wheel. He was dressed in khakis and a faded Lacoste shirt and had not shaved. Valentine got in.

Higgins stared intently at the road as he drove. In profile, he looked one hundred percent American Indian, his proud features chiseled into his deeply tanned face.

Valentine had always wanted to ask him about his ancestry but didn't know how to go about it without sounding racist or insensitive. He supposed being politically correct meant never having to say you're sorry.

"Heard you were a hero down at the airport," Higgins said when they were on Maryland Parkway heading south. "You never told me you were into the martial arts. Ever compete?"

"I was New Jersey state judo champ five years running."

"Wow. You still practice?"

"There's a dojo within walking distance of my house. Sometimes when I'm in a bad mood I go down and throw the kids around."

"That must make you feel good."

They drove for a while in silence. Valentine touched the empty pocket where his wallet had once resided. He'd looked at that picture every day since the funeral. Maybe it was time for him to get on with his life, whatever that meant.

"What are you doing at the courthouse on a Sunday morning, anyway?" Valentine asked.

"Looking for you," Higgins replied.

Valentine eyed his friend. Longo had not bothered to notify Bill when he'd decided to collar Nola. It was a childish thing to do, as Bill would quickly find out. But that didn't explain how Bill had known his whereabouts.

"Who told you where I was?" Valentine asked.

"A little bird," Higgins said, hitting the signal arm as the exit appeared. "Don't act so pissed off."

"I'm curious—that's all."

"I have a snitch on my payroll."

"You want me to figure it out?"

"Go ahead."

"How much?"

"How much what?"

"How much says I can't figure out who your snitch is?"

"Ten bucks," Higgins said.

"Make it fifty."

"Fifty? That's pretty steep."

"We're talking about my reputation here, Bill."

"How many guesses?"

"Just one."

"Fifty it is."

"Roxanne," Valentine said.

At the light, Higgins threw the Volvo into park and dug out his wallet. He extracted one of the new fifties that looked like Monopoly money and handed it over. Valentine stuffed the bill into his pocket, no longer broke.

"Remind me never to gamble with you."

They drove through a borderline slum on the northern tip of the Strip. Valentine did not think he'd been in a more depressing place on a Sunday morning in a long time. The streets were run-down and littered with trash, the people on them dragging their asses as if strung out, pulses barely registering.

"Why Roxanne?" Valentine wanted to know.

"She's smart and dependable. Her dad was a cop."

"So she told me."

"She called me last night after you got the fax from your son. At first I couldn't believe it was Sonny Fontana. But the more I thought about it, the more sense it made. I was always suspicious about his dying in Tahoe. No autopsy. So I decided to do a little snooping. I had my records department pull up Sonny's Social Security number; then I went online to the Social Security Web site. They keep a death index of all deceased Americans, and Sonny wasn't on it. That means his Social Security number is still being used. I contacted the

IRS, and guess what? They had a record. Last known address was three months ago. He's been living in Vegas."

"Scoping out the Acropolis," Valentine said.

"That would be my guess."

"Why would he use his old Social Security number?"

"It's his way of having fun."

They turned onto Las Vegas Boulevard. The Acropolis stuck out like a dwarf standing among giants. Maybe that was it; just like any other bully, Sonny had chosen to rob the littlest kid on the block.

"I heard some disturbing news," Higgins said as they waited at a light. "Someone in town put a contract out on your life."

Valentine turned sideways in his seat.

"No one wanted to take it. Whacking tourists is a no-no. I put the word out on the street that you were an ex-cop, and if anyone even tried, I'd make them pay."

"Thanks, Bill."

"So here's my question," Higgins said. "Is there someone in town who hates you that much, or is this Sonny's doing?"

"It's Sonny," Valentine said.

"You guys got something personal going on?"

"Yeah."

"Mind filling me in?"

"Back in '84, a mob Sonny was running ripped off Resorts International in Atlantic City. There was a detective on duty who got wise and chased them outside. Sonny and his boys beat the detective to death. I got there too late."

"This detective a friend of yours?" Higgins asked.

"My brother-in-law," Valentine replied.

The light changed and Higgins drove a hundred yards to the next red light. Throwing the car into park, he said, "So this is personal."

"You bet."

"Mind telling me what you plan to do if you catch Fontana?"

"That all depends."

"On what?"

"Where and when I catch him."

"You're saying you'll kill him."

"It could happen."

The light turned green, but Higgins wasn't going anywhere. Eyeing Valentine, he said, "Do that, and I'll arrest you, Tony."

"I'm sure you will, Bill," Valentine said.

Nola Briggs's injuries were not as serious as first believed. Her wrist was only sprained and her ribs were badly bruised; she was back in the city jail cooling her heels when Underman finally got to her.

A plate of two-inch Plexiglas separated Underman from his shell-shocked client. It was obvious she'd been through a war, and he found it hard to imagine someone so small and helpless taking down four of Las Vegas's finest. He'd completely underestimated her, which he supposed had been his first mistake.

"I'm afraid I've got some bad news," Underman said, knowing no other way to put it. "The police would like to give you their own polygraph test."

"Can they do that?"

"No. But if you don't, Judge Burke won't release you."

"What do they want to ask me that I haven't already told them?" she said, massaging her bandaged arm. "How many times can I say I didn't do anything?"

"Nola, listen to me—"

"No, you listen," she said, her eyes burning a hole through the protective glass. "I didn't do anything, and they know it."

Underman paused as a burly female guard escorted a prisoner into the adjacent booth. When the guard was gone, he brought his face to the plastic and placed his mouth against the oval wire mesh that allowed them to talk.

"Nola, I had a very unpleasant thing happen to me in the courtroom this morning," he whispered. "I stepped on a land mine. I discovered I wasn't really representing an innocent blackjack dealer. I was representing an accomplice of Sonny Fontana, probably the single most hated individual in the state of Nevada. No attorney in his right mind would do that, at least not one who had his practice based here. You set me up, you little bitch."

Nola began to speak, then stopped, her mouth moving silently up and down. "Sonny Fontana? Why are you bringing him up?"

So she knew him. Underman forged ahead. "The money you used to pay me. Was it yours?"

"No," she mumbled.

"Damn you," he swore angrily. "That's the Acropolis's money, isn't it? I know how the casinos work. The numbers on those bills are in consecutive order so the GCB can trace whose bank account it ends up in. It's tainted, and you knew it."

"No," Nola sputtered, beginning to tear up. "I swear—"

"I'm going to the judge and tell him I want off this case unless you come clean with me," Underman said, his eyes spitting venom. "You understand what I'm saying? I'm going to tell the judge that you paid me with the casino's money, stolen money, and that will be that."

"You can't do that," she cried. "You're my attorney."

"Not for much longer."

"Mr. Underman—"

"Come clean, or I'm going to walk. The choice is yours."

Nola drew closer, the tip of her freckled nose touching the plastic, desperately trying to win him back. *"I didn't do anything.* Everything I said to you before was true."

"That's a clever play on words," he said. "'Didn't do anything.' That's what the examiner asked when you were polygraphed. 'Did you *do anything,* Nola?' Well, maybe you didn't do anything, but that still doesn't mean that you didn't participate. Here's a question. Have you ever known a man named Sonny Fontana?"

"What if I have?"

Underman pushed his chair out of the booth and motioned for the guard.

"Please," Nola hissed through the wire mesh. "Don't leave me high and dry, Mr. Underman."

Her attorney glared at her. "The truth, Nola. What does it take for me to hear the truth? Do you know him or not?"

"I did know him. He's dead."

"No, he's not. He got a face-lift, and now goes by the name *Frank Fontaine."*

"What?!"

Nola's hand went to her mouth, the shock on her face all too real. The female guard waddled over. She weighed two hundred pounds and was shaped like a bowling pin. Underman said, "Please. I need another minute with my client."

The guard scowled. "Don't use me as leverage, mister."

"No, ma'am," Underman replied.

The guard waddled back to her high chair and sat down.

"That bastard," Nola swore under her breath. "He used me."

Underman dragged his chair back into the booth.

"You're saying Fontana set you up," he whispered.

Nola nodded her head savagely.

"And you never saw it coming."

"Not until you just told me."

"How long have you known him?"

"Too long."

"How long is that?"

"Since we were kids."

"Were you involved?"

"Excuse me?"

"I mean, were you in love with him?"

Nola let out a bitter laugh, the sound shaped by a lifetime of hurt and betrayal. She dug a nasty-looking hankie from her pocket and honked her nose into it.

"Was I 'involved'?" she said, mocking him. "Hell, Mr. Underman, I was married to the son of a bitch."

14

Barely seventeen, Nola Briggs was married on a rainy Saturday morning in a Catholic church on the south side of the Bronx. The priest, Father Murphy, had at first said no—he did not marry children—then changed his mind when Sonny slipped him a C note, and he forever bonded them in holy matrimony.

"I wish I didn't have to leave," Sonny said as they stood on the church steps. "You know that, don't you?"

"Yes," Nola replied. "I know that."

"I'm sorry it has to be like this," he said.

"So am I."

"I'll come back for you. I promise. I will come back."

"Stop saying it, then."

Nola twirled the gold band encircling the third finger on her left hand. Rain spit on their heads. She had wanted her wedding day to be the *Sound of Music;* instead, it was *On the Waterfront.* Sonny took his leather jacket off and covered her shoulders. She shut her eyes as he kissed her on the lips, wishing the moment would last forever.

The shrill blast of a car's horn ruined the moment. Sonny's father, Elvis Fontana, owner of Elvis's House of Billiards, sat in a rusted-out Lincoln across the street, looking homicidal. He pointed at his wristwatch and mouthed the words *Hurry up.*

"I'll call you every day—and write letters," Sonny promised, holding Nola in his arms. "I swear. Every day."

"Sure you will."

"Don't make it sound like that. I wouldn't have asked you to marry me if I didn't mean it, would I?"

"Why doesn't your father just work it out?" Nola said, her eyes brimming with tears. "Why doesn't he just say he's sorry and give the money back?"

"You don't understand," Sonny said. "He didn't just take their money—he cheated them."

"So?" Nola said. "That doesn't give them the right to kill him."

"To these men, it does," Sonny told her.

Elvis Fontana did a U-turn and pulled the Lincoln up to the curb. He hit the horn again. Nola got the feeling that if she stalled long enough, he might have a heart attack and die right there.

"Good-bye," Sonny said. "I'll call you in a few days."

They kissed a final time, his mouth warm and sweet. Then Sonny ran down the church steps and jumped into the car, his father peeling out before the passenger door was shut.

"I love you," his voice trailed down the empty street.

Nola hugged herself, trying to fight off the cold. She thought about what Father Murphy had said about love and friendship and patience and all the other things that made up a true marriage. Then she began to cry, knowing it was all lies.

"I had a miscarriage the following week," Nola said, crushing out her cigarette and ending her story.

"Did you ever hear from Sonny again?"

"No," she said.

The airless interrogation room in the basement of Metro LVPD headquarters fell silent. Nola shifted un-

comfortably in her chair. Underman lit up a fresh cigarette and placed it between his client's trembling lips.
Longo, who was doing the questioning, glanced across
the room at his standing-room only crowd, which included Valentine, a freshly shaved Bill Higgins, Sammy
Mann, and, on the other side of the two-way mirror,
Wily and Nick Nicocropolis.

"That's not true," Nola suddenly said. "I got a couple
of postcards. He bounced around for a while. Miami,
Atlanta, Myrtle Beach. Then the postcards stopped. Not
a peep for twenty years."

She inhaled pleasurably, then crushed the cigarette
out in a tin ashtray—and kept crushing after the flame
was long dead. It was something a crazy person might
do, and Valentine stared at her, then her attorney. Underman had his best poker face on and had not uttered
a syllable during her entire confession.

"How did Sonny find you?" Longo said.

"He didn't," Nola said. "I found him."

"Explain yourself."

Suddenly, Sammy Mann broke in. "You had it in for
Nick, so you went looking for Sonny Fontana."

Nola flipped the butt out of the ashtray and hit
Sammy square in the chest with it. "Who asked you
here, you stupid cretin?"

"I did," Longo snapped, sliding the ashtray off the
table. "Do that again, and I'll cuff you to the chair. Answer the question."

"I never had it in for Nick," Nola insisted. "I worked
for him for ten years. I was loyal. Doesn't that count for
something?"

"He dumped you," Sammy said. "He asked you to
get your tits blown up, and you said no. He hurt you."

Nola stared at Sammy in bewilderment, then at
Longo. "Who fed you that line of crap?"

"Your old friend Sherry Solomon," Sammy said.

"Sherry's lying," she shot back. "Nick never said that to me. It had nothing to do with my tits, you dried up pencil-dick!"

"It's the truth," Sammy swore.

"No, it's not! Ask Nick."

"Nick doesn't remember—"

Longo looked ready to erupt. "Shut up, Sammy!"

Had it been Valentine's interrogation, he would have dragged Sammy into the hallway and throttled him. The ex-hustler had just ripped the heart out of the state's case. Because Nick had no recollection of his affair with Nola, whatever Nola said about the relationship had to stick.

"Whatever Sherry Solomon told you is not to be discussed," Longo said, his cheeks burning. "I don't want you bringing her up again, okay?"

"Sherry Solomon is a lesbian," Nola told the room. "We slept together once, and she's been trying to get me in the sack ever since."

"You slept with Sherry Solomon?" Longo asked incredulously.

"That's right. A few weeks after I broke up with Nick."

"Christ Almighty," Bill Higgins said under his breath.

Valentine glanced at the room's two-way mirror, wondering if Nick and Wily understood what had just happened. Sherry Solomon had slept with too many of the players to be considered a credible witness. The state's case had just flown out the window. Only Nola and her attorney didn't know it.

Longo was sweating. To Nola, he said, "You said you found Sonny. How?"

Nola stared gloomily at the floor. "Last February, Wily gave the dealers the *Griffin Book*. He told us to memorize the faces of the known blackjack hustlers so we wouldn't get cheated. One day I was looking through it and saw Sonny's picture. It brought back a lot of memories. I still had our marriage papers with Sonny's Social Security number on it, so I hired one of those services to track him down. Eventually they found him in Mexico, living in this walled estate inside a country club."

"And you contacted him?" Longo said.

"I sent him a postcard with my e-mail address," she explained. "He e-mailed me a letter; I wrote him back. That went on for a while. I think he wanted to make sure it was really me and not someone else."

"Were people after him?"

Nola smiled tiredly. "People have always been chasing Sonny. Anyway, he finally called and we talked for a few hours. It was great. Sonny was always so . . . I don't know . . . so easy to be around. Not much to look at, but a real charmer. I hung up feeling like Cinderella at the ball.

"The next day, a FedEx package arrives. One first-class ticket to Mexico City and a dozen roses. I called in sick and took off. I figured, what did I have to lose?"

Nola took a deep breath, suddenly looking about as pissed off as a woman could look. "Looking back, I guess you could say Sonny set me up. He lived in a swanky estate with more security than the Pentagon. We ate and drank and fucked and hung around the pool and played cards all day long."

"How is that a setup?" Longo wanted to know.

"We always played for money, and it was always competitive. When Sonny and I were kids, we flipped baseball cards and tossed nickels every day. It was just like old times. We must have played five or six hours a day for the whole week."

"And?" Longo said, not seeing the significance.

Nola shot a weary glance at Sammy. All the talking was wearing her out. "You explain it to him," she said.

"Fontana was looking for tells," Sammy told the detective. "Little tics in Nola's personality that would tip him off to the cards she was holding. Until now, it's only been used in poker."

"So Fontana taught himself to read you," Longo said.

"Right," Nola said. "By the end of the trip, I couldn't beat him at anything. It was amazing."

"Okay. What happened after you left Mexico?"

"Nothing," Nola said. "He put me on a plane and I didn't hear from him. A month later, I overheard Wily saying that some gorilla had beaten Sonny to death in Reno. I went home, had a good cry, and got on with my life."

"That's it?" Longo asked.

"That's it," she said.

At two o'clock, they took a break. The basement was a warren of small rooms, and Valentine got lost looking for the john. Stacks of cardboard boxes stood outside the offices, making each doorway identical. Finally, a sympathetic secretary showed him the way.

It was Higgins who took over the questioning when everyone reappeared in the interrogation room ten minutes later.

"Let's jump to Wednesday night," he began. "Frank Fontaine sits down at your blackjack table and takes you to the cleaners. You practically couldn't win a hand. He comes back the next night and does the same thing. Didn't you see a connection?"

"No," Nola said adamantly.

"Come on, Nola," Higgins said, leaning on the table, getting in her face. "You're a professional dealer. How many times has a player done this to you?"

"Hey," she protested, "it happens."

"What are you saying?" Higgins said, the edge creeping into his voice. "You thought this was luck?"

"A blind pig gets an acorn every once in a while."

"Not like this," Higgins said forcefully. "Twenty grand the first day, thirty the second. You must have suspected something."

"You think I knew it was him? Look at the photos of Fontaine," she said, a fresh cigarette glowing angrily in her mouth. "Fontaine's chin's chiseled and his hair's thicker than Sonny's. Even his voice was different. I didn't realize it was Sonny until Mr. Underman told me."

Higgins frowned. "Why didn't you tell the police about Sonny before? It's against the law for a dealer to have a relationship with a hustler. You know that, don't you?"

"The law does not require my client to make her relationship with Sonny Fontana known," Underman said, speaking for the first time.

"What are you talking about?" Higgins said.

"Nola is still technically married to Sonny and has a certificate to prove it," the defense attorney said. "By law, spouses are immune from having to implicate their partners."

"You think that applies here?"

"Well, because they were married before Nola went to work at the Acropolis, yes, I do."

"Look," Nola declared, her nostrils flaring angrily. "I loved the guy, okay? But I didn't know it was him. The only reason I got arrested is because Sammy let Sonny fly out the door."

Sammy Mann erupted. "That's a lie!"

"Keep your mouth shut," Higgins told the head of security. To Nola, he said, "You're saying the casino is using you as a scapegoat."

She blew a monster cloud of smoke across the room. "You're goddamned right I am."

"You spent a week with him," Sammy said accusingly, ignoring Higgins's command.

"So?" Nola shot back.

"You were in from the start," Sammy said. "You broke the law, and you know it."

Nola cast an evil eye at Sammy, then the others. When no one corrected him, she jammed her cigarette into the tin ashtray, fighting to control herself. "Which law is that? The one for being naive? Or maybe there's one for letting your heart be broken by every sweet-talking guy you meet. Yeah, I broke both of those laws. Go ahead, put me in jail and throw away the key. I deserve to be punished."

"So who you picking?" Wily asked, slurping a Mountain Dew while staring at Nola through the two-way mirror.

"Holyfield," Nick replied, eating a bag of stale pretzels.

"They're giving two-to-one odds over at the Golden Nugget."

"They're morons," Nick snapped.

"You read the paper?" Wily asked. "Guy who writes sports for the *Sun*, Joe Taylor, says the Animal is in the best shape of his life. Running five miles a day, knocking out his sparring partners. Joe Taylor says—"

Nick turned around in his seat and cuffed Wily in the head.

"Holyfield! You hear what I'm saying? Holyfield!"

Wily refused to give in. "But the Animal looks great."

Nick tossed a handful of pretzels into the air, just to get Wily's attention. "No buts, stupid. The winner is gonna be Evander Holyfield. The casinos in this town have lost more money giving odds against Holyfield than any athlete who's ever lived. Three-to-one underdog against Buster Douglas; five-to-one underdog against

Riddick Bowe in the rematch; twenty-to-one against Iron Mike in the first fight, even money the second. Now you're telling me some punk who just got out of prison is gonna win. Holyfield. Let me hear you say it."

"Jesus," Wily said. "Can't I have an opinion?"

"A what?"

"An opinion."

"No. Now say it."

"All right already. Holyfield."

Nick patted him on the shoulder. "You're learning, kid."

Through the glass, they saw Longo escorting Nola and her attorney out of the interrogation room. Something important had happened and they'd missed it. Valentine appeared in the doorway with a disgusted look on his face.

"What's going on?" Nick asked.

"Everyone's going out to Nola's house," Valentine said. "Nola says she has e-mail letters from Fontaine that will prove she's innocent."

Nick tossed the pretzels into the wastebasket. The Holyfield fight was two days away. Tomorrow the whales would start rolling into town, deep-pocket guys who knew how to throw money around. All he needed was one to walk into his joint and his financial troubles would be gone. He was sick of Nola, ready to move on to grander things.

"So?" Nick grumbled.

"If the letters are real, Longo will have to let her walk."

"What about my fifty grand?"

"Kiss it good-bye," Valentine said.

Nick jumped up, knocking his chair over.

"Over my dead body," he said, running out the door.

15

Chewing on an unlit cigar, Nick drove his Cadillac Seville through the prefab development Nola Briggs called home. A hundred yards ahead, Longo's unmarked sedan turned down a dead-end street. Nick flipped his turn indicator on, then fiddled with the AC. They'd been on the road twenty minutes and the vents were still blowing hot air.

Valentine rode shotgun, Wily and Sammy Mann in the back. No one had spoken since leaving Metro LVPD headquarters, and it made the ride seem twice as long. Finally, Wily broke the silence. Sponging his face with a hankie, he said, "Where the hell are we, anyway?"

No one knew. Sammy griped about not being able to find his way around the burbs anymore, the developments choking the desert like weeds. Nick slowed down for a mob of kids on roller blades.

"You still think Nola's guilty?" Wily asked Valentine.

Valentine fanned himself with a magazine. "I sure do."

"I don't know," Wily said, drawing glares from everyone in the car. He quickly added, "I mean, she's looking at five to ten years. Why doesn't she turn state's evidence and rat on Fontaine? They'd probably let her go."

Wily was talking like a moron. Valentine tried to explain it to him. "Because she's in too deep. She's switched sides."

"How can you be so sure?"

"Because I've seen it a hundred times before."

"You have?"

Valentine turned around to look at him. "When the circumstances are right, most people will cheat. It's human nature."

Wily said, "Define *most people.*"

"*Most people* means everybody who gambles," Valentine replied. "Look, my own grandmother used to cheat. I'm talking about family games, mind you. She'd hold her cards in one hand and her rosary in the other. I used to think she was praying, but one day I noticed her lips moving, and I went out of the room, then snuck back in behind her. Guess what? She was using the rosary like an abacus. Granny was card-counting."

"Your own grandmother," Wily said, astonished.

"It was a real eye-opener," Valentine admitted.

Longo pulled his sedan up Nola's driveway. Nola's house was identical to every other one on the block, the sameness giving Valentine pause. How could someone live here ten years, he wondered, and not get angry?

Nick parked across the street. The four men got out and crossed together. Handcuffed, Nola huddled on her front lawn with Longo, Higgins, and her defense attorney.

"Let's make this fast," Longo said as they converged. He had pinned a silver badge to his lapel to make it clear to everyone that he was in charge.

"I want to see those letters," Nick said.

"They're real," Nola told him. "You'll see."

A pubescent horde had gathered curbside. Nola raised her manacled wrists and called to them. "Hey, Johnny; hey, Taylor; hey, Josh. You boys staying out of trouble?"

"Yes, ma'am," they chorused, heads nodding in unison.

To her attorney, Nola said, "There isn't a boy on this block that I haven't changed diapers for."

"It must be hard to have them see you like this," Underman said.

"It sure is." Pointing her manacled hands at a potted cactus by the front door, Nola said, "The key's under there, Lieutenant."

Longo lifted the plant and retrieved it.

"You have a security system?" he asked, slipping the key into the front door.

"No," she said, "and I don't own a dog."

"Thanks." Longo opened the front door and went inside. A blast of cold air hit the front lawn, momentarily cooling everyone down. Valentine took a direct hit, the sudden drop in temperature making him shiver. He watched Wily stroll to the curb and pull out his wallet.

"Here," the pit boss said, tossing each kid a dollar. "Do everybody a favor and get lost."

Pocketing the money, the boys sauntered down the street, stopping at the corner to resume watching.

Longo appeared in the doorway. "House is clean."

Nola marched inside with her attorney and Bill Higgins on her heels. Nick and Valentine followed. As Sammy Mann and Wily tried to follow them, Longo filled the doorway.

"Six is a crowd," the lieutenant said. "You boys wait out here."

"Why?" Wily asked petulantly. "We're part of this, too."

"I know," Longo said. "You fingered her. That's why you're staying."

Then the lieutenant slammed the door in their faces.

Back in Nick's Caddy, Wily said, "What do we do now?"

Sammy turned on the engine and flipped on the AC. More hot air blew in their faces. Nick's Caddies never worked right, yet he was more loyal to them than he was to his women.

"*Hut eeduck be thesuck ou shoufut,*" Sammy said.

"What the hell you saying?"

"It's Arabic," Sammy explained. "It was my father's favorite expression."

"I didn't know you were A-rab," Wily said.

"Well, now you know."

"So what does it mean?"

"It means 'Put your finger up your butt and whistle.'"

"Same to you," Wily said.

At first, Valentine thought Nick was having a stroke.

On stepping foot inside Nola's tiny house, the little Greek had started to babble, the drab interior dredging up long-forgotten memories. Clutching Valentine's arm, he said, "*Jesus Christ,* I remember this place."

"You do?"

Nick nodded, pointing at the floor. "Same cheap orange shag carpet. Has to be the ugliest carpet ever, next to the stuff in my casino." He laughed timidly, eyes sweeping the barren living room.

"Maybe she couldn't afford to replace it," Valentine suggested.

"The house is *the same,* Tony. She hasn't changed a thing in ten years. Not since that night."

Valentine got Nick a glass of water from the kitchen. "What night was that?"

"We were fighting," Nick said, standing by the sliding glass door and staring at the rock garden in the backyard. "God, I can see it like it was yesterday. Me standing here, Nola where you are, screeching at the top of her lungs."

"Why was she yelling?"

Nick put his hand to his forehead. "I don't know. I must have said *something.* You know how women get.

A few wrong words and *pow!*—you're dealing with a demon." He stared into space, struggling to remember. "She threw a flowerpot at me—nearly took my head off. Then she says, 'I'll castrate you, you fucking son of a bitch.'"

Nick stopped, looking confused.

"What's wrong," Valentine said.

"Did Nola really say that," he questioned himself aloud, "or was it another crazy babe?" Scratching his belly, he said, "I've had so much pussy over the years I sometimes forget where one relationship ended and a new one began, the sex and booze and crazy things I did to impress them all flowing together. Know what I mean?"

Valentine didn't know what Nick meant at all—because he was one of those strange birds who'd slept with the same woman his entire adult life.

"Any regrets?" Valentine asked.

"Yeah," Nick said. "I should have written it all down."

Nola's pitiful cries carried from the back of the house. Valentine went down a hallway with Nick on his heels. He found the others standing in Nola's bedroom. The space was small and dark, the blinds tightly drawn. No longer handcuffed, Nola knelt on the floor, a slender cardboard box she'd pulled from beneath the bed lying open before her.

"Sonny's e-mail letters were *here*," she insisted tearfully. "I kept them in an envelope with the marriage certificate." She looked up into their faces. "I swear to God I'm telling the truth."

"Anyplace else you might have put them?" Higgins said, giving her the benefit of the doubt. "Think hard."

"No!" she said, rummaging through the box one more time. "They were here. He must have come and taken them."

"Who?" Higgins said.

Nola dropped her chin on her chest and began to weep.

"Sonny set me up," she sobbed, her chest heaving with each word. "I let him into my life, and look what the fucker did to me."

She was racked by sobs, unwilling to accept this latest setback. Even Valentine felt his heartstrings take a little tug. Nick dug out a silk hankie, suddenly feeling bad about the whole thing.

"Don't," Longo cautioned him.

Nick ignored the lieutenant and knelt beside her.

"Here," he said.

"Thanks, Nick," she said, wiping her eyes.

"Tell me something," the little Greek said. "I remember being here a long time ago. You and I had a fight."

"It was more like World War III."

"I really pissed you off, huh?"

"You sure did."

Nick glanced at Underman, wondering if he should be having this conversation in his presence. He asked anyway. "What did I do?"

"You don't remember?"

Nick shook his head. "Was it a whopper?"

"Maybe this will spark your memory."

With Longo's permission, Nola crossed the hall and entered the bathroom. Opening the medicine cabinet, she removed a can of hair spray and tossed it to the lieutenant.

"I couldn't afford a safe," she explained.

Longo turned the can upside down. It wasn't a can of hair spray at all but a fake with a removable bottom. A ring box fell into the lieutenant's hand. He opened it and whistled. Then he handed it to Nick. "Look familiar?"

Nick stared at the diamond engagement ring that had

been hidden in Nola's bathroom for ten years. Judging by its clarity, he guessed it had come from Mordechai's, the finest jeweler in town.

"I bought this for you?" he asked in astonishment.

"You got down on your knees in that living room and asked me to marry you," Nola blurted out, her face flushed, the years of pent-up rage spilling over. "Asked me to be your bride, your honey, your sweetheart. Only there was a stipulation."

Nick closed the box, finally remembering. The ring had cost him twenty grand. He'd paid cash. Nola was the best lay he'd ever had. At the time, it seemed like a bargain.

"You wanted me to get my tits done before the wedding," she went on. "I said no, I'd do it after. You said no, before—you wanted me to come down the aisle with big tits, and I said, 'What are you marrying, me or my tits?' and you said, 'I want the whole package.' And I said, 'Aren't I good enough for you the way I am?' And you just shook your head and said, 'That's not the point. I want big tits.' And we fought, and finally I threw you out."

Nick tried to give the ring back. When Nola refused to take it, his face grew pink with embarrassment. It was Higgins who spoke next.

"Wait a minute," the GCB chief said. "Back at the station, you said Nick never asked you to have your breasts done."

"That's right," Nola said.

Higgins burned her with a glare.

"I lied," Nola explained.

Her defense attorney groaned. Longo and Higgins stared at him, then at each other. Valentine looked at everyone in the room. Only Nick wasn't getting it. Nola had set them up.

Which was why it didn't come as a complete surprise

when Valentine heard the bedroom window shatter. The blinds came down, and something round and heavy rolled across the floor and came to rest at Longo's feet. It was a police-issue smoke bomb, normally used to quell riots. Within seconds, a black mushroom cloud enveloped the bedroom.

Valentine reached the door first. Leave it to Longo not to have any backup. In the hall, he encountered a wall of smoke and saw ribbons of gray pouring out of the air-conditioning vent. He tried to remember the layout of the house as he stumbled through it. Back in the bedroom, Nola was screaming for help.

"Let me go! Let me go!"

Valentine hesitated. Emotion was hard to fake, and Nola's cries sounded real. What the hell was going on? Or had Sonny set her up as well?

Underman burst through a wall of smoke and ran into him. Together they staggered out the front door. Nick appeared behind them, puffing furiously. Upon reaching the lawn, he viciously kicked Underman's legs out from under him and sent the defense attorney sprawling to the grass.

Valentine's heart was pounding furiously, his breath gone. The world was spinning, and he heard the neighborhood kids having a laugh at his expense. He sat down on the grass and waited for his head to clear.

Moments later, Higgins and Longo burst through the front door and onto the lawn. Odorless smoke poured through the front door. Later, they would learn that it had been created by a dry-ice machine and was harmless.

"Where's Nola?" Valentine asked them.

No one knew.

"Let me go, let me go," Nola screamed at a man wearing a black ski mask who'd come through her window.

Instead, the man knocked her down. Nola felt a cloth bag being fitted over her head, then felt the man toss her over his shoulder and climb out the shattered window. His body was solid muscle. Nola pounded his back until her hands ached. Laughing, her kidnapper slapped Nola's fanny.

"Stop it!" she screamed through the hood.

The ground became macadam. Her kidnapper stopped running and Nola felt him dig a key ring out of his pants pocket, then heard the trunk of a car pop open. He stuffed her into the trunk, forcing her body into the cavity where a spare tire had been.

"Don't worry, honey," he said, his drawl pure Texan. "I drilled plenty of air holes. You won't croak."

Then he slammed the trunk closed. Moments later, the car's tires were squealing. Her kidnapper hit his horn; the unmistakable shouts of the neighborhood kids rang out. *Please, God,* Nola prayed in the darkness, *don't let him hit one of them.*

The car went up a steep incline, and Nola guessed they were on the parkway entrance right outside her development. She waited for the wail of police sirens, her last chance. But soon they were speeding down the highway, and she felt the fight leave her body.

Her kidnapper played let's-get-laid music as he drove. Guns 'n' Roses, Van Halen, Aerosmith. Women were horny bitches, and men, beer-guzzling predators. Nola pressed her hands against her ears as Aerosmith's Steve Tyler implored her to "Sit on my big ten-inch." She wanted to cry, but her conscience would not let her.

You did this to yourself. You hung around men because you thought they were the answer, that the love of a decent guy was all you needed to be free of the loneliness you grew up with. You opened the door each time they came calling. Nick was the worst, but did you leave Vegas after splitting up with him? No, you had to hang

*around and prove that you could make it on your own.
And how did you do that? By taking a job in his casino
and becoming his slave. "Sit on my big ten-inch" is right.*

Twenty minutes later, her kidnapper's car left the
parkway. Nola worked the bag off her head and stared
at the road through the tiny air holes he had mercifully
drilled. They drove for miles without passing another
vehicle, and she guessed that they were out in the desert,
in a place where no one would ever find her.

The car pulled off the road and went down a long
gravel drive. Braking, her kidnapper beeped the horn
three times. Nola heard a roll-up metal door being
lifted. He drove into a building and the door came
down behind them.

Moments later, the trunk popped open and Nola was
momentarily blinded by a surge of fluorescent light.

"Rise and shine," her kidnapper said. Nola climbed
out rubbing her eyes, the cavernous interior gradually
coming into focus.

"It's not much, but we call it home," her kidnapper
said.

It was a warehouse with bare walls, the air as cold as
a meat locker. In the room's center sat a replica of the
Acropolis's outdated blackjack pit, the tables arranged
in a tight hub. Behind one table stood Frank Fontaine in
a red silk shirt, effortlessly riffle-shuffling a deck of
cards.

Nola's eyes shifted to a large easel beside the pit. It
contained a map of the floor of the Acropolis, the yellow and blue thumbtacks arranged like a battle plan.

When she looked back at Fontaine, he was staring at
her.

"Hey," he said.

"Hey, yourself," she whispered.

"Big surprise, huh?"

"You're telling me."

"You okay?"

"I've been better," she admitted.

"I didn't hurt her none, Frank," her kidnapper said, standing beside her. He'd exchanged the ski mask for a ten-gallon hat. He was tall and rangy with straw-colored hair and a leathery complexion. *A real cowboy,* Nola thought. Turning, she slapped the cowboy's face hard.

"You redneck bastard!"

The cowboy smiled like she'd paid him a compliment. Fontaine came out of the pit. To the cowboy, he said, "Good work."

"Thanks," the cowboy said.

Tipping his hat to Nola, the cowboy crossed the warehouse floor, opened a door, and disappeared into the bright sunlight.

Nola stiffened as Fontaine got close, then began to cry.

"Miss me?" he asked.

"Fuck you, Frank—or Sonny or whatever the hell you're calling yourself," Nola sobbed. She raised her arms and tried to beat her hands against his chest, only to have Fontaine grab her wrists. "Fuck you and your crazy fucking schemes!"

Fontaine let her cry herself out, then released her wrists.

"I missed you, too," he said.

16

Valentine stood in the blazing sun and tended to Sammy Mann while they waited for an ambulance to arrive. Nola's kidnapper was as sharp as they come. First he'd gone next door and tied Longo's dim-witted undercover men to a chair. Then he'd crossed the street and pulled a .380 Magnum on Wily and Sammy. Handcuffing Wily to the steering wheel, he'd made Sammy get out; then he'd done a Tonya Harding on Sammy's good leg with the gun's barrel.

"You get a look at the guy?" Valentine asked.

"Wearing a ski mask," Sammy groaned, lying on the grass.

"Think he was a pro?"

"Uh-huh. All business."

"Why'd he pick you and not Wily?"

Sammy grimaced, the pain shooting through his eyes. "Dunno."

"Think Wily was in on it?"

"No way."

"How can you be sure?"

"He peed his pants."

Only after Sammy was strapped to a gurney and getting pumped with morphine did Valentine venture back inside. Longo had dragged everyone into the living room and was pacing the ugly shag carpet, yelling at the top of his lungs.

"This is fucked! We get dragged out here to see some fucking letters that don't fucking exist and get ambushed by some fucking guy no one gets a good look at. It doesn't take a fucking genius to figure out that we were set up. The question is, by who?"

Longo's eyes narrowed as he searched the men's faces.

"It was Nola," Wily blurted out. He had removed his soiled pants and wore a man's bathrobe he'd borrowed from Nola's closet.

"Nola?" Longo said incredulously. "The only thing Nola Briggs is guilty of is hating Nick. Judging by the size of that ring, I think the little lady has a real gripe with you, mister."

Standing in the corner, Nick hung his head in shame.

"Story of my life," the casino owner mumbled.

"So that means one of you is guilty," Longo said, his eyes doing another sweep. "One of you orchestrated this."

The detective looked at Underman. So did everyone else. The defense attorney sat on a stool they'd dragged in from the kitchen, the knees of his silk trousers bloodied by his fall. He returned their sullen looks, seemingly as perplexed as everyone else.

"I had nothing to do with this," he stated flatly.

Longo bellowed like a mad bull. "You think I'm going to take the fall for this? Get real, asshole. My reputation isn't going down the drain because I got snookered by some smart-mouth attorney. This is your problem. You're under arrest."

Underman shook his head. "You're crazy."

"Am I? Look at the facts. You were the only one who knew where this was headed. Nola was your baby."

"I was just along for the ride," Underman said lamely.

An evil laugh came out of Longo's mouth. "You think

I can't talk some jailhouse snitch into saying he saw you and Frank Fontaine together?"

"It will never stick."

"You'll do four years minimum. And not in a country club, either. The federal pen. With a three-hundred-pound cellmate named Bunny."

"Stop it!" Underman roared at him. "I won't stand for this."

"Want to call your attorney?"

Underman began to reply, then hesitated. "No," he mumbled.

"Oh," Longo said, turning playful. "Now we're getting somewhere. Like to cut a deal instead?"

"What kind of deal?"

"One that keeps you out of prison."

Underman's lower lip began to tremble. "I'm listening," the defense attorney said.

"Find Nola for us," Longo said.

Underman's face twisted in confusion. "How am I going to do that?"

"I'll give you a hint. She's with Fontaine."

"But he's invisible."

"Only to us," Longo said.

"What is that supposed to mean?"

"Fontaine is a criminal. You deal with criminals. Talk to them, ask them to sniff around. Someone will know where he's hiding."

"All right," Underman said. "I suppose I can do that."

"You'll find him?"

"I'll try."

"That's not good enough."

"All right. I'll find him."

"We have a deal?"

The defense attorney nodded stiffly. TV reporters were knocking at the front door, their garish van parked in the driveway. The cruisers Longo had radioed for were nowhere to be seen.

While Longo went to deal with the reporters, Valentine caught Higgins's attention and the two men slipped into the kitchen. Touching his friend's shoulder, Valentine said, "This is some of the worst police work I've ever seen."

"Longo was never the sharpest knife in the drawer," Higgins admitted. "You think Underman's involved?"

"Of course not," Valentine said.

"How can you be so sure?"

"What does he stand to gain? He's got to be as rich as Croesus. Nola set him up."

"You think she orchestrated her own kidnapping?"

"No, Sonny did. But Nola's still involved. She has to be."

Higgins and Valentine stood in the doorway, watching Longo and Underman. The chubby lieutenant had his hand out. The defense attorney reluctantly shook it, sealing their deal.

"What a prick," Valentine said.

"You never extorted a suspect?" Higgins asked.

No, he hadn't. Nor had he ever stood up in court and lied under oath or taken a bribe to look the other way or robbed the dead. By today's standards he was a square, and he wasn't afraid to admit it.

"Never," Valentine said.

"You're a better man than I am," Higgins said.

"I didn't mean *that*, Bill."

"I know you didn't. You want a ride back to town?"

"I'll hitch one off Nick. Thanks anyway."

Valentine rode shotgun in Nick's Caddy, the vent blowing hot air on his face. His heart was pounding, so he took his pulse while staring at the clock on Nick's dashboard. Ninety-four beats a minute. There was a reason cops retired young: The work ruined your health. Nick was equally flummoxed and mumbled to himself as he drove. Wily sat in back, still wearing the borrowed bathrobe.

Valentine watched the monotonous scenery, wishing he were home. The rules were different out here and always would be. The casinos were built by gangsters and bootleggers, and although the mob's influence was gone, their way of doing business remained. Ruthless men still ran the town; they just happened to be small-time thugs like Nick or renegade cops like Pete Longo.

Nick stopped at Wily's house so Wily could change. The pit boss bolted from the car and hopscotched across the lawn, the in-ground sprinklers shooting his robe open. At the front door, he was met by his wife, a big blonde in spandex. She pointed at his robe and demanded an explanation. Just then, his two stepdaughters walked out of the garage wearing postage-stamp-size bikinis. They pointed and laughed at their stepfather like he was a freak. Valentine did a double take: He had never seen two young girls dressed so provocatively.

Nick shook his head sadly. "Somebody once said that marriage was the single biggest enemy of love."

"I think it was Sinatra," Valentine said.

"Old Blue Eyes said that? Sinatra sure knew dames."

"Wasn't he married a bunch of times?"

"Four or five," Nick said. "Why?"

Valentine shrugged. Nick was not the person with whom he wanted to have a conversation about the virtues of monogamy. No one ever said marriage was easy, or that raising kids was particularly fun, but it was what you did because it worked better than anything else. He gave Wily credit for toughing it out.

Finally, Wily managed to get into his house and the commotion died down. Turning, Nick said, "Mind my asking you a personal question?"

Valentine eyed him. "Go ahead."

"I noticed you don't drink. You a rummy?"

"My old man," Valentine said. "I swore it off before I had my first drink."

"You've never touched the sauce?"

"No."

"I admire people who don't drink," Nick confessed. "It screwed up my life in a big way. Your father a jerk?"

"Pretty much."

"You ever patch things up?"

Valentine fell silent, wishing his employer would drop the subject. He had tried to patch things up and had chased his old man around Atlantic City for years, bailing him out of jail and cleaning him up dozens of times, only to watch his father drink himself into oblivion and, eventually, to death. Clearing his throat, he said, "No."

It was Nick's turn to start clearing his own throat. Valentine stared at his watch, then the dashboard, then out the window.

"How'd you like to make a quick five grand?" Nick asked.

"On top of what you already owe me?"

"How much is that?"

"Two grand."

Nick pulled a wad of cash out of his pocket and peeled off twenty hundred-dollar bills. Handing them to Valentine, he said, "On top of that."

"What do you want me to do?"

Nick hesitated. "This is going to sound stupid."

"Try me."

"I want you to find Nola."

"I thought you'd be glad to be rid of her."

"I've had a change of heart."

"Nick, she hates your guts."

Nick stared through the windshield, swallowing hard. "I know."

"She's also guilty as sin."

He swallowed hard again. "Probably."

"She really did a number on you back there, didn't she?" Valentine said.

"Hey," Nick said. "I did it to myself."

"How's that?"

"I had an epiphany," he explained.

Nick had been having epiphanies a lot longer than Valentine had. His first epiphany occurred, oddly enough, during a religious festival that bore the same name. He had been all of sixteen.

Every January sixth, the tiny Greek fishing village in Florida where Nick grew up celebrated *the* Epiphany. This day had been chosen to commemorate the baptism of Christ in the River Jordan, when the Holy Spirit descended on the young Jesus in the form of a dove. In the view of the Orthodox Church, this event above all others revealed Christ's divine nature and mission.

"Bigger than Christmas," Nick explained.

The day was always the same. The town would shut down and everyone would pack into the Orthodox Church of St. Nicholas. After a brief service, clergy and congregation would form a procession and walk to Spring Bayou, the priests dressed in embroidered robes and bearing jeweled crosses and croziers and magnificent silk banners. They were followed by a young girl dressed in white, her hands cradling a pure white dove.

"She was always the prettiest girl in the town," Nick explained, the memory making his face light up. "One year, they chose a girl I was in love with, Zelda Callas."

After an invocation by the archbishop, the dove is released to fly over Spring Bayou. The archbishop then casts a white cross into the water, and fifty boys leap out of a semicircle of small boats in a mad scramble to retrieve it.

"The kid who gets the cross, he brings it back to the

archbishop, and he gets a blessing and is guaranteed a year of good fortune, courtesy of Jesus Christ."

"Not a bad deal," Valentine remarked.

"You said it," Nick said, shaking his head. "I needed some good fortune back then. I'd lost my father and my grandfather and had to quit school to support my mom and sisters. Let me tell you, I was determined to get that white cross and get blessed and impress Zelda Callas. I mean, I was ready."

Nick kept shaking his head. Valentine said, "And then?"

"Didn't happen."

"You didn't find the cross?"

"They didn't let me jump. The priest asked my mother to keep me on shore, out of respect for my father and grandfather. To tell you the truth, I don't think they wanted me in the water, scared I might drown. You know how it is."

"Sure," Valentine said.

"Then the damnedest thing happened," Nick went on. "I was standing on the shore, watching all my pals jumping into the water, and I had my first epiphany. Right there, my father appeared to me, and he shook his finger in my face. *'Never give in,'* he said. Then he was gone. Poof, just like that."

"You really saw him?"

"Sure did," Nick replied. "And he was mad. *Never give in.* It was like he was scolding me. And you want to know something, Tony? I haven't given in to anybody ever since. That's been my mantra, and it's gotten me where I am. It's who I am, you know?"

"I understand," Valentine said.

"And then I'm standing in Nola's house and I have another epiphany. It was in that house that I learned that my father was wrong. Sometimes, you have to give in. God, what a mistake I made."

"You loved her?"

Nick filled his lungs with air. "Yeah. And she loved me. She even signed a prenup. What more could I ask for? I got down on my knees for her, Tony. Got down on that ugly carpet and slipped that giant rock on her finger and asked her to marry me. And she says yes, and what do I say? Stupid fucking me. I say, 'But you've got to get your tits done.' And then the excrement hit the air-conditioning."

"So you got drunk and wiped it from your memory," Valentine said.

"That and a lot of other stupid things," Nick admitted. He stared at him. "So, will you do it?"

"You mean find Nola?"

"Yeah. I need to see her one more time."

"You really feel bad about this, huh?"

Nick grunted in the affirmative.

Valentine gave it some thought. He hadn't tracked anyone down in years. Still, five grand was a lot of dough, and there was a fringe benefit. Along the way, he just might stumble across Frank Fontaine and get to extract a little payback. What was that old expression? Revenge is a dish best served cold. Suddenly, a few more days sweating through his clothes did not seem like such a bad idea.

"Why not," Valentine said.

His suite was still being cleaned when Valentine returned later that afternoon. Ushering the Mexican chambermaid out of the bathroom, he locked himself in, stripped off his smelly clothes, and took a long, ice-cold shower. He emerged shivering and revitalized.

The suite was clean, the air reeking of Windex and fresh flowers. He found the remote on the dining-room table and flicked on the Yankees–Devil Rays game. Top of the seventh, Devil Rays ahead by two. He'd have to track Gerry down, rub it in. It was a crummy thing to do, but it would make him feel good, so it couldn't be all that bad.

He searched his bedroom closet for something light-weight to wear. All he'd packed were long-sleeved shirts, all solid colors; three pairs of slacks, all black; and a couple of navy blazers. He was still dressing like a cop, and he supposed it would be his uniform until the day he died.

All the booze had been removed from the bar and replaced with Evian and Diet Cokes. What service. He popped a soda and lay down on the couch. Seventh-inning stretch, the announcers hawking dog food and motor oil. You didn't last on TV these days if you didn't know how to sell. A Bud Light commercial came on, its stars two smart-ass ball players, one with a lengthy criminal record. At home, he listened to baseball on the radio, the way it was meant to be experienced, and limited his TV watching as much as possible.

The Yankees tied it up in the ninth and sent the game into extra innings. In the eleventh, Boggs hit a solo shot into the bleachers, and the Devil Rays chalked up another win. Gerry would be going insane right about now. Going into the bedroom, he dialed Mabel's number.

"He's gone," his neighbor informed him. "Left on the twelve-o'clock flight. Said he had some business to take care of. He's a wonderful young man, Tony. I can't see why you dislike him so."

"Someday over a milkshake I'll give you my side of it," Valentine replied, sinking into the bed's soft mattress. In the ceiling mirror he watched himself wiggle around, then said, "You're not going to believe this Mabel, but there's a mirror above my bed."

"That must be nice, lying there watching yourself shave."

"Touché," he said. "I appreciate your taking care of him."

"My pleasure. You know, he eats like you."

"With his hands?"

"*No!* The way he addresses his food. Mealtime was obviously serious business in your house. Are you having a good time out there?"

"It could be worse."

"You *sound* miserable. Are they paying you?"

"Like a king," he said.

"Well, then stop complaining."

"Who's complaining?"

"You were about to start. I looked at the weather report in the paper. It said it hit a hundred and twelve in Las Vegas yesterday."

"It's dry heat. You remember to feed the bird?"

"Feed the—" Mabel's voice got caught on the words. Hesitation, then, *"You don't own a bird!"*

"No, but I had you going. Hey, I got your message. Did you come up with a new ad to replace the last one?"

"I sure did," Mabel said. "I faxed it to your hotel an hour ago."

"You did?" Valentine glanced at the phone to see if the message light was blinking. Sitting up, he said, "The front desk hasn't called. Look, let me hang up and check. If it didn't come in, I'll call you back, and you can fax it again."

"Gerry helped me," she informed him.

He put the receiver back to his ear. As far as he knew, his son hadn't helped anyone in years. "Come again?"

"He came up with the concept. He's a very clever young man. I think it's my best yet."

"Better than the 'tattooed man seeks tattooed lady' ad you ran in the religious section of the paper?"

"It's light-years ahead of that."

This he had to see. Saying good-bye, Valentine slipped on his loafers while trying to picture Gerry writing an ad. Maybe Mabel was the dose of reality his son needed. She had certainly done him a world of good.

Going into the living room, Valentine was looking for his plastic room key when a man wearing a cowboy hat stepped out of the kitchen and pointed a .380 Magnum in his face. He was tall and rangy, with yellow hair past his collar and ice-cold eyes.

"On your knees," the cowboy said.

Valentine sank to the floor. The icy tiles sent an unpleasant sensation up his legs. He watched the cowboy reach into his breast pocket.

"Look familiar?"

In his hand was Valentine's honeymoon snapshot.

"Yeah," Valentine said.

Holding a corner of the photo between his teeth, the cowboy ripped the snapshot in half, then in quarters. Valentine watched the pieces float to the floor, remembering that day on the Steel Pier as if it were yesterday.

"I've got a message from Frank Fontaine," the cowboy said.

"I'm all ears," Valentine said.

The cowboy flashed a lopsided grin. "Fontaine wants you to know that he's got a flag in every state. You know what that means, old man?"

Valentine nodded. It meant that Fontaine had gangsters he could call in every city in the country who'd do a job for him, no questions asked. He watched the cowboy reach into his pocket again.

"Look familiar?"

This time, he was holding Valentine's address book.

"Yeah," Valentine said.

"Leave town by tomorrow," the cowboy said. "Or Frank will make a call, and someone you love will get hurt. Get it?"

"Got it," Valentine said.

The cowboy made him go into the bathroom and shut

the door. The bathroom phone had been ripped out of the wall. Valentine dropped his pants and checked his Jockeys. Still dry.

"Stay in there a while," the cowboy said.

"You got it," Valentine replied.

He pulled his pants back on and sat on the toilet. Having nothing better to do, he mulled over Fontaine's threat. Why hadn't Fontaine just whacked him? The only answer he could come up with was because Fontaine didn't want that kind of heat.

Which could only mean one thing: Fontaine planned to rip off the Acropolis one more time.

Five minutes later, Valentine emerged from the bathroom. His honeymoon snapshot was still on the floor. Retrieving it, he slipped the pieces into his breast pocket. Two pieces of Scotch tape and it would be as good as new.

He cased the suite, just to be sure the cowboy was gone. Then he sat down on the bed and came to a decision.

He wasn't going to run. If he did, he might as well quit the consulting racket and learn to play shuffleboard or bingo or whatever it was retired people did in Florida. He couldn't be in Fontaine's back pocket and be any good at what he did.

No, he was going to stay and track Fontaine down. Most of his friends, he was not worried about; many were cops and could take care of themselves. Two people who weren't cops—Mabel and Gerry—he was sure he could keep out of harm's way until Fontaine was in the arms of the law. There could be only one reason why Fontaine was threatening him—because he was scared. Not just of getting caught, but of *losing*. His pride was at stake, and his reputation.

And so was Valentine's.

17

Roxanne was busier than a one-armed paperhanger, the line of guests waiting to check in twenty deep. Valentine had forgotten that Tuesday night was the Holyfield title fight, and he grabbed a table in Nick's Place and waited for her to go on break.

His heart was still pounding from having a gun shoved in his face. There was no worse experience, unless the gun happened to go off. Roxanne appeared and joined him at the table.

"I heard you did a Chuck Norris out at the airport," she said when their drinks came. She sipped her Chardonnay and made a face. "I didn't peg you as a martial arts expert."

"I spent nearly twenty years working inside casinos," he said, sipping his tap water. "Guns don't work with that many people around."

"Is that why you took it up?"

"Yes."

"Let me guess: You're really the quiet type."

Valentine smiled. His heart had finally stopped racing and he felt himself starting to relax.

"That's me. You want something else to drink?"

"That's okay."

Roxanne gave him a dreamy, faraway look. She looked older than the other day, the wrinkles showing

through when she was tired, and for some reason it
made him like her even more, the chasm between them
not as big as he'd first thought.

"How long you've been working for Bill?" he asked.

"About a year. Bill told me you figured it out."

"Does anyone else know?"

"No. Unless you decide to tell Nick."

"I wasn't planning on it."

She laid her hand on top of his and flashed a weary
smile. Her cigarette had died without her taking two
puffs. "Does it bother you that I like you as much as I
do?"

"I'm getting used to it," he admitted.

"Any other women in your life?"

"Just Mabel. She's my neighbor back in Florida."

"The same Mabel who sent you the funny fax?"

"That's her. Speaking of which, did you happen to see
a fax for me in the past hour or so?"

"God, Tony, I've been so busy, the casino could have
caught on fire and I probably wouldn't have noticed."

"Holyfield really draws the crowds, huh?"

"It's like Fourth of July and New Year's rolled into
one."

Valentine motioned to the waitress for another round.

"So," Roxanne said, "are you serious about Mabel?"

Serious about Mabel? He'd never looked at their
friendship in that light. With a smile he said, "It's not
that kind of relationship."

"Oh." She twirled the rim of her wineglass with her
manicured fingernail. "What kind of relationship is it?"

"We tread water together."

"No other girlfriends?"

"No."

Their drinks came. The waitress said, "This one's on
the house," and nodded at the bar. Valentine caught the
eye of his favorite bartender and lifted his glass to him.

"You know," Roxanne said, "I'm older than you think I am."

Valentine almost said "I know" and wisely stopped himself. "How old are you, twenty-eight?"

"Very funny. How old are you?"

"I'm sixty-two," he confessed.

She didn't blink. "I'm thirty-eight."

Sixty-two plus thirty-eight was one hundred—divided by two was fifty, the prime of life. He could live with that.

"So what's holding you back from dating," she said. "Your health?"

"Everything worked the last time I checked."

She cracked a smile. "Then what?"

"You ever been married?"

"Stop avoiding the question."

"I'm not. Have you ever taken the plunge?"

"Yeah. It lasted a couple of years."

"Mine lasted thirty-five. My wife died in November. Part of me is still married to her. Letting go isn't easy."

"Ever thought about seeing a therapist?" she said quietly.

"It hasn't been a problem until now," he admitted.

There were a stack of faxes in the tray when Roxanne checked a few minutes later. Mabel's latest parody was on the bottom of the pile, and Roxanne brought it to the front desk and handed it to him.

"I need another favor," Valentine said. "Can you make it look like I've checked out of the hotel?"

"Sure," she said. "You feuding with your son again?"

"No, no, just trying to send up a smoke screen."

"Consider it done."

"Thanks a lot."

"I'm off tomorrow," she said as he started to walk away.

Valentine came back to the desk. "Any plans?"

She shrugged. "Sleep in, watch the soaps. Maybe rent a movie. I've been wanting to see *The Full Monty.*"

The Full Monty? Did she really want to watch a bunch of pasty-skinned Limeys get naked? Women had sure changed since he'd last checked in. It was his turn to say something, but he was not sure what. Should he ask her to grab a cheeseburger, go see a movie, get an ice cream cone? None of those activities sounded with it anymore.

"Can I call you?" he asked timidly.

"Sure." She jotted her number on a blank receipt. "I know a great little vegetarian burger place on the south side of town."

Vegetarian burger? Wasn't that an oxymoron? And who'd said anything about dinner? A phone call was all he was promising—only, she was beaming like a lantern and he was not about to shut her off.

"Sounds great," he said.

There was a mob at the elevators. Valentine got behind two African-American couples wearing EVAN-DER HOLYFIELD—PEOPLE'S CHAMPION T-shirts who seemed to be part of a tour group. They chatted excitedly, their voices filled with the kind of electricity that only a heavyweight contest can produce. Unfolding Mabel's fax, his eyes quickly skimmed the page. She'd gone back to what she did best, parodying the classifieds.

Attention, internet sex junkies. Tired of the same old porn? Young naked girls in voyeur dorms no longer turn you on? Pamela Lee starting to look like someone's old coat? Grandma Mabel has got just the solution. That's right, naked pictures of old ladies. Don't laugh—they turned your old man on! Send $5.00 to P.O. Box 1005, Palm Harbor, Florida, 34682.

● ● ●

"Mabel, Mabel, Mabel," he was saying into the phone a minute later, staring at himself in the mirror over the bed. "This has nothing to do with Gerry and me. You can't run this ad."

"Of course I can," she insisted.

"I'm not saying it isn't funny," he said. "It's very funny, and it will probably make a lot of people laugh."

"So what's your gripe?" she snapped irritably. When he didn't call back right away, she had gone outside to feed the birds and now answered the phone breathless and out of sorts. "Afraid your little boy is starting to usurp you?"

Valentine stared at the receiver clutched in his hand. Suddenly Roxanne's question about the nature of their relationship was taking on new meaning. "Are you angry at me?" he asked.

"Yes."

"A thousand apologies," he said from his heart.

"Thank you. Now, what's wrong with my little parody?"

"You're breaking the law, that's all."

She let out a gasp. "Are you going to explain," she said after a lengthy pause, "or is this your version of Chinese water torture?"

"You put your real P.O. box in the ad. The post office will have a problem with that. They'll probably fine you."

"I can live with that."

"If some idiot sends you a check, then it's mail fraud, which is a felony. You don't have a previous record, so they'd probably go easy on you. Six months' probation and a few hundred hours' community work down at the library. And you'll get your picture in the paper—or should I say your mug shot."

"You're serious about this," she said.

"Dead serious. You can commit a crime without having intent to commit a crime. You understand what I'm saying? The law doesn't cut you much slack in that regard. I tried to explain this to Gerry a few years ago when he was running a mail-order business out of his basement. He didn't listen."

"What was he selling?"

"Edible condoms. He called it A Taste of Paris. He shipped a few boxes to some state like Utah where everything is illegal and he got nailed. I had to bail him out of jail."

"Oh, Tony, I hope I can get this ad out of the paper."

Valentine sat up on the bed. "You already faxed it in?"

"This afternoon. They have a twenty-four-hour line."

"Call them and cancel. Better yet, drive down and cancel it. Mabel, you've got to kill this thing."

"All right, all right. I'll do it."

She sounded hurt and defeated. Leave it to Gerry to screw up the one thing that made her happy. How long had it taken him, two whole days? That had to be a record, even for his son.

"I've got some more bad news for you," Valentine said.

"What?"

"You need to get out of town for a couple of days."

"Why on earth . . . ?"

"A guy in Vegas is threatening to kill one of my friends."

"How does he know I'm your friend?"

"He's got my address book."

"Oh, Tony . . ."

"I'm sorry, Mabel. Look, there's a Carnival Cruise sailing out of Tampa every day. Go to Mexico for a week. My treat."

"Sure," she said, "if I'm not in jail."

Valentine felt his neck burn.

"Good-bye, Tony."

Valentine stared at the dead receiver in his hand. Then he dialed his son's apartment in New York. The answering machine picked up. After the beep, he said, "Gerry, it's Pop. Listen up. Some thugs got ahold of my address book and may come looking for you. You'd better lay low for a while. I know this is a real pain in the ass, but these guys are serious. I hear Bermuda is nice this time of year. And Gerry, this is on me."

He started to hang up, then thought better of it and said, "You take care of yourself, kid."

The words sounded wooden. He and Gerry had been in so many wars over the years it was hard to be civil. He dropped the receiver into its cradle, wondering who was the bigger jerk, him or his son.

18

Wearing a floppy I LOVE LAS VEGAS hat and a pair of Terminator shades, Felix Underman crawled across the broiling desert in a rented Dodge Intrepid. Doing the speed limit was annoying, especially on a quiet Sunday afternoon, but he didn't want to risk getting pulled over.

Soon he crossed the county line. A garish billboard welcomed him to Armagosa Valley, soon-to-be-home of a U.S. Army MX missile site. Underman smiled at the ingenuity of the local boosters. This was Nye County, birthplace of bordello-style prostitution in Nevada, its founder the legendary Bugsy Siegel. The only business here was whoredom, and building an army base would insure huge profits for years to come.

A green exit sign shimmered in the distance. Seeing empty road in his mirror, Underman flicked on his indicator.

Soon he was on a two-lane service road. Signage was sparse. A man had to know where he was going out here. Turning down a rural road, he glanced in his mirror. If there was anything he had learned over the years, it was that you could never be too careful.

Five minutes later, the Pleasuredome appeared in front of him. The original building had been razed in 1984 during the Nye County brothel wars, and in its place stood a two-story Victorian with sloped roofs and minarets, the windows stained glass. As whorehouses went, it had an ounce of class. He pulled up, popped open his door, and stepped onto the baking macadam. Desert heat was different from city heat, and sweat poured down his face as he hiked the short distance to the entrance.

A sleepy-eyed bouncer held the door for him. The interior was dark and cool, and Underman sat on a red leather couch and looked for a hostess. The parlor had been designed with a Roaring '20s theme and had red carpet, red velvet drapes, and a white baby grand on a raised stage with a sparkling Tiffany chandelier hanging above it. The pianist, a chalky-complexioned woman in her fifties, sang Cole Porter. He didn't look important, so they weren't hurrying. He twiddled his thumbs, waiting.

The truth be known, Underman was against prostitution, especially the way it was practiced in Nevada. Legally, the whole issue was a disaster. There was not a general law specifically allowing prostitution, nor was there one prohibiting it. Since 1949, brothels had existed in nearly all of the state's seventeen counties. Only Clark County, which comprised all of Las Vegas, specifically prohibited it. Everywhere else the law was vague.

But that wasn't the only issue. There was the problem in how the women were treated. Their regimen was extreme: one week off, three weeks on. Being on meant on call twenty-four hours a day, just an intercom away from crawling out of bed and standing in a lineup before a potential customer. Conditions were harsh, alcohol and drug abuse rampant. The women came from all walks of life—rich, poor, middle class, and all ethnic backgrounds—but one thing was always the same. They lasted a year or two, then left damaged beyond repair, their self-esteem destroyed.

A cocktail waitress slipped through the curtains. She wore a tasteful ruffled dress, her face heavily painted.

"Cup of coffee, black," he ordered.

"We got a special on the piña coladas," she said meekly.

"No, thanks. I'd like to see someone in charge."

"Sure. I'll get Charlene."

The coffee came before Charlene. It was very hot and tasted very good. He guessed it was a Columbian blend. His waitress reappeared with a menu, which she stuck in his hands.

"Charlene's kinda busy," she explained. "So she asked me to take care of you. My name's Sassy."

"I'm looking for someone," Underman explained.

Sassy sat down on the couch beside him. Beneath the makeup, he saw a young woman from the Midwest, maybe Ohio, who'd come out here chasing a dream and gotten behind on her bills and sucked into this crummy situation. Underman smiled at her pleasantly. To his surprise, she smiled just as pleasantly back.

"Aren't we all," she said sweetly. Taking the menu from his hands, she read aloud his choices. "Everything's à la carte. First, there are Warm-ups: sensual massage or a lingerie show, or you can have a party starter. That's where a girl gets you hard with her mouth. Next is Ready, Baby. That's your basic sucking and fucking: missionary, on your back, half and half, reverse it, or on your knees. You with me so far?"

Underman nodded. Her matter-of-fact delivery reminded him of the pizza boy reading the choice of toppings over the phone.

"Next is Keep It Going. Your choices are a Jacuzzi party; Show Time, which is two or more girls having sex with each other; or the Orgy Fantasy, which is just about whatever your little heart could desire. Then we've got One Step Further. That's for guys who like to indulge. There's Dominance, Pajama Party, Bondage, and Fantasy. Then we offer a refreshing massage and shower. Each lady is an independent contractor, and prices vary with different activities. We accept cash, Visa, MasterCard and traveler's checks, with proper ID, of course."

She stopped and smiled. Before Underman could tell her what he wanted, her hand flew up to her mouth.

"Whoops, I almost forgot. There's something new that isn't on the menu. Titty Fucking. That's where you put your erection between a girl's breasts and you come or she sucks you off. Your choice."

Underman took a deep breath. Just imagining this creative little endeavor was getting him aroused. He would turn seventy in October, which put any idea of experimentation out of the question. It wouldn't be the actual act that would kill him. The heart attack would come a few days later, just remembering it.

"So," Sassy said abruptly, "you ready to see the lineup?"

"I actually had something else in mind," he confessed.

"What's that, big boy?"

He dropped his voice. "I'm looking for Al."

The name didn't register. Sassy said, "You want a guy? Mister, I think you made a wrong turn. This is a whorehouse."

"I know what it is," Underman said, her patronizing tone losing its charm. "Al works here, at least the last time I checked."

"Never heard of him," she said.

"You must be new," Underman said.

That got her mad. "I've been working here two years next week, buster, and I've never heard of him."

"Al Scarpi," Underman said.

"Not ringing any bells."

"Little Hands," he said.

"You want to see Little Hands? Why didn't you say so?"

"I just did. His name's Al."

"No one calls him that," she said defensively.

"His friends do."

"Little Hands has friends? That's a new one to me."

Sassy approached the stage. The pianist stopped her playing and they had a little chat; the pianist raised her eyes and gave Underman a hard look. Underman stared right back while sipping his coffee. It had grown ice cold but still tasted great. Maybe he could talk the management into putting a bluebird special on the menu: coffee, talk dirty to a hostess, more coffee. It was about all he was good for these days.

"Follow me," Sassy said, offering Underman her hand. She escorted him to the entrance and then outside into the sweltering desert inferno. Instantly, her face turned old, the harsh sunlight keeper of few secrets. She pointed down the road in the opposite direction from which he'd come.

"Get in your car and go west five miles. There're a couple of trailers down there, girls who service the migrants. Little Hands lives there."

"Thanks," he said, reaching for his wallet.

She slipped the fifty between her breasts and pecked his cheek.

"Stop back in if you need anything."

"I'll do that," Underman said.

The Intrepid was too hot to drive. Underman started the engine and got out, letting the AC run while he hid in the building's shadow, thinking about Sassy. She was a hostess, not a hooker, so her offer intrigued him. She probably talked to a thousand sex-starved men a week, which made her a real pro on the male condition. With a selection like that, why service him?

Driving down a miserable gravel road ten minutes later, Underman was still wondering about it. Just about all he was good for these days was playing chess and listening to records. Wouldn't Sassy have figured that out? He'd lost his vanity long ago and assumed everyone saw the same old crow he saw in the mirror each morning. How bad *was* the light in there?

The migrant brothel was an ugly sore on the landscape. Four inhospitable double-wide trailers surrounded by a row of razor-sharp cyclone fencing. Underman pulled up to a guard booth and rolled down his window. Inside sat a dark-skinned Mexican with a shotgun, a small electric fan beating back his stringy hair.

"What you want?" the Mexican said.

"I'm looking for someone," Underman said.

The Mexican raised an expectant eyebrow.

"Little Hands."

The Mexican had a face of stone. Underman decided he wasn't nearly as stupid as he looked. For all he knew, the Mexican owned the place.

"Who?" the Mexican asked.

Underman held up his hands and wiggled his fingers. "Little Hands."

The Mexican frowned, not seeing the humor. "Who you?"

"A friend."

"Never seen you before," the Mexican said.

The Intrepid's interior was heating up, his precious cool air escaping. With sweat pouring down his brow, Underman said, "Look, do I look like trouble to you?"

The Mexican lifted his head, peering inside the rental.

"Maybe," he said. He picked up a walkie-talkie from the floor and called inside. "What your name?"

"Don't push it," Underman said.

The Mexican's brow furrowed suspiciously.

"You not gonna tell me your name?"

"I don't think so," Underman said through clenched teeth. "Let me ask you a question. How well do you know Little Hands?"

The Mexican's face turned blank.

Underman smiled. "Good. I just wanted to be sure we understood each other."

The Mexican chewed his lip, considering. Then said, "He's behind trailer with red door."

Underman pulled into the squalid compound and got out of his car. The ground was soft beneath his feet and he saw a squashed scorpion where his tires had been. He walked around the trailer with the red door, the sun beating down mercilessly on his head and shoulders. It was like descending into hell, one step at a time.

Little Hands was in the back with his shirt off. It was a frightening sight, his muscles popping grotesquely as he stuck a crowbar into the dashboard of a Volkswagen Beetle and tore it from the car. The Beetle was brand new, a temporary license taped to the rear window. Its owner, a freckle-faced whore wearing a pink nightshirt, stood helplessly nearby, kicking the ground with her bare feet.

Underman found a shady spot and watched Little Hands dismantle the vehicle. The rules against the women stashing money were strict. Every room was wired, allowing management to listen in as negotiations were made and prices settled on. Once the money was collected, it was the woman's responsibility to deliver it to the office, where it was held, to be split in half later.

"You gonna tell me where you're hiding it?" Little Hands said when he had reduced the Beetle to a worthless shell. He ripped the last seat apart and tossed the stuffing at the freckle-faced whore's feet. "Or what?"

"Ain't nothing to tell," she said sullenly.

"You think I'm fucking stupid?"

"Never gave it much thought."

Little Hands went to work on the body. German engineering was no match for American bodybuilding, and soon the car looked like a hot rod, its frame stripped down to almost nothing.

"These Michelins are worth something," Little Hands said, whacking the front tires with the crowbar. "You want me to puncture them, or are you going to tell me where it is?"

The freckle-faced whore crossed her arms. Little Hands jabbed the right front tire, causing it to explode. Underman jumped as the hubcap went flying. A small, tightly wrapped plastic bag fell out of a hollow cavity in the tire. The whore burst into tears, then ran into one of the trailers.

Underman approached Little Hands, his floppy hat in his hand. Little Hands squinted at him.

"Mr. Underman," he said with surprise. "Fancy seeing you out here. Looking for a little action?"

"You and I need to talk," Underman said under his breath.

Little Hands pulled a sleeveless T-shirt on over his sweaty, bulging torso. "I got my own trailer; nobody will bother us."

"In my car," Underman said.

"I'm not supposed to leave the premises. I'm locked up in here, just like the whores."

"Can you get a pass?"

Picking up a towel, Little Hands wiped the sweat from his little hands. Underman tried not to stare, knowing how it would set his client into a rampage.

"What's this all about, Mr. Underman?"

Underman got right up next to him. "Guess who ripped off the Acropolis the other night."

"I dunno. Who?"

"Sonny Fontana."

"Come on, Mr. Underman. You and I both know that ain't so. I snuffed that greaseball up in Lake Tahoe."

"You killed someone else," Underman said.

"Can't be."

Underman nodded. "Fontana's alive. Now, how about you and I take a little drive?"

Underman had defended Little Hands four times in jury trials, all of which ended in acquittals. In each trial, the charge had been murder in the first degree, and in each case Underman had swayed the jury to believe his client's side of the story without ever putting his client on the witness stand. To do otherwise would have been suicide.

Underman drove to a spot in the desert directly between the two brothels and pulled off the road. Leaving the engine running, he reached beneath his seat and removed a manila envelope. Little Hands was watching a rattler crawl beneath the car and did not seem to notice when the envelope was dropped into his lap.

"They threw a big party for me at Caesars," he said, glancing Underman's way. "There were girls and booze and a band."

"I heard about it," Underman said.

"And there was a cake. No one ever threw a party for me for snuffing somebody before. It was special, you know?"

"I'm sure it was," Underman said.

"And now you're telling me it wasn't Sonny Fontana. Shit. You think they're going to ask for their money back?"

"They might," Underman said truthfully.

"So what am I gonna do?"

"Find Fontana," Underman said. "Do the job right this time."

Little Hands tore the envelope open. Two black-and-white photographs fell in his lap. He picked up Fontaine's first and examined it.

"This what the greaseball looks like now?"

Underman nodded. "My sources say he's living near the Strip."

"Cute bitch," Little Hands said, examining the second photo.

"Name's Nola Briggs," Underman said. "She's a blackjack dealer at the casino. She's holed up with Fontana."

"So what you're saying is, I find her, he'll be nearby."

"That's exactly what I'm saying."

"This might take a while," Little Hands said.

For an old man, Underman could move like lightning when he had to. Jumping out of the rental, he popped the trunk, retrieved a heavy paper bag, and was back behind the wheel before a drop of sweat could form on his forehead. The paper bag landed with a loud *thump!* in Little Hands's lap.

Little Hands peered inside the bag. "Jesus. There must be—"

"Fifty grand," Underman said. "Turn the town upside down if you have to. Just find that son of a bitch. You think you can do that?"

Little Hands was all smiles. "Mr. Underman, with this much money, I could invade a country."

"It shouldn't be that hard."

"No, sir."

On the drive back, Little Hands memorized the photos, shredded them and tossed them out the window. Underman had once visited an apartment where Little Hands had holed up for a while. Every single thing that could be torn into little pieces had been. It was simply the way he was.

"The casino bosses sent you, didn't they?" Little Hands asked as the migrant brothel came into view.

Underman said nothing, letting him believe what he wanted.

"I appreciate it, is what I'm saying. Getting a second chance and all. I won't let them down. That's a promise."

"I'll pass it along," Underman said.

"What about the bitch?"

"What about her?"

"I find her . . . what?"

Underman had wondered about that very thing during the drive up. Having Fontaine killed wasn't going to bother anyone—hell, the casino owners might throw Little Hands another party—but Nola was a different story. She appeared to be an unwilling pawn, and he felt genuinely sorry for her. Still, she had dragged him into this, and he was not prepared to lose his license or go to jail because of her misfortune. The best thing that could happen to her would be if she disappeared as well.

"I'll leave that up to you," the defense attorney said.

19

Only in Las Vegas did Valentine think he could start his day by having an argument over whether a guy was dead.

He'd been waiting for an elevator to take him downstairs when two medics pushing a corpse on a gurney came out of a room. Ignoring him, one of the medics punched the button for the service elevator, then popped a piece of gum into his mouth.

Valentine tried to act nonchalant. The corpse's feet were visible, and he guessed the deceased to be a middle-aged white male of medium height and above-average weight. Back in Atlantic City, guys fitting this profile had dropped about once a week. Their stories were always the same: In for a convention or trade show, they'd hit the town like a runaway train, gambling and drinking and whoring for a few days without sleep or proper nourishment until the ole ticker finally had enough and quit.

"Service elevator must be out of order," the gum-chewing medic remarked, the name skull stitched above his breast pocket. "We're going to have to wheel him through the lobby, Larry."

"That's just swell," Larry said. "Better pull the sheet back."

A regular elevator came and Valentine held the door.

As they descended, he watched Larry draw the sheet back and expose the deceased's head, which bore the bemused expression of someone who'd died doing something he probably shouldn't have been.

"So how long's he been dead?" Valentine asked.

"He's not dead," Larry said.

"Beg your pardon?"

"You heard me," Larry said. "Man's not dead."

Valentine put his hand on the deceased's neck. The pulse was long gone, the skin ice cold. He guessed six hours.

"You willing to swear to that?" Valentine asked.

"Why?" Larry said. "You a cop?"

"Ex. And having been around a few corpses, I'd say you'd be doing this gentleman's memory a disservice by claiming he's still alive."

"Man's not dead," Larry said, stone-faced.

Valentine became incensed. What kind of fool did this gruesome twosome take him for? Reaching the lobby, he put his hand on the gurney, halting the medics' departure.

"You'll lose your license if I report you," Valentine said.

"Like hell we will," Larry said.

"Man's not dead," Skull said, cracking a loopy smile. When Valentine would not let go, he added, "It's a game, mister. Make a scene, and you'll get thrown out of the casino."

"Like hell I will!"

The two medics burst out laughing. They both had a ghoulish sense of humor, which Valentine found distasteful. Respect the dead, and they won't come back to haunt you. Releasing the gurney, he ran to the front desk. It was empty; he went into the casino looking for someone who wasn't sleepwalking.

The casino was empty except for an old lady with

liver-spotted forearms as big as two-by-fours pumping the slots. Desperate, he ducked into the alcove that housed One-Armed Billy and grabbed Joe Smith by the arm.

"Come here," Valentine said, pulling Joe toward the front door as the medics loaded the corpse into a waiting ambulance. "I want you to be a witness to something."

"I'm not supposed to leave my post," Joe said without conviction, eager for something to do. "What's up?"

"I want you to look at this guy."

"What guy?"

"This dead guy."

Outside, Valentine stopped the medics and drew the sheet back. Joe put his giant hand on the dead guy's chest and felt for a heartbeat.

"He's mighty cold," Joe said, crossing himself.

"Does he appear to be breathing?" Valentine asked.

The dead guy broke wind, cracking up the medics. Holding a smile, Joe said, "No, sir."

"Any signs of life?"

"Not that I can see."

"So you'd agree that he's dead?"

Joe shook his head in the negative.

"What is that supposed to mean?"

"Man's not dead," Joe muttered.

The medics slapped their sides and laughed some more. Thinking the whole world crazy, Valentine ran back inside, hoping Roxanne was in the back room doing the books, only to hear the ambulance turn on its siren and peel out. Joe came inside, and Valentine followed him into the alcove.

"You just broke the law, you know that," Valentine said, steaming.

"Law's different here," Joe said, sitting on his stool.

"Care to fill me in?"

"Nobody dies in the Acropolis," Joe replied.

"Excuse me?"

"Nick's rule."

"Well, it didn't work with that guy. He was as dead as roadkill."

Joe flashed a toothy grin. "Yes, he was. But it don't get reported until they reach the hospital."

"You're saying that Nick pays the coroner's office to say that every stiff that gets wheeled out of here still has a pulse."

"You catch on fast."

"Any other rules of King Nick that I should be aware of?"

Joe rubbed his chin, his pose reminiscent of a great thinker. "Well, there's the rule about me and this chair. I'm supposed to keep my butt glued to it."

"All the time?"

"Uh-huh. Ain't supposed to leave Billy."

"You mean what I just did could have gotten you fired?"

"Yes, sir. Nick's afraid of getting ripped off."

"Doesn't want to make that twenty-six million payoff unless he has to, huh?"

"You got that."

"Mind if I examine your bride?"

"Be my guest."

One-Armed Billy was made of cast iron and had six reels and a single pay line—line up the cherries and win the jackpot. It was an antique, its popularity probably the only thing keeping it from the scrap heap. Today's slots were computer driven, with microprocessors controlling the reels and sophisticated silicon chips to deter tampering. Slots like Billy were easily ripped off, but Valentine didn't think Nick had anything to worry about. By law, all gaming areas in a casino had to be under the watchful eye of a surveillance camera. Slots came under the heaviest scrutiny, and Billy's alcove had two ceiling-mounted pan/tilt/zoom cameras, commonly called PTZs.

"Why's Nick so paranoid?" Valentine asked.

Joe shrugged his broad shoulders. "Beats me. I just do what I'm told, you know?"

"Sure. I'd better run."

"Don't go turning up any more dead guys."

"I'll try not to," Valentine promised.

"I figured you'd be back in Florida counting your money," Sammy Mann said from behind a gauzy white curtain.

Valentine stood in an otherwise empty hospital room, a plastic bag from the gift shop dangling between his hands. Shadows played on the curtain's hot fabric, and he watched a nurse stick a needle in Sammy's arm.

"Ouch," Sammy yelped. "Take it easy, will you, honey?" To Valentine, he said, "So how's the joint holding up without me?"

"Nick's got Wily running security."

Sammy emitted a deathly groan, its timbre sending a shiver down Valentine's spine. He whisked away the curtain to see the nurse frantically shaking her patient. Sammy looked like he'd just checked out and the poor nurse looked ready to join him. Valentine caught the nurse's eye, then grabbed the black onyx ring on Sammy's third finger and tugged. Sammy's eyes snapped open.

"That's not funny," the patient said.

"You know what they say. You can't take it with you."

The nurse got out of their hair. Valentine tossed the gift-shop bag onto Sammy's chest and pulled up a chair. Sammy was in traction, his left leg dangling from a

Rube Goldberg contraption hanging from the ceiling. He wore a loose-fitting cotton gown that exposed the tired, ropy flesh of his neck and spindly arms. On the night table sat the TV remote, a buzzer for the nurse, water, and a stack of crossword puzzle books. Sammy beamed as two decks of Bees, one red, the other blue, fell from the bag.

"You remembered," he mumbled.

"I figured you still practiced," Valentine said.

"Every day."

Tearing away the plastic, Sammy removed the red deck from its cardboard box. Tossing away the junk cards and jokers, he began to expertly riffle-shuffle and cut the cards on the sheet, which lay flat across his stomach, the pasteboards moving with such unerring precision that even to Valentine's trained eye there did not appear to be a hint of subterfuge. Squaring the deck, Sammy turned the cards face up and ribbon-spread them in a wide arc. Not a single card was out of the deck's original order.

Valentine let out a whistle. Back in the fifties, a New Jersey certified public accountant named Herb Zarrow had devised a revolutionary way to false-shuffle a deck, the mechanics perfectly miming a real mix. Sammy's rendition was pure poetry, and Valentine guessed he had a game on the side he was working; probably a bunch of old geezers he squeezed for pocket change.

"I need your help," Valentine said.

"You still on the case?"

"Nick's got me on a new assignment. He wants me to find Nola."

"Has Cupid's bow struck again?"

"Afraid so."

"I think Nola's dead," Sammy said.

"I don't," Valentine replied. "But I'd like to hear your theory."

Gathering the cards, Sammy spoke as if he'd already given the matter serious thought. "I think Nola went to Mexico with some cockamamie notion that she could rip off Nick and pay him back for humiliating her. Sonny played along until he realized she was the perfect patsy."

"Learned how to read her and sent her home?"

"Exactly. There's no law against reading a dealer. He's done nothing illegal, and neither has she."

"Then why did do you think he killed her?"

"Because she knows where he lives. Mexico City isn't as far away as you might think. She's a risk."

"And he kneecapped you for old times' sake," Valentine said.

"Exactly. You agree?"

"I'm sticking with my original theory."

"Which is?"

"Nola is as crooked as a corkscrew," Valentine said. "There's something bigger going on here, just like you said two days ago. Fontaine spent a long time planning this one, and Nola helped him."

Sammy boxed the deck, deep in thought.

"How's Wily really doing?"

"He's trying," Valentine said.

"Like a dog trying to walk on its hind legs?"

Valentine smiled. "Something like that."

"One day, I caught Wily eating fried chicken behind the craps table. The guy shooting the dice is taking us to the cleaners. Wily goes over and throws the chicken bones under the table. I ask why, he says, 'Well, it was bad luck for the chicken, wasn't it?'"

"The place hasn't fallen down yet," Valentine said. "He's beefed up security, has everybody on his toes."

"I begged Nick to do that years ago. We get so many hustlers it isn't funny."

"Why's that? The $4.99 buffet?"

"Very funny," Sammy said, suddenly getting cranky. He pushed a button and the bed tilted so he was sitting erect. "When it comes to running a casino, Nick's the squarest operator around. He gives people better value. We play handheld games of blackjack, and at craps we let punters press their frontline bets up to ten times at stake. That's true odds. Tell me another house on the Strip that does that."

There were a handful of casinos on Fremont Street that shaded the odds in the player's favor, but Valentine knew of no others on the Strip, which was where all the action was.

"None."

"None is right. You don't have to cheat very hard to tilt the odds Nick's giving. When I arrived, the place was a candy store."

"Why doesn't Nick play the same odds as everyone else?"

"I tried to talk him into it," Sammy said. "Nick wouldn't budge."

"Why not?"

"He's got principles."

Valentine thought Sammy was making a joke, and he laughed.

Sammy's face turned to a snarl. "You spent your whole life in Atlantic City," he said, making it sound like grade school. "Las Vegas is different. The turnover at most casinos is a hundred percent. Nick's a saint compared to the rest of these owners. He's got profit sharing and health insurance. This stay ain't costing me a dime. What more can I ask for?"

Valentine looked around the room, which was sleek and contemporary. What was missing was a get-well card, or flowers, or balloons. But maybe that was too much to ask for. In that regard, Las Vegas really was different.

"I had a visitor yesterday," Valentine told him.

"Someone I know?"

Valentine told him about the cowboy's visit and Fontaine's threat.

"You think it was the same guy that kneecapped me?"

"Sure do," Valentine said.

"How the hell did he get into your room?"

"Someone inside the hotel gave him a key."

Sammy sat up very straight. "Who?"

"Could be anybody. A dishwasher, a bellboy, even Wily."

"Jesus Christ." The head of surveillance turned pale. "Okay, so what are you going to do?"

"Find Nola," Valentine said.

"If she's still alive, you mean."

"Trust me, she is."

Sammy took the blue Bees out of their box and put them through the motions. Valentine had watched a lot of top-notch mechanics over the years, but no one in Sammy's league. Others manipulated the cards; Sammy's fingers made love to them.

"Start with Sherry Solomon," Sammy suggested. "If anyone knows Nola's haunts, it's her. She works the graveyard shift, so you'll probably catch her at home."

Valentine scribbled the address on a paper napkin. "Thanks. I'll drop by tomorrow."

"Bring a good cigar, will you?"

"You can't smoke in here."

"I just want to smell it," Sammy said.

In the hallway, Valentine ran into a bearded doctor clutching a clipboard. He wore a troubled expression, and Valentine got the sinking feeling that the news he was about to share with Sammy was not good. The doctor had a good Irish face, filled with freckles and lots of character, and Valentine guessed he was from Boston or

New York or some other bastion of civilization back east.

"How bad?" Valentine asked.

"Bad enough," the doctor replied.

Normally, Valentine would have hung around and lent Sammy some moral support. But his friend lived in a world where compassion was seen as weakness, and Valentine didn't think he'd appreciate the gesture.

"Take care of my friend," he whispered.

Sherry Solomon lived in a futuristic development built on the rocky plains leading up to Red Rock Canyon. Turning the car off the highway, Valentine stared at the endless repetition of yellow stucco homes, their terra-cotta roofs framed by an angry copper sky, the color so vibrant it made his eyes hurt. A cheerful billboard welcomed him to Rainbow Valley, home to future country clubs, Pete Dye golf courses, schools, a hospital, police and fire departments, and, he imagined, lots of ugly strip malls.

He drove for miles, the rows of identical homes nearly putting him to sleep. As habitats went, it was about as inviting as the surface of the moon. Sherry lived in the last cluster, the remnants of a yard sale littering her front lawn.

He parked and strolled up the walk. On a card table sat mismatched dishes, plastic coffee mugs, and assorted knickknacks, twenty-five cents each. Also for sale was an assortment of furniture, a deflated waterbed, a ThighMaster, and a box of Cindy Crawford workout tapes. Post-its had been stuck to each with the words *Best Offer*.

The front door was ajar. Sticking his head in, Valentine said, "Anybody home?" and heard a shrill voice bid him entrance. It did not sound at all like the young woman he remembered from Nick's office.

"Is this Sherry Solomon's house?" he inquired.

"*Damn straight*. I said come on in!"

So much for first impressions. Shutting the door behind him, he was greeted by a miniature canine with a pink ribbon in its hair. It was a cockapoo, normally a docile breed. This one was all teeth, and Valentine kicked it in the mouth.

"Scram," he said.

He found Sherry in the dining room yakking on a cell phone. She wore ultratight gym shorts and a sleeveless UNLV jersey, her bronzed skin looking radioactive in the bright sunlight that poured through the curtainless windows. She gave him a puzzled look.

"You the real estate guy?"

"Tony Valentine," he said. "We met in Nick's office."

"Oh yeah. What can I do for you, Tony?"

"I'm helping the police look for Nola," he lied.

"I gotta run," she said into the phone, and killed the power. She eyed him suspiciously. "You're helping the police? I thought you were working for Nick."

Valentine swallowed hard. There was no dumber lie than the one he'd just told. All Sherry had to do was call Longo and his goose was cooked. In answer to his prayers, the dog staggered in looking as drunk as a sailor and peed on the salmon-colored carpet.

"Aw, for the love of Christ," Sherry screeched, running to the kitchen to grab a roll of paper towels. Sponging up the mess, she said, "Look, Tony, I don't know what you're up to, and I don't care. Personally, I don't give a rat's ass what happens to Nola. She had her chance to grab the brass ring and she blew it."

The brass ring. Valentine had to think hard about that one.

"Any idea where she might be hiding out?"

"In the arms of Frank Fontaine."

"You think so? The police don't think she had anything to do with it. Neither does Sammy Mann."

"Screw Sammy and screw the police," Sherry swore.
"She's guilty as sin."

The cockapoo was peeing again. Bending down, she
cleaned the mess up, then stuck the wet paper towel in
the dog's face. "See this, you stupid little mutt? Keep it
up and you can live at the pound."

"Maybe there's something wrong with its bladder,"
Valentine said, not wanting to see the dog punished on
his account.

"It's always something," Sherry replied, without a
hint of sympathy. "Look, I need to run."

"One more question," he said.

"You're a real pain in the ass, you know that?"

He'd been called a lot worse over the years, but never
by someone as downright mean as this snake. In a measured tone, he said, "You and Nola were living together
when she and Nick had their fling, right?"

"Yeah, so?"

"The night Nick took Nola on the catwalk and they
had sex, Nola told you she saw something that wasn't
kosher with the casino's security."

"That's right. She said there was a fight or something."

"A fight?"

"Some drunk broad took a swing at a dealer and all
hell broke loose. Broad's husband went ballistic, started
beating people up. Guy was a professional wrestler or
something."

"And during the commotion, Nola saw the flaw."

"I guess."

"She never elaborated?"

"She said that she could close Nick down if she
wanted to. I tried to pump her, but she wouldn't tell. I

think it made her feel powerful, knowing she had Nick by the balls."

The cockapoo was clawing her leg, feeling better, and Sherry scooped him up and let him lick her face.

"That's momma's little boy," she cooed, trading kisses. "Nasty man got you all upset, didn't he? Coming in here and pissing Mommy off. We won't let that happen again, will we?"

To her visitor she said, "Anything else?"

"You moving in with Nick?"

"What business is that of yours?"

"Just curious."

"Yeah, I'm moving in with Nick."

"Does he know, or were you going to make it a surprise?"

Sherry marched him to the front door. Stepping outside into the desert inferno, Valentine spied a three-hundred-pound whale of a woman lugging the ThighMaster down the street. On the card table, she'd left three dollars as payment.

"Can I give you some advice?" he asked.

"Get lost," Sherry replied, slamming the door.

"Don't sell your house," he said anyway, then traipsed across the lawn to his baking car.

On the way back into town, Valentine stopped by Bill Higgins's office on Clark Street and talked his friend into going off campus for a cup of coffee and a chat. Higgins chose a greasy spoon within spitting distance of Glitter Gulch, a four-block galaxy of neon and twinkling lights that defined the original downtown of Las Vegas. The Gulch was the epitome of Old West boomtown decadence, the smaller hotels and casinos still clinging to their seedy homespun ways.

"Coffee's okay, but the food will kill you," Higgins cautioned as a sullen waitress approached their booth.

"I once saw a guy nearly choke to death on a jelly doughnut."

"Thanks for the warning."

The waitress took their order and sauntered off. Higgins pointed out the window at a row of dilapidated buildings across the street. "See that gym on the second floor? The toughest guys in Vegas hang out in that gym, guys who used boxing to climb out of the ghetto. When Marvin Hagler fought Tommy Hearns, that was where he worked out. No air-conditioned tent at Caesars for him."

Valentine remembered the bout well, nine minutes of glorious mayhem that ended with Hagler's arm raised in triumph and Hearns on his back counting stars. Hearns had been younger, taller, and the superior ring technician. Hagler's only advantage had been his heart.

"You get to see Hagler train?"

"I went one day at lunch. The gym was like an oven. I lasted twenty minutes."

"How long was Hagler there?"

"Three weeks."

Their coffee came, a witch's brew that Higgins tempered with two packets of cream and plenty of sugar. Valentine drank his black.

"Any luck finding Nola?" Higgins asked, blowing on his cup.

"Not yet. How about you?"

"Nothing. We're kind of strapped right now with all the big hitters rolling into town for the Holyfield fight."

"Wouldn't be too hard for Fontaine to go out to the airport and come back in as a tourist, would it?"

Higgins put his cup down. "That's an interesting idea. You really think he'd try something as brazen as that?"

"He did it in Atlantic City once," Valentine said. "We missed him completely."

"You think Nola's with him?"

"I do. In disguise, of course."

"Where's he staying?"

"Hard to say. Someplace large and impersonal that's in walking distance to the Acropolis. He's probably checking out the new security measures as we speak."

"What's his identity this time?"

"Something ordinary, like a lightbulb salesman from Minnesota with two-point-four kids and a doting wife. His hair is a different color and he's wearing elevators in his shoes. He probably has some new facial hair and a really ugly wardrobe."

"You know this guy pretty well."

"Not well enough to catch him."

"When's he going to take another stab at Nick's?"

"Soon. He'll wait until the casino is packed. The day after the fight might be an opportune time. Lots of noise and adrenaline."

"Any idea how he'll do it?"

"No. But I think someone inside the casino will be helping him."

Higgins winced like he'd been kicked in the solar plexus. Inventory was impossible to track on a casino floor, and if an employee was involved in a scam, millions of dollars could walk out the front door.

"You're giving me an ulcer, you know that?"

"There's still time," Valentine said.

"To do what? Update my résumé? Look Tony, every time a casino gets whacked in this town, I get my tit put in a wringer. I'm going to be out of work if this thing comes down."

"I can stop him."

"What makes you so sure?"

"I'm not a cop anymore. I don't have to stay within the letter of the law, if you know what I mean." Valentine leaned back from the table as their waitress rudely slapped down a check. Only when she was out of earshot did he speak again. "Give me the information you have, including the wiretaps of Nola's phone."

"No," Higgins said.

"Why not?"

"Let's say you hunt Fontana down and you end up killing him. That makes me an accessory to murder."

Valentine saw where he was going. "So I won't kill him."

"Is that a promise?"

Valentine nodded.

"Come again?"

"Yes, it's a promise."

Higgins finished his coffee, grimacing until the very last drop. He tossed a few dollars on the table and wiped his mouth with a paper napkin. "I'm off at six. I'll come by the Acropolis and drop off what I have. I'll bring a tape recorder so you can listen to the wiretaps."

"I really appreciate it, Bill."

"Hey, look," Higgins said.

Valentine followed Higgins's gaze out the window. Across the street, four black gladiators in skimpy gym clothes emerged, their sinewy bodies dripping perspiration. A playful exchange of punches quickly escalated into warfare. A hooded figure, taller and broader in the shoulders, came out of the stairwell and began to mix it up with them, slapping the combatants with his open palms, sending them reeling into parked cars until they begged uncle.

"Is that who I think it is?" Valentine asked.

"The People's Champ," Higgins said. "I got two hundred bucks riding on his winning. How about you?"

Valentine shrugged. Holyfield's opponent was a foul-mouthed tattoo-covered ex-con who exemplified everything wrong with sports in America. Valentine wanted to see him lose, but the desire was not great enough to overcome the even greater aversion he had for wagering on sporting events.

"You should," Higgins said.

Valentine shrugged again.

"I'm serious."

"Give me one good reason why."

"Because it's good versus evil, that's why."

"And betting on Holyfield is good?"

"It most certainly is."

Valentine had never looked at it that way. Betting tended to bring out the worst in people, and it had never occurred to him that by putting a few bucks down, he'd be striking a blow for the sake of humanity. He slid out of the booth.

"I'll have to think about it," Valentine said.

20

Twenty minutes later, Valentine found himself stuck in traffic on the Strip. Thousands of newly arrived tourists had hit the streets and transformed the city's main thoroughfare into a pedestrian walkway. Horns blared, engines overheated, and cabbies stood on the hoods of their cars and shouted in murderous rage.

Where's a cop when you need one? he wondered. He'd promised to call Roxanne and like an idiot had left her home number on his night table. It hadn't helped that he didn't know her last name and couldn't look her up. He glanced at his watch—nearly five. Flipping the turn indicator on, he maneuvered the Cadillac Nick had loaned him into the front entrance of the Desert Inn. Tossing the valet a twenty, he threw his sports jacket over his shoulder and hit the pavement, the Acropolis shimmering miragelike in the distance.

Florida was never this hot. You could go out at night, walk around, and not be afraid of bursting into flames. He crossed the street in slow motion and caught his breath in the welcome shade of a bus stop. It wasn't any cooler.

By the next block, the heat had risen through his loafers and his feet were burning up. Hundreds of people streamed around him, oblivious to his condition. He looked hopelessly up and down the street. In any other city, there would be someone hawking ice-cold drinks and umbrellas. Not Las Vegas—the only free enterprise here was located inside the casinos.

He heard voices. Women singing, the melodious words floating above his head. No one else seemed to notice. What the hell was going on? Crossing at the light, the voices grew stronger, and he shaded his eyes and stared straight ahead. A block away, he saw Nick's harem of ex-wives standing in the fountains, serenading him.

He was hallucinating, the heat doing tricks with his head. It didn't matter. He'd heard women singing the day before Lois died. God talked to people in strange ways, and there was no doubt in his mind that God was talking to him right now. He started to run.

He was sopping wet by the time he reached Nick's joint, his heart racing out of control. The check-in line was twenty deep, T-shirts flapping over Day-Glo Bermudas, and he went straight to the elevators and bullied his way onto the first available car.

The message light on his bedside phone was flashing. Tearing his shirt off, he placed the receiver to his ear and punched in the code for voice mail.

There was only one message. Mabel.

"Oh, Tony, you were right," his neighbor said, her voice trembling. "The ad ran this morning and I got a call from the postmaster. The police had called him, asked who owned the box. The next thing I know, one of Palm Harbor's finest is standing on my porch. Oh, Tony, it was so embarrassing. He *arrested* me."

Valentine sat on the bed. Gerry's brilliant idea had gotten Mabel thrown in the pokey. His son was a bad-news buffet.

"They gave me one phone call. Thank God for my MCI calling card. The judge told me I'd better hire an attorney. Who do I call? I've never broken the law. You think F. Lee Bailey would be interested?"

Mabel's voice was drowned out by a drunk woman mutilating an old Carole King song. She'd called him from a payphone in a holding cell.

"That's Sally. She's a bag lady. Anyway, I got arraigned an hour ago. Judge set bail at one thousand dollars. I laughed in his face, told him it would be a cold day in hell before I'd fork over a thousand bucks to him. You should have seen his face!"

Valentine fell backward on the bed.

"Well, I guess I got him pretty mad. He banged his gavel like Judge Wapner and gave me a lecture about propriety in his court. I tried to keep my mouth shut, but you know me . . . I let him have it right between the eyes. Told him to calm down before he had a stroke. Then I asked him why he was wasting the taxpayers' money arresting me, when every day I drive over to Clearwater Beach and see a hooker on Alternate 19 with her thumb out. Guess what he did then?"

"Here it comes," Valentine said, shutting his eyes.

"Well, he starts to talk, only his face is beet red and there's sweat on his brow, and no words come out. So I say, 'Cat got your tongue, Judge?' and that gets him even madder, and he takes a big gulp of water and looks at me, and I think, *You're screwed, Mabel,* and then I see him start to froth at the mouth and his eyes roll up into his head and he just keels over right there."

"Sweet Jesus," Valentine groaned.

"Had a stroke. They carried him out on a stretcher. I can't tell you how horrible I felt. Still, he had no right to treat me like a common criminal."

The line went silent and he heard Mabel blow her nose. "Well, now the judge's in the hospital and no one in the jail wants to talk to me. I don't know what to do.

I'm sorry to be bothering you, but who else am I going to call?"

Why not Gerry? he thought. *He got you into this.*

"I'm sure you're mad at your son, but it's not his fault. I'm an old woman prone to stupid deeds. It's my nature, so don't blame him, okay? Well, I guess I've babbled long enough. Can't wait to see the phone bill when I get out of here. If you do get home in the next few days, I'd appreciate it if you'd come down to the Clearwater jail and bail me out."

She honked her nose again and he realized she was crying. Tears of sympathy poured down his face, and he rubbed them away with his sleeve. Grow old enough, and Father Time will find a way to rob you of all your dignity.

A dial tone filled his ear. Valentine dropped the receiver on the pillow and covered his face with his hands.

Rising from the bed, he tore off his smelly clothes and took a cold shower, but not before chaining the door and propping a chair up against it. When he came out, he grabbed a Diet Coke from the bar and sat down at the dining-room table, the phone before him, and he began to hunt for his beloved Gerald.

Burned in his memory were five different phone numbers for his son. They included the apartment in Brooklyn, his saloon, his ex-wife, an ex-girlfriend with whom Gerry had cohabited for two years, and his cell phone. It was Pee Wee, Gerry's bartender, who answered the phone at the saloon, his tongue thickened by whiskey.

"Hey, Mr. Valentine, how's it hanging?"

"Longer than yours," Valentine growled. "Where's my son?"

"Out making the rounds," Pee Wee said. "Wanna leave a message?"

Valentine swallowed hard. Bar owners didn't make rounds.

"You're telling me Gerry is out collecting money?" Valentine said.

"I didn't say that—"

"Is Gerry still running a bookmaking operation?"

"I don't have to answer that question," Pee Wee said.

"It's my bar," Valentine reminded him.

Pee Wee hiccupped into the phone. He was in his early forties and probably wouldn't make it to fifty, the booze taking him down a one-way street with no detours.

"You're on parole, aren't you?" Valentine said. "If I call the cops and they find Gerry's taking bets, they'll put you back in jail, Pee Wee."

"You'd turn in your own son?"

"Goddamn straight I would."

"You're something else," Pee Wee said.

"Answer the question."

"Yeah, he's still taking bets."

Valentine slammed down the phone. Seething, he began dialing Gerry's other numbers, working his way through the list until an unfamiliar young miss with a sultry Puerto Rican accent answered Gerry's cell phone, a radio blaring samba music in the background. He sensed that his son was nearby, perhaps lying in bed beside her, and barked louder than he should have.

"Gerry's not here," she replied timidly. Lowering the radio, she said, "Are you really Gerry's father?"

"That's me. Where is he?"

"I don't know. Why are you such a prick?"

"Is that what Gerry told you? That I'm a prick?"

"He said you were the biggest prick on the planet."

"He wasn't off by much. Where'd he go?"

"I don't know. Why are you such a prick?"

"Maybe I'm just a prick with Gerry."

"Gerry's *wonderful*," she said, the word melting on her tongue. "Nobody else hates him like you."

That was a lie. Valentine gave her Gerry's ex-wife's and ex-girlfriend's phone numbers and suggested they start a support group. The Puerto Rican woman cursed him and the line went dead.

Valentine sat on the bed and felt his blood pressure rise. As criminal endeavors went, being a bookie required a lot of social skills, and he could see his son being good at many other things, like selling real estate or cars or even stock. It wouldn't be hard to make the switch; it just took desire.

Ten minutes later he called Gerry's saloon again.

"Gerry just came back," Pee Wee informed him. "You want to talk to him?"

"You're psychic," Valentine said.

"Hold on."

When Pee Wee returned, his voice was subdued. "Gerry's in his office on the other line. He asked me to ask you if you had a conversation with a young lady on his cell phone."

"I most certainly did," Valentine said.

"Oh, man," Pee Wee said. "Why'd you give Yolanda those phone numbers?"

"Because he deserved it."

"Hold on."

"Pop, you're killing me," Gerry said moments later, barely able to control his anger. "I've got this crazy bitch on the other line who wants to castrate me on account of something you said. What the hell's wrong now? I thought we had a truce."

When did one conversation constitute a truce? His son was going to have to grovel a lot more before things would ever be right between them. Feeling something inside him snap, Valentine lost control of himself.

"Son of mine, you are one useless piece of garbage.

What a mistake I made thinking you had changed. You know that crazy ad you helped Mabel write? Well guess what, meatball: She got arrested for mail fraud. She's sitting in a holding cell down in Clearwater not knowing where to turn."

"Mabel got arrested?" Gerry said. "Geeze, that's too bad."

Too bad? He lost it. "Let me tell you what's too bad. Too bad is when I call the police and have them close you down. Too bad is when I stop bailing you out every time you land in jail."

"Pop, stop it," Gerry said, the edge leaving his voice. "I was just trying to have fun with the old bird. She's a little off in the head, you know? I mean, she's wasting her money running those ads, thinking people care. She gave me a business card. Mabel, Queen of Spoofs. I mean, come on."

"People *do* care," Valentine bellowed at him. "I care! Just because she's retired doesn't mean she can't make a statement. You think Mabel no longer matters? Well, let me tell you something: She matters plenty. She's decent and strong and God-fearing and likes to make people laugh. I can't remember the last time you embraced any of those things, Gerry."

"Stop it, Pop."

"You hurt my friend, you little shit."

"I'm sorry. I didn't mean to."

"You've run out of sorrys."

"What is that supposed to mean?"

"It means I want you to fix the problem."

"What are you talking about?"

Valentine glanced at his watch. It was nine p.m. East Coast time and probably too late for his son to catch a plane. He hated the thought of Mabel spending the night in jail, but he saw no other solution. He said, "I want you to fly down to Clearwater tomorrow and bail

Mabel out of jail. Then the two of you need to get out of town. Go on a cruise or something. I'll pick up the tab."

"What?" his son said, growing belligerent. "Why don't you help her? She's your friend."

"Because you messed up her life," Valentine barked. "It's called cause and effect. You make a mess, you clean it up. That's the way the world works. Irresponsible little pricks like you are what throws everything out of whack."

"That's right," Gerry said, "blame me for the world's problems."

"You'd better do as I tell you."

"Or what?"

The words left his mouth before he had a chance to catch them. "Or I'll never talk to you for as long as I live."

Gerry coughed. "You mean that?"

Valentine cleared his throat. He'd stepped over the imaginary line that he and Gerry had drawn in the sand a long time ago. They'd been sparring since his son was a teenager—over twenty years—and they'd always remained somewhat civil, until now.

"Yeah," Valentine replied. "I do."

"Jesus Christ," Gerry said.

There was a long silence. Finally his son spoke.

"All right, Pop. You win."

Another silence. Again, it was his son who broke it.

"I'm on the next plane."

"You better be," his father replied.

Valentine was hanging up when there was a knock at his door. Through the peephole he spied Bill Higgins cradling a cardboard box in his arms. He ushered his friend into the suite.

"Wow," Higgins said. "This is some setup. Is Nick comping you?"

"Of course he's comping me," Valentine said.

"You know what they say," Higgins said. "There are a lot of free things in this town, only nobody can afford them." Taking the lid off the box, he dumped its contents onto the dining-room table. "I stopped by Longo's office and got the evidence. He asked me to bring everything back tomorrow, the case still being open."

Higgins pulled up a chair and together they sorted through the evidence. Valentine remained standing, still reeling from his conversation with Gerry. It would be just like his son not to come through. And that would be it, the end of the line. Somehow, he'd always imagined a reconciliation between them, the years of butting heads finally put to rest, the bond between them stronger than it had ever been. Deep down, that was what he had always wanted.

Higgins gave him a funny look. "You okay?"

"I've felt better," Valentine replied. "What have we got?"

"Usual crap. The wiretaps are worth listening to."

From the box Higgins removed a cassette tape and popped it into the tape player he'd brought with him. "We caught Fontaine leaving a message on Nola's answering machine. Call came from a joint called Brother's Lounge. What you're about to hear is Nola trying to call him back and having an acrimonious conversation with the bartender."

Higgins hit Play and they listened to an agitated Nola Briggs calling Brother's Lounge and asking the bartender for Fontaine.

"Sounds like Fontaine was harassing her," Valentine said.

"It does, doesn't it?" Higgins said.

"Anyone talk to the bartender?"

"Yeah. He says Fontaine was a regular until last week."

"You give him a polygraph?"

Higgins scratched the late-afternoon stubble on his chin. "No. But that's not a bad idea, come to think of it."

"Mind if I talk to him first?"

"Go ahead. Only you've got to share with me whatever he tells you."

"Share's my middle name," Valentine said.

"Good," Higgins said. "Then maybe you'd like to tell me what happened at Sherry Solomon's place earlier."

Valentine felt something catch in his throat. Sherry had called Longo and lodged a complaint, and Longo had called Higgins. The question was, who were the police going to believe, a snitch or an ex-cop?

"Nothing much," he lied. "Why?"

"She said you leaned on her. Is that true?"

"I was just poking around."

"Do it again, and Longo will bust you."

"Sorry."

They sorted through the rest of the tagged evidence. Most of it was junk, scraps of paper, scribbled phone messages, the usual bills. In the bottom of the box, Valentine found Nola's diary. He started reading. Every day had an entry, even if it was only a sentence long.

"Anyone study this?" he asked.

"One of Longo's detectives went through it," Higgins replied. "He found seven entries Nola wrote during her trip to Mexico. It's the same story she told us at the station."

"You're saying she's telling the truth."

"The evidence sure looks that way. You still think she's guilty?"

"I sure do," Valentine said.

"You're in the minority, you know."

"I usually am."

The last envelope was tagged with a question mark. In it Valentine found two twisted metal coat hangers.

"Cops found those in a closet," Higgins explained.

"Mind if I straighten them out?"

"Be my guest."

Valentine straightened the hangers out. Both were three feet long and bent in the same spots, with a curved fish hook on one end. They reminded him of the contraptions people used to open locked cars, only he was certain that was not what they were intended for.

Standing, he held one hanger at chest height so the curved end was pointing at the ceiling. He moved the hanger up and down, using the hook to move an imaginary object above his head. The first piece of the puzzle fell into place, and he felt a sense of relief. He'd been right about Nola from the start. She despised Nick, so much that she hadn't replaced the shag carpeting in her house. It had served as a reminder, all these years.

"So what do you think?" Higgins said.

Valentine folded up the hangers and handed them back to him.

"Beats me," he replied.

Twenty minutes later, Higgins left, taking the box of evidence with him. Valentine was chaining the door when the phone rang.

"Why did you poison Sherry's dog?" Nick shouted at him.

"I didn't poison Sherry's dog," he replied stiffly.

"Don't bullshit a bullshitter," his employer retorted. "It ain't healthy."

"I kicked the little floor mop in the mouth."

"Why'd you do that?"

"Sherry sicced him on me."

"Oh," Nick said, backing down. "She does that sometimes when she's in a pissy mood."

"How sweet. Did she move in?"

"Yeah, and I moved out," Nick said. "You and I are neighbors."

Valentine was standing by the picture window in his living room just as the Mirage's volcano spit a mammoth fireball into the pinkish sky. Without thinking, he said, "You're staying at the Mirage?"

"Fuck the Mirage, you stupid Jersey asshole," Nick bellowed. "I'm staying down the hall, room 1201. We're neighbors, as in next door." One of the luxuries of being the boss was not having to watch your tongue.

"Sorry. What happened?"

"None of your fucking business," Nick said testily. "I called because I wanted to hear how your day went."

"Well," Valentine said, "I started out—"

"Not over the phone!"

"Sorry. I'll be right over."

Nick's suite was unlocked and Valentine entered without knocking. The living room was a throwback to the glorious seventies, the walls covered with splashy LeRoy Niemans, the furnishings sparkling chrome and glass. He crossed the tiled floor and noticed a boxy RCA television set propped against the wall. It did not fit in with the cheesy decor, and he noticed a brass plaque screwed into the top. On May 4, 1972, Elvis Presley had stayed in the suite, distinguishing himself by putting a bullet through the TV. The plaque did not say why.

Valentine found Nick sitting at the dining room table while a doctor attended to a puncture wound on his hand. The doctor removed a needle from his bag and swabbed Nick's forearm with alcohol.

"This is going to sting," the doctor warned.

"Great," Nick said, clenching his teeth as the booster was jammed in. To Valentine, he said, "What kind of guy kicks a little dog?"

"One who doesn't want to get bit."

"Only W. C. Fields didn't like dogs," Nick said, flexing his arm as the doctor tried to apply a bandage.

"It was self-defense."

"Me, I love animals. Sherry says she has a dog, I say, 'Bring it over.' Dog comes into the house, sniffs my leg, I bend down to pet it, suddenly the little monster attacks me."

"You let her move in?" Valentine asked, unable to hide his astonishment at Nick's lack of judgment.

"No! I invited her over for some sex and a little dinner," Nick said, feigning innocence. "The next thing I know, she's got a U-Haul parked at the front door. I tried to talk some sense into her, but she wouldn't listen." He shook his head. "Crazy broads. I'm a magnet for them."

"So you moved out."

"Temporarily. If she's not gone by tomorrow, Hoss and Tiny will toss her." The doctor was packing his bag. Nick dug out his wad and tossed him several hundred dollars. "Hey, Doc, I really appreciate you coming over. You're a lifesaver."

Pocketing the money, the doctor handed him a vial of white pills. "These are antibiotics. Take three a day for the next two weeks. And no alcohol."

"Sure thing. Thanks, Doc."

The doctor showed himself out and Nick threw the vial into the garbage. "So, on to more important things. You find any trace of Nola?"

Valentine told him how his day had gone, leaving out Higgins's visit. Bill had stepped over the line by sharing police evidence with him, and telling Nick now would only compromise his friend for the rest of his days. In conclusion, he said, "Look, Nick, you may not want to hear this, but the way I see it, Fontaine's going to show up in your casino again, and Nola's going to be with him. Maybe not physically with him, but with him nonetheless. The more I look at what happened, the more I'm convinced she's the one pulling the strings. Shakespeare said all the world's a stage, and this is Nola's stage we're playing on."

Nick's face was emotionless. His fingers fumbled with a half-smoked stogie that lay in a heart-shaped marble ashtray on the table. As it reached his lips, the tip magically turned orange.

"I still want to see her."

Valentine said, "I just wanted to warn you."

"I want to make peace, you know? Clean the slate."

"She might gouge your eyes out."

"You're a real positive guy, you know that?"

Valentine nearly told him to go to hell. His argument with Gerry was eating a hole in him. It was growing dark outside, and across the street, the Mirage had turned its lights on, the mammoth structure glowing like a thousand-watt bulb.

"You think Fontaine will try to rob us when Holy-field's fighting tomorrow night?" Nick asked.

Valentine gave it some thought. The casino would be dead during the fight, and he said, "Probably not."

"Good. Being that Sherry won't be joining me, I was wondering if you wanted to come."

Valentine did not know what to say. Why was Nick offering him the hottest ticket in town? Then it dawned on him: Nick had lived in Las Vegas for over thirty years but didn't have any friends. He suddenly felt sorry for the guy, even if he was a flaming jerk.

"Sure," he mumbled.

"I'll give it to the bellman if that's the way you feel about it."

"No," Valentine said. "I'd like to go."

"You could have fooled me."

"Seriously."

"You a fight fan?"

Valentine acknowledged that he was. Nick slapped his hand on the empty seat beside him, begging for company. Valentine moved to join him. Then it hit him like a thunderbolt: He hadn't called Roxanne. He glanced at his watch. It was nearly seven. He imagined her at home right now, the steam pouring out of her ears.

Nick practically pulled Valentine into the chair.

"Sit down, sit down," the little Greek said. "I got a story about Muhammad Ali you're not going to believe."

21

Valentine didn't sleep much knowing that Mabel was in jail, Roxanne was angry at him, and he and Gerry had come close to never speaking again. While doing ceiling patrol at three A.M., he realized that his propensity for angering the people he cared about most had gotten steadily worse since Lois's death, and he came to the sad conclusion that his unerring ability to find the negative in everything came from missing Lois as much as he did. And so he made others suffer.

He got up for good at six, ordered coffee and some plain white-bread toast from room service, then got on the horn and started making noise. It was nine o'clock back east, and he located the captain of the Clearwater police without much trouble. Luckily, the captain remembered a cruise ship gambling case Valentine helped the department solve, and he promised to move Mabel into a private cell once he got out of a staff meeting. As a rule, cops didn't lie to other cops the way they lied to practically everyone else, and Valentine hung up feeling better than he had before making the call.

Breakfast came, and he munched on toast while watching the sun rise. It was going to be another brutally hot day, and down the block he saw bare-chested men putting the finishing touches on the outdoor arena that had been erected behind Caesars Palace for tonight's extravaganza. He had seen many prizefights, but never one in Vegas, where probably every member of the audience, except him, would have a financial stake in the outcome. He had never placed a bet in his life and did not think tonight's bout would be any different. But it would still be fun to watch.

The food lifted his spirits, and at six-thirty he began trying to reach his son with a renewed sense of purpose. He'd done a real number on Gerry the night before and had probably made him feel a lot more guilty than he should have. It was time to fall on his sword and start over. He felt certain Gerry would let him.

Only . . . he couldn't find his son. No one answered at the saloon, and Gerry's cell phone emitted a frantic busy signal. He waited a few minutes, then called Gerry's cell phone again. This time Gerry's Puerto Rican girlfriend answered sleepily.

"This is Tony Valentine. I'm looking for Gerry."

He heard the phone hit the floor, then cursing. When Yolanda came back on, she was on fire. "Jesus Christ. Can't I get a decent night's sleep once in a while? First, some guys bang on my door; now, his old man's looking for him. I work late, you know."

Valentine mumbled a lame apology. "You work in a club or something?"

"A club? You think I'm a stripper?"

The sun was streaming into his suite, and Valentine covered his face with his hand. "No. I figured you were a bartender or a waitress. Gerry owns a bar, so I assumed that was how he met you."

"You think I hustle tips?"

He took a deep breath. "I didn't say that. Look, I didn't mean to offend you. Your name's Yolanda, isn't it?"

"That's right."

"So what do you do, Yolanda?"

"I'm an intern at Bellevue."

It was Valentine's turn to lose the phone. Retrieving it, he said, "You're studying to be a doctor?"

"That's right," she said icily. "Not your usual Puerto Rican success story, huh?"

"I didn't mean that."

"Sure you did, Tony. Because I'm Puerto Rican, you took me for some lowlife. Gerry was the same way when we first met."

"No, I didn't," he said forcefully. "I was just surprised to hear that my son is seeing someone who didn't flunk out of high school."

Yolanda let out a laugh. "Gerry likes them stupid, huh?"

Valentine wanted to say, "No, they like *him*," but he decided to shelve the line. As voices on the phone went, she sounded trustworthy, what the Jews called a mensch, and he said, "Used to. Listen, you said some guys were banging on your door."

"That's right."

"You know them?"

"Never seen them before," she said.

"Can you describe them?"

"Sure. Big, Italian, midthirties. One didn't talk; the other had a zipper scar down the side of his face. Kind of scary looking."

"Did they say what they wanted?"

"Yeah. They wanted Gerry."

Being a bookie, his son did business with a nefarious group of people, and those two could easily have been customers or even runners for him. Or they could have been thugs sent by Sonny Fontana.

"What did you tell them?"

"I told them Gerry had gone to Florida for a few days, which is what he told me. They acted pissed off and left."

Valentine smiled into the phone.

"Thank you, Yolanda," he said.

Valentine hung up feeling even better about the world. Twenty years earlier, when Gerry had started giving him and Lois problems, they'd gone to a family counselor. What Valentine had learned about himself had been surprising. Adult children of alcoholics, of which he was one, fell into four categories. Some ran away from their problems; others became loners; others made jokes about it. The fourth category, into which he fell, tried to right the world's wrongs in the mistaken belief it will heal their own wounds. Children of these people, he'd learned, often feel neglected or ignored.

So he'd set aside time for Gerry and gotten to know him better. A few hours a week had narrowed the chasm between them. Baseball games, movies, sometimes a long walk on the beach. And although they fought constantly—and probably always would—in the end they'd always come to terms. It was a harsh kind of love, never easy, but what was easy in this world?

Which was why it elated Valentine to know that Gerry had kept his word and had gone to Florida to rescue Mabel.

At eight he went downstairs to try and patch things up with Roxanne. The casino was packed, and as he crossed the floor the drone of a hundred discarded conversations was shattered by the electronic buzzer of a jackpot being paid. As he passed the craps table, a stickman bellowed "Winner eleven!" and the table went wild.

Roxanne was running the front desk. She looked almost radiant, her long red hair tied back in a bun, revealing her perfectly symmetrical Irish face. Slapping his hands on the counter, he wondered how many hot-blooded guys walked into the casino and offered to chuck their jobs and whisk her away to a tropical island.

"Hey," he said, "think you could find it in yourself to give a smelly old guy like me a second chance?"

"Not on your life," she said stiffly. "Get lost."

He returned a minute later with a dozen white roses.

"You're sweet," she said, sniffing the flowers. "But it doesn't make up for not calling me."

"I was going to, but Nick moved in across the hall," he explained. "He grabbed me and I couldn't get away."

"You spent the night with that little prick?" She tossed the flowers at his head, missing by inches. "Goddamn you!"

He picked the flowers off the floor, wondering how he'd lasted so long without understanding the opposite sex. Meeting her gaze, he saw a scowl so mean that it nearly made him run.

"I'm sorry," he stammered. "I'll make it up to you."

She had a customer. Out of the side of her mouth, she said, "I'm going to hold you to that, Tony. Why don't you make yourself useful until I go on my break."

"Sure. What do you want me to do?"

From her pocket, Roxanne removed five silver dollars and slid them across the counter. "Go play One-Armed Billy for me. I was in such a hurry this morning I forgot."

"You play that stupid thing?" he said without thinking.

"Every stupid day," she replied.

They met up twenty minutes later in Nick's Place, which had transformed itself from a sleepy hole-in-the-wall to a jumpin' speakeasy with a jazz band and cocktail waitresses in leotards and more customers than places to sit. Valentine pounced on the first available table and had two cups of coffee waiting when Roxanne came in. She'd let her hair down. She managed to snap around the head of every guy in the place as she crossed the room to join him.

"How'd you do?" she asked.

"Give me your hand," he said.

Roxanne obliged, and he placed three cherries, a slice of orange, and a wedge of lime into her palm.

"I put your money in the slot machine and that's what came out." He smiled and said, "I really did mean to call you."

She put the steaming coffee beneath her nose and sipped. "I fell asleep by the phone. I thought something horrible had happened to you."

Valentine squirmed in his chair. Wounding people he cared about was becoming a real specialty. He put his hand on the table and drummed it nervously with his fingers. He was pleasantly surprised when she placed her own atop his and gave his fingers a squeeze.

"Don't let it happen again," she said quietly.

"I won't."

They listened to the band play "New York, New York." It was one of those songs that could get him stirred up even if a trio of Shriners were blowing it on kazoos, and he hummed along. As the story went, Sinatra was going to name it "New Jersey, New Jersey" until a crowd in Hoboken had booed him offstage one night. What a way to get even.

When the song was over, Roxanne was grinning from ear to ear. She said, "I didn't know you were musical."

"Men have died for having voices like mine."

"But you have rhythm."

"No, I have a pulse."

"Do you play an instrument?"

"Just the radio."

She slapped the table. "You win. Look, I've got to get

back to work. How about we have dinner later and make up for last night?"

"I need to hang around tonight, in case Fontaine sneaks in."

"You think he will?"

"It's a distinct possibility," Valentine said.

"So we have dinner here."

"What time?"

"My second shift ends at ten."

Valentine took a deep breath. The fight was scheduled to begin at eight to accommodate everyone back east who'd be watching on Pay-Per-View. Nick would want to get back once it was over, freeing him up. So what if they were light-years apart and probably totally incompatible? She was the real thing, and that didn't come along very often.

Roxanne squeezed his hand. "Cat got your tongue?"

"Ten it is," he said.

"You sure you can stay awake that long?" she teased him.

"Only if I nap this afternoon."

She got up and kissed him on the cheek.

"Sweet dreams," she said.

There was nothing like a pretty woman's smile to start the day. Braving the heat, he walked to the Desert Inn and paid the valet twenty bucks for Nick's loaner. Las Vegas was not a morning town, and he cruised the Strip in a minimum of traffic.

Brother's Lounge was located on a desolate side street named Audrie. As bars went, it was a rathole, its neighbors a pawnshop and a tanning salon, and his shoes crunched broken glass as he entered the dimly lit establishment.

The bartender had a hockey player's blunt, proudly damaged face. His name was Mike, and he wore a ruffled tuxedo shirt with stained armpits and a yellow collar. "Can or tap?" he inquired when Valentine ordered a Diet Coke.

"Can's fine," Valentine said, casing the room. In the back, a guy sat nursing a draft beer; otherwise, the place was empty. He drew a C-note from his wallet and let it float to the laminated counter. "Can you change that?"

"Sorry," Mike said. "It's too early."

"Mind if I ask you a couple of questions?"

"Depends," Mike said.

Valentine nudged the C-note toward him. "There was a guy who used to come in here named Frank Fontaine."

Mike crossed his arms in front of his chest. "You a cop?"

Valentine nearly said no, then stopped himself. He would always be a cop, and this joker knew it. "Retired," he confessed.

"Private dick?"

"Consultant."

"That's a new one."

"Welcome to the nineties."

In the mirror behind the bar Valentine saw the guy in back kill his beer. He was built like one of those behemoths that carried refrigerators on their backs on ESPN. As he strolled out the front door, Mike pocketed the C-note.

"You know that dude?" Mike asked.

"No—should I?"

"He's looking for Fontaine, too."

Valentine spun around in his chair, wishing he'd gotten a better look at the guy. "Did he say why?"

"Said Fontaine owes him money."

"I wouldn't want to owe money to a guy that big."

Mike popped a can of Diet Coke and poured it into a plastic mug. He put a big head on it, which Valentine found insulting. He was sure Mike was capable of pouring a soda without making it look like a root beer float.

"Look, I'll tell you exactly what I told the cops," Mike said. "Fontaine came in a few times, mostly to use the phone. Never drank anything hard. Always left a fat tip."

Valentine waited. "That's it?"

"He liked to play video poker."

"He win much?"

"Hell, he never lost."

"Which machine?"

"Get out of here," Mike said with a laugh. The cordless phone beside the register warbled. Mike took the call in the kitchen.

After five minutes, Valentine realized Mike wasn't coming back. He finished his soda while reflecting on how little a hundred bucks bought these days. Instinct told him that Mike knew more than he was telling; the problem would be getting him to flip. Maybe a subpoena would do the trick, or Longo's doing a number on him. He threw a few pennies on the bar, just to piss Mike off.

On his way to the john, Valentine found the video poker machines. Video poker was a tough game to beat consistently, and he patted both machines down. A dime-size hole had been drilled into each, and he guessed Fontaine had found a way to rig the machines' silicon chips to pull up specific cards. It was one more headache for Bill Higgins to deal with.

The johns were crudely marked POINTERS and SITTERS. Valentine went through the appropriate door and the smell nearly knocked him over. Taking a deep breath, he soldiered up to a urinal.

As he'd aged, taking a piss had started to feel about as good as having sex, and he was lost in the moment when he heard someone barrel into the room. Jerking

his head around, he saw the big guy hovering menac-
ingly behind him, his eyes glazed over like he'd just inhaled a popper.

"Yeah?" Valentine said.

He put his hand on Valentine's face and pressed it into
the wall. Valentine kissed the condom dispenser above
the urinal, his nose pressing the button for a ribbed
Black Mambo.

"Let me see your hands," he said.

"I'm pissing, for Christ's sake."

"You heard what I said."

"What are you trying to do," Valentine said belliger-
ently, "make me wet my pants?"

Valentine's head banged the condom dispenser. Hug-
ging the urinal, he said, "Look, pal, I'm sixty-two years
old and wearing a pacemaker. Unless you came in here
to kill me, how about cutting out the rough stuff?"

"I heard you asking the bartender about Fontaine,"
the big guy said. "Tell me what you know."

"Sure," Valentine said. "But first let me breathe."

"Stick your hands out."

Valentine obeyed and the big guy frisked him like he
knew what he was doing. Then he reached around and
grabbed Valentine's dick, shook it, and shoved it into
his trousers and yanked up the zipper. Valentine had
never had a guy handle his balls before, and once he got
over the initial revulsion, he decided it wasn't the worst
thing that had ever happened to him. Close, but definitely not the worst.

Valentine felt the guy relax. Dropping his arms,
Valentine grabbed his assailant's fingers and pushed the
guy's thumb back at an unnatural angle. His attacker
corkscrewed to the floor, the pain ripping through him.
Valentine stepped away from the urinal.

"What's your name?"

"Al," his attacker gasped, gnashing his teeth.

"Why are you looking for Frank Fontaine, Al?"

"Because . . ."

"You want to kill him?"

"Let go of my thumb!"

Valentine did the opposite. The bigger they were, the harder they screamed. Al was no exception.

"You the guy who squeezed his head in a door in Tahoe?"

Al nodded that he was.

"Who're you working for, Al?"

"I can't tell you that."

Valentine bent his thumb back a little more. As thumbs went, it was awfully small, and he noticed how freakishly small Al's other fingers were as well, the tiny appendages attached to an even smaller hand. The rest of him looked normal, at least what was visible.

Al screamed some more. The bathroom door swung open and Mike stuck his head in. The bartender blinked, then blinked again. Valentine shot him a murderous glance.

"Where've you been hiding?"

"I was on the phone. Jesus, I thought *he* was killing *you.*"

"Thanks for the concern," Valentine said.

"You want me to call the police?"

Valentine looked at Al. "How about it? You want to have a chat with the boys in blue?"

Al shook his head. He was clutching his wrist with his other hand, trying to stop the pain from spreading to other parts of his body. Judging by the agonized look on his face, it wasn't working.

"I'll take that as a no." To Mike he said, "I'll try to keep the screaming down to a minimum."

"Sure," Mike said.

He left, and Valentine said, "Who're you working for?"

"I can't tell you," Al said. "They'll kill me."

"Like this is better?"

When Al didn't respond, he gave the thumb a little more juice. Al's face turned crimson and his eyes popped out like a comic-book character.

"How about their initials?" Valentine said. "Tell me their initials, and I'll figure it out."

"F. U.," Al whispered.

"What's that?"

"*F. U.! F. U.!*"

"You saying 'fuck you' to me? Why, you stupid punk . . ."

Valentine's anger rose to the surface like the lava in a volcano. Why someone cursing him bothered him more than having his balls squeezed, he didn't know. He brought his knee up into Al's jaw and sent him into dreamland.

Valentine laid him out in a stall, then rifled his pockets. A few hundred bucks and an empty inhaler. Typical.

Back in the bar, he found Mike standing stiffly at his post. Al's screaming had put the fear of God into him, and his upper lip was sweating BBs. Valentine slipped onto his former stool, pleased to see a fresh Diet Coke awaiting him, sans a frothy head. He raised the plastic mug to his lips and took a healthy swallow.

"Where's Muscles?" Mike asked.

"Napping," Valentine said.

He finished the soda and reached for his wallet.

"On the house," Mike said.

"I knew there was a reason I liked you," Valentine said.

22

"So when are they going to let you out of here?" Valentine asked, pulling a chair up to Sammy Mann's hospital bed.

"Not anytime soon," the patient said gloomily.

Visiting hours did not start for several hours, and Valentine had taken the service elevator up to the third floor and stolen down a hallway to Sammy's room, the nurses at the station too busy watching monitors to see him slip past. The hospital ran a tight ship, and he felt bad about breaking the rules, but he needed to talk to Sammy in private and this was the best way to do it.

Valentine noticed an uneaten breakfast on a tray sitting beside Sammy's bed, the scrambled eggs cold and runny. He felt a lump form in his throat. "You sick?"

"You got that right."

"What's wrong?"

"Big guy's getting the range."

"Cancer?"

"Prostate."

"What stage?"

"Stage two," Sammy said. "Doctor said it was lucky I got my knee whacked; a few more weeks, and it might have started spreading."

"When can you start chemo?"

"Two weeks," Sammy said, using the remote to kill

the picture on the silent TV. "They've got to put a pin in my leg first, let it heal, then start in with the rough stuff. Tell you the truth, I'm scared. I'm not in the best of shape, you know."

Valentine didn't know what to say, so he didn't say anything. He looked around the room and didn't see the faintest evidence that Sammy had received any visitors other than himself. Sammy wasn't much older than him, which made it easy to put himself in the sick man's shoes. One day you feel fine; the next, a doctor is giving you a death sentence. Life was like that; the shame was suffering through it alone.

"Can I make a suggestion?" Valentine said. When Sammy nodded, he continued. "My wife had breast cancer, pretty advanced. She had this great doctor at Sloan-Kettering. He convinced her that her mental outlook in dealing with her disease was critical to her getting well. So Lois started planning things to do once the chemo treatment was over. Like going to school and taking a trip."

"You're saying I should start planning a new life?"

"Why not?"

"Doing what? Flipping burgers? I've seen those retired people working at McD's. No thanks."

"I can get you a job working on gambling ships in Florida," Valentine offered. "You go out at noon, come back at night; they feed you a buffet and everything. Two hundred a day to watch some drunk tourists squander their money."

"Sounds sweet. Why don't you do it?"

"I get seasick."

"I'll think about it. Thanks."

"I need to ask you a couple of questions." Pulling his chair close to the metal bed, Valentine dropped his voice. "There's a guy on the prowl for Fontaine. Real nutcase. He's got the tiniest hands I've ever seen."

"That's Little Hands Scarpi," Sammy said. "Whatever you do, don't get in the same room with him. Rumor has it the casino bosses threw him a party after he murdered Fontana."

"You think they might have rehired him once word got out that Sonny wasn't dead?"

"It's possible."

"Is Nick one of those bosses?"

"No," Sammy said. "The worst Nick's ever done is have somebody's legs broken. Nick respects human life."

Valentine said, "Here's my next question. How trustworthy is Wily?"

Sammy gave him a hard look. "Wily? Why?"

"Fontaine has someone inside the Acropolis helping him. If I'm going to catch Fontaine, I'll need someone on the inside helping me."

"And you don't want that someone to be the same person who's working with Fontaine."

"Precisely."

"Well," Sammy said, "you can trust Wily. He may be as dumb as a bucket of nails, but he's square. Just don't tell him too much. You'll only confuse him."

Valentine rose to leave. "Thanks. I've got to run."

"You said they served a buffet. What kind of food?"

"Mostly seafood. Lobster, shrimp, stone crab when it's in season. You ever have stone crab? It's the greatest; they tear only one claw off the crab, then throw it back in. They also have a carving board with roast beef. And a dessert table. Éclairs, ice cream, chocolate cake."

"They have a bar?"

"The ship *is* a bar," Valentine replied.

"They let you smoke cigars?"

"All night long. Cigars are the in thing. Everybody on the ship smokes them—even the ladies."

"That's too bad," Sammy said sadly. "You didn't happen to remember to bring one along, did you?"

Valentine wanted to slap himself in the head. He'd been too distracted to remember half the promises he'd made in the past two days. He apologized profusely to Sammy.

"Bring one next time," Sammy told him.

Valentine stopped in the doorway. "You want me to make a call? I know the guy who owns the ship."

"I'd better deal with my cancer first."

"It's never too late to plan for the future."

Sammy smiled, his teeth stained by years of smoking and neglect, his eyes dancing with the possibility of what might be.

"Let me think about it," he said.

Down in the lobby, Valentine dropped a quarter in the pay phone and dialed the main number of the Acropolis.

"Ten cents, please. Please deposit an additional ten cents."

He searched his pockets for more coinage. Since when did local calls cost thirty-five cents? How much did they *really* cost, with fibers optics and all the satellites circling the earth? Probably a nickel, the same as when he was a kid. The rest went for advertising. He reluctantly fed another dime into the slot.

The hotel operator connected him to his room and he dialed into his voice mail. Although he was not officially registered in the hotel, he'd asked Roxanne to alert the operators to take any calls from Mabel, knowing she'd probably try to reach him again. Three messages awaited him, so he punched in the code to retrieve them.

"Hi, Tony," Mabel said. "Well, I guess you didn't get my first message, because I'm still here in the pokey with a hooker with AIDS and some Mexican girl that stabbed her boyfriend to death."

Valentine bowed his head, his forehead touching the cold hospital wall. The captain of the Clearwater police had *promised* him he'd move Mabel into a decent cell. Wasn't a man's word worth anything anymore?

"The good news is, the judge looks like he's going to make a full recovery," she said. "Not that I wish the man harm, but he had no right to treat me the way he did. Anyway, he's not paralyzed or drooling, so I suppose my prayers were answered."

Mabel had prayed for the judge. Valentine found himself smiling in spite of everything.

"Well, I figure I can take another couple of days of this, and then I'm going to break out of here, ha-ha. Seriously, I'm starting to feel pretty bad. Food is just lousy and I can't sleep. I guess that's why they call it jail. Well, hope all is well with you. Good-bye, Tony, wherever you are."

A dial tone filled his ear. He glanced at his watch. Gerry would be in Florida soon and Mabel would be saved. He played the next message.

"Pop . . . it's me . . . Gerry. Listen—I've got trouble."

Valentine cupped his free hand over his ear. He could hardly hear his son, a jukebox in the background spitting out the Stones' "Honky Tonk Woman."

"The operator said you checked out, but when I called back and talked to Roxanne, she said you were still there. Anyway, I hope you get this, because there are two Mafia guys looking for me."

"Sweet Jesus," Valentine said into the phone.

"I went to the saloon to get some cash, and they were waiting for me," his son went on. "I asked them what they wanted, and they said this had to do with you. I threw a table at them and then hightailed it out the back, and I've been running ever since. These guys are acting like they want to kill me, Pop."

Valentine gripped the phone, his heart racing out of control.

"Anyway, I missed my flight. I'm sorry about Mabel,

but I've got to watch out for my own rear end. I'm sure you understand. I'm going down to Atlantic City to hide out. I'll call you from there."

Valentine played the message again, this time listening to his son's voice. Gerry was scared. Valentine closed his eyes and said a prayer for his son's safety, then played the final message.

"Hey, Tony!" Nick shouted over the wail of sirens. "Get your butt over to my place. Somebody tried to burn my house down!"

The fire trucks were long gone by the time Valentine arrived at the smoldering palace that Nick called home. Muddy tire tracks crisscrossed the front lawn, the shrubbery trampled beyond recognition. He parked behind Nick's Caddy, got out of his car, and surveyed the damage. Whatever ugly charm the grounds had once was now gone.

A shroud of soot covered the portico and he wiped his feet on the mat before entering. Inside the foyer, he found Nick engaged in a heated discussion with a claims adjustor who was lamely trying to explain why State Farm wouldn't issue a check until the fire marshal had issued a report and ruled out arson.

"Of course it was arson," Nick bellowed at him. "She tried to burn the place down. Hoss and Tiny saw her. Didn't she, boys?"

The two gridiron stars sat at the phallic bar in the living room. Hoss sported a wounded hand, Tiny a line of scratches across his cheek. Both nodded, then stared shamefully at the floor.

"What more proof do you want?" Nick asked.

The claims adjuster glanced rudely at his watch. In an impatient voice, he said, "I meant deliberate arson, Mr. Nicocropolis. If the fire marshal concludes that it was Ms. Solomon who set the fire, your claim will fall under vandalism, which you're covered for. Until then, I can't do anything except put you up in a hotel."

"Put me up in a hotel? I own a hotel, nimrod!"

"Mr. Nicocropolis, just give me a little time, okay?"

"How much is a little?"

"Three, four days."

"That's a little?"

"To get a claim put through, yes."

"Aw, get out of my face," Nick said, dismissing him with a wave of the hand. To Valentine, he said, "Where the hell you been?"

The claims adjustor did not move. Slowly, almost mechanically, he removed his glasses and stuffed them in his shirt pocket, and Valentine got the feeling he was about to do something really stupid. He touched the man's arm.

"Don't," Valentine said under his breath.

The adjustor looked at him out of the corner of his eye, not knowing if Valentine was threatening him or offering advice.

"You work for him?" the adjustor asked.

"Part time."

"Too bad," he said. Then he walked out of the house.

Nick went to the bar and put his hands on Hoss's and Tiny's broad shoulders. There was not enough floor for the two men to stare at.

"How much am I paying each of you boys?" Nick asked them.

"Forty grand," Hoss said.

"The same," Tiny said.

"For what?"

Pulling an O'Doul's from the bar, Nick said, "Think about it," and then led Valentine down the hallway to the master suite. The house had suffered little damage, the blaze being isolated to Nick's chambers. The bedroom door had been splintered with a fire axe, and Nick kicked at it upon entering.

"Sherry went nuts when Hoss and Tiny tried to evict her," he explained. "Locked herself in my bedroom and started destroying my clothes. Real little-girl stuff. Then she came across an album I keep of all the broads I've known. It didn't sit too well."

Valentine canvassed the bedroom and found the album in a corner. It had been used to start the fire, the flame's path easy to trace. Up the curtains, across the ceiling, and down into Nick's dresser, the collection of sharkskin suits and silk shirts going up in one big nova. The flames had taken out the wall, which now offered a nice view of the bocci court in Nick's backyard.

The album was still warm. That the police hadn't tagged it as evidence spoke volumes. Valentine pulled away the cover and thumbed through dozens of melted glossies of Nick's lady friends posed in the buff. Several faces from the hotel popped up, startling him.

"You shot your girlfriends in the nude?" Valentine asked.

"Sure. With my memory being so lousy, I figured I'd better start keeping records."

"They didn't mind?"

"They love it."

"You're kidding me."

"They always want me to shoot their faces. That way, I'll know it was them later. Ha-ha."

"You're kidding me."

"You never took any pictures of your old lady naked?"

Valentine shook his head. If he'd ever tried to photograph Lois without her clothes on, she probably would have shot him.

"You shouldn't be screwing all these women on your staff."

"Oh, for the love of Christ," Nick said. "Don't start preaching to me, okay? Next you'll be telling me how to run my life. I don't want to hear it."

Valentine felt something inside of him snap. The claims adjustor was right: Too bad he had to work for this jerk. Removing his wallet, he extracted Nick's two thousand and threw it at him.

"What are you doing?"

"Quitting," Valentine said.

"What?!"

"You heard me."

"You can't run out on me now. I *need* you."

"You got yourself into this mess," Valentine said, "and you deserve whatever you get."

Nick's pug face hardened. He pulled a cigar from his shirt pocket and chewed on it furiously. "You having a bad day or something?"

"It's running neck and neck with yours."

Nick's expression changed. Misery was something he understood all too well. Scooping the money off the floor, he wiped it on his pants, then handed it back to Valentine.

"You win."

"Meaning what?" Valentine asked.

"Meaning I'm sorry."

Valentine put the money back into his wallet.

"I'm still leaving," he told his employer.

"But—"

"You hired me to finger Fontaine, and I did, and now it's time to go."

"But you haven't found Nola . . ."

Valentine shrugged. His son needed him more than Nola Briggs did, and so did Mabel, and they mattered more to him than all the tea in China. He'd started entertaining the thought of taking a cruise with them and found it oddly appealing.

"She'll turn up," Valentine said.

A tired look spread across Nick's face. His waterbed had not been touched by the flames, and he plopped down on the mattress. Streams of water shot up all around him, soaking the ceiling.

"That little bitch!" he roared.

Valentine got some towels from the bathroom and helped Nick dry off. By the time they were done, Nick was cracking jokes and reminiscing about an old flame who'd tried to run him over with her car. When it came to bad relationships, he had no equal, and Valentine couldn't help but like him, even though he liked practically nothing about him.

"Look," Nick said a few minutes later, residing on the heart-shaped couch, "how about we strike a deal?"

"What kind of deal?"

"If Fontaine is going to rip me off, he'll probably do it tonight—you told me so yourself."

"That's right."

"Without Sammy around, I'm vulnerable. Hang around and I'll pay you five grand."

"I've got to leave, Nick."

"I'm talking about a night's work."

"Sorry," Valentine said.

Nick chewed his unlit stogie, thinking. "You got a seat on a plane?"

Valentine hadn't thought that far ahead; he shook his head no. Pulling out his cell phone, Nick said, "A hundred bucks says you can't find one."

Using Nick's phone book, Valentine called the various airlines. The first plane out was tomorrow night. He'd forgotten that Las Vegas drew the crowds like no other city in the world.

"I lease a private jet," Nick told him. "You want it— it's yours."

"What's the catch?" Valentine said.

"They require twelve hours' notice."

Valentine looked at his watch. It was nearly three. If Nick's jet was the fastest way out of town, then he owed it to Gerry and Mabel to take it. Even if he was ready to pack it in.

Nick poked him in the arm. "So what do you say? Deal?"

"Okay," he mumbled.

Nick punched him in the biceps, sealing the agreement.

Walking through the hole in the wall in Nick's suite, they stood in the backyard and inspected the damage. By the pool, a statue of Michelangelo's *David* had been castrated with a blunt object. Finding the stone penis in the grass, Nick pocketed it.

"I think you ought to consider putting some special security measures into play at your casino tonight," Valentine said.

Nick eyed him. "What kind of measures?"

"Add more security but tell Wily not to let them on the floor until the casino is packed. That way they'll blend in."

"Okay," Nick said.

"You should also stagger your shifts in the surveillance control room," Valentine said. "Let the team that knocks off at midnight leave an hour early and replace them with fresh people."

"How come?"

"Most scams in casinos go down during shift changes. People are going home; others are coming in. It's easy to get distracted and not watch the monitors for a few minutes. Fontaine knows this."

"You've got this all figured out, haven't you?"

Valentine nodded solemnly. He knew exactly how

Frank Fontaine thought—not that it had ever done him any good.

"What about Nola?" Nick said.

"Nick, she's as guilty as the day is long."

Nick winced, his face turning sour. "You're sure?"

"One hundred percent positive sure," Valentine said.

Nick took the stone penis out of his pocket and examined it. His face had a faraway look, the memory of her still haunting him. The penis seemed the perfect metaphor for the life he'd led. He took a running start before pitching it over the hedges.

23

Leaving Hoss and Tiny to guard his smoldering domicile, Nick drove Valentine down the block to a neighbor's gated driveway, buzzed himself in, and parked in the shadows of an elegant Tudor mansion. Behind the house sat a gleaming Sikorsky on a helipad, a blond pilot wearing Ray-Bans posed smartly by the door.

"We'll never reach the Strip by car," Nick explained. "Too many tourists. This is the only way to go."

They crossed the lawn, and Valentine spotted a bald, heavyset man lying on a towel by the pool. A curvaceous miss with red floss riding up the crack in her behind knelt beside him, giving him a rubdown. Nick whistled wolfishly and the woman looked up. The bald man turned his head, ignoring them.

"Who's he?" Valentine asked.

"Some hotshot surgeon," Nick replied. "Dropped a hundred grand playing craps in my casino one night. Turned out he was in debt and couldn't pay his marker. I could've foreclosed on his place, but I figured he's a neighbor, so I let him work it off. His yard man does my lawn, I use his chopper when I want, and I bang his wife when he's out of town."

"You're kidding me," Valentine said.

"Thousand bucks' credit a whack," Nick said, winking at him.

"Hope you didn't give her a house key."

"Stop picking on me."

Nick exchanged high-fives with the grinning pilot. His name was Ken, and when they were strapped in and had headsets on, Ken took the chopper up and made a bee-line for the Strip, the colorful casinos spread out before them like an overturned pirate's chest. Valentine had ridden in plenty of choppers and knew the pitfalls of staring at stationary objects for more than a few seconds at a time. You threw up. So he kept his eyes shut and held on to the door.

"I want to show my friend something," Nick told Ken. "Think your boss will mind if we take a side trip?"

Ken laughed loudly.

A minute later, Ken dropped down near a desolate trailer park on the north end of town. Climbing out, Valentine followed Nick down a dusty dirt road that dissected a honeycomb of dilapidated trailers. A shirtless migrant and his snarling dog emerged to stare at them.

After a half mile, the trailer park ended and so did the road. A sea of numbered graves lay before them. It was a pauper's field. The plots were laid out haphazardly, the final punishment for dying broke. Nick zigzagged down a narrow path, walking quickly between graves. Valentine did a tightrope walk behind him as he tried to avoid stepping on the dead.

In the corner of the cemetery sat a manicured plot with a decorative headstone. Kneeling at the grave site, Nick crossed himself and mumbled a prayer. Valentine crossed himself as well, squinting to read the tombstone.

James Dandalos
"The Greek"
6/4/10–9/12/94
"If it's worth doing,
it's worth overdoing."

"My mentor," Nick explained, getting up and fishing a black hundred-dollar chip from his pocket. "I came out here in sixty-five and the Greek took me under his wing. He was a real gambler, maybe the best who's ever lived. One night we went out and won forty grand playing craps. We bought a car and decided to press our luck at the tables. We lost all our dough, then went out and wrecked the car. It was the best lesson I ever learned."

Nick dug a hole and buried the chip, patting the ground smooth when he was done. "I told the Greek that gambling full time was a losing proposition. The house was always going to win. He laughed and said the only way to make money in a casino is to own one."

"So you went and bought one."

"As soon as I could scrape the money together."

"He must have died pretty broke to end up here."

"Four million in the hole, not counting what he owed me," Nick said, wiping the sand off his knees. "He died a John Doe. I didn't find out he was gone until he was already in the ground."

"How much do you think he lost over the years?"

Nick laughed. "Thirty million, forty, maybe more."

"You'd think someone could have given him a proper burial."

"The Greek lived large and died small," Nick said fondly. "He wouldn't have wanted it any other way."

Ten minutes later, the Sikorsky dropped them off at the Mirage's helipad, which was jointly used by several casinos on the Strip. Out of principle, Nick would not step foot in his competitor's establishment, so they walked clear around the mammoth hotel. It was a good hike, and by the time they reached the Acropolis's front doors, they were both dripping with perspiration.

"Look at all these people," Nick said gleefully.

The front doors were propped open, and a long line of tourists waiting to play One-Armed Billy snaked past the valet stand. Like a politician, Nick began pumping the flesh and handing out comps for free meals. Two minutes later, everyone in line was beaming, and Nick and Valentine entered the casino to a round of applause.

The casino floor was a madhouse of noise and blinking lights and people yelling at the roll of the dice or the turn of a single card. There was the sound of a hundred silver dollars hitting a metal tray, of a man in a baseball cap having won twenty grand bluffing at poker, of fortunes won and bankrolls lost. By the time they reached the elevators, Nick was walking on air.

"You see that action?" he said when the doors had closed and they were rising. "Nothing like a prizefight to get people to open their wallets. We'll gross two, maybe three million, easy."

Which was what Fontaine was counting on, Valentine thought as the elevator raced to the twelfth floor. So much money coming in at once that it blinded you—the perfect misdirection for a heist.

Nick called Wily once he reached his suite. The disheveled pit boss came upstairs in a suit so wrinkled it looked slept in. In an exhausted voice, he read the numbers off a spreadsheet.

"Since noon, we've done five hundred big ones on blackjack, three eighty on the slots, eighty-five on the wheel, sixty on pai gow, and fifty on craps."

"What's the take on Billy?" Nick asked. He'd parked himself in a recliner in the living room and was sucking on an O'Doul's.

"We've emptied him out twice already," Wily said.

"Beautiful," Nick said. "Listen. Tony wants to put some special security measures into play tonight. Just in case Fontaine shows his face."

Valentine explained to Wily what he wanted done. The pit boss brightened, sensing a trap being set.

"You think we'll nail him?" Wily asked.

"Only if you stay on your toes," Nick told him.

Wily's shoulders sagged, as if the weight of what he was being asked to handle was too great. He excused himself to the john. When he returned, his hair was parted and his tie had a fresh knot.

"No one's going to rip us off while I'm on duty," he announced.

Nick ushered him to the door. "Tony and I are going to the fights. Call me on my cell phone if anything comes up."

"Yes, sir."

"I'm depending on you."

"I won't let you down," the pit boss said resolutely.

"Go make my money grow," Nick said.

The orange message light on his phone was blinking when Valentine returned to his suite a few minutes later.

There was only one message. Gerry.

"Hey, Pop—just wanted to give you a status report. I'm still in New York. Those goons rammed my car on the FDR Drive; I got off in Midtown and left the car in a garage by the UN. I thought about calling the cops, but since I've got a record, well, you know . . ."

"Hang tough," his father said into the phone.

"I got ahold of Pee Wee, told him to shut down the bar, so I guess you're getting your wish—no more book-making for me. Ha-ha. Anyway, Yolanda is going to pick me up in about twenty minutes and we're going to hit the Jersey shore. I'll call you when I get settled in, let you know where I'm staying. And Pop, I'm sorry about Mabel. I keep thinking about her down there in jail. . . . It's eating at me, you know?"

Gerry was sorry about Mabel. Valentine couldn't remember his son ever being sorry about anything.

"And Pop, I guess I should be mad at you, but I'm not. I mean, what goes around comes around, you know? I mean, what I'm trying to say is, I guess I'm getting a taste of what I've put you through over the years, and it doesn't taste very good. I'll call you."

The line went dead. He considered playing the message again, just to hear Gerry eat crow a second time, but he erased it instead. Once was more than enough.

He sat on the edge of his bed and thought back to Nick's burying the chip for the Greek, a guy who died owing him lots of money. How far do you go for the ones you love? All the way, he realized.

"Undercard starts in twenty minutes," Nick said, having materialized in Valentine's doorway. "There's a welterweight fighting who I've got money on."

Nick had changed into white slacks and a purple silk shirt, his snowy chest hair contrasting sharply with the jet-black mop on his head. Around his neck hung several thick gold ropes.

"Give me a minute," Valentine said.

Nick let out a disapproving howl when Valentine emerged from the bedroom sixty seconds later.

"You can't go to the fights dressed like that!" his host exclaimed. "You look like a cop! Everybody will shun us."

It was the last set of clean clothes Valentine had.

"I'm open to suggestions," he said.

"Bag everything but the pants," Nick told him. "You can wear some of my clothes."

The clothes Nick had in mind were classic seventies hoodlum attire; a skintight, bloodred silk shirt and a creamy linen sports jacket with mother-of-pearl buttons and wide pointy lapels. Standing in the dressing room in

Nick's suite, Valentine grimaced at his reflection in the mirror. Put some grease in his hair and he could pass for one of Moe Greene's henchmen in *The Godfather*.

Nick tapped his watch. "Let's get moving. I've got two grand riding on my boy winning inside three rounds."

Valentine followed him out of the suite. By the door, Nick stopped and pointed at a framed head shot of Elvis Presley on the bookshelf. The inscription read *To Nick—you're the greatest! Elvis*.

"I helped him once," Nick explained.

They went into the hall and waited for an elevator.

"How?" Valentine asked.

"I'd just opened," Nick said. "This was back in '70. Elvis worked the main room, packed the place every show. It was like printing money. Cha-ching! One night he was in his suite and he saw something on the TV that got him pissed off, so he shot it. Bullet went through the wall—nearly killed the couple next door."

"What did you do?"

"I had the screen replaced."

"What?!"

"What do you mean, what?"

"You repaired the TV for him?"

"Sure. What else could I do?"

Nick's logic escaped him. Calling the police would have been one solution. Getting him some good psychiatric help another.

"What set him off?"

A blue-haired couple wearing matching polyester outfits stepped off the elevator, their Midwestern voices raised in agitation. The woman, who appeared to be getting the worst of it, wagged a disapproving finger in her companion's face.

"Stop making me out to be the big loser," she said.

"Well," the elderly man said, "you are."

"I lost four hundred playing keno," she practically shouted. "You lost *four thousand* playing craps."

"Yeah," her companion said, "but I know how to gamble."

The couple disappeared into one of the suites. Nick and Valentine got into the elevator and Nick punched the Lobby button. The doors closed and they started to descend.

"He was watching Robert Goulet," Nick said.

24

On their way out the door, Nick ducked into One-Armed Billy's brightly lit alcove. The giant slot machine was idle, and the little Greek planted his lips on his favorite employee. Sitting on his stool, Joe Smith chuckled silently.

"Billy was the smartest thing I ever did," Nick confided to Valentine. "Every day, rain or shine, Billy makes money."

"You can't beat that," Valentine said.

Outside, Nick's monogrammed golf cart was parked at the valet stand, a perspiring O'Doul's in the drink holder. Valentine got into the passenger seat, then held on for dear life as Nick floored the accelerator and sped down the Acropolis's front entrance.

The Strip was jammed, the mob rivaling New Year's in Times Square. Nick darted in and out of traffic, hopped a median, and ran a red light, all for the sake of traveling a few short blocks. When they reached Caesars' entrance, he hit the brakes and nearly sent Valentine through the windshield. A line of stretch limousines blocked traffic in both directions. Spinning the wheel, Nick hopped the cart onto the sidewalk with his hand on the cart's Harpo Marx horn.

"I've got a sick man here," he announced to a sharply dressed contingent in their path. "Gangway, folks."

The crowd parted and Nick drove through.

"He doesn't look sick," a man in a tuxedo yelled.

"He married his sister," Nick yelled back. "That sick enough for you, buddy?"

The cart still on the sidewalk, Nick pulled up to the busy valet stand, hopped out, and tossed the uniformed kid a fifty.

"I'll take good care of her, Mr. Nicocropolis," the kid promised.

"You'd better," Nick said.

Valentine followed his host into Caesars plush casino. The tables were jumping, the players wall to wall. Nick did a little jig as they sifted through the crowd, the electric atmosphere putting a noticeable jump in his step. Jay Sarno, the impresario who had single-handedly built Caesars, had themed the hotel after a Roman orgy. It had not been planned as a family destination and never would be one.

Passing a sea of blinking slots, they detoured into a shopping promenade with artificial waterfalls and life-like statues that shifted poses every few minutes. Pleasant 3-D images lit up the domed ceiling, the air filled with the soothing sounds of a rain forest.

"I hate this crap," Nick swore under his breath. "Casinos are supposed to sell dreams, not illusions. You know what I'm saying?"

Valentine nodded, remembering Sammy Mann's comments about the odds Nick offered. "No magic acts for you, huh?"

"Never," Nick swore.

Signs directed them to a bank of doors, which opened onto a parking lot. The boxing ring sat a hundred yards behind the casino, hemmed in by rows of bleachers that rose straight up into the sky. Nick handed his tickets to an attendant, and a toga-clad waitress escorted them to their seats, which were fifth row center. Then she took their drink order.

"Jay Sarno is the smartest guy who's ever lived," Nick said when their drinks came. "Back in '78 when Atlantic City opened, everyone out here panicked. But not Jay. Instead, he started staging prizefights. Each fight got a little better, then Jay went and staked fifteen million for Leonard–Hearns. What a night that was!"

Valentine remembered the fight well. Sugar Ray Leonard and Tommy Hearns, two undefeated, charismatic boxers, fought in Caesars parking lot for the undisputed welterweight championship. The fight had attracted every major gambler in the world and disappointed no one. Atlantic City never recovered.

Nick clicked his fake beer against Valentine's bottled water.

"Here's to catching Frank Fontaine."

"I'll drink to that," Valentine said.

Two Hispanic flyweights entered the diamond-bright boxing ring. A referee gave them their instructions. The bell rang. The fighters met in the ring's center and whaled away at each other.

They fought to a draw and a chorus of boos. Valentine clapped anyway. Fighting to a draw was considered noble in most parts of the world, even worthy of celebration. So what if the kids stunk? They'd fought their hearts out and deserved something for it.

"My boy's up next," Nick announced.

"Is he any good?"

Nick's eyes twinkled. "Yeah, and nobody knows it."

The wind shifted and the rumble of traffic from the nearby highway infused the air with a sense of impending combat. Colored spotlights perched above the ring came on, bathing the canvas in soft hues. The arena was filling quickly, and in the front rows sat several male movie stars and their stunning dates. This was the "exposure section," and Nick explained that the studios paid obscene sums to put their stars in these seats.

Nick's ringer performed as expected and pounded his opponent like a hammer pounding a nail, winning in two rounds. Standing, Nick said, "I'd better go collect my dough. Want anything?"

"No thanks."

"Be back in a few."

Nick strode down the aisle. The next bout was about to start and the referee motioned two snarling females to the center of the ring. Then the bell sounded and they started brawling like alley cats. It was ugly, and the crowd quickly made its displeasure known. Luckily, it ended quickly, a physician climbing into the ring to tend to a young skinny black woman sitting on a stool. Nick returned with his cash.

"If you or I did that," he remarked, "we'd do time."

"No kidding."

"Look," Nick said, elbowing him in the ribs.

Valentine stared across the ring at a well-known movie actor getting his picture taken with a star-struck fan.

"I hate that prick," Nick swore.

It took a moment for Valentine to realize that Nick was referring not to the actor but to Nola Briggs's defense attorney, who rose from a nearby seat. He was small in stature and looked even smaller in the company of the larger-than-life characters that stood yukking it up around the ring apron. Cupping his hands over his mouth, Nick yelled, "Hey, Felix, how's the leg holding up?"

Valentine stiffened. And it hit him: Felix Underman was the F. U. who'd hired Little Hands. He seemed smarter than that, but people often did stupid things when backed into a corner.

Valentine watched Underman leave the arena. Then he rose himself.

"I'll be right back," he said.

Underman wasn't walking very fast and seemed to favor the leg that Nick had kicked, and Valentine quickly caught up to him. Valentine followed him into the casino and through a buzzing mob of gamblers whose excitement was palpable: The odds had dropped, making Holyfield's opponent a two-to-one proposition. Underman went into the men's room, and Valentine followed.

Caesars' johns were something special. Travertine marble ran floor to ceiling and the brass fixtures were so shiny you could see well enough in them to shave. Valentine stood at the sinks and watched Underman enter a stall; then he dropped two fifties in the attendant's tip basket.

"Get lost for a few minutes."

"I could lose my job," the attendant said.

Valentine tossed another hundred into the basket.

"You a cop?" the attendant asked.

"What do you think?"

The attendant left without another word. At the sink, Valentine wadded a handful of paper towels and soaked them with cold water. Then he went to Underman's stall and waited. The defense attorney emerged tugging up his fly. Valentine slapped the towels over his mouth, pushed him into the stall, and shut the door, latching it with his free hand.

"Sit down," he said.

Trembling, Underman lowered himself onto the toilet.

"Look at me," Valentine said.

Underman stared into his eyes.

"See the purple bump on my nose?"

Underman nodded his head vigorously.

"Know who put it there?"

Underman made a noise that sounded like no.

"You sure you don't know?"

A sound like *no* again.

"A guy you hired put it there. Little Hands Scarpi. Said you sent him to find Fontaine. This ringing any bells?"

Underman took the Fifth.

Valentine cuffed him in the head the way his own old man used to. With feeling. Underman made a sound like *stop*. Valentine cuffed him again. The defense attorney's breathing grew shallow. Valentine took the towels away and heard Underman's chest rattle.

"I made a mistake," Underman gasped. "I was out of my mind with worry."

"That's no excuse for breaking the law," Valentine said.

"You think I don't know that?" Underman said, sounding more defiant than he had any right to. He tore off a sheet of toilet paper and wiped the spittle that had gathered at the corners of his mouth. "Look, you seem like a reasonable man. I'll give you fifty thousand dollars to forget about this."

Valentine slammed Underman's head against the imported marble. "I don't take bribes, asshole."

"Seventy-five," Underman gasped.

Valentine brought his mouth an inch from the defense attorney's ear. "You're busted, Underman. I'm going to make sure you spend your golden years teaching lifers how to file appeals."

"Now you listen to me—"

Attorneys always had to get in the last word; it was why people hated them so much. A short, quick uppercut snapped Underman's head straight back. His body turned to jelly and he slid off the toilet.

Valentine left him lying on the bathroom floor to think about his future.

The next fight turned out to be the real thing and let Valentine forget his troubles for a little while. The bout was a twelve-round light heavyweight contest for one of the alphabet-soup championship belts. The challenger—a Compton kid named Benny "Lightning" Gonzalez—had more talent than experience and a murderous right hand. His opponent, champion Barry "the Blarney Stone" Ross, had started his career kickboxing in Europe, switched to the sweet science, and won his first thirty fights, knocking out all. It was a classic match-up, boxer versus brawler, age versus experience.

"Something you and I can relate to," Nick said.

As fights went, it was pure drama, with each man pressing the action only to have the other come roaring back. First Gonzalez was ahead, then Ross; then Gonzalez charged back; then Ross asserted himself. When the final bell sounded, both men were still standing, and the crowd rose, cheering itself hoarse.

Valentine had lost his voice in the eighth during one of Gonzalez's furious attempts to finish Ross off, and he stomped his feet and whistled. As the scorecards were read and Ross's arm was raised in triumph, Nick screamed at Ross's corner.

"Who says white guys can't fight?"

A tuxedoed announcer climbed through the ropes. Mike in hand, he introduced the boxing luminaries at ringside, the names spanning several decades. Over the PA system, gospel music was being played, the singer the great Mahalia Jackson.

"It's part of Holyfield's contract," Nick explained. "Gotta play gospel music before every fight. He says it inspires him. Personally, I wish he'd tone down the religious stuff."

"You think it's a put-on?"

"Naw," Nick said. "He's religious. I just think it's silly. After every bout, he thanks God for letting him win. Do you really think God gets some kind of joy out of him turning a guy's face into a pizza?"

"Probably not."

"I'm hungry. Want anything?"

"No, thanks. Mind if I borrow your cell phone?"

"Sure," said Nick as he handed over his phone and left. Taking a scrap of paper with Bill Higgins's cell number on it from his wallet, Valentine punched in the numbers. His friend answered from a bar, shouting to be heard over the televised highlights of the Ross—Gonzalez fight. "I'm not talking to you," Higgins said, sounding drunk.

"Why not?"

"Because you're holding out, that's why. I show you the police evidence and you suddenly clam up."

Valentine heard real anger in Bill's voice. He wanted to explain that he had his reasons, but he knew that would only upset his friend more. He tried another tack.

"I've got a hot tip for you," Valentine said.

"Sure you do," Higgins said sarcastically.

Cupping his hand over the mouthpiece, Valentine said, "Felix Underman hired Little Hands Scarpi to kill Frank Fontaine."

Higgins's tone changed. "You can prove this?"

"I sure can."

"Where's Underman now?"

"Probably trying to get out of town."

"Where are you?"

"I'm at Caesars with Nick."

Higgins belched into the phone. "I hate you."

"I'm sure it's nothing personal," Valentine replied.

Nick returned with a bag of peanuts, which he shared, along with the latest line from Caesars' sports book.

"They're giving even money inside," he said breathlessly. "Can you believe that? I put ten grand on Holyfield. You'd better hurry before they stop taking bets."

"I don't bet on sports," Valentine replied.

Nick looked at him like he was an alien.

"It makes you root for the wrong reason," Valentine explained.

"How so?"

"There's a difference between wanting someone to win and wanting someone to win because you've got money on them."

"Betting on Holyfield is different," Nick said.

"How so?"

"Holyfield's a great fighter who has never broken the law. How many boxers can you say that about these days? By betting on him, you're supporting him. Trust me: He'll know what the odds are before he steps in that ring. Fighters always do."

Valentine found Nick's argument oddly appealing. He'd always liked Holyfield, and those feelings turned into adulation the night Holyfield had dethroned Mike Tyson. You could attribute his victory to many things, but what it had boiled down to was a decent guy fighting a not-so-decent guy. And the decent guy won. It was sweet redemption for every person who believed in playing by the rules.

"All right," he told his host. "I'll do it."

Following Nick's instructions, Valentine entered the casino and sifted his way to Caesars' sports book. It was a large, windowless room with cages for bets and a big electronic board that flashed the odds. He got on the end of a long line. As he waited, he watched the odds change. It was like bingo—pick the right combination and win a prize. Five had always been his lucky number and he checked the odds of Holyfield's winning in that many rounds. Thirty to one. He extracted a crisp C-note from his wallet.

The line inched ahead. As if by magic, the big board turned into a digital TV screen. Holyfield and the Animal were in the ring being introduced by the announcer.

When the announcer was done, a bloated Wayne Newton look-alike belted out the national anthem. Reaching the betting cages, Valentine saw that the singer *was* Wayne Newton.

He threw his money down. "Holyfield in five."

"You're in the minority on that one," the man in the cage informed him.

"Keep it that way."

Valentine shoved the ticket into his pocket and felt a hand on his shoulder. It was Nick, and his face was flushed.

"Wily just called. He just spoke to Nola," Nick said excitedly.

"Where is she?"

"Hiding out on the west side of town. She escaped from Fontaine."

"Did Wily call the police?"

"No. I want to talk to her first."

"Nick," Valentine said. "Call the police."

"I've got to talk to her," Nick insisted. "Come on."

They jogged through Caesars to the front doors. All gambling had stopped and all eyes were glued to the giant-screen TVs that had been erected throughout the casino. The fight was less than a minute old and Holyfield had already eaten a punch and was lying flat on his back. The Animal stood in a neutral corner, taunting him. The champ staggered to his feet on the count of eight.

"There goes my hard-earned dough," Nick lamented. "Come on Evander, you lousy bum!"

Valentine found himself thinking the same thing and realized he was more concerned about his C-note than Holyfield's health. He took the bet ticket from his pocket and tore it into pieces. They left the casino and got into Nick's golf cart.

"You've got to call the police," Valentine said as Nick sped them up the Strip.

"No, I don't," Nick replied.

"Nola's a fugitive. Knowing where she's hiding makes you an accomplice. That's a felony."

Nick gave him a sideways glance.

"You, too," Nick said.

"You want me to make the call?"

"No," Nick said. He raced to the entrance to the Acropolis, where the harem of his ex-wives glowed eerily beneath amber spotlights. "Look—I want to apologize to her like a gentleman. You think Longo will let me do that?"

Valentine wanted to say yes, but knew he'd be telling a lie. Sympathy was for doctors and the clergy, not the police.

"No," he said.

"I just want five minutes with her," Nick said. "That's all."

"Just five minutes?"

"That's all."

"Is that a promise?" Valentine said skeptically.

"On my mother's grave," Nick swore.

25

Nola was holed up at the Lucky Boy, a motel on the west side of town. Las Vegas got progressively worse the farther you strayed from the Strip, and the Lucky Boy was a wrecking ball away from being turned into a parking lot, the broken neon sign spelling something slightly obscene. Nick parked his Caddy in the motel's deserted lot and killed the headlights. For a long moment, neither man cared to speak.

"I still think you should call the police," Valentine said.

"Fuck the police."

"What if there's trouble?"

Reaching across Valentine's lap, Nick opened the glove compartment and removed a pearl-handled .38 that looked like a novelty-store item.

"Put that thing away before you hurt yourself," Valentine said.

"I'm not going in there unprotected," Nick said, slipping the piece under his belt. "Anything else on your mind?"

"Yeah," Valentine said. "You'd better call Wily."

Nick wiped his face on his sleeve. Twenty seconds without AC and the car was already an oven. "What for?"

"Tell him to put everyone on alert."

"Why?"

Valentine stared at him in the dark. Why couldn't Nick see it? Or was it one of those things that was so obvious it somehow became invisible? "Because the last act of Frank Fontaine and Nola Briggs is about to start."

"You think I'm about to get ripped off?"

"I sure do."

Sweat poured off Nick's nose. "How can you be sure?"

"I can feel it in my bones," Valentine said.

"What are you, psychic?"

"For this kind of thing, yes."

Nick made the call. Valentine played with the radio and found the news. A loudmouthed announcer was reading the sporting news. The fight was still on and Holyfield was getting the living daylights beat out of him. At the end of the fourth round, he'd eaten another vicious right and taken a breather on one knee. The champ sounded finished.

They got out of the Caddy. A nasty wind blew invisible grains of sand in their faces. Blinded, Valentine rubbed his eyes with his sleeve. He'd take Florida's blood-sucking mosquitos any day. Nick banged loudly on the peeling red door of 66-A.

"Who's there?" a woman's voice said meekly.

"Guess," Nick said.

The door opened and a sliver of yellow light leaked out from within.

"Hey, Nick," Nola whispered.

They slipped into the room. The accommodations were the kind you rented by the hour, with a waterbed and a TV bolted to the floor that took coins and showed porno. Valentine checked the bathroom, then went to the window and lifted a blind with one finger. In a loud voice, he said, "Mind telling us how you got here?"

Nola stared at him blankly. She sat on the bed with Nick, holding hands. If Valentine didn't know better, he would have sworn they'd just gotten married.

"You didn't walk here," Valentine said accusingly. "Did you?"

"Leave her alone," Nick said.

"Why should I?"

"Because somebody beat her up, that's why."

Valentine got down on one knee to have a look at her. She'd been worked over by a pro. Her eyes were blackened, her nostrils were bloodied, and her lower lip sported a little purple pig. Ugly, but nothing disfiguring: no teeth gone, the pretty little nose intact. To Nick, he said, "I hope you're not buying this little charade."

Nick blinked. "What are you talking about?"

"Somebody did this with some oranges stuffed into a nylon stocking," Valentine explained. "It's an old trick, causes lots of bruises." To Nola he said, "Didn't they?"

Nola stifled a pathetic little sob. Nick put his arm around her, shielding her from Valentine's accusation.

"Tony, you're a real asshole," Nick said.

Valentine's face grew hot. He stood up and pointed a finger at Nick. "Five minutes, like we agreed."

"Yeah," Nick said. "Five minutes."

"I'm calling the cops in five."

"Five minutes," Nick repeated. "Now just get the hell out, okay?"

"Sure."

Valentine went to the door. He'd done what he'd been hired to do. Now it was time to extricate himself from Nick's crazy world and go back to his own. His son needed him, and so did Mabel. And he desperately needed them. He opened the door and stepped outside.

The loudmouthed announcer had said that Holyfield had taken more punishment tonight than most boxers endure in a lifetime, but none of the blows that had bounced off the champ's skull were as unexpected as the one that awaited Valentine in the parking lot. It snapped his head straight back and he took a few wobbly steps backward. Then he collapsed in the open doorway of room 66-A.

His eyes snapped open to the sound of Nola's screams, followed by the unmistakable bark of Nick's toy .38. A punch followed, bone hitting bone. Nola's screams stopped and were replaced by the sound of someone choking the life out of her. Clutching the doorsill, Valentine tried to move his fingers and found them frozen in a spastic claw. Slowly he pushed himself off the floor and staggered back into the room.

Little Hands stood over the bed, holding Nola by the throat.

"Where's Fontaine?" he demanded.

"I . . . don't . . . know," she gasped.

"Like hell you don't."

Nick had wrapped his arms around Little Hands's massive leg and was biting him. Little Hands swatted him away like a flea.

"Help us," Nick begged.

Valentine wasn't sure he knew how. Judo was great if someone was attacking you but offered little offense of its own. And Little Hands was a pro and not likely to let Valentine get the jump on him. The best he could try for was getting Little Hands outside, in the hope that someone would pass by and come to their aid.

Stepping forward, Valentine kicked Little Hands in the rump. It was like kicking a piece of rock. Little Hands glared murderously at him.

"You're next," he said to Valentine, while putting the squeeze on Nola.

Valentine kicked him again.

"I'm going to mutilate you, old man."

Valentine's instincts told him to run—only, Nola's

face was turning blue, her time running out. He tried another approach.

"Felix Underman said your mother got drunk and screwed a dwarf," Valentine said. "Is it true?"

Little Hands dropped Nola on the bed, the demented look on his face suggesting Valentine had pushed all the wrong buttons. He rushed forward, screaming like a banshee, and Nick pulled the rug out from under him. Little Hands fell forward, catching himself on the TV.

The force of his body turned the TV on and porno filled the screen. A naked woman was on a bed with a black guy, who for some reason wore a sombrero. Their screwing bordered on violence, and it seemed to make Little Hands go crazy. He made another mad-bull charge at Valentine.

Most contract killers are proficient in the martial arts, but whatever training Little Hands had went out the window. Valentine grabbed the collars of his open shirt and threw him sideways into the wall. Then he elbowed Little Hands in the face. He heard cartilage break, and Little Hands sank to the floor.

Valentine retrieved Nick's .38 and aimed it at Little Hands. The giant man rolled over, his face sheeted with blood, and pointed at the TV just as the guy with the sombrero started to climax.

"Turn the TV off," he cried. *"Please, turn it off!"*

Valentine had never seen a guy lose his marbles over dirty movies. Maybe in prison, the state could get a psychiatrist to drill a hole in Little Hand's head and find out what was wrong with him.

"How did you find us?" Valentine said.

"Turn it off!"

Nola, who'd been lying motionless on the bed, rose and went to the TV. Finding no knobs, she said, "I can't turn it off."

"Kick it," Valentine told her.

She did and the screen slowly faded, the sombrero vanishing like a sunset. Valentine turned to Little Hands and said, "You got your wish."

"Mr. Underman called me," he whimpered, a disturbed little man lurking beneath his tough-guy surface slowly emerging. "I went to Caesars and saw you leave. I took a chance you were on to Fontaine and I followed you here."

"Anybody with you?"

Little Hands shook his head. "I work solo."

The TV came back on. Same woman, new guy, real small, almost a midget except for his organ. Little Hands covered his face, screaming like he was being stuck with a knife.

"Jesus Christ," Nick muttered. "What should we do?"

Valentine backed out of the room. As long as the porno was on, he didn't think Little Hands was a threat to anyone.

"Call 911," Valentine said. "Let the cops deal with him."

The longer Valentine was retired, the more he understood why people hated the police. All of the sterotypes were unfortunately true, especially the one about a cop never being there when you needed one. Nick, sitting in the back of the Caddy with Nola, dialed 911 on his cell phone for the third time.

"The dispatcher says every cop on duty is at Caesars," Nick said, cupping his hand over the mouthpiece. "Some kind of riot."

"Any idea how long it's going to take?"

Nick asked the dispatcher, then reported, "She says a half hour, maybe longer."

"What happened?"

"She doesn't know."

Valentine turned on the radio. The loudmouthed announcer was back, talking by phone to a reporter at Caesars. Loudmouth said, "Can you tell us what happened that led to the melee between corners?"

The other reporter said, "In round five, Holyfield got his act together and started to use his jab. He opened up a cut over the Animal's left eye. The Animal got frustrated and took a shot at Holyfield after the bell. Holyfield retaliated with a short uppercut. I was a few rows back and heard the punch land. The Animal had been warned for fouling, and I think the last one got Holyfield really angry."

Loudmouth said, "Did the melee start then?"

The other reporter replied, "No, it happened when the Animal couldn't continue and the ref declared Holyfield the winner. Then the corners started to tango."

Loudmouth said, "And the fight spilled into the crowd." To which the other man said, "Like a brush fire."

"Holyfield won," Nick said gleefully. "We win!"

Valentine groaned. He'd torn up a ticket worth three grand. That would teach him to gamble.

Nick's cell phone rang. It was Wily. Nick listened intently, then killed the power.

"Wily's shitting in his pants," the little Greek said. "He's got three big hitters doing a number on us, and he thinks one is Fontaine. I gotta get back to my casino."

"We can't leave Little Hands," Valentine said.

"Then do whatever you gotta do," Nick said.

Valentine went back to 66-A and poked his head in the door. Little Hands was on the bed. The porno was still on and every moan of pleasure was driving him that much closer to insanity. Valentine silently shut the door. Then he had an idea.

His eyes swept the near-empty lot and settled on a bloodred Mustang with a souped-up engine, the bumpers adorned with stickers from Gold's Gym. He smashed the driver's window with a rock, then got in behind the wheel. The ashtray was filled with inhalers. This was definitely the right car.

Intent on disabling the engine, Valentine pulled the lever that popped the hood, then noticed a suitcase sitting on the passenger's seat. He popped the clasps and let out a whistle. It was full of the stuff dreams are made of.

Back in the Caddy, Valentine tossed Nick his fifty grand.

"Merry Christmas," he said.

Nola didn't say much during the ride back to the Acropolis. Laying her head on Nick's lap, she cried softly most of the way, the perfect image of the damsel in distress. She was pretty in a way that none of Nick's other wives were pretty, her looks pure and clean. Valentine wanted to ask her which of the three guys beating the Acropolis was Fontaine, but he decided to wait until they got inside, where he could get her under a bright light and look into her eyes while she answered his questions.

Valentine pulled up to the Acropolis's entrance and a valet ran out to assist them. Nick made him get a wheelchair, and they rolled Nola inside.

The casino was jammed, the action at the tables out of control. Guys in T-shirts and rundown Nikes were betting like high rollers. Tens of thousands of dollars were flowing back and forth on every roll of the dice. It was pure madness, and every single player was involved. *Holyfield beat the odds,* the collective reasoning seemed to be saying, *so why can't we?*

They took the service elevator to the surveillance control room, where a different brand of insanity was going on. Five men were working the master console, each talking frantically into a walkie-talkie in an effort to track the frantic play below.

They found Wily standing in front of the wall of monitors. He'd removed his tie and was nervously gulping coffee.

"Hey, boss," he muttered.

"Who's ripping me off?" Nick demanded.

Wily pointed at a screen to his left. "Suspect number one. Australian named Martini. Was staying at the Mirage. He somehow got thirty hookers into his suite. He made them strip and do a lineup, three hundred apiece. The ones he liked, he asked to stay. Management tossed him."

"And you took him in," Nick said.

"His money's as green as anyone else's."

Valentine stared at the black-and-white monitor. Martini had a shaved head and rings in each ear. He also had a big nose and an overbite. He was playing blackjack and winning big.

"How much we into him for?" Nick asked.

"Sixty grand." Wily pointed at a screen to his right. "Suspect number two, Joey Joseph, calls himself the pizza king of L.A. He demanded we lift the table limit and then started beating us into the ground."

Grimacing, Nick said, "How much?"

"He just hit a hundred grand," Wily said. "He's a wild man. I tried to talk to him, and he told me to get lost."

Valentine went and stared at Joey Joseph. The pizza king wore Coke-bottle glasses and a cheap wig. He had a cleft in his chin like Fontaine, and there was something familiar about the way he banged his fist on the table.

"Suspect number three doesn't have a name. Says he's a Texas oilman," Wily said, pointing at a man wearing cowboy clothes and a string tie. "He strolled in an hour ago."

"How much?" Nick bellowed.

"Eighty."

"You're killing me," Nick said.

"What do you want me to do? All three of them can't be Fontaine."

Valentine watched the Texan play. He was the same age as the other two and played the same game, blackjack. He was betting big and winning big, just like the others. Then he noticed something else. The dealers at all three tables were women, all attractive, and all chatting up a storm with the three guys who were beating them silly.

It was beautiful, absolutely beautiful, the kind of scam that bordered on true genius. He knelt next to Nola's wheelchair.

"Listen to me and listen good," Valentine said quietly. "I'm going to give you a chance to come clean. I know what's going on, and I think you do, too. Help us, and you won't go to jail."

Nick and Wily were listening intently. Nola looked at them, then back at Valentine. The harsh fluorescent light caught her face at a bad angle, robbing it of all beauty.

"Okay," she mumbled.

"Martini, Joseph, and the Texan are a team, aren't they?"

"Uh-huh."

"They're all reading different dealers, just like Fontaine read you. They're girls you know, and you tipped Fontaine off to the things that turn them on, like cowboy clothes and foreign accents."

"That's right," she mumbled.

"Fontaine slapped you around and put you in that motel, hoping we'd stay away from the casino. With

Sammy out of the way, and us across town, he figured he'd have easy pickings."

"Go to the head of the class," she said.

"Which one's Fontaine?"

"The Aussie."

Valentine was stunned. He would have put his money on the pizza king. Sensing his disbelief, she said, "The overbite is a bridge. He made his nose bigger by sticking a piece of plastic tubing up each nostril."

Valentine looked at Nick. "Heard enough?"

Nick bent toward Nola, his face twisted by the grief that only lost love can cause. "You don't love me anymore, do you?"

Nola started to cry. "I used to. I really did."

"But not now?"

"Oh, Nick, don't you get it?" she said. "I'm always going to love you, no matter how much I hate you."

Truer words had never been spoken. Nick embraced her from a crouch, kissing the top of Nola's head as she wept into his chest. Just then, Nick's cell phone rang. He answered it, then handed Valentine the phone.

"Someone's looking for you."

Valentine put the phone to his ear. "Hello?"

"Oh, Tony," he heard Roxanne cry, "I came up to your suite to surprise you, and the phone rang a dozen times so I answered it. It was a woman in New York, Yolanda somebody-or-other."

Valentine felt his stomach turn upside down. Roxanne began to cry hysterically.

"Tony, something terrible has happened to Gerry."

"What?" he said.

Roxanne could not stop crying.

"Sweet Jesus," he said into the phone. "I'll be right up."

Valentine handed Nick the cell phone. "I've got to go."

He started to walk across the surveillance control room, his thoughts a thousand miles away.

"*Where the hell are you going?*" Nick yelled across the room.

Valentine kept walking. Why hadn't he called the New York police after he'd gotten Gerry's first call? Why hadn't he tried to do something? Why?

"Tony," Nick called after him, "don't do this to me!"

Valentine stopped at the door. He hesitated, then he put his hand firmly on the doorknob.

"Tony—look at me!"

Valentine jerked open the heavy steel door. Glancing back, his eyes met Nick's and he saw pure hatred.

"You Jersey piece of shit!" Nick shouted as Valentine left the surveillance room.

Valentine rode up to his room in an elevator crammed with drunks. In the corner, a man was having a heated discussion with his wife about their current financial situation.

"Give me the money I told you not to give me," the man insisted.

"No," the wife said emphatically.

"Give it to me!"

"No!"

At the sixth floor, the last passenger got off and Valentine rode alone to his suite. His jaw had started throbbing from the punch he'd taken, and he shut his eyes, trying to ignore the pain.

His suite was unlocked, the lights were muted, and vintage Sinatra was playing on the stereo. Two places had been set at the dining-room table. In the table's center, a pair of skinny candles burned seductively.

He found Roxanne on the couch bawling like a baby. She wore a red silk blouse and a leather mini and looked like a supermodel. She'd teased her hair, and a lazy curl formed a question mark on her forehead. *Do you dare?* it seemed to ask.

"I was going to surprise you," she said with a sniffle as Valentine sat down.

"What happened to my son," he asked quietly.

Roxanne put her hand on his knee and dug her fingernails into his skin. "You need to call Yolanda."

"Tell me."

"Call her, Tony. She's hysterical."

"Is he alive?"

"Yolanda said—"

"Is he alive?" Valentine put his hand on Roxanne's chin and made her look at him. "Is he?"

"Please . . . call her."

Valentine buried his head in his hands. Sinatra's melancholy "Only the Lonely" filled the suite and he began to weep. The cell phone in Roxanne's lap warbled. She answered it, then pressed the receiver against her chest. "It's Nick. He says he's giving you one more chance."

"Tell him to go to hell."

Roxanne did as she was asked, and Tony could hear Nick screaming through the phone. Valentine got up and went to the picture window and stared down onto the neon Strip. He tried to imagine his son the last time he'd seen him. It had been at the saloon, Valentine whipping him with his belt. Would that be last image he would have?

"You stupid bastard," he said to himself.

Then he cried some more.

"Good-bye," Roxanne said curtly, and hung up.

"What did he say?" Valentine asked her.

"He's going to shoot you."

It sounded like the perfect antidote for the way he was feeling. Valentine took a deep breath, then said, "Give me the phone."

Roxanne crossed the room and handed him the phone. Then she gave him a hug. Valentine held her tight, his heart about to break.

Then he went into the bedroom and shut the door.

Sitting on the bed, Valentine suddenly felt like an old man. No wife, no son, nothing left. His eyes fell on a long-stemmed yellow rose lying on the pillow. He picked it up and smelled it. Roxanne had thought of everything.

He dialed Gerry's cell phone and heard the call go through.

"Hello," a woman said hoarsely.

"Yolanda, it's Tony Valentine."

"Oh God, Mr. Valentine." She let out a sob, and Valentine joined her.

"The goons caught up with you," he said.

"Yeah."

"Where?"

"Holland Tunnel. Traffic was so bad, we couldn't move."

"Did they hurt him?"

"Yeah."

"Did you run?"

Another sob.

"It's okay," he told her.

"Yeah," she said, "I ran like hell."

"It's okay," he said.

"No, it's not," she said.

"You call the police?"

"Yeah. They looked around. No Gerry."

Which meant they hadn't really looked at all. Taking a deep breath, he said, "Maybe we could go look for him together."

"Okay," Yolanda whispered.

"I'll call you when I get in."

"Okay."

He started to hang up, but she said, "Mr. Valentine?"

"Yes, Yolanda?"

"I really loved him."

"Me, too," Valentine said.

He killed the power and tossed the phone on the bed. Then he went into the bathroom and looked at his puffy face in the mirror. Would he spend the rest of his days cursing himself for not getting Gerry out of New York? Yeah, he probably would.

The numbness from the punch had worn off and his jaw was throbbing. Hearing Roxanne enter the bedroom, he went out to face her.

"Got any aspirin handy?" he asked, coming out of the bathroom.

Only it wasn't Roxanne standing before him. The closet door was wide open and the cowboy who'd aimed a .350 Magnum in his face a couple of days ago was standing in his bedroom. Now he was holding a three-foot steel pipe, ready to begin the final act in the drama of Nola Briggs and Frank Fontaine.

"Didn't I tell you to get out of town?" the cowboy said.

Valentine took a step back and nearly fell down. His balance was gone, his body having forgotten how to defend itself. The cowboy flashed him a crooked smile.

The cowboy's movements were swift and deliberate, and Valentine lifted his arms helplessly as the steel pipe came down forcefully on his skull.

26

"That low-life fucking Jersey bastard," Nick roared, feeling as forsaken as the day he'd buried his father and kissed his childhood good-bye. "How dare he run out on me!"

Nick paced the surveillance control room and swore some more. Wily stood by the master console, watching his boss with one eye while keeping the other on the monitors. "Boss! They're into us for four hundred grand."

Picking up a house phone, Nick called the people working the cage and instructed them not to pay Fontaine's gang if they tried to cash out. Then he went and stuck his head into Sammy Mann's corner office. Nola lay on the busted couch, facing the wall. He could not wait to get her out of his life, and he said, "You gonna live?"

"Yeah," she said.

"I'm sorry about ten years ago. Sorry I blew it."

"Sure you are."

"You want a drink or something?"

Nola shook her head stiffly. Nick thought he understood. She didn't want *anything* from him. Wily tapped him on the shoulder and Nick followed the pit boss out into the hall.

Hoss, Tiny, and four other security guards stood at

the ready. They all power-lifted together and were behemoths. Nick walked the line, appraising each man.
"Wily says you're ready. That true?"

The guards nodded their heads in unison.

"I didn't hear you," he said.

"Yes, sir!"

"This is the plan," Nick told them. "Hoss and Tiny
get the Aussie at table six. John and Brett, the Texan at
eleven; Karl and Leroy, the pizza king at fifteen. I'll back
you up if you have to break bones. Got it?"

"Yes, sir!"

Wily made them synchronize their watches. It was
10:05. He said, "Go downstairs and get near your as-
signed table without being conspicuous. At 10:08, grab
your man. Any questions?"

This was not a talkative group. Hoss, their leader,
said, "That doesn't sound too hard."

The guards disappeared into the stairwell, their footsteps as loud as jackhammers. Nick and Wily returned
to the surveillance control room and stood before the
wall of monitors.

"Think we should call the cops?" Wily asked.

"Fuck the cops," Nick said.

The door to Sammy Mann's office opened. Nola
emerged, her hair standing on end like Frankenstein's
bride. Pointing a finger at Nick, she emptied her lungs
out.

"What the hell is she doing here?"

Nick didn't understand. "Who?"

"Her, you idiot!"

Nick glanced over his shoulder. Sherry Solomon had
found her way into the surveillance control room, and
was still wearing the same sooty clothes she'd worn
when she set fire to Nick's mansion.

"Beats me," he confessed.

Then it was Sherry's turn to start screaming.

"You told me you and Nola were finished!"

Nick shrugged like it was no big deal. "Hey, baby, I mean, stuff happens. You know?"

Sherry grabbed a wastepaper basket and threw it at him. A lamp followed, coming from Nola's side of the room.

"Don't tell me you fucked her," Nola screamed.

"Only in the biblical sense," Nick said.

"What the hell is that supposed to mean?"

"It means it was a fling, no big deal," he said. "I didn't ask her to marry me or anything."

"You two-timing, good-for-nothing prick!"

"Get away from him!" Sherry screamed at Nola.

"Make me, bitch!"

The two women met in the middle of the room, scattering everyone working at the master console. Sherry was in better shape and threw punches like she'd had lessons, while Nola was more of a scratch-and-pull kind of fighter. Within seconds, they were rolling around on the floor, tangled in each other's arms. Nick grabbed a fire extinguisher and doused them both with white foam.

"Don't just stand there," he told Wily. "Do something!"

Wily did. He grabbed Nick by the shoulders and spun him around. There were a hundred eighty-four monitors on the wall and each showed absolute bedlam downstairs. The Texan and pizza king were whupping their security boys good, the hustlers as skilled in the martial arts as they were in cheating at cards.

"Are we recording this?" Nick bellowed.

"I think so," Wily said.

"You think so?" Nick stuck his head into the adjacent room, which housed the VCRs the monitors were hooked up to. Each machine had a red light on, indicating it was recording. Fontaine's gang was going to jail for a long time. He shut the door and locked it.

"Come on," Nick said.

"What about the girls?" Wily asked.

Lying beneath the console, Sherry had gotten Nola in a half nelson and was systematically pulling out clumps of her hair, while Nola retaliated by biting her nemesis savagely in the bosom. That Sherry didn't feel it did not come as a surprise. Standing in the room's open doorway, Nick shrugged his shoulders.

Then he ran out.

Nick had never seen anything like it. Guys fighting guys, women fighting women, his employees trying to break up one fight while others erupted all around them. Chips and glasses and chairs were flying through the air; people were ruining his joint just for the hell of it. Nick had never understood the impulse, but he recognized it in others: the appetite for destruction.

He quickly marshaled his troops. First he commandeered a dozen dishwashers and his front desk staff, then the dealers who were on break or hiding. Each was given something solid to hold—golf clubs from the pro shop for the ladies, brooms and pool cues for the gents—and then sent into battle with these simple instructions: "If they put up a fight, beat them into the ground."

Nick's employees streamed into the casino. The craps table had been turned on its side by two dealers attempting to protect a rack of chips from a mob's greedy hands. With a handful of dishwashers backing him up, Wily descended on the mob, their war whoops sending shock waves through the casino.

It was Nick's distinction to have nothing but ladies in his gang. There was Betty, the sixty-year-old chip girl, and Louise, who ran Housekeeping and who claimed to have changed more of Nick's dirty sheets than his own mother. Over the years, he'd pissed off every single one of these women, yet every single one had stayed. They were *his people*, and as he led them toward the black-jack pit, a chant went up.

Nick, Nick, Nick.

At table fifteen the pizza king was kicking Karl and Leroy senseless. Clutching a Big Bertha, Nick moved in, swinging the driver around his head like a bolo. He hated guys who fought with their feet. You want to kick, take up tap dancing. He slammed the driver into the pizza king's back and sent him sprawling.

Nick, Nick, Nick.

"I'm just getting warmed up," Nick told the crowd, charging to the other end of the pit. Several tables had been overturned, and the Texan was dancing around and karate-chopping his security men silly. He was Chuck Norris and *Lethal Weapon* rolled into one, and Nick wisely steered clear. Two tables away, he saw Wily pounding the daylights out of someone and he went to investigate.

It was Fontaine. Wily had pinned him to the table and was driving his right fist repeatedly into the hustler's face.

"Call the Texan off," Wily said, drawing his fist back. "Make him stop before he kills someone."

"Fuck you," Fontaine said.

"Get off him," Nick said.

Wily did, and Nick grabbed Fontaine's ear and twisted until the skin turned a violent purple. The hustler fell to his knees in agony.

"You want me to tear it off?" Nick asked, being polite about it. "I can do that. It's your call."

"I *can't* call him off," Fontaine cried, writhing beneath Nick's hand. "He's an ex-con. Swears he won't go back to the joint. You're going to have to kill him."

"That can be arranged," Nick said. He released Fontaine's ear, then kicked him in the nuts for good measure. To Wily, he said, "Sit on him!"

The pit boss complied. "What are you going to do?"

"I'm going to get Joe," Nick said.

His employees had gotten the mob under control, so Nick ran across his ravaged casino and ducked into One-Armed Billy's alcove. Just as he was paid to do, Joe Smith sat on his stool, looking bored out of his mind.

"How'd you like to get in on this action?" Nick asked.

Joe brightened. He was still young and in great shape, all seven feet and three hundred pounds of him, and he jumped off his stool like a sprinter coming out of the blocks.

"You mean that, Mr. Nicocropolis?" he said. "You gonna let me break the rules?"

"I sure am. Come on."

Joe was so conditioned to staying with Billy that Nick had to drag him out of the alcove. Once outside, he stiffened, his eyes traveling the length of the casino and coming to rest on the Texan, who was hopping around on one foot, like a crane.

"Who's that dude?" Joe snarled.

"The enemy. Think you can handle him?"

"Looks like a bird. Maybe I'd better pluck his feathers."

Nick smiled gleefully. This was going to be great. Too bad Valentine was going to miss it, that dumb Jersey greaseball.

Mike Turkowski, ex-hockey player and bartender at Brother's Lounge, had been standing beside the Acropolis's notorious fountain for twenty minutes, staring into the casino with a pair of infrared binoculars no bigger than a cigarette pack. Over the years, he'd been involved in a dozen casino rip-offs, all of them successful, and one thing had been true with each. The last people the casinos called were the cops. No one trusted them, especially when large sums of money were lying around. Which made his job that much easier.

Mike brought his wristwatch to his face, noting the time with one eye: 10:14. Fontaine told him to wait until 10:20, and if the ruse didn't work, run. His car was parked across the street, a one-way ticket to Seattle in the glove box, a suitcase in the trunk. Leaving town without telling his friends didn't thrill him, but that was part of the business.

At 10:16, he saw Nick duck into One-Armed Billy's alcove. Only one guy in the whole world could move Joe Smith off his stool, and that was Nick Nicocropolis. Fontaine had called it perfectly.

Mike tossed the binoculars into the fountain and started walking toward the front entrance. He saw Nick and Joe Smith leave the alcove and run across the casino, just like Fontaine said they would. Pushing open the front doors, Mike slipped into Billy's empty alcove.

Taking five silver dollars from his pocket, Mike quickly fed them into the machine. Then he pulled the giant arm.

The reels flashed by, stopping on two watermelons and four lemons. Which was where the expression "a lemon" came from. Taking a tennis ball from his pocket, Mike wedged it into the base of the arm so it could not spring back. From the sleeve of his jacket, he removed a pair of coat hangers and fitted them together in an L, then he bent a fishhook into one end. Kneeling, he inserted the hook into Billy's coin tray and shoved the hangers into the machine, his eyes fixed on Billy's twenty-six-million-dollar jackpot. Billy was insured by Lloyd's of London, and Fontaine had done his homework; he knew the policy was paid up. It was the little details that screwed you up, he'd once told Mike.

Billy had six reels, which made it harder to manipulate than hand-cranked slots, and Mike was probably the last guy in Vegas who knew how to manipulate an old-time machine, having learned on a pair of cast-iron Ballys in Brother's backroom. He had expected to put this talent to work on cruise ships, where old machines were still common. The payoffs weren't so hot, but it was easy work for the mentally challenged, a club of which Mike had considered himself a lifetime member until now.

From the alcove, he could hear the Texan hollering. Poor bastard. Fontaine had not given each member of the team a complete script. For the Texan and pizza king, this meant a beating and jail time; for everyone else, a life of wine and roses. Mike felt bad for the two ex-cons, but he wouldn't lose any sleep over them.

Twenty seconds later, he was done. Snapping the hangers back to their original shape, he slipped them up his sleeve. He found himself laughing. Instead of cherries, Nick's six ex-wives made up Billy's jackpot, their titties exaggerated to comic proportions.

"Beautiful," he said, kissing the glass they stood behind.

Then he ran out of the casino as fast as his legs would carry him.

Not everyone who worked at the Acropolis was taking part in the battle royale on the casino floor. People were getting *hurt* out there, and many of Nick's less courageous employees chose not to participate. These included the waitresses and bartender at Nick's Place, a group of Mexican dishwashers and chambermaids, and several bookkeepers. Together they cowered in the employee lounge, waiting for the bedlam to subside.

Roxanne sat among them, biting her nails. She'd stepped out of the elevator five minutes earlier and had nearly been hit by a flying chair. Running to the lounge, she'd bummed a cigarette off a slow-witted chambermaid named Dolores and waited it out with the rest of them.

"I thought you had a date?" Dolores said, always the snoop. "What happened?"

"It didn't work out," Roxanne said coolly.

Dolores cackled. Earlier, she'd caught Roxanne in the bathroom preening, her perfume heavy enough to choke a horse.

"Didn't work out," Dolores squawked like a parrot. "Honey, you were gone only forty-five minutes."

"It sure seemed longer," Roxanne said, trying to make light of it.

"What happened?"

"You heard what I said—it didn't work out," Roxanne snapped. "It happens, okay?"

"Was he that bad?"

Roxanne stomped her foot and the kitchen help looked up in alarm. Not a one had a green card, and they were all scared as hell.

"Stop it," she told Dolores.

Dolores cackled again. "My, my. Aren't we sensitive tonight."

"Must I tell you the gory details?" Roxanne said.

"Yeah!" Dolores said.

Roxanne lowered her voice to a whisper. "I went to his room, had room service bring up two surf and turfs, then set the table, and put on some music. Then I got a call. His son's missing and presumed dead. I call around the casino and find him and he comes upstairs. It was so sad; I figured the least I could do was console him."

Dolores, who couldn't buy a social life, looked ready to pee in her pants. "*Yeah,*" she said breathlessly. "*What happened then?*"

"Nothing," Roxanne said sadly.

Dolores's face caved in. "What do you mean, nothing?"

"I mean, nothing happened."

"But . . ."

"He fell asleep," Roxanne said, stifling a little sob and rubbing her eye with the sleeve of her silk blouse. "He went into his room to make a call. When he didn't come out, I went in and found him lying on the bed. God, I just can't win."

"Oh, baby," Dolores said, putting her arm around Roxanne's shoulder. "I'm so sorry."

"Me, too," Roxanne said, crying silently.

At 10:20, Roxanne stuck her head out of the lounge. Nick and his troops were in the pit applauding Joe Smith, who stood on a blackjack table with his shirt off, doing tricks with his muscles. A man in cowboy clothes lay on the floor, sleeping soundly.

Stubbing out her cigarette, Roxanne said her good-byes. Then, just as she had a thousand times before, she walked across the casino floor to the front entrance, opting to take the long way to her car, which was parked in the employee lot in back. Everyone who worked in the casino had seen her do it, and everyone knew why.

Because Roxanne had a dream, no different from the rest of them. A dream of a better life, one without alarm clocks and mailboxes filled with bills and time clocks to punch. It was the dream of wealth, and it had made her leave her husband and come to Las Vegas. As she walked, she removed five silver dollars from her purse, kissing Eisenhower's profile on each. Then she shook them in her hand like a pair of dice. Every day for a thousand days, she'd gone through this ritual. The long walk, the coins, the kiss, the shake, and finally the moment of truth, when she'd feed her money into One-Armed Billy and blow a kiss at Joe Smith, who'd always wished her luck.

Every day the same ritual. She'd become part of the

fabric. Some of the employees found it funny, others a little sad. *Look, there goes Roxanne and her silver dollars. She kisses them for luck, you know. If anyone deserves to win the jackpot, it's her.*

She slipped into the alcove and stared at Joe Smith's vacant stool. How careless of Nick to pull him out. When the casino's surveillance cameras had been updated, Nick had installed dummy cameras over One-Armed Billy, too cheap to rewire the ceiling at this end of the casino. Nick was his own man, and now he was going to pay for it.

Roxanne stepped up to Billy and held onto the giant arm while she removed the tennis ball and dropped it into her purse. For a split second, she caught her reflection in the polished brass. Words could not describe the look of exultation on her face.

She hesitated, savoring the moment before she released the giant arm and set the bells off that would bring Nick and the rest of the gang running. They'd see her jumping up and down, and once the initial shock wore off, they'd be happy for her good fortune. Everyone loved a winner, and everyone was going to love her.

Roxanne was sure of it.

But when she tried to release Billy's arm, her fingers became stuck. A man's hand had clasped itself over hers and was holding Billy's arm in place.

"Let go," she begged.

"No," the man said.

"Please."

But the man would not let go. She did not have the courage to look him in the eye, and instead looked into Billy's polished brass. It was Valentine, his face a bloody mess. Behind him, Wily stood in the alcove's entrance, filming her every move with a camcorder.

"I was hoping like hell it wasn't going to be you," she heard Valentine say.

27

"You've got some balls," Bill Higgins said a few hours later, sitting on the edge of the mammoth granite desk in Nick's office and blowing steam off a cup of coffee.

Valentine sat on the couch, an ice pack pressed to his forehead. One of his judo exercises required him to stand on his head a few minutes a day to keep his neck strong, and he supposed this was why the cowboy had not split his skull open with the steel pipe. Bill was showing little sympathy, their twenty years of friendship about to go up in flames.

"You ride into my town like Wyatt Earp," Higgins went on, "conduct your own investigation, then nail the bastards without consulting the GCB or the police. I should haul you in."

"I called you first, didn't I?"

"So?"

"It's your collar," Valentine mumbled.

"My collar?" Higgins laughed derisively. "I can't take this in front of a judge without a story to go with it. It's nobody's collar until you explain to me what's going on."

Rising on shaky legs, Valentine went to the window behind Nick's desk and stared down. Eight police cruisers jammed the Acropolis's front entrance, their bubbles throwing an eerie red light onto the gawking crowd pushing at the wooden sawhorses. Three thousand miles away, he imagined another crowd was gathered, staring at a body lying beneath a sheet. His son's.

Valentine felt the pain well up in his chest. He needed to be alone for a while, to stare into the darkness. But if he didn't explain to Bill what had happened, Fontaine and his gang might walk. And no matter how bad he felt, he was not about to let that happen.

"How about I start at the beginning?" Valentine said.

"You mean when you rode into town?"

"No, I mean when this really started."

"I'm all ears," Higgins said.

"Ten years ago, Nick fell in love with Nola," Valentine began. "One night, they go on the catwalk and start screwing. A fight breaks out below. The guard who baby-sits One-Armed Billy comes running, and Nick goes ballistic. Nola's not stupid and she makes the connection. The guard beside Billy isn't for show. He's for real."

"The flaw Sherry Solomon was taking about."

"Right."

"Why did Sammy Mann say it didn't exist?"

Valentine shrugged. "Nick probably swore Sammy to secrecy— didn't want to risk losing his license."

"Okay."

"Jump to six months ago. Nola goes to Mexico, falls back in love with Sonny. She tells Sonny about the flaw, and they decide to rip Nick off.

"Nola leaves Mexico. Sonny thinks it through, realizes the scam is flawed. Nola knows too much; she'll never pass a polygraph. So Sonny changes the plan. He gets plastic surgery, then finds a look-alike and sends him to Tahoe."

"And that's who Little Hands whacked."

Valentine nodded. "Sonny, aka Frank Fontaine,

moves to Vegas. He scouts the Acropolis and hears about Roxanne's ritual of playing Billy every day. He also learns that Roxanne hates Nick. Seems they had an affair—"

"*Who told you that?*"

"I saw an album that Nick keeps of all the ladies he's slept with. Roxanne was in it."

Higgins shot him an angry look. "Why didn't you tell me?"

Valentine shrugged.

"You fell for her."

Valentine shrugged again.

"You sly dog."

Old blind dog was more like it, Valentine thought.

"Roxanne joins the team," he went on. "They rehearse, then try their scam last week. Fontaine beats the house silly, hoping he'll get barred so he can start a fight. It's all a ruse to get Joe Smith out of his chair so Roxanne can rob Billy. On the third night, Fontaine gets his wish, and Sammy Mann bars him. Fontaine starts brawling, but Joe Smith stays put. The whole thing's a dud."

"I'm with you so far," Higgins said.

All the talking was giving Valentine a headache. They were up high enough to see behind Caesars, and he watched a legion of shirtless men dismantle the canvas ring where Holyfield had beaten his unworthy opponent. In a week, they'd show a replay on TV, and he'd make it a point not to watch it. It was never the same after it was over.

"Go on," Higgins prodded him.

"Nola gets arrested. Fontaine springs her, brings her into the gang. Then hatches a new plan. He puts Nola in a motel. She calls Nick, who rescues her and takes her back to the Acropolis. Nola fingers the gang to Nick.

Nick sends his men into the casino, not realizing it's a ruse to get Joe Smith out of his chair."

"You're saying Fontaine set himself up," Higgins said.

"Uh-huh."

"But we arrested him. What kind of plan is that?"

"He'll be out of jail in a few hours," Valentine said.

"How can you be so sure?"

"Because he didn't break any law," Valentine said, wishing Bill would wisen up so he could go find Gerry's body. "Reading a blackjack dealer isn't illegal. And you can't prove Fontaine grabbed Nola at the house."

"But Nola fingered him."

"To Nick. I'm sure her story will change when she talks to the police."

"But Fontaine started a brawl in the casino."

"Nick's men started the brawl. Look at the video. The only thing Fontaine's gang did was resist Nick's men. And Fontaine didn't even do that. The only law *he* broke was stepping foot in Nevada, which you can only fine him for."

Higgins considered Valentine's point. "Jesus," he muttered.

"Am I right?"

"Of course you're right. Stop rubbing it in."

"Sorry."

Higgins made a face. "When I brought you the hangers, you realized Nola had been planning this a long time, didn't you?"

Valentine nodded.

"Why didn't you tell me?"

"I was afraid you'd tell Roxanne."

"You suspected her?"

Valentine nodded again.

"Why?"

"Because I'm sixty-two and she's thirty-eight," he

blurted out, his eyes fixed on the sea of flashing neon that defined the Vegas skyline. "I wanted to believe she liked me, but deep down I knew it wasn't real."

Higgins heard something in Valentine's voice that made his own soften. He put his hand on Valentine's shoulder and gave it a squeeze.

"Hey, it really happens sometimes," he consoled him.

"Only in the movies," Valentine replied.

Higgins dropped his hand. "So how do I go about prosecuting these people?"

"Put the screws to Roxanne," Valentine said. "Threaten her with hard time, then offer to cut her a deal."

"You think she'll squawk?"

"Like a chicken with its head on the block." Valentine turned from the window. "Look, Bill, I need to beat it."

"Longo's going to want to talk to you some more," Higgins said.

"Think you can explain it to him?"

"Why? Where are you going?"

"To New York."

"Something wrong?"

"Family emergency."

Higgins looked hard and saw the grief balled up behind his friend's face. "You got a flight to catch, then go."

The truth was, Valentine didn't have a flight to catch, but he figured he could talk his way onto one. Higgins walked him to the elevator. Valentine had run out of things to say and so he stared at the hideous carpet. Pushing the button, the GCB chief said, "You want to tell me what's wrong?"

Valentine lifted his eyes and met Bill's sympathetic gaze. It was a small consolation that in the past three days he hadn't ruined every one of his friendships, and he said, "My son got whacked this afternoon."

Higgins swallowed hard. "No, Tony . . ."

"It was Fontaine," he said. "He threatened me a few days ago."

A shadow passed over Higgins's face.

"Why didn't you tell me?"

Valentine shrugged. "Maybe I thought I was Wyatt Earp."

The elevator doors parted.

"You want me to have him hurt?" Higgins said. "I can talk to Longo. He'll break Fontaine's legs if I tell him."

Valentine knew that. But it wouldn't bring Gerry back, and it wouldn't make him feel any better. He shook his head and got into the elevator.

"Call me if you change your mind," he heard Higgins say as the doors closed. "You hear?"

28

Back in his suite, Valentine sat on the couch and stared into space. Every part of his body hurt, his head most of all. And tomorrow, he was going to hurt a lot more.

The scent of Roxanne's lilac perfume clung heavily to the air. On the couch were the dents she'd left in the cushions; on the coffee table, a half-smoked cigarette and her lipstick-stained drink. She was everywhere, her lovely memory haunting him. He fired up a book of casino matches to erase the intoxicating smell.

A knock on the door interrupted him. Not every member of Fontaine's gang had been apprehended, and so he approached the door cautiously. Through the peephole he saw a uniformed waiter. He cracked open the door.

"What's up?"

"Mr. Valentine?" the waiter inquired.

"That's me."

The waiter handed Valentine a cream-colored envelope. "Mr. Nicocropolis apologizes for not delivering this in person, but he's busy with the police."

Valentine reached for his wallet and the waiter shook his head.

"No need, Mr. Valentine. Good night."

He walked away and Valentine tore the envelope open. Inside were fifty hundred-dollar bills. And a note.

Tony,
Billy's jackpot would have busted me—I'm liable
for the first three million. Thanks.
Wily told me about your son. Really sorry. My jet is
still available.

Nick

P.S. You're a good guy, even if you are from Jersey.

Valentine took out his wallet and added the bills to
his growing collection. Then he slipped Nick's note in
behind his torn honeymoon photo. After Lois died, he
found a scrapbook in her closet filled with newspaper
clippings and commendations he'd received as a cop.
She'd cared about that stuff, and he would add Nick's
note to the collection, knowing how happy it would
have made her.

He was tossing his dirty clothes into his suitcase when
the phone rang. He ignored it, not wanting to talk. But
to his annoyance, it continued to ring. Apparently this
call was not going to voice mail. He lifted the receiver
to his ear and said, "Yeah?"

"Tony? Is that you?"

"*Mabel?*"

"I'm free," she squealed with delight. "I know it's late
out there, but I had to call and tell you my good news."

"You're out of jail?"

"I most certainly am!"

Valentine heard a screen door slam in the background, then a familiar voice. "Mabel, where'd you say
the ice cream was?"

"Gerry?" he said in astonishment.

"In the icebox in the garage," Mabel said. "I've got
your father on the line."

"Hey, Pop," Gerry said from afar.

"*Gerry?*" Tears rolled down Valentine's face. "*Gerry!*"

"Hey," his son said, coming on the line.

"You're alive!"

"You bet I'm alive. Those judo moves you taught me as a kid finally came in handy."

"What happened?"

"Guy was choking me to death in the Holland Tunnel and I snapped his arm back. He fell over, hit his partner, bidda-bang, bidda-boom, they're both out cold. I cabbed it to the airport, jumped on a plane."

Valentine could not remember when his son's voice had sounded so good. "You called Yolanda, didn't you?"

"She's flying down tomorrow," his son said. "We're going away for a few days."

"Good boy."

"Mabel's dying to talk to you."

Valentine heard the screen door open and close. Ice cream. His son had gone to get some ice cream. Did he have any idea the anguish his father had been through, thinking him dead?

No, Valentine realized, probably not.

Mabel came on, her voice filled with schoolgirl glee. "Oh, Tony. You would have been so proud."

"Tell me," he said.

"Your son flew down an hour ago and drove straight to the courthouse. He begged a judge to hear my case, and they dragged me out of jail. Your son told that judge exactly what happened, how he was to blame, and how he should have come down and straightened things out, and how his father was a cop, and that he'd been raised knowing right from wrong, and this time there was no doubt he was wrong. Then he begged the judge to let me go—"

"Mabel," Valentine said, "slow down before you croak!"

His neighbor took a deep breath, then plunged back in. "Tony, it was so touching, I cried. Gerry told the judge that just a few hours ago, two hoodlums had tried to murder him and that he'd had this amazing life-changing experience. He had a strange name for it—"

"An epiphany?"

"That's it. Anyway, he said it was a real wake-up call. He told the judge that he had to take responsibility for his life and that this was as good a way as any to start."

"Gerry said that?"

"I know," she laughed merrily. "Tony, for a minute I thought I was listening to you!"

"What did the judge say?"

"Well, the judge was a she and a real tough nut. She praised Gerry for his honesty, but then told him the law was the law, and fined him fifty-five hundred dollars."

"Fifty-five hundred bucks!" he shouted into the phone. "That's highway robbery. She ought to be run out of town."

"Well, your son doesn't feel that way."

"What do you mean? What did he do?"

"He paid up."

"*What?*"

"He said, and I quote, 'I broke the law, and I'll pay whatever fine you see fit.'"

Valentine heard the screen door slam. "Put him on, will you?"

"Hey," his son said a moment later.

"Mabel told me what you did. I'm proud of you, boy."

"Yeah, well, now that you mention it, I was wondering if I could ask you a favor," his son said.

"Sure."

"I paid the court with a check, and my cash flow's been kinda short lately, if you know what I mean."

Valentine pushed himself off the bed, not believing his ears.

"You want me to cover you?"

"Well, yeah," his son said.

Valentine kicked the night table and got violent feedback from his big toe. The more things changed, the more they remained the same.

"I'll pay you back," his son mumbled.

An uncomfortable silence followed. Gerry cleared his throat. "Pop."

"What?"

"I know this is hard to believe, but I'm trying."

"You're trying," Valentine echoed.

"Yeah, I'm trying."

Across the street the Mirage's volcano spit a doughnut-shaped cloud into the air. The police cruisers were leaving the Acropolis, their wailing sirens drowning out all other sound. Roxanne was in one of those cruisers, getting her first taste of her new life. She would do a minimum of five years in the state pen and her life would never be the same again. Only when the cruisers were gone did Valentine speak.

"Well," he said, "it's about time."

Read on for
an exciting look
at James Swain's
next novel,

SUCKER BET

Available in hardcover wherever books are sold.
Published by Ballantine Books.

THE TURN OF A CARD

The mark's name was Nigel Moon.

Jack Lightfoot recognized Moon the moment he stepped into the Micanopy Indian reservation casino. Back in the eighties, Moon had played drums for an English rock band called One-Eyed Pig, his ransacking of hotel rooms as well-publicized as his manic solos. Unlike the other band members, who'd fried their brains on drugs and booze, Moon had opened a chain of popular hamburger joints that now stretched across two continents.

As Moon crossed the casino, Jack eyed the delicious redhead on his arm. She was a plant, or what his partner Rico called a raggle. "The raggle will convince Moon to come to your casino," Rico had explained the day before, "and try his luck at blackjack. She'll bring him to your table. The rest is up to you."

She looked familiar. Jack frequented Fort Lauderdale's many adult clubs and often picked up free magazines filled with ads of local prostitutes. The raggle was a hooker named Candy Hart. Her ad said she was on call twenty-four hours a day, Visa and MasterCard accepted.

"Good evening," Jack said as they sat down at his empty table.

Moon reeked of beer. He was pushing fifty, unshaven,

his gray hair pulled back in a pigtail like a matador's *coleta*. He removed a monster wad from his pocket and dropped it on the table. All hundreds.

"Table limit is ten dollars," Jack informed him.

Moon made a face. Candy touched Moon's arm.

"You can't bet more than ten dollars a hand," she said sweetly. "All of the table games have limits."

Moon drew back in his chair. "Ten bloody dollars? What kind of toilet have you brought me to, my dear? I can get a game of dominos with a bunch of old Jews on Miami Beach with higher stakes than that."

Candy dug her fingernails into Moon's arm. "You *promised* me, remember?"

"I did?"

"In the car."

Moon smiled wickedly. "Oh, yes. A moment of weakness, I suppose."

"Shhhh," she said, glancing Jack's way.

Moon patted her hand reassuringly. "A promise is a promise."

Moon slid five hundred dollars Jack's way. Jack cut up his chips. During a stretch in prison, Jack heard One-Eyed Pig's music blasting through the cell block at all hours, and he knew many of the lyrics by heart.

Jack slid the chips across the table. Moon put ten dollars into each of the seven betting circles on the felt. Jack played a two-deck game, handheld. He shuffled the cards and offered them to be cut.

"Count them," Moon said.

"Excuse me?" Jack said.

"I want you to count the cards," Moon demanded.

Jack brought the pit boss over, and Moon repeated himself again.

"Okay," the pit boss said.

Jack started to count the cards onto the table.

"Faceup," Moon barked.

"Excuse me?" Jack said.

"You heard me."

Jack looked to the pit boss for help.

"Okay," the pit boss said.

Jack turned the two decks faceup. Then he counted them on the table.

"What are you doing?" Candy asked.

"Making sure they're all there," Moon said, watching intently. "I ran up against a dealer in Puerto Rico playing with a short deck and lost my bloody shirt."

Jack finished counting. One hundred and four cards. Satisfied, Moon leaned back into his chair.

"A short dick?" Candy said, giggling.

"Short *deck*. It's where the dealer purposely removes a number of high-valued cards. It gives the house an unbeatable edge."

"And you figured that out," she said.

"Yes, my dear, I figured it out."

Jack saw Candy's hand slip beneath the table and into Moon's lap. Moon's face lit up like a lantern. "You're *so smart*," she cooed.

Jack reshuffled the cards. For Moon to have figured out that a dealer was playing with a short deck meant that Moon was an experienced card-counter. Card-counters were instinctively observant, and Jack realized that he was going to have to be especially careful tonight, or risk blowing their scam before it ever got off the ground. He slid the two decks in front of Moon, who cut them with a plastic cut card.

"Good luck," Jack said.

Then he started to deal.

Jack Lightfoot was not your typical card mechanic.

Born on the Navajo Indian reservation in New Mexico, he'd been in trouble almost from the time he'd started walking. At seventeen, he'd gone to federal prison for a string of convenience store robberies and spent the next six years doing hard time.

The prison was filled with gangs. Jack had gravitated to a Mexican gang and hung out in their cell block. The Mexicans were heavy gamblers and often played cards all day long. They liked different games—seven-card stud, Omaha, razzle-dazzle, Texas hold 'em. Each game had its subtleties, but the game Jack fell in love with was blackjack. And whenever it was Jack's turn to deal, blackjack was the game he chose.

Dealing blackjack gave Jack an edge over the other players. He'd worked it out and figured it was slightly less than 2 percent. It was offset by the fact that if he lost a round, he had to pay off the other players, and that could be devastating to his bankroll. But if he won, the other players *had to pay him*. Blackjack was the game with the greatest risk but also the greatest reward.

One night, Jack had lain on his cot, thinking. He'd seen a lot of cheating among the Mexicans. They marked cards with shoe polish or palmed out a pair before a hand began. It occurred to him that if he was going to cheat, wouldn't blackjack be the game to do it in?

He thought about it for months. The Mexicans were suspicious guys, and manipulating the cards was out of the question. But instead of manipulating the cards, why not manipulate the other players into making bad decisions? Guys did it in poker all the time. It was called bluffing.

Why not blackjack?

One night, one of the Mexicans gave Jack a magic mushroom. Jack ate it, then went to bed. When he woke up a few hours later, he was screaming, his body temperature a hundred and six.

While Jack was strapped to a bed in the prison infirmary for two days, his brain turned itself inside out.

When he finally came out of it, a single thought filled his head.

With the turn of a single card, he could change the odds at blackjack.

With the turn of a single card, he could force other players into making bad decisions.

With the turn of a single card, he could master a game that had no masters.

One card, that was all it took.

And all Jack had to do was turn it over.

He howled so hard, they kept him strapped to the bed for an extra day.

Nigel Moon's stack of chips soon resembled a small castle. A crowd of gaping tourists had assembled behind the table to watch the carnage. The Brit cast a disparaging look over his shoulder, like he was pissed off by all the attention.

"You've got groupies," Candy said.

Moon's eyes danced behind his sour expression. He sipped his martini, trying to act nonchalant. Candy stared at him dreamily.

"Congratulations, sir," Jack said, his lines committed to memory. "You just broke the house record."

Moon fished the olive out of his martini glass. "And what record is that, my good man?"

"No one has ever won eighty-four hands before," Jack informed him.

The Brit sat up stiffly, basking in the moment. "Is that how many I've won?"

"Eighty-four, yes, sir."

"And no one's ever done that before."

"Not in a row, no, sir."

"So I'm the champ?"

"Yes, sir, you're the champ."

Moon snapped his fingers, and a cocktail waitress came scurrying over.

"Drinks for everyone," he said benevolently.

The crowd gave him a round of applause. Candy brought her mouth up to Moon's ear and whispered something dirty. Moon's eyes danced with possibilities.

Jack gathered up the cards. He'd dealt winning hands to players before, and the transformation was always fun to watch. Weak men turned brave, the shy outspoken. It changed them, and it changed how others saw them. And all because of the *turn of a single card*.

"A question," Moon said.

Jack waited expectantly.

"Is there a limit on tipping?"

"Sir?"

"I know there's a limit on betting," Moon said. "Is there a limit on tipping?"

"Not that I'm aware of," Jack said.

Moon shoved half his winnings Jack's way. Standing, he leaned over the table and breathed his martini onto Jack's face. "Do something wicked tonight. On me."

"Yes, sir," Jack replied.

Jack's shift ended at midnight.

He changed out of his dealer's clothes into jeans and a sports shirt and drifted outside through the back door. Standing in the parking lot were his other dealer buddies. They were planning an excursion to the Cheetah in Fort Lauderdale to gape at naked college girls. Jack told them he had plans and begged off. His buddies got into their cars and left.

Jack lit a cigarette. A full moon had cast a creamy patina across the macadam. The casino backed onto a lake, and across its surface floated a dozen pairs of greenish eyes. The Micanopy reservation was in the

Everglades, and alligators were always hanging around, eyeing you like a meal.

He smoked his cigarette down to a stub while thinking about the raggle. She had melted when Moon had started winning, and Jack had watched her leave the casino draped to his side. Was she falling for him? He sure hoped not.

A black limo pulled into the lot. Behind the wheel sat Rico's driver, a spooky Cuban guy named Splinters. The limo pulled up and the back door popped open. Rico Blanco sat in back, jabbering on his cell phone.

Jack got in.

"South Beach," Rico told his driver.

The limo glided out of the lot. Rico was a New Yorker and liked to boast that he was the only member of John Gotti's crime family currently not in jail. Tonight he wore a designer tux with a red bow tie and looked like a million bucks. Rico put his hand over the phone's mouthpiece. "I hear you were a star tonight."

"Who told you that?"

"Candy," Rico said. "She called me a little while ago."

"It went great."

"Let me ask you something. You think she's in love with him?"

Jack nodded.

"Damn hookers," Rico said. "They smell money, their brains melt. Every time I use one, know what I tell them?"

Jack had no idea what Rico told them. But Rico had a line for everybody, and if you hung around him long enough, you got to hear it. Jack opened the minibar and helped himself to a beer. "No, what do you tell them?"

"I tell them, honey, you know it's time to quit the business when you start coming with the customers. Think any of them listen?"

"No," Jack said.

"Fucking-a they don't," Rico said. Taking his hand away from the mouthpiece, he said, "Yeah, Victor, I'm still here. No, Victor, I'm not driving while I'm talking on the phone; I've got someone to drive for me." Rico looked at Jack and rolled his eyes. Victor was the senior partner in the operation and often treated Rico like a kid. "Yeah, Victor. I'll see you tomorrow. Nine sharp. Brunch at the Breakers. Bye." He killed the power. "So where were we?"

"Hookers," Jack said.

"Speaking of which, I've got some girls lined up you're going to love."

"They like Indians?"

"They like who I tell them to like," Rico said. He took a Heineken out of a holder and clinked it against Jack's bottle. "To the best blackjack cheat in the world."

Only one road led back to civilization, and it was long and very dark. The limo jumped into the air as it hit a bump in the road, then bounced hard on the macadam.

"What the hell you doing?" Rico yelled.

"Sorry," Splinters said, not sounding sorry at all.

Jack looked at his shirt. Beer had jumped out of the bottle and soaked it. He swore under his breath. Rico laughed like it was the funniest thing he'd ever seen.

"Jack's all wet," Rico said with mock indignation. "Apologize."

"Sorry," Splinters said.

Jack swallowed hard. "No problem."

"You got a towel up there?" Rico said. "I got some on me, too, for Christ's sake."

A handkerchief flew into the backseat. Rico plucked it out of the air and balled it up. He pressed it against the wet spot on his knee, then leaned forward and pressed the handkerchief against Jack's shirt. Jack pulled back, and Rico's eyes grew wide. Then his hand turned into a rock-hard fist.

"You fucking bastard!" Rico roared.

At seven the next morning, Chief Running Bear, leader of the Micanopy nation, sat in his double-wide trailer a hundred yards behind the casino, staring at a pair of identical TV sets. Two hours earlier, a phone call had awoken him from a deep sleep, and now he rubbed his eyes tiredly while staring at the dueling images.

On one TV, a casino surveillance film showed an employee named Jack Lightfoot dealing blackjack. A player at Lightfoot's table had won eighty-four hands in a row, a feat that Running Bear knew was statistically impossible. The player had never touched the cards, ruling out sleight of hand. There was only one logical explanation: Lightfoot had rigged the game.

On the other TV, a second surveillance film showed Lightfoot standing in the casino parking lot, smoking a cigarette.

Before running the tapes, Running Bear had gone through Lightfoot's personnel file. He was a Navajo and had come to work for the Micanopys with a glowing reference from Bill Higgins, another Navajo, who happened to run the Nevada Gaming Control Board. Indians did not lie to other Indians, and Running Bear could remember Higgins's words as if it were yesterday.

"Jack won't let you down," Higgins had said.

Running Bear shook his head. Jack Lightfoot *had* let him down. He was a cheat, and a damn good one. Bill Higgins had once bragged to Running Bear that he knew every goddamned cheater in the country. So why hadn't he known about this one?

On the second TV a stretch limo appeared. Running Bear leaned forward to stare. The passenger door opened. Sitting in back was an Italian with wavy hair and a mustache. Running Bear found most white men identical, their faces as bland as pudding. Italians were particularly annoying. The men all wore mustaches, or snot-catchers as Indians called them. This one looked like a gangster.

Running Bear stopped the tapes. Sipping his coffee, he listened to the air conditioner outside his window. His casino had been ripped off by a dealer recommended by the most respected gaming official in the country. And that dealer was working with a mobster. *It doesn't get any worse than this,* he thought.

The door opened. The casino's head of security, Harry Smooth Stone, stepped in. He was out of breath.

"More problems," Smooth Stone said.

Running Bear pushed himself out of his chair. Thirty years wrestling alligators had put arthritis in every joint in his body, and he grimaced as his bones sang their painful song. Had he disgraced a dead ancestor recently and not realized it? There had to be some reason for this sudden spate of bad luck.

They drove Smooth Stone's Jeep across the casino parking lot. Jumping a concrete median, they went down a narrow dirt road through thick mangroves that led into the heart of the Everglades. For centuries, the Micanopys had lived in harmony with the alligators, panthers, and bears that called this land home, and had been rewarded in ways that few humans could appreciate.

Ten minutes later, Smooth Stone pulled into a clearing and parked beside a large pool of water. Running Bear knew the spot well; in the spring, alligators came here to mate and, later, raise their young. A half-dozen tribe members with fishing poles stood by the water's edge, looking scared.

Running Bear got out of the Jeep. The men stepped aside, revealing a body lying facedown in the water. It was a man, and he'd been shot once in the head. His left forearm had been chewed off, as had both his feet. Someone had hooked him by the collar. Running Bear said, "Flip him over."

The men obeyed. The dead man was covered with mud, and one of the men filled a bucket out of the lake and dumped it on his face. Running Bear knelt down, just to be sure.

Back in his trailer, Running Bear thumbed through the stack of business cards he kept in his desk. He had decided to dump Jack Lightfoot's body in nearby Broward County—the men in the limo had been white, so let white men deal with the crime—and Smooth Stone was on the phone making arrangements.

"Done," his head of security said, hanging up.

Running Bear found the card he was looking for and handed it to Smooth Stone. "Call this guy and hire him. Tell him everything, except our finding the body."

Smooth Stone stared at the card in his hand.

Grift Sense
International Gaming Consultant
Tony Valentine, President
(727) 591-5115

"He catches people who cheat casinos," Running Bear explained.

"You think he can help us?"

Running Bear heard the suspicion in Smooth Stone's voice. Bringing in an outsider was a risk, but it was a chance he had to take. Jack Lightfoot had cheated them. If word got out that his dealers were crooked, their business would dry up overnight. The casino was the reservation's main revenue source: It paid for health care, education, and a three-thousand-dollar monthly stipend to every adult. If it fell, so did his people.

"I heard him lecture at a gambling seminar," Running Bear said.

"Any good?"

Running Bear nodded. He'd learned more about cheating listening to Tony Valentine for a few hours than he'd learned running a casino for ten years.

"The best," he said.

**Don't miss James Swain's thrilling
second novel featuring Tony Valentine**

FUNNY MONEY

With his old partner murdered in a bomb blast,
Tony Valentine returns to Atlantic City to retrace
Doyle Flanagan's last case. Investigating a six-
million-dollar casino takedown, a square cop soon
meets a whole lot of bent people, from a beautiful
lady wrestler to some Manhattan mobsters; from a
trio of beautiful casino "consultants" to a team of
Eurotrash blackjack card counters. But while
everyone around Tony Valentine (including Tony's
own son) is playing some kind of angle,
Tony is determined to find a killer who is
playing for keeps. . . .

"Fascinating . . . Dazzling . . . Entertaining."
—*Los Angeles Times*

"Smart, snappy . . . Tremendously infectious."
—*St. Petersburg Times*

Published by Ballantine Books.
Available wherever books are sold.